# SURRENDERING INTO SOUL

# A Heroine's Journey

**Second Edition**

Dr. Janet Smith Warfield has inspired me since the first time we met. Dr. Janet is a talented, best-selling author, international speaker and host, a consciousness thought leader and soul. She has won more prestigious awards than I can mention. In light of these achievements, she is humble, generous, and accessible. Dr. Janet welcomes us all on an energetic level to create a rich inner circle of conscious luminaries and a world-class network of change agents.

**Ellema Albert Neal, Ed.D., Author**
**In a Perfect World: Man in Relationship with Self**

I have learned so much from Janet about the power and magic of words! I love the work Janet has done and continues to do to enlighten humanity!

It is an honor to be a steward of Janet's work, and a partner in making sure Janet's work is nurtured and expanded! I am here to be sure that who Janet is, and has been, lives on forever!

Through Janet we are all coming together to create a most powerful synergy to alter humanity!

Janet stands for integrity, impeccability with word and deed, oneness and, don't tell Janet, LOVE! In other words, say what you mean, mean what you say, be thoughtful and kind!

Janet reminds me all the time to claim my power as a woman and as a part of humanity!

Thank you, dear Janet, for gracing our world with your presence!

**Gail Kaplan**
**Aroma Therapist**

I've known Dr. Janet Smith Warfield for many years now, and I am so grateful she has come into my life. She carries so much vitality, wisdom, and love in all that she does; and, what she does, is to share and constantly promote and expand that love and wisdom with others. She engages her vast experience from lawyer to present day talk show host, where she lays bridges, connects and supports the awakening of people from around the world toward greater peace, power, and prosperity.

She tirelessly pursues the journey of greater conscious awareness and unity for all.

**Taveta K. Grant, Founder**
**Awakening Pathways**

Dr. Janet Smith Warfield is one of the most authentic persons I know. Whether it be in her writing, speaking, or just plain living, if you want veritable, and worthwhile messages, dial into Dr. Janet. She has a remarkable IQ, and an equally exceptional EQ - Emotional Intelligence or Emotional Quotient. She has the ability to understand, use, and manage her own emotions in positive ways. Her ability to communicate effectively, empathize with others, and overcome challenges is shown in her writings, because she knows how to live her truths.

**Constance d'Angelis, J.D.**
**Author, Speaker, Facilitator**

Dr. Janet is a solution to world peace and prosperity. She understands the dynamics to creating a life you love. Her desire to inspire the world to embrace powerful communication, relationships and self-love are several reasons I feel she is comparable to a feminine version of Gandhi.

Because of her knowledge of words and her intention to empower others, she is a relentless force for a world of hope and smiles.

**Dr. Ken Rochon, Co-Founder**
**The Keep Smiling Movement**

Dr. Janet's devotion to the cause of uplifting humanity and her boundless energy are inspiring. The way she shows up in service is a powerful example for us all.

**Stephen Dynako**
**Social Entrepreneur**

Dr. Janet Smith Warfield is a treasure. Her passion for the power of words to heal and transform her world and, indeed, all of Humanity, is exemplary. She has traversed many challenges, heartbreaks, and setbacks, but Dr. Janet is an extremely resilient being. I have learned so much from her as she has navigated, and championed, and alchemized her experiences in life into a book of wisdom, website, and a very popular podcast. Dr. Warfield is an internationally recognized speaker, and once you hear her – you'll know why. I urge you to read her book and benefit from her magical approach to life.

**Noel K. Marshall, Ph.D.**
**Co-Founder, LightPartners.org and**
**Co-Creators Convergence.com**

I know Dr. Janet as an open and loving woman who invites all of us to find our internal power and intelligence and use it wisely. Her book about her journey is an invitation to all of us to learn more about her story of transformation, strength, and "humanness." I am in awe of her willingness to be so transparent, and of the strength that she possesses to model empowerment for all of us. She is a treasure.

**Elsie Ritzenhein, Author**
*Awakening Your Creative Voice/Women*
*in a World of Possibility* **(2017)**

*Surrendering into Soul* gives words to guide us in spiritual activism. When we organize around the higher vibration of the good, the dream for a just and peaceful world happens and with joy. Dr. Janet's years of being on this path to change our words shines through in her personal stories, and invites us to be on the same journey of enlightenment and empowerment. I am eager to tell others of this most needed book in mining the good of humanity. Namaste!!!

**Ann Smith**
**Director of Circle Connections,**
**Changing the World, Circle by Circle**

Janet's work is a gift to anyone who is searching for meaning and purpose in life. It all starts inside with our perceptions of what is happening around us, and then our choice of words and the actions that follow. Such beautiful teaching, and really so simple -- it's wonderful that she is helping us all to wake up to this very accessible power that we have to transform our lives and our world! Her insights are astute and show a deep understanding of our human experience.

**Melissa Nuwaysir**
**Owner, Awakened Heart Coaching**

Janet puts down her ideas in amazingly clear and uncomplicated language. Her Biblical references are numerous, and yet she sees the ancient book through a new lens, a modern, evolved way of understanding.

**Deborah DeNicola**
**Dream Image Worker, Editor, Professor**

From the first few moments of speaking with Dr. Janet Smith Warfield, I knew she was deeply inquisitive, bright minded, backed by a buoyant spirit that soars into new paradigms. And all the while one is dancing with her in inquiry, she is welcoming and accessible. I am delighted to walk the path with Janet, dive into her meanderings, or set her teachings into action whenever the opportunity presents itself. She is truly a wise guide for the times, leading us to our living, breathing humanity, while also reminding us that we are of the stars.

**Lulu Delphine**
**National Development, Outreach, Facilitation:**
**Turning the Wheel**
**M.Ed., Certified Body Now Facilitator &**
**Arts Integration Instructor**

Published by

Word Sculptures Publishing, LLC.

3225 McLeod Drive, Suite 100,

Las Vegas, NV 89121



Manufactured in the United States of America, or in the United Kingdom when distributed elsewhere.

Warfield, Janet.

eBook ISBN: 979-8-89795-014-0
Paperback ISBN: 979-8-89795-015-7
Hardback ISBN: 979-8-89795-016-4

LCCN: 2024917332

Cover design by: Frank Watson Copyediting by: Wendie Percharsky Interior design by: Suba Murugan Author photo by: Nikki Incandela

www.planetarypeacepowerandprosperity.org

# Table of Contents

# Preface

Why do I write this book? The simple answer is that I am both driven and guided. I do not know why, how, or by what.

Am I driven by my love of problem-solving? My love of exploration? My deep need for clarity, courage, and inner peace?

Am I driven to answer that age-old question, "Who am I?" to discover the Pearl of Great Price, the Philosopher's Stone, the Hidden Treasure, the Holy Grail, the Elixir of Immortality, the wisdom that comes from a life well-lived? To make sense of the path I have been given to walk?

I do not know.

What I do know is that my mother's clear intentions for her only child, a daughter, were that I marry, become an excellent cook, housekeeper, and gardener, and birth the children my mother had been unable to birth. I fulfilled those intentions impeccably for years—until I could no longer walk the path my mother wanted me to walk.

I never dreamed that something, somewhere, somehow, would gift me with mystical, transformational, eye-opening experiences. I never dreamed I would become an attorney, author, speaker, TV show host, and founder of a nonprofit organization, Planetary Peace, Power, and Prosperity Legacy Foundation, Inc. I never dreamed I would create a consciousness diagram that, from hindsight, maps the psychic and spiritual journey my own life has taken. I never dreamed I would develop the skill to connect what appear to be disparate and dissonant conceptual worldviews with the underlying experiences from which the words emerged and transform those apparent conceptual dissonances into exploratory, creative, respectful, and meaningful exchanges of information among unique human beings.

The challenge of writing this book has been huge.

What are the right words when talking about eye-opening experiences that instantaneously shift understanding, emotions, and conduct? What are the right words to put into this book when I know that the same words impact different people in different ways?

There are no right words. There are only many different words, all pointing to the same underlying personal and planetary transformation.

We humans created words. I have created the words in this book.

What do words do? They separate, divide, and categorize. They emerge spontaneously from human experiences and a desire to connect and communicate. But words are simply static placeholders that, for a single moment in time, stop the flow of something ineffable that moves, lives, breathes, and constantly changes as it flows through us and around us.

How can I capture and communicate, by means of human-created, static placeholders, something ineffable that moves, lives, breathes, and constantly changes? I can't.

Whenever I try to capture and communicate this ineffable, living, breathing energy or spirit by using human-created words, I separate myself from it and create a subject/object duality. When instead, I allow myself to trust it, experience it, and allow it to guide my steps in each and every moment, the subject/object duality dissolves. There is only peaceful, powerful, prosperous energetic flow.

My original intention for the structure of this book was simply to tell the stories of my own life journey through my own lens of perception and allow readers to take what they liked and leave the rest. Telling stories kept me out of self-righteousness. That was vital.

But then editors began reading my words and looking at them through their own left-brain, conceptual, analytic lenses. In some cases, they appeared to be looking at them through the cultural lenses within which they had been educated, unconsciously conditioned, and, perhaps unconsciously imprisoned. They looked for what they perceived was wrong—what, in their views, should be added, deleted, or rearranged. They failed to look for what was interesting, meaningful, and impactful.

I *did* listen to their words. I did integrate some of their suggestions into this book. But the words you read here are not "Truth," never will be Truth, and never can be Truth. They are nothing but the story of my own Heroine's Journey and the truths, practices, and experiences that have informed and supported me throughout my own life.

When one editor suggested using the heroine's journey conceptual framework as a container for my stories, I liked that suggestion. My life experiences have certainly felt like a heroine's journey.

I read Joseph Campbell's *Hero's Journey*. But then, I began reading works by Maureen Murdock, who was teaching that the Hero's Journey was different from the Heroine's Journey. It certainly did feel that way to me. I attended one of Maureen's workshops. I delved deeper and made more supportive and clarifying connections.

I researched Heroine's Journey images and structures on the internet. Again, each image and structure was a bit different. Each felt like a tiny little brick in the great wall of Heroine's Journey knowledge.

Which was the right structure? Which was the right image?

I was also doing in-depth reading and research within biblical texts, particularly the Book of Revelation in the New

Testament. I learned about the Buddhist Four Noble Truths and Eightfold Path, the Hindu Piercing the Veil of Illusion, the Eternal Tao. Each of these provided a different conceptual structure for my own life experiences.

My intention with this book is that perhaps the words I have created within my own little "Heroine's Journey" microcosm will resonate with something within your own "Hero's or Heroine's Journey" microcosm. I have seen this happen many times, and almost always in ways I never could have planned or predicted. Read the Amazon Reviews of my first book, *Shift: Change Your Words, Change Your World* to see the viability of that statement.

Some people use it like a Tarot deck, opening it to a random page each morning and reading the words on the page. They report that they always receive exactly what they needed that morning in a way they did not expect.

Others read it once, put it down, and then pick it up three months later. The second time they read it, they receive something new and different, not because the words in the book have changed, but because they have changed.

Is this resonance the creation and co-creation of a living, breathing macrocosm, connecting and reconnecting, like an Indra's Web, all the little individual unique microcosms, suddenly seeing the similarities and patterns? Suddenly gaining clarity and understanding? Suddenly shifting into compassion and gratitude for the one precious life they have been given? Is this how we co-create a peaceful, powerful, prosperous planet—together and forever?

I do not know. All I know is that something, somewhere, somehow, is driving and guiding me along the path I have been given to walk and the work I am here to do until my physical body takes its last breath and my Soul sinks back into that living, breathing energy that lives and breathes forever.

# Introduction

This is a book about connecting and reconnecting—with Soul, Family, Community, Nation, and Planet. It is about connecting our personal experiences with the multitude of words with which we map and conceptualize those experiences.

It is about noticing the thoughts that fly through our minds and the words that fly out of our mouths. It is about answering the question, "Who am I?" It is about answering the questions, "Whom do I choose to be? What do I choose to do with my one precious life?"

It is about listening deeply to the words that others speak about themselves, about me, about you, and about our planet. It is about observing body language. It is about feeling the underlying emotions, both our own and those of others.

It is about overcoming shame, not feeling good enough, fear, terror, anger, and rage, and standing tall in our full creative and co-creative strength and power.

It is about searching for clarity, meaning, and integration. It is about weaving the unique colors of multifaceted experiences into our own beautiful, life tapestry. It is also about weaving our own unique life journey into the unique life journeys of others we encounter along the way.

It is about looking for similarities, not differences. It is about discernment, not judgment.

It is about learning the art of Word Energy Alchemy, an art that connects and reconnects us all.

It is also about protecting the Sanctuary of our Soul, Family, Community, Nation, and Planet from all the human-created dysfunctional dissonances we have created with our ignorance of what words do and what we humans do with words.

My intention behind the words in this book is simply to create a beautiful and fascinating tapestry of word art, using a variety of words, concepts, and methods to create meaning for the reader—perhaps even an aha moment. This is not logical, linear writing. It is pure creative art form.

Just like the colored threads in a beautiful tapestry, the reader may notice that certain themes emerge, recede, and then reappear in new contexts, locations, and conceptual forms. Some of these themes include:

- The impact of raging male hormones on men, women, and children.
- Sudden transformational experiences.
- The dynamics and experience of power over, power under, power against, and Power With human interactions.
- The integration of conceptual opposites through clarification of the experiential referents.
- Archetypes and archetypal patterns.
- Trust and betrayal of trust.
- Personal integrity.
- Microcosms and macrocosms.
- Going wide versus going deep.
- The lens of perception.
- Piercing the veil of word illusions.
- Integrity, transparency, and accountability.
- Clear speaking and deep listening.

Perhaps you will notice and observe other themes that I have not noticed, observed, or remembered. Please add your observations and unique colors to the beautiful word tapestry we create, co-create, and manifest together.

If my word art has the impact I would like it to have, your eyes, heart, and mind will simply open and expand. You may become more aware of the infinite number of choices you have in each moment to weave your own unique, beautiful, fascinating tapestry of word art, bringing inner peace, personal empowerment, and prosperity into your own precious life. When you manifest from this State of Connection and Reconnection, your own inner peace, personal (em)power(ment), and prosperity impact the lives of all around you without any effort on your part—simply with pure ease, grace, and flow.

If each of us were to bring inner peace, personal empowerment, and prosperity (by which I mean a sense of gratitude and abundance) into our own one precious life, peace, power, and prosperity would become planetary, not because some human authority is standing over us with a whip, but because this is the way we want to live and be.

You may notice that, in most contexts, I use specific linguistic forms:

- Stories
- Poetry
- Questions
- The right questions with the intention of creating and co-creating the connections and eye-opening experiences I want to create.
- Metaphor
- Analogy

- Quotations from other writers.

Occasionally, I use images. All of these forms are intentional. They keep me manifesting within the creative and co-creative role of artist and educator rather than the authoritarian role of power over didactic teacher and expert.

For the most part, I avoid didactic teaching. Avoiding didactic teaching keeps me out of self-righteousness. It prevents me from taking on the persona of the authoritative teacher and controller.

The one exception is when I am writing about words. When I write about words, I *do* use didactic teaching because, in that context, I *am* an authority. My entire life has been spent studying words and the supportive or traumatic impacts they have on human lives, as well as living the underlying experiences from which the words have emanated.

Welcome to my world of words, Welcome to my "Heroine's Journey."

# Chapter 1
# The Journey - An Overview

**Evolving into:**
**Self-Awareness and Other-Awareness**
**Self-Forgiveness and Other-Forgiveness**
**Self-Compassion and Other-Compassion**
**Self-Respect and Other-Respect**
**Freedom, Personal Integrity, and Accountability**

*"Out beyond ideas of wrong-doing and right-doing, there is a field. I'll meet you there. When the soul lies down in that grass, the world is too full to talk about. Ideas, language, even the phrase 'each other' doesn't make any sense."*

—Rumi, "A Great Wagon"

## THE CONSCIOUSNESS DIAGRAM

The consciousness diagram below is a map of my Heroine's Journey. It appears in modified form on the cover of this book.

It is not new. I birthed it on page 83 of my first book, *Shift: Change Your Words, Change Your World*, in a chapter entitled Science and Religion: Hypothesis, Faith, and Creativity, which is included within Part Three, Words as Dualistic Dividers. The diagram also appears on the website of our recently created educational foundation, Planetary Peace, Power, and Prosperity Legacy Foundation, Inc.[1]

---

[1] https://planetarypeacepowerandprosperity.org/

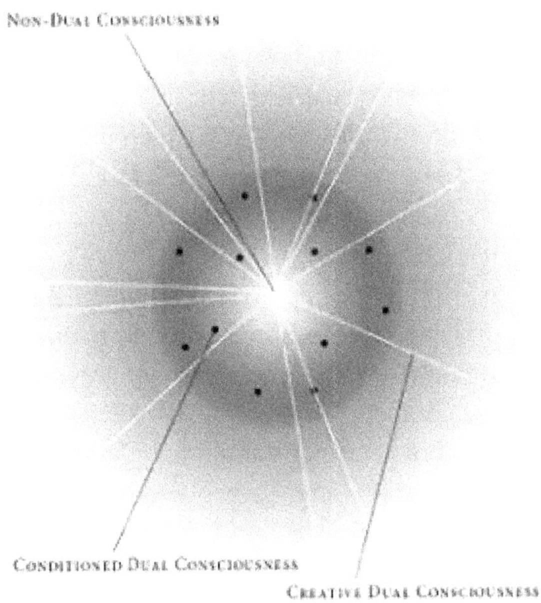


**Non-Dual Consciousness** is a center point of pure Beingness—that pure connection with all that is—a state of pure awareness. It cannot be conceptualized with words. It can only be experienced and allowed to flow through like a stream of pure, cleansing water. People have called that center point of Non-Dual Consciousness God, Jehovah, Allah, Brahma, the Tao, a Power Greater than Myself, and many other human-created words.

**Conditioned-Dual Consciousness** consists of all those little, limited, separated black boxes (seen as black dots in the diagram) of human-created words and worldviews, which the human mind has manifested through the creation of separating, dividing, and categorizing words. These words and worldviews are exceptionally useful tools, but they are not what has been called "Truth."

When we disconnect from the *experience* of Non-Dual Consciousness and believe that our human-created words are

Truth, the little black boxes fight with one another about whose words are right and whose words are wrong. Our human challenge is to learn to release ourselves from the limiting words and worldviews into which our souls, spirits, and life forces have been imprisoned. Through release, we free ourselves to reconnect with an "Energy" I sometimes call Non- Dual Consciousness.[2]

**Creative-Dual Consciousness** is a human skill of *using* separating, divisive, categorizing words to manifest, within our physical world, a clear intention that serves ourselves, others, and our planet. We can use that skill to reconnect back to that core, experiential energy of Non-Dual Consciousness, or to create, co-create, and manifest outwardly the kind of world in which we want to live. Ultimately, the inner and outer movements integrate into a moral/ethical, functional, integrated practice and way of life. We can analogize it to the breath—breathing in and out, expanding and contracting, with or without consciously thinking about it.

I don't remember exactly when I created this diagram, but clearly, before 2007, when I first published *Shift*. At that point, I was attempting to create a map of my own Heroine's Journey out of my then seventy years of life experience, walking step by step through the labyrinth of my own existential, experiential Heroine's Journey. I hoped that somehow the words that flowed through me might resonate with other hearts and minds.

I still find the Consciousness Diagram useful. Perhaps it will be useful to you.

---

[2] Even the term "Non-Dual Consciousness" is simply one of many possible, human-created placeholders for an ineffable experience.

In 2007, I talked about the Consciousness Diagram within a specific context, with a specific focus and a specific conscious intention. The specific context and focus were science and religion. My conscious intention was to open and conceptually explore new ideas and opportunities and then connect what I understood to a single broader conceptual context: what appeared to be the conflict or paradox between the worldviews and disciplines of science and religion.

It is now 2024. I am now using different words to talk about the Consciousness Diagram.

I now see this Consciousness Diagram as a possible consciousness map of the psyche for all humans, particularly those stuck in some little black box of a single conceptual worldview, suffering either consciously or unconsciously, from terror, rage, shame, or not feeling good enough. I now see this Consciousness Diagram as having meaning and offering guidance to every human who has the perseverance, commitment, and courage to take that first step on his or her own Hero's or Heroine's Journey.

Sometimes, as we walk along our life path, we are simply thrust into circumstances over which we have no control despite our best intentions. A flood destroys our home. We lose a son to a drunk driver on the wrong side of a divided highway. We lose a parent to a sudden heart attack. Our home is brutally reduced to rubble by bombs in an attack ordered by a dictator, orchestrated by a butcher, and implemented by soldiers willing to simply follow orders to earn a living to support their wives and children.

Suddenly, we are devastated. Our everyday lives have been turned upside down and inside out. We are suddenly thrust into suffering and grief. We face hard moral choices. Are we going to die alongside those crucial parts of our lives that we have lost, or take another breath, pick ourselves up, and take the next step, and the next, and the next?

Ultimately, the Hero's or Heroine's Journey through what we call "Kronos" or "Chronos" time collapses into that non-dual center point of pure, present-moment, energetic, creative, and co-creative awareness and manifestation.

That non-dual center point is the state of consciousness that Ram Dass refers to as *Be Here Now*.[3] It is T.S. Eliot's "still point of the turning world."[4] It is Rumi's "field."

Is this Consciousness Diagram a possible map of human consciousness for each person on this planet? Is it a map of each Hero's and Heroine's internal, consciousness-shifting, and mentally expanding, deepening, and heightening Journey? Does it map a journey through the psyche, into the depths of the subconscious and unconscious mind and then out again to Abraham Maslow's state of self-actualization[5] or Carl Jung's individuation[6]?

## BLACK BOXES

In the Consciousness Diagram, I use the words "Conditioned Dual Consciousness" to point to the small black dots in the image. I further use the words "little, limited, separated black boxes" to add deeper meaning, context, and focus. But when I research the meaning of that one word, "black," I discover it has a multitude of meanings,

---

[3] https://www.amazon.com/Be-Here-Now-Ram-Dass/dp/0517543052
[4] https://www.uvm.edu/~mjk/013%20Intro%20to%20Wildlife%20Tracking/ BURNT_NORTON_by_TS_Eliot.pdf
[5] See Abraham Maslow's Self-Actualization Diagram in the Appendix.
[6] https://scottjeffrey.com/individuation-process/

as well as different meanings to different people.[7] I would like to clarify the sense in which I am using the words "black boxes" within the context of a discussion of the Consciousness Diagram.

I am *not* intending to inject the word "black" with any pejorative meaning, such as evil, or childhood experiences of having been whipped or raped by an angry father. I am using it simply to describe a consciousness that has limited experience, education, and skill—a consciousness shaped by the limited experience, education, and skill of our parents and teachers.

## MY LITTLE BLACK BOX

I was born into that center point of Non-Dual Consciousness totally naïve, innocent, unaware, and fully dependent on the earthly resources that supported me—the archetype of the Innocent, Magical Child. I was born into a nonconceptually structured world of pure experience with which I constantly interacted. When I was hungry, I cried

---

[7] "It can be linked with death, mourning, evil magic, and darkness, but it can also symbolize elegance, wealth, restraint, and power." "In Latin, the word for 'black,' ater, is associated with cruelty and evil. Atrocious and atrocity are derived from this Latinate stem." "The Benedictine monks wore black robes as a sign of humility and penitence. In the 12th century, the *Black monks*, as they came to be called, were challenged by the Cistercian monks, who wore white. The Benedictines accused the Cistercians of being prideful, as demonstrated by their white robes. The Cistercians prepared their comeback: Black, they responded, was the color of the devil, death, and sin, while their own white symbolized purity and innocence." "'Vantablack,' as the scientists called it, traps light to such an extent that the surface looks like a void. (T)he artist Anisk Kapoor…uses it to give the viewer the impression that they are looking into a black hole. https://artsandculture.google.com/story/the-secret-history-of-the-color-black/fwISZyrkPUt0IA

until my mother fed me. When my body needed restoration, I slept. When I had gas in my belly, I cried until my mother burped me. My tiny, little human, dependent body simply did whatever it needed to do to live, breathe, and survive. I was born into Non-Dual consciousness.

Then my parents, teachers, peers, and the environment began conditioning me, without my knowledge, through words and experiences, into one of those little black boxes of a specific environment, culture, language, and values. As a young child, it was my *known world.*

Mommy and Daddy, on whom I was dependent for food, water, and shelter, were eager to teach me human-created language so that I could learn to talk, think, conceptualize, and become successful in the world. "This is Mommy. That is Daddy. This is our dog, Rascal. That is a tree."

I was fortunate. I was born to kind, loving parents, both of whom were teachers. They both truly desired the child born of their physical union. As a child, that little, black, conceptual worldview box created by my parents felt very safe and secure. My parents loved and supported me, allowing me to learn, grow, and explore within a safe, loving, supportive family structure. I thought that every child's life was just like mine.

But as I left that beautiful, nurturing worldview cocoon into which I had been born and began moving out into the world, I started bumping into other worldviews. I encountered the worldviews of children abused by ignorant parents—parents who didn't want their children—children born solely out of raging male hormones and sexual lust. These resented, abused, ignored, and battered children had never learned a better way.

As I grew, I became exposed to other little black boxes of environments, cultures, languages, and values. Each was slightly different from my own. All were fascinating.

Some were fun and exciting. Some were supportive. Some were educational.

Some hurt. Some were terrifying.

That was my Heroine's Journey—one tiny step at a time, trying to make sense of it all and integrate everything into a coherent pattern so that I could live a peaceful, powerful, prosperous, meaningful life.

Ultimately, through my own "Dark Nights of the Soul,"[8] I had no choice but to surrender back to that center point of Non-Dual Consciousness or pure, present-moment awareness. Having lived every human archetype and experienced every human emotion, having lived in five different cultures and environments with different languages and societal structures, having visited many other cultures and environments, I ultimately chose to settle into navigating my own mind, emotions, and actions in each and every moment, fully immersed in and supported only by that center point of "Living, Breathing Energy" that my mind could not conceptualize, but that my Soul had learned to trust and allow to flow through me.

From one perspective, I had returned to the point where my life began—Non-Dual Consciousness. From another perspective, I was a new person, no longer naïve and dependent on other people as I had been as an infant. I had now acquired years of breadth, depth, context, and experience within a myriad of little black worldview boxes

---

[8] For one of these stories, see *Shift: Change Your Words, Change Your World, p. 117*. I will be telling many more of these soul-challenging stories throughout this book.

of what appears to be a physical world. During my Heroine's Journey, I had weathered trials and tribulations, defeats and successes, hell and purgatory, and then emerged again—like a diver returning to the water's surface, gasping for life-giving air, like a phoenix emerging from the ashes—centered, restabilized, reconnected, safe, empowered, and aware—detached from all the human-created turmoil and chaos—compassionate, grateful, appreciative, and serene.

I had now acquired an entire toolbox of useful human understandings. I now knew how to detach from other peoples' unconscious emotional reactivity, protect my own soul, release fear, transform rage into right action, and shift an entire human dynamic by merely choosing my own thoughts, actions, words, and presence. Everything became a constant living, breathing, dynamic, energetic creativity, co-creativity, and manifestation. Human-created concepts of time, space, and separation collapsed into an *experience* of infinite immersion in all that is. Greeks and many religions call this kairos[9] time.

I was fully connected with everyone and everything. I now was experiencing myself as a minuscule but vital part of that infinite, co-creative dance of eternity.

## SUBJECT/OBJECT DUALITY

Words separate, divide, and categorize. Early in life, we are taught by other, separating, dividing, and categorizing human beings how to separate ourselves from and stand outside of this pure flow of energy and experience. We stop the flow at a single frame, chop it up into pieces with our minds, analyze what we have chopped up, chop it up into

---

[9] https://en.wikipedia.org/wiki/Kairos

smaller and smaller pieces, and move the pieces around to make it all "work better." Our parents have taught us how to step into dual consciousness by creating a subject/object duality.

This human-created tool of subject/object duality is extremely useful for many purposes. We can communicate with one another—at least to some extent. We can separate the pure flow of experience into tinier and tinier parts, and then put the pieces back together again in new ways. We can build cars, skyscrapers, and rockets that go to the moon. We can go on forever, creating and co-creating our tiny little conceptual black boxes—our individual worldviews—to achieve what we want to accomplish in what appears to be a very physical world.

But while our minds separate us from the pure, energetic, spiritual flow of experience, the flow continues on, carrying us with it.

When we believe our own little, human-created, limited, conceptual black box or worldview is Truth and other people's little human-created, limited, conceptual black box or worldview is Not Truth, we fall into self-righteousness (Jewish and Christian words), stray from the path of righteousness, sin (Christian words), or function from ignorance (Buddhist words).

The human mind has used human-created words to separate, divide, and categorize so that it can feel good about itself when controlling, abusing, and using others or enabling the dysfunctional conduct of others—a "power over/power under" dynamic.

We start using words to call each other names—stupid, wrong, ugly, incompetent. Those abusive words hurt, particularly when we are small children, dependent on the adults who are sticking those word labels on us, or when we are mothers, dependent on the man who impregnated us if we are going to continue to thrive and nurture the child we together brought into this physical world.

We try harder to please the parents who are calling us negative names, the husbands who are running off to have affairs with other women or screaming at us and slamming their fists on the table.

To protect our own body and soul, we sink into a "power under" position. Like the tortoise, we pull into our shell. Like the embattled warrior, we crouch into our foxhole and pull camouflage over our heads. We cower in corners. We become victims and slaves.

Why do we do this?

Because we are dependent on these bullies/abusers for food and shelter; because we have been taught to honor our parents and support our husbands regardless of their conduct; and, finally, because we want to be perceived by others as kind, loving, and patient.

Sometimes, out of pure anger and frustration, we fight back and become rebels or destroyers. Then, we shift into a "power against" dynamic.

We want to feel okay. We want to feel loved. We want to feel safe. Yet, as children and women, we rarely do. It is easy to find fault with ourselves because so many other confused, dysfunctional human beings have found fault with us. The self-righteousness and fault-finding cut us off from that center point of Non-Dual Consciousness—contracting and limiting our creative energy field, imprisoning us, turning us into servants whose only use is to support another human being's unconscious ignorance and egotistical control.

# RECONNECTION WITH NON-DUAL CONSCIOUSNESS

So how can we use analytic, divisive words consciously and intentionally to attract lost, confused, constricted, imprisoned, suffering human beings (including ourselves) to their original connection with that center point of Non-Dual Consciousness? How can each of us regain our birthright and become the powerful, aligned co-creators we were intended to be? How can we manifest and maintain a peaceful, powerful, prosperous planet—together and forever?

Can we learn to use the Art of Word Energy Alchemy?[10] Ask questions? Tell stories? Use consistent grammar? Learn to use metaphor and analogy to clarify abstract terms through example and down-to-earth simile?

Can we share transparently what we think, feel, need, and need to know? Can we do this with as much clarity, transparency, and excellence as our current resources and understanding allow?

Do we understand that we always have choices? Do we think about what matters most to us and what we want to do with our one precious life?

Can we learn to listen openly, without judgment, to the words of others, through practices like Vistar Circles[11] and engage in conscious and intentional conversation to explore how we can work together to co-create a peaceful, powerful, prosperous planet?

---

[10] https://wordenergyalchemy.com/
[11] http://www.vistarfoundation.org

Can we stay in the Buddhist "Witness," "Beginner's Mind," "Right Speech," and "Right Action"?[12]

Can we live the Tikkun Olam[13] (Hebrew for repairing the world) according to Judaism? Participate in the return to the Promised Land?"

Can we follow the Christian edict "Judge not, that ye be not judged?"[14]

Can we pierce the Hindu "Veil of Illusion?"[15]

Can we simply BE in Taoism's "The Eternal Tao that cannot be spoken while living the Tao (the way) of carefully chosen words and practices?

Can every one of us work on our own "overcoming," experience the "Alpha and Omega," and be part of the descent of "the holy Jerusalem" portrayed in the Christian Book of Revelation?[16]

---

[12]https://extension.illinois.edu/blogs/refill-your-cup-self-care/2020-10-14-power-witness;
https://encyclopediaobuddhism.org/wiki/Noble_Eightfold_Path
[13] https://www.myjewishlearning.com/article/tikkun-olam-repairing-the-world/
[14] (Matt. 7:1)
[15] (https://www.yogabasics.com/connect/yoga-blog/lifting-the-veil-the-maya-of-comparison-critique-and-envy/,
https://www.britannica.com/topic/maya-Indian-philosophy,
http://janetsmithwarfield.com/tag/piercing-the-veil/
[16] (Warfield, J. (2007): Shift: Change Your Words, Change Your World, pp 165-178.)

# Chapter 2
# The Ineffable Call

## The Passion to Solve Problems

*"Uncover what you long for and you will discover who you are."*

—Phil Cousineau

DRIVEN TO UNDERSTAND

In 2007, when I published *Shift: Change Your Words, Change Your World*, the Ineffable Call was the three eye-opening experiences I had after reading A.S. Neill's book, *Summerhill.* See *Shift*, Part One, Chapter 1.

The first experience was stopping a bed-wetting problem by giving my son a penny.

The second was allowing young boys to decide whether or not they wanted to fight. The third was apologizing to a furious man at my front door and asking how I could make things right.

Before reading *Summerhill,* I was trying to solve the bed-wetting problem by:

- Ignoring it
- Explaining to my son why a five-year-old was too old to wet the bed
- Spanking him

I would have tried to solve the problem of young boys calling each other names and raising their fists at each other by lecturing them about why they shouldn't fight. I would have tried to solve the problem of the furious man at my front door by saying something like, "Oh, you shouldn't be angry over a little thing like that."

These three experiences happened around 1966, but I didn't share them with the world until 2007, when I felt driven to write and publish my first book. What I learned in 1966 was that by changing my own conduct, everything around me changed. It was fascinating and so much easier than trying to follow someone else's rules or trying to get somebody else to do what I wanted them to do. Changing my own conduct was also entirely within my own control.

Now, in 2024, I see the Ineffable Call as something much bigger and much more all-encompassing. Is it a call for every human on this planet to look deeply into their own soul, change their own conduct, and transform our entire planet into one that is peaceful, powerful, and prosperous?

None of us can do this alone. We need all of us.

That's when the personal peace, (em)power(ment), and prosperity that each of us brings into our own life by Surrendering into Soul becomes planetary. We do this together by first doing it for ourselves.

It is not easy. It is the individual Hero's or Heroine's Journey. Each of us must question everything we have ever been taught. We need to notice where the generalizations we have been taught don't support us, pay attention to what matters to each of us, release our fear, and transform our rage into what the Buddhists call "right action."

Instead of pretending we are not afraid when we are trembling, we start watching our mind, choose to bring it back to the present moment, and ask ourselves what we can do, right here, right now, to move our life in the direction we want it to go. Instead of fighting against injustice, we stand for justice.

In my own Ineffable Call and my personal Heroine's Journey, a single archetype keeps appearing and reappearing. How do I deal with the Bully (Coward), who keeps showing up, time after time, in my life?

There is also a second type of archetype who keeps showing up—the person who is so focused on what they want or need that they don't listen or pay attention to what I need. I haven't found an archetypal name for this person, but the pattern is one of "ignorance" (to use a Buddhist term) or just not paying attention to the whole.

I do this, too, but never intentionally. I'm not omniscient, omnipotent, and omnipresent. None of us is in these limited physical bodies, including the would-be dictators.

Is there a correlation between the Bully (Coward) and the person who is simply unaware? In some sense, is each purely ignorant, unwilling, or unable to face the formidable challenges of this physical life?

Does each believe they already know everything and that everyone else should fall in line with their momentary, unconscious whims? Are both merely self-righteous, believing that their way of looking at the world is the only way of looking at the world? Does each assume that everyone else agrees—or should agree?

Is each of them stuck in one of those little black boxes on my consciousness diagram into which they have unconsciously been conditioned? Have I, too, been stuck in one of those little black boxes into which I was unconsciously conditioned?

And how does male testosterone, our monetary system, and our patriarchal societal conditioning play into this bully/coward dynamic?

## EARLY CHILDHOOD

There were certain experiences and themes running through my birth family that shaped the little black box in which I grew up. As a child, I didn't think of these as themes. In many cases, I only learned later about things that had happened or understood them in greater depth through words spoken or written by others.

When I look back now at my life through the lens of all the words I have ever been taught, all the words others have spoken or written about my life experience or their own, and all the experiences I have had, I can see the themes and patterns of my own family conditioning repeatedly emerging, each time in a new experiential context.

What themes do I now see? Deep parental love and commitment; husband and wife working together as a team; father as protector of wife and child; wife and child as dearly loved by the father; wife and child as supporting the father and allowing him to make final decisions; hard moral choices.

Here are some of the stories from which those themes emerged.

I was born one month early, on September 6, 1936, at 10:44 a.m., in Lying-In Hospital in Philadelphia, Pennsylvania. My parents gave me the name "Janet." Janet means "Gift of God." My mother always said it meant "wonderful gift of God," although I'm sure there were times when she questioned her choice of name.

One day, my little friend Sammy Wanamaker and I climbed up on a studio couch to reach the mineral oil on top of the bureau. I loved mineral oil. Together, Sammy and I drank the whole bottle—except for what we spilled all over my mother's studio couch.

My mother didn't scold us. She just cleaned us both up and sent us happily out to play.

Another time, on a hot summer day, our neighbors' sprinkler was on. What a wonderful opportunity! Why not cool off?

I stripped off all my clothes so they wouldn't get wet, carefully folded them as my mother had taught me, and ran naked through the sprinkler with the other neighborhood children. My mother laughed, then retrieved both me and the clothes and brought us inside.

I always felt my parents love and support. I never questioned it. I didn't even think about it. It was just always there.

Both of my parents were educators. My father taught music at Central High School in Philadelphia. My mother taught elementary education. Our home life was structured and orderly but always fun and interesting. There were always new games to play and new learning experiences.

Behind my parents' little twin home on Brighton Street in Mayfair in northeast Philadelphia, there was a back alley. A monkey grinder would stroll up the alley, dressed-up monkey on rope, playing his grinder. My mother would take me out to talk with the man and give the monkey a penny to put in the man's cup.

We had a dog, Rascal. When my parents moved to a larger, single-family home in Custis Woods, in Cheltenham Township, Pennsylvania, they introduced baby rabbits and ducks into our family. My father, an exceptional carpenter as well as a music teacher, built a hutch for the rabbits to keep them safe from predators and created a small pond for the ducks.

On summer evenings, my mother would organize the neighborhood children into games, like Red Rover or I See Something Red. On winter evenings, the family would play board games together or work on putting together the pieces of a jigsaw puzzle before we went to bed. After my mother tucked me in, she'd read me stories and sing songs.

Two years after I was born, my mother became pregnant again. The pregnancy was lopsided. The doctor anesthetized her so he could do a thorough internal examination. He discovered a membrane dividing my mother's uterus into two parts.

I had been conceived on the larger side. My sibling had been conceived on the smaller side. There was simply not enough room for the fetus to develop to full term.

With my mother still under anesthesia, the doctor advised my father that both the fetus and my mother would die of peritonitis unless a hysterectomy were performed. My father gave his permission.

When my mother came out of anesthesia, her second biological child was gone, her uterus was gone, and she would never be able to bear the other three children she had so passionately desired.

Had my mother been given the opportunity to participate in the decision made by the doctor and my father, perhaps she would ultimately have agreed. However, she was never given that choice. In our patriarchal culture, the men simply made that life-changing decision for her.

Would the decision-making power have been different had it been my father who had been anesthetized and threatened by an impending surgery that would determine whether he could continue to father children? What if it were the doctor and my mother who had to decide what to do? Would the doctor and my mother have decided without first consulting my father?

I remember a time when I was three years old. I suddenly found myself flat on my back on the garage floor of my home, a neighbor's child pummeling me with her fists.

I was stunned. I had had no previous experience with being so viciously attacked and didn't know what to do.

My parents heard the commotion and came out. They didn't break up the fight and give us a lecture on why we shouldn't fight. Instead, they stood on the sidelines and cheered me on to defend myself.

Hearing their cheers, I began pummeling the neighbor's child back. She stopped her attacks and ran home crying.

The little girl who had attacked me was not as fortunate as I to have had kind, fair, creative, loving, supportive parents. Abused and belittled by her mother and father, it was the only way she knew how to treat others.

Although I didn't understand archetypes at age three, this was one of many preludes to my own Heroine's Journey. In my childlike way, I had become a tiny Spiritual Warrior for a single moment in time.

This was not because I was following somebody else's rules. It was because my parents were supporting me, cheering me on.

I had learned a valuable lesson. I had the ability to protect myself from abusive attackers. I could preserve my own safe space. Many years later, I saw this as protecting not only my body and safe space, but also my soul, my personal integrity, and my one precious life.

I did not have to passively succumb. There were times when I had to fight for my life and the principles that mattered to me, even if I couldn't articulate those principles at age three.

In early 1942, my parents adopted a second child, James Albright. Upon completion of the adoption, James Albright became Norman James Smith.

The baby didn't change. Only his name changed.

Most of the time, Jimmy and I played harmoniously together, despite the differences in genetics, age, and gender. However, on occasion, we would squabble.

My mother never lectured us about why we shouldn't fight. She didn't spank us. She simply sent us both to our rooms. We could come out whenever we decided we could live harmoniously together in the same house.

Spending time alone in my room was never a punishment for me. I could always find something interesting to do. I would read or color or clean out a bureau drawer. Often, I rediscovered toys I had forgotten, pulled them out, and brought them back to life.

For Jimmy, being sent to his room was hell. He would lie on his bed, suck his thumb, and stare at the ceiling.

When each of us was ready to come out, we did and began playing peacefully together again.

The way my mother managed the squabbles between Jimmy and me became a model for the way I handled conflicts later in my own life when my mother was no longer there to guide and protect me.

Shortly after the beginning of World War II, my parents sold their car and Custis Woods home and bought a home in Glenside, Pennsylvania, within walking distance of schools and stores. Our new home was big, old, and had three floors and a cellar. I can remember the big coal bins in our basement and the coal trucks that would dump the coal down a chute through a basement window into the bins. I can remember my father shoveling coal into the furnace every morning to keep his wife and children warm.

The living room, dining room, pantry, and kitchen were on the first floor. Three bedrooms and two baths were on the second floor. The third floor was used for storage and children's play. In an old cedar chest, my mother had saved dresses from the 1800s, belonging to my maternal grandmother's sisters, dead in their teens from tuberculosis.

My friends and I delighted in climbing the two flights of stairs to that third floor, pulling the dresses out of the chest, putting them on, and allowing our imaginations to soar. Weren't we the loveliest of ladies dressed in the finest of clothes, waiting to magnetize the perfect prince of our dreams into our lives?

As a child, I had little interest in playing with dolls. While my parents bought me one or two, they never pushed me to play with them. I was much more interested in climbing cherry trees, skating around the block, solving puzzles, and playing board games. That is precisely what my parents allowed and encouraged me to do. They always supported my desire to hone new skills, explore new experiences, and simply learn, grow, play, and create.

My mother's father worked as a clerk for the Pennsylvania Railroad. One of the benefits he received as an employee was free passes on trains.

I was his first grandchild. Thanks to the free passes, he was able to take me on trips to New York City and Washington, DC.

I can remember my mother putting her young daughter on a train in Glenside and telling both me and the conductor that I must get off at Wayne Junction, where my grandfather was always waiting to walk me back to the little row home on 18th Street, where he and my grandmother lived. My grandfather called my grandmother his "little rosebud."

Frequently, my grandfather and I would walk to nearby Stenton Park, where I played in the playground. We toured the museum. I remember my grandparents' little backyard with its pretty flowers and small goldfish pond, kept private and protected by a high wooden fence.

My mother had been reared Methodist. My father had been reared Presbyterian. Early in their marriage, they had migrated to Unitarianism. Neither wanted to be forced to accept rigid doctrines to join a religious community, even though they had to drive a half hour to attend church.

In Unitarian Sunday School, I was encouraged to think for myself. While we were taught stories from the Bible such as feeding five thousand people with only five loaves of bread and two fishes, the telling of the story was generally followed with questions like, 'What do you think happened here? How would you explain how five thousand people could be fed with only five loaves of bread and two fishes?'

Unitarian Sunday School was a valuable part of the conditioning that shaped me into thinking for myself and asking questions. However, Unitarians in my childhood church were intellectuals and scientists. They never talked about "salvation" or "mysticism." Many considered themselves agnostics or atheists.

As a young adult, I, too, thought of myself as an intellectual agnostic. I was quite clear that I did not believe in an old man sitting on a cloud with a thunderbolt in his hand, waiting to strike me dead if I did something he didn't want me to do. But I had no idea what this "God" thing was that so many people talked about, worshipped, and idolized.

Years later, when, around age thirty, I had that "mystical" experience with the man at the door (see Chapter

1 of *Shift*), the Unitarian lack of interest in "salvation" and "mysticism" felt like a glaring omission from my education. I suddenly *knew*, from personal experience, what "God" feels like, what "God" is.

I had been given no preconditioned vocabulary with which to think about that experience. I had to search for vocabularies in other religions to name it, conceptualize it, and try to understand it.

I found many different vocabularies in many different religions, all describing the same patterns of human experience.

While the words were different, the underlying experience I had had could have been described by any of those words.

## THE ERUPTION OF RAGE. THE ACHILLES HEEL OF MY PARENTS' CONDITIONING. BETRAYALS OF TRUST

In junior high school, I was editor of the school newspaper. Since my creative schoolteacher parents had always encouraged me to explore my world and think for myself, I decided to write an editorial on freedom of speech. The English teacher responsible for the newspaper was appalled!

She quickly rewrote my editorial, returned it to me with the "right" way to express my thoughts, and "kindly" told me she would nevertheless publish the "corrected" version using my name as the author.

I had never before experienced rage. At that moment, I did. The editorial was about freedom of speech. Why was my teacher, who had been given role power and authority over me, not allowing me to use my own words to express my own thoughts when I wrote about freedom of speech?

These were not grammar corrections. They were content changes. Was my teacher afraid of how she would be perceived by the male principal and supervisor who had role power over her if she didn't reshape my content?

Shocked and stunned, I exploded in what I later viewed as moral outrage. "You wrote it! You put your name on it."

I stormed out of the classroom, desperately seeking a place to process what had just happened. Retreating to a stall in the girls' room, I sobbed uncontrollably.

As stunned as I was by my teacher's words and conduct, I was even more stunned by my own rage. In my little, peaceful, supportive, nurturing family, I had never experienced that powerful emotion. There had been no need to.

I had always been a model student. I had always respected my teachers and learned from them. I had never before experienced such explosive emotional reactivity.

Where had it come from? What did it mean?

Who was I? A model, respectful student, or a raging rebel?

Suddenly, I felt the unexpected tension between who I thought I was and the behavior I had just exhibited. I didn't like the fact that I had disrespected a teacher, but I could not have done anything else, conditioned by the very stable and supportive family environment into which I had been blessed. I had absolutely no conscious intention as a young teen of stepping further into my own power. At age 14, I wasn't even thinking about personal empowerment or protecting my own sense of integrity, authenticity, soul, and energy field. I was simply reacting emotionally in the only way I could.

Looking at the experience from hindsight, not only was I protecting my own sense of integrity and authenticity, my soul, and my energy field, I was also standing in my own personal (em)power(ment). Suddenly, I had shifted into the Rebel archetype, with the unconscious intention of bringing integrity back into the whole dynamic between my teacher and me.

Were the teacher's motives conscious and intentional? Did she simply believe she was teaching me how to express myself in ways that would not conflict with the standard acceptable forms of expression or upset the male authorities who held role power? Did she believe she was protecting me from an unpleasant backlash? Was she afraid that if I stepped outside the walls of the little conceptual prison within which she herself was existing, she would be criticized and punished?

Did she want to be seen by the principal and superintendent of schools as a competent teacher, guiding her students in "proper" ways? Was she afraid of becoming embroiled in controversy over something one of her students had written? Afraid she might be fired and lose her source of income?

I will never know the teacher's motives for doing what she did. However, the cultural structures of the time required me to remain in her class, regardless of how she had treated me. Today, I can and do walk out when I am not treated with respect.

## DIFFERING WORLDVIEWS, PAINFUL EXPERIENCES

I constantly felt driven to understand and integrate other dissonant experiences, both with high school classmates and the cultural norms of the time. Who was I, separate and apart from what I had been taught and from my relationships with other people?

In high school, I once overheard a popular classmate call me "queer." The word didn't have the same connotation then as it does now, but her casual remark felt like an arrow piercing my heart.

I suffered from that wound for twenty years as I tried to integrate my mother's praise with my classmate's condemnation. Who was right? Who was wrong? Who was I?

I became anxious and nervous. My hands shook when I ate. I tried to hide the shaking so no one would see a part of me I didn't like. The harder I tried, the worse it became. I thought about committing suicide.

I so wanted to be loved and appreciated by everyone I met. But who was I supposed to believe? Whose worldview was right? Whose worldview was wrong?

Who was I? A beautiful, intelligent child and model student, adored by her parents and appreciated by her teachers, or "queer"?

As time passes and a painful experience recedes into the background, or you receive more information about the other players, experiences that once stunned and tormented you suddenly make sense.

Twenty years later, I attended a high school reunion. The classmate who had called me queer was in a wheelchair, recovering from hip surgery. She greeted me like a long-lost friend, totally oblivious to the pain and anguish her casual remark had caused me so many years before.

While I don't remember where I learned that the classmate who had called me queer had grown up in an abusive household where both wife and children were constantly terrorized by an alcoholic father, that one piece of information suddenly brought clarity to that painful life dynamic.

The sins of the parents are visited upon their children.[17] We continue to perpetuate this dysfunctional cycle of abuse, generation after generation, parent after parent, child after child.

My high school class has its own Facebook page. In 2021, only eighteen members were on that page out of an original three hundred-member graduating class. One of them was the classmate who called me queer.

I posted all the time. No one else ever did. While a few of my fellow students viewed my posts, no one ever commented.

In the spring of 2020, a different dynamic emerged. I had posted a notice about a talk I intended to give on April 20, 2020, on my blog talk radio show, Dancing with Words, Dancing with Wisdom. The title was "The Heroine's Journey."

That post generated more comments than I had ever seen before and developed some transparent communication that had never before appeared on that page.

One of my closest high school friends commented, "My world is shattered, and there is no solution." Was my friend a tiny part of our human collective trauma about which Thomas Hübl teaches?[18]

I replied, "Yes, Barbara, all of our worlds are shattered. Our trust has been betrayed. We are all going through "Dark Nights of the Soul" because all we have been taught by other human beings is no longer working. But there are many solutions. Each and every one of us is always in choice. Do

---

[17] https://biblia.com/bible/niv/jeremiah/32/18
[18] See, e.g., https://www.youtube.com/watch?v=Ur7b0pCuO2E

we choose to roll over and die, or do we choose to live and take our next step? If we choose to live, we have to trust that there is some larger purpose for our lives that we cannot fully see or understand. If so, the simple questions are:

- What do I think?
- What do I feel?
- What do I need?
- What are my choices?
- What do I need to know?
- Whom can I trust?"

My friend replied, "The last on your list is too hard at this time for me."

I responded, "I get it, Barbara. My trust, too, has been betrayed, over and over, by one human being after another. The high school classmate who called me queer. That single word was like an arrow through my heart, shattering it for years. The boys who wanted to borrow my homework but were too afraid to ask me out on a date. What was wrong with me?

"The armed East German soldiers, standing on the platform in Potsdam, Germany, when our American troop train pulled in early in the morning during the summer when I was an exchange student to Berlin during the Cold War. East German soldiers that were pointing their guns at my German brother and me when we were biking two hundred feet from the border.

"The father of my children, a man who had made vows to love, honor, and obey until death do us part, who decided it would be macho to have an affair with another woman and was unavailable to support either our children or me. We are now divorced. A once-beautiful soul mate turned hell mate when we lived together, smashing glasses into walls and viciously screaming at my children and me.

"An Atlantic City councilman, when I practiced law there, (who) slandered me and threatened to pull my contracts because I refused to put his political sign in my front yard.

"Managers of the community in which I once owned a beautiful home overlooking the Caribbean on Roatan, Honduras, who spent most of their days trying to figure out how to steal money from the homeowners.

"Builders of what I once believed would become my dream home in Boquete, Panama, who took my money, began laying foundations with hand-mixed concrete that wasn't strong enough to hold up the building, altered plans without my consent, built a septic system that was too high to drain properly, installed a plumbing system that leaked, and finally walked off the job. They refused to let me finish with other contractors unless I paid them an exorbitant amount of money. I declined, and lost one-third of my investment, but was finally able to sell the property—back to Panamanians—and recover at least some of my investment.

"An American landlord in Boquete with whom I had a continually renewing contract as long as I paid my rent on time and took care of the property, who found someone who would pay him more and evicted me.

"Robbers who cut a hole in a chain-link fence surrounding a rental home in which I was living in Boquete and came onto the property at night.

"An American woodworker in Boquete, who sold all the custom furniture he was building for me for drugs.

"A man I once trusted, who asked me for a 'short-term loan,' and then refused to repay it when I needed the money to pay my bills.

"So, whom can you trust? Only yourself and whatever God, Higher Power, Universal Energy, Allah, Brahma, Tao, pure present-moment awareness that works for you, right here, right now, in each and every moment. When, as Ram Dass said, you can just 'Be here now,' life becomes very simple and serene. It's all inner work. Much love to you, Barbara. You have been such a wonderful friend over the years."

But the kicker was the comment from the classmate who had called me "queer" so many years ago: "Although we graduated the same year from Abington, I had no idea that you were bullied or picked on and miss treated (sic) that way, and I am so sorry for that as well the people who (sic) trusted who treated you so badly. You have accomplished so much, and I wish you the best now."

I never told her she was the one who had called me queer.

Amends had been made, and the wound fully healed.

There was another tension among worldviews that arose for me during high school. I was an excellent student. I graduated fourth in a class of almost three hundred students. I was a graduation speaker. I sang soprano in the chorus, trios, and sextets and sang well enough to sing in the Pennsylvania State Chorus. I swam backstroke on the women's varsity swimming team. I acted in school plays and was co-editor of the high school yearbook. I was chosen as my school's American Field Service summer exchange student to Berlin, Germany, between my junior and senior years.

My parents had given me opportunities to take tap dancing lessons, ballet lessons, ballroom dancing lessons, art lessons, and piano lessons. All these opportunities and honors integrated with my parents' and teachers' perceptions of me.

Boys with similar accomplishments were liked by the teachers and admired by both male and female students. I had my own small, supportive group of female friends, yet boys and some of the other girls seemed to avoid me. What was wrong with me?

As a teenager, I had always wished my father had told me, just once, that I was beautiful. Born into a strict German family, devoid of emotion, fathers from that culture didn't tell their daughters they were beautiful. I felt awkward, unattractive, and out of place. What was wrong with me?

I was not part of the clique of "popular girls," the louder, less studious girls whom the boys seemed to prefer. What did these girls have that I did not? They were always painting their nails or fixing their hair. They talked more loudly than I did and more often. They were more interested in teasing or poking at the boys than studying or climbing cherry trees. I so wanted boys to like me. What was wrong with me?

No one had ever told me about the raging hormones flooding boys' bodies as they approach puberty. Sex was a topic my parents never discussed, nor did they ever educate me about what to expect on my wedding night. Perhaps they simply didn't know what to say about such an intimate experience.

Years later, my mother told me that sex had been my mother and father's Waterloo. She had always desired it more than my father. She once wrote that the words on her tombstone should read, "I blew it!"

During one of my solitary excursions to the third floor of my childhood home, while exploring the books in an upstairs bookcase, I *did* discover a copy of the Kama Sutra,[19] hidden behind other books. I read it with great interest and then began exploring experientially with Jimmy. That didn't last long. Jimmy was still too young to be experiencing his own raging hormones and couldn't have an erection.

Although I didn't know it in high school, I was clearly being culturally conditioned to be a wife and mother. I was required to take classes in cooking and sewing. I was not permitted to take classes in carpentry or mechanics.

My tension over feeling not good enough in the eyes of boys was exacerbated because my mother had made my role in life quite clear. I was to follow the family tradition; marry a nice man; learn to cook, wash, and iron clothes; bake delicious pies, cakes, bread, and cookies; clean the home; care for the garden; bear children; and become a wonderful steward and caretaker of home, husband, and family.

Was it also her personal, unconscious intention that her only daughter bear the children she had been unable to bear? God forbid that I should pursue my love of math and science and become an old maid, living a dull, drab life in a laboratory.

I deliberately started to dumb myself down. I tried to learn how to apply makeup to appear more beautiful. I practiced walking in high heels. I even got a job one summer as a model in one of the local department stores.

Only one boy in high school ever asked me out. He was very religious, but he did kiss me. It was a slobbery kiss that didn't feel good, but he did take me to a prom. Maybe, somewhere, somehow, I had a few redeeming qualities, at least in the eyes of one boy.

---

[19] https://www.amazon.com/Complete-Kama-Sutra-Unabridged-Translation/ dp/0892815256

The cultural conditioning at that time was that girls were supposed to be physically beautiful to please and attract boys. Being smart didn't matter. Being competent didn't matter. Being kind and considerate didn't matter. All that mattered was physical attractiveness and a willingness to have sex.

I lay out on the Ocean City, New Jersey, beach for hours so I could acquire a beautiful tan that might attract some boy. Today, a dermatologist regularly treats me for skin cancer.

As a teenage girl, I didn't think about cultural conditioning. Between my mother's pressure to marry and the fact that boys didn't ask me out on dates, I simply felt constant tension between what my mother wanted for me, what I loved to do, and the fact that boys seemed not to like me. I felt not good enough. I felt as if this was the one area of my life where I was a failure.

My mother's messages were subtle but present. Guided by my mother's perhaps justified fear of the plight of an unmarried woman in the 1960s workplace and her desire for grandchildren, I went to college not to develop my mind and intellectual interests but to find a husband—someone who would financially provide for me and our children and tolerate an ugly duckling as a wife.

Was my mother living the unfulfilled parts of her own life through me, her only biological daughter? Did she unconsciously want me to bear the children she had desired and been unable to bear?

She was such an exceptional mother in so many ways. I tried very hard to become the woman she wanted me to be— until her life for me was no longer the life my soul demanded I live.

On summer days, I donned my roller skates and took our two little dogs for runs around the block. The family picked blueberries and blackberries on the vacant lots near Custis Woods.

When I was older, my father organized the neighborhood children into softball teams. We played ball in the street in front of our Glenside home.

I was good at hitting the ball. Everyone would shout and cheer when someone scored a home run.

This kind of sports competition was a functional use of "power against." Yes, we wanted to hit a home run. Yes, we wanted our team to win. But we were also improving our individual skills, as well as our teamwork. When one person won, everyone won. It was just a fun and challenging game.

On summer weekends, when we weren't at our little rental cottage on Beverly Lake, near Delta, Ontario, Canada, my parents would take the family to the beach in Ocean City, New Jersey. I loved the water, jumped the waves, got knocked down, and picked myself up again. Together, we spent hours building beautiful sandcastles, only to see them washed away by the incoming tide. This experience was such an excellent metaphor for my later experience with all my culturally conditioned worldviews. One by one, they were washed away by new information and experiences.

In the evenings, we would walk on the boardwalk and ride the rides. I loved the roller coaster—the suspense of slowly climbing to the top of the track, followed by the thrill of barreling down the other side. Other children would scream. I never did. I was simply living my childhood life full out.

I remember, at the beginning of World War II, living in that nice suburban home in Custis Woods. My Uncle Gene, my father's oldest brother, lived with us after his wife, Jane, died.

Uncle Gene was the neighborhood air raid warden. We had an air raid siren on top of our home. Whenever the siren sounded, we closed the heavy black drapes covering all our windows, turned off the lights, and remained silent. I never questioned why. I just followed my parents' instructions.

Little did I know that German submarines were lurking three miles off the East Coast of the United States. At age five, I would never have understood what German submarines were, why they were there, why the sirens on our rooftop were blasting, or why we were closing the black drapes, turning off the lights, and remaining silent until the "all clear" signal sounded.

Toward the end of World War II, my father was drafted into the Navy as an enlisted man. He served as a chaplain's assistant because of his musical training. In 1945, he was assigned to the Naval Base in Pensacola, Florida. Our family moved into a small, basic wooden house in a Naval subdivision. I remember my mother leaning over the bathtub, washing our clothes on a washboard. I remember pigs wandering through our backyard, and watermelon growing wild from discarded seeds.

I went to school in the mornings. I remember recess and sitting on pine needles in the schoolyard under tall trees. I remember my beautiful teacher with her slow Southern drawl gently stimulating our minds. For me, it was a lovely experience. For the rest of the world, it was hell.

On August 15, 1945, I was sitting in a theater at the Pensacola, Florida, Naval Base, watching a fascinating movie. Suddenly, the movie stopped. The auditorium lights burst on. Emperor Hirohito had just announced the surrender of Imperial Japan—nine days after two devastating atomic bombs had been dropped on the cities of Hiroshima and Nagasaki. Within my little, protected worldview, I knew nothing about atomic bombs. I was just frustrated that I never saw the end of that fascinating movie.

## WIDENING MY WORLDVIEW

In 1953 during the Cold War, the American Field Service (AFS) selected me as a summer exchange student to Berlin, Germany. The experience opened my mind to different cultures, traditions, languages, and ways of thinking. It also opened my mind to the suffering and desecration we humans created during World War II.

Most remarkable was the fact that my parents let their only daughter go, even though there had been riots in Berlin three weeks before our departure. AFS was desperately working to create a backup plan and find substitute homes and families in West Germany if the Berlin riots worsened.

My parents had such a strong and unshakeable love of life that they simply trusted that all would end well. It was more important for them to gift their daughter with an experience of a lifetime than to fear her possible physical death.

In 1953, Berlin was an island surrounded by Russian-controlled East Germany. To get to West Berlin, we had to take a United States troop train in the dead of night from Frankfurt in the United States Zone of West Germany. Heavy black drapes covered all the windows, just like the heavy black drapes over the windows of our home during the Second World War. We had strict instructions not to open the drapes.

In early morning, the train stopped. As a curious, adventuresome 16-year-old, I carefully opened the drapes a crack, and peeked out. The train had stopped in Potsdam, right outside Berlin, still in the German East Zone. Soldiers carrying guns crammed the platform. I quickly closed the drapes, suddenly understanding why we had been instructed not to open them.

That summer, I lived with a German family in Spandau, part of the British-controlled sector of West Berlin. My German "father" worked in the Spandau prison.

Spandau Prison, during World War II, was a predecessor to the Nazi concentration camps of Dachau, Osthofen, Oranienburg, Sonnenburg, Lichtenburg, and the marshland camps around Esterwegen. Journalists and opponents of Adolf Hitler were incarcerated and tortured there. By 1953, Spandau was housing Nazi war criminals, sentenced to imprisonment during the Nuremburg trials, among them, Rudolf Hess.[20]

My German "mother" scolded me when I brushed my hair in my bedroom. She had no vacuum cleaner with which to remove my hair from her carpet.

My German brother, Peter, and sister, Brigitte, wanted to use my visit to improve their English. Although I had studied Latin and French in high school, I had never studied German. As a result, I learned only a few German words.

Peter and his male friends seemed to like me more than American boys did. How nice to be treated with respect!

One day, Peter and I went swimming in the Havel, a river running through Berlin. Where we were swimming, the river was divided by a rope marking the boundary between East

---

[20] https://en.wikipedia.org/wiki/Spandau_Prison

and West Berlin. Of course, Peter and I swam under the rope so we could say we had swum in East Berlin.

Another time, Peter and I rode bikes toward the border between Spandau, in the British Sector of West Berlin, and the Eastern, Russian-controlled Zone of Germany. As we approached, a soldier patrolling the border raised his gun and pointed it toward us. We quickly turned our bikes around and rode back to what then felt like safety.

The family had no car or refrigerator. Every morning, Peter and I would ride our bikes to the little, nearby grocery store to shop for fresh food for the day, supplementing the food my German mother grew in the small garden in her backyard.

Peter and I went on long bike rides together. Peter escorted me all over East and West Berlin on the U-Bahn and S-Bahn, the Berlin underground and above-ground trains that traversed the city. He showed me the devastation World War II had wrought. He took me to the opera.

What opened my mind most were the experiences of seeing so many armed soldiers, the devastation the war had wrought on so many of the buildings, and the differences between German and American culture and lifestyles.

In my American home, we ate bacon, eggs, toast, and orange juice for breakfast. In Germany, we ate open-faced sandwiches with meats and cheeses on delicious, homemade, hearty bread. In America, I took a bath every night before I went to bed. In Germany, I took a bath once a week, the water heated on the kitchen stove.

A friend recently asked me whether I was aware of how unpopular Germans were during this period in the Western world. No, I wasn't. Was I simply not paying attention to what was happening outside of my immediate experience?

In my world, people were just people. Yes, each one looked different from me; many acted in ways I didn't understand, but they were just other, unique people I wanted to get to know and understand.

We had no TV in my childhood home. We had no smartphones. We had newspapers, but I didn't read them. I was too busy exploring my own immediate world with friends and family, playing games, learning exciting new things in school, and just enjoying life.

## REFLECTIONS FROM HINDSIGHT

When I look back upon these early years, I see the seeds of who I am today—someone willing to take risks and step into her own power, yet cautious when confronted with dissonant worldviews and cultures. Although I grew up trying to meet the standards that a patriarchal culture and my mother had placed on me as a female, I felt confused by the paradox and dissonance but still longed for the acceptance it would bring if I followed the rules. But whose rules?

Little did I then know how little I knew and how many hard, challenging, devastating experiences I would have to navigate, to sink or swim, to die or survive. Little did I know how many times I would be challenged in this physical body and physical world; how many mountains I would have to climb; how many deep, dark valleys and torrential streams I would have to cross. Little did I know the strength, courage, skill, persistence, and commitment I would need to find ways to overcome those challenges.

Finally, fully Surrendering into Soul, I allowed that powerful center point of energetic/spiritual Non-Dual Consciousness or pure Spiritual Energy to guide my every step and word in every moment. In this physical world, life had taught me that far too often, other humans, whether intentionally or unintentionally, would betray my trust.

I could not live my life without support. I simply had to trust that Spiritual Energetic guidance, even though I couldn't conceptualize it, understand it, or even know that it was *real* in the sense that we generally use that word in what we perceive as our physical world.

What I *did* experience was that whenever I set a clear, high-integrity intention, it was always fulfilled, although often not in ways my little left brain could ever have figured out.

I can now see the injustices I experienced as a child at the hands of others as the others struggling with what they believed to be the right thing for themselves and me. It doesn't make their conduct right, ethical, and moral, but it *does* allow me to move on and accept the fact that the others were doing the best they could, given their own upbringing and cultural conditioning.

My experiences of betrayal were long-term lessons in patience and compassion; how perspectives can change when we receive new information; about learning to set boundaries; about detaching from other people's harmful and abusive words; about moving out of abusive relationships and seeking supportive relationships.[21]

---

[21] Using different words, but pointing to the same conduct, see Don Miguel Ruiz's *The Four Agreements*. 1) Be impeccable with your word. 2) Don't take anything personally. 3) Don't make assumptions. 4) Always do your best.

# Chapter 3
# The Threshold - Exploring the Unknown

*"Neither an outside observer nor the Subject who undergoes the process can explain fully how particular experiences are able to change one's center of energy so decisively, or why they so often have to bide their hour to do so. We have a thought, or we perform an act, repeatedly, but on a certain day the real meaning of the thought peals through us for the first time, or the act has suddenly turned into a moral impossibility."*
—William James, "The Varieties of Religious Experience"

## COMMUNICATING THE EXPERIENCE

The experiences I wrote about in Chapter 1 of *Shift* were so amazing I had to tell others. The words came tumbling out of my mouth and were met with blank stares. I was talking, but I was not communicating.

At that point in time, I was pursuing the path of Matthew Fox's "Via Positiva."[22]

The question I was asking fifty-five years ago was, "How could I use analytical, divisive words to communicate a unifying, holistic experience?" Like a Zen koan[23], the

---

[22] https://dailymeditationswithmatthewfox.org/2019/08/28/via-positiva-via-negativa-intertwining/;
https://en.wikipedia.org/wiki/Apophatic_theology#:~:text=Etymolog y%20and%20definition,-%22Apophatic%22%2C%20 Ancient&text=From%20Online%20Etymology%20Dictionary%3A,ap ophatic%20 (adj.)&text=Via%20negativa%20or%20via%20negationis,the%20katap hatic%20 or%20positive%20way.

[23] https://tricycle.org/magazine/what-is-a-koan/.

question was a paradoxical riddle, demonstrating the limitations of conceptual thinking and a shift into pure present-moment awareness.

I felt driven to find the answer, but it was like trying to hammer a nail using a screwdriver. I had no choice but to cross the threshold of my own Heroine's Journey into the unknown.

I journaled. I wrote poetry. I wrote essays and stories. I asked questions. Words were illusions, dancing at a masked ball. "Words are only fingers pointing at the moon. They are not the moon."[24]

Nevertheless, there *was* a moon behind the word illusions. There was a "Human Truth Puzzle" that could be put together. In fact, it had been put together, over and over, by person after person throughout history. Words were one piece of that Human Truth Puzzle. Each person who solved the puzzle used different words to point to the solution.

People who are connected to and immersed in that existential center point of Non-Dual Consciousness can hear, understand, and connect with the words of all the different worldviews because they have personally experienced the existential moments from which the words have emanated. Because they have walked in the existential shoes of another, they can understand, be compassionate, forgive, and serve the present moment needs to shift *power over*, *power under*, and *power against* into *Power With.*

There *was* that unifying, holistic moment of experience—that sudden insight—that connected those

---

[24] http://www.cttbusa.org/shurangama/shurangama6.asp.html; Shurangama Sutra, 2.61.

Biblical words I had been taught as a child[25] with my own unifying experience. For a single moment in time, my consciousness had jumped out of that little protective, conceptual, black box within which my parents had so conscientiously conditioned and protected me, back into that center point of Non-Dual Consciousness or pure present-moment awareness.

It felt as if I had found the lost gold mine, the pearl of great price. How could I share that treasure with the world? How could I use analytical, divisive words to communicate a unifying, holistic experience?

Little did I then know that all I had been given at that moment was a single, tiny opening in that little protective, conceptual, black box into which my parents had conditioned me and through which, as a child, they had protected me. But that one moment in time blinded, mesmerized, and magnetized me with its brilliance. It would not let me go.

## NEW EXPERIENCES, NEW ARCHETYPES

My journey since that first eye-opening experience in 1966, which I wrote about in *Shift*, has been filled with archetypes. I have named them as I have been able to connect their energies with roles I have either played, encountered along my path, or been forced to play.

Archetypes make me think of Jacques' statement in *As You Like It*, by William Shakespeare,

"All the world's a stage,

---

[25] "But I say unto you, that ye resist not evil; but whosoever shall smite thee on thy right check, turn to him the other also." (Matt. 5:39.KJV)

And all the men and women merely players; They have their exits and their entrances;

And one man in his time plays many parts…"[26]

As the terrain and archetypal patterns changed, both the archetypal roles I was required to play and the words I spoke changed. My clear intention was always to shift dysfunction into function, to shift power over, power under, and power against into Power With[27], and to shift top-down patriarchal control structures into aligned creativity, co-creativity, connection, and manifestation.

Even though I was not always aware of the Buddhist Eightfold Path,[28] I am now aware of how my own intention parallels "right intention" in that teaching.

As previously stated, one worldly archetype frequently and repeatedly appeared to challenge me on this new and more encompassing Journey—the bully (coward). Carolyn Myss[29] describes this archetype as follows:

*"Consider whether, on your life path, you confront one experience and relationship after another that appears to have more power than you and ultimately leads you to ask, "Will I stand up to this challenge?" People are often called to take on bullies for the sake of others, as David did Goliath, and this is another criterion of your connection to this archetype."*

Conventional wisdom holds that underneath a bully is a coward trying to keep others from discovering his true identity. Symbolically, the Coward within must stand up to

---

[26] https://literarydevices.net/all-the-worlds-a-stage/
[27] Masters, Robert Augustus, PhD (2018) "To Be a Man: A Guide to True Masculine Power."
[28] https://tricycle.org/magazine/noble-eightfold-path/
[29] https://www.myss.com/free-resources/sacred-contracts-and-your-archetypes/archetypes/

being bullied by his own inner fears, which is the path to empowerment through these two archetypes.[30]

SEARCHING FOR ANSWERS

Fifty-five years ago, I was trying to learn from other people and other people's words how to answer that life purpose question that seemed to be driving me forward: "How can I use analytical, divisive words to communicate a unifying, holistic experience?" I kept having new experiences, meeting new people, and reading more books. Yet, I still didn't find the answer I was seeking.

Little did I then understand that by trying to find the answers "out there," I was separating myself from that amazing energetic connection I had experienced as a young mother. I kept falling back into creating a subject/object duality: me, as subject, looking "out there" to find the answer to my question. I was also looking at other worldly authorities for my answers, rather than to that energetic, spiritual connection within, which I could experience, but which my mind was conceptualizing in an infinite number of ways. At that time, I did not fully realize that the answers did not lie "out there." The answers lay "in here."

"Know thyself." Those were words written over the portal at the Temple of Apollo at Delphi, Greece, in the seventh century BC. Those same words were spoken by Socrates, according to the writings of his student Plato, over twenty-four hundred years ago. And now, I was again asking the question, "Who am I?" to which, so many years ago, the Temple of Delphi, Socrates, and Plato had all offered

---

[30] https://www.myss.com/free-resources/sacred-contracts-and-your-archetypes/appendix-a-gallery-of-archtypes/

identical answers, the same word fingers pointing at the same moon.

Was the question that kept tormenting me given to me alone to explore? Was it my task alone to bring the answer back to the world?

The task felt gargantuan. It felt like *Mission Impossible*. It felt like David standing before Goliath. It felt like the task given to Frodo in *Lord of the Rings*. Who or what would guide me through this void of conceptual unknowing?

A friend once talked about "shaman sickness" when describing his own life path. Is shaman sickness simply the fear or overwhelm of stepping into your full spiritual purpose and power?

Could I do this? I didn't know. What I did know was that I had to take the next step. And the next. And the next, until the moment I took my last breath.

## CROSSING THE THRESHOLD

Now, fifty-five years after that initial eye-opening mystical, unifying experience, I understand the threshold in a much broader, inclusive, and more encompassing sense. Originally, it was simply *my* threshold.

But what if the Heroine's (or Hero's) Journey is one that every human must take? What if each of us has been differently culturally conditioned? What if each of us is living in his or her own little black, conceptual worldview box? What if we don't even see that we've been conditioned into a particular worldview?

Our worldview feels very safe and secure. It is comfortable.

We believe it is the only "right" way to think and act.

Occasionally, we bump into dissonant worldviews. We perceive these as clearly "wrong." We believe they must be corrected and forced to conform to our own, human-created doctrines. We sit in self-righteousness and judgment, clutching our illusory worldviews, projecting our fear and rage out onto those whose worldviews are different.

"It is all their fault! They are wrong! They are dangerous!

They are evil! They must either be controlled or destroyed!"

We don't want to look at, or perhaps can't even see, the smallness of our own, little, conceptual black box or the prison walls within which it has entrapped us. We certainly don't want to pull aside the heavy black drapes hung tightly over our windows and peek outside. After all, if we don't adhere to the doctrines our parents, teachers, priests, and rabbis have taught us, we shall certainly be cast into hell and forever consumed by its fiery flames. Far better to conform and remain silent.

I grew into present-moment awareness—one moment at a time—one experience at a time. Curiously pulling aside the black drapes of my beautiful little protected world, sneaking a peek at the horror, the guns, the violence, the abuse, the human suffering, I quickly closed those drapes again. I began thinking about what, if anything, I could do to change this. It was a vicious, self-perpetrating cycle of worldview against worldview, human against human, all disconnected from self, from others, and from a Power greater than themselves.

As I stepped out of my own highly protected childhood family into interaction with the rest of the world, the innocent female child I had been conditioned to be, frequently and unexpectedly became the victim of other people's desperate needs to feel good enough, the male patriarchal, top-down control system, and male testosterone. (Are the latter two related?) As previously stated, my innocence, desire to connect, play, and co-create were simultaneously my Achilles heel.

The abusers continued to abuse. The unaware continued to harm through their ignorance. The controllers continued to control. Each was still stuck in his or her little conceptual worldview, terrified of opening the black drapes that imprisoned him, terrified of crossing his own threshold and reconnecting with that center point of Non-Dual Consciousness—that conceptual void of pure present-moment awareness.

To protect and enhance my own energetic field and continue to share the gifts given to me with those who were suffering and open to receiving, I had to learn many mental and physical skills. I learned skills such as detaching from other people's negative words about me, moving out of the physical range of abusers if possible, and, if not immediately possible, defending myself by using my mind, my awareness, my problem-solving abilities, and my verbal and legal skills to manifest my strengths and bring my abusers' façades into transparency. This has been my Heroine's Journey. It continues to this day.

# Chapter 4
# Challenges - Moving through the Unknown World, the Void, the Mystery, Seeking Answers

*"You have your identity when you find out, not what you can keep your mind on, but what you can't keep your mind off."*

—A.R. Ammons

## MY PERSONAL CHALLENGES

The dissonant experiences I had with the neighbor's child, my junior high school teacher, the teenage boys in my high school, and the classmate who called me "queer," tortured my soul. The eye-opening experiences I had as a young mother enlivened my spirit. The dissonance between the two emerged as a series of existential questions that hurled me onward:

- Do I stand strong in personal integrity, or do I follow someone else's rules and orders?

- Who am I?

- How can I use analytical, divisive words to communicate a unifying, holistic experience?

- What is my purpose on the planet?

- How can I best protect my soul from the projection, self-righteousness, and abuse hurled at me by others?

- How much time do I have?

These were not theoretical or conceptual questions. These were gut-wrenching, experiential questions that would not let me go. The questions forced me to make constant, existential choices as I walked one step at a time through that unknown void. I was free, but I had no idea where I was going or how to get there. Where could I find trustworthy maps that would guide me? Where could I find mentors who would support me?

The questions I was asking and the choices I was making brought emotional and mental challenges as my own existential choices bumped into, rattled, or threatened other people's conditioned worldviews. For the most part, I experienced myself as a living, breathing, playful, loving, exploring human being whose greatest joy was connecting, playing with, learning from, and growing with other living, breathing, exploring human beings.

The emotional challenges arose when I felt ignored, abused, misunderstood, or treated as an object by the people I depended on for my safety, food, shelter, and sense of identity. I was not willing or able to be their slave or a pawn on their chessboard. The emotional challenges manifested as fear, terror, anger, rage, shame, and a deep sense of betrayal by, and distrust of, other human beings, particularly unaware or abusive men.

Did my emotional challenges mirror and reflect the emotional challenges my abusers were experiencing? Was there a mirroring in the bully/coward archetype?

Like the Emperor in Hans Christian Anderson's parable, "The Emperor's New Clothes," or the Wizard in L. Frank Baum's *The Wonderful Wizard of Oz*, is the bully really a coward, hiding behind a façade of pomp and circumstance, fine clothing, money, and an imposing exterior while cowering under an interior of fear, terror, anger, rage, and shame?

My Heroine's Journey was about overcoming those emotional challenges and protecting my soul, my authenticity, my integrity, my life force, and my own energy field from the dysfunctional conduct of other ignorant, suffering human beings. Each was on his or her own Hero's or Heroine's Journey, with different needs, intentions, and culturally conditioned expectations.

My Heroine's Journey was also about noticing how others sometimes experienced my pure intentions as disruptive or controlling. My intention was often so different from the effect my speech and actions had on others.

## CHALLENGES WITH WORDS AND WORLDVIEWS

I felt driven to discover ways to burrow beneath the words to understand the underlying disconnections and dissonances, so that together we could return our relationships to fun, play, creativity, co-creativity, teamwork, and aligned manifestation.

The emotional challenges spawned mental and physical challenges.

- How could I protect myself from verbal and physical abuse?
- How could I find people with whom I could have transparent, eye-opening conversations?
- How could I find people with whom I could learn and grow?

# CHALLENGES WITH MALE TESTOSTERONE AND OUR PATRIARCHAL CULTURE

- How could I earn a decent living and provide for my safety, food, and shelter in a culture in which both men and women were taught that a woman's role in life was to be nothing more than the bearer of a man's children, his cook, housekeeper, and gardener; a support to her husband in any way he dictated, directed, or needed, regardless of whether it honored her own sense of integrity; that paid women far less than men for the same or superior work; where schoolgirls were required to learn home economics and sewing and were not permitted to study mechanics and carpentry?
- How could I earn respect?
- How could I give back to the world what had been so freely given to me?

Was our culturally conditioned patriarchal system driven solely by male testosterone, raging hormones, and the rhetoric young men hear in teenage locker rooms? Are they bragging to one another about their sexual conquests, their "scores"? Are they hearing that their masculinity depends on their ability to master and control women, children, and physically weaker men and force them to serve the strong man and do his bidding? Are they hearing that their power should be used to kill, rape, abuse, and desecrate in bully/coward "power over," "power under," and "power against" dynamics?

Or is a culture of mature, elder wisdom-keeping males teaching young men that their role in life is to bring their raging hormones to the surface of their consciousness and learn to master their testosterone and use its power to respect, protect, and serve all needs to the best of their ability, including those of themselves, women, children, and physically weaker men. Are these cultural and rhetorical differences the differences between dictatorships and democracies?

Is this testosterone drive so profoundly hidden in the male unconscious that men are unable to bring it to the surface of their consciousness into transparency, own it, and transform it in ways that respect both their own biological needs and other woman's and men's needs for support and respect? Do women also have a responsibility to help men master their testosterone? Is this driving testosterone part of Sigmund Freud's Id?

Positive Psychology describes Freud's Id as follows:

The id operates at an unconscious level and focuses solely on instinctual drives and desires. Two biological instincts make up the id, according to Freud: eros, or the instinct to survive that drives us to engage in life-sustaining activities, and Thanatos, or the death instinct that drives destructive, aggressive, and violent behavior.[31]

A beautiful, mature male friend recently commented that young men think "below the belt." They think with their penises, not with their heads and hearts. Another male friend once commented that every woman with whom he had ever had sex was an angel. And a third once told me a story about how, as a young man, he would just "pop it off" and then take off. But then, one time, the woman with whom he had just "popped it off" told him she had not yet gotten her period, and all he could think was, "OMG, what do I do now?"

---

[31] https://positivepsychology.com/psychoanalysis/

A fourth male friend, now committed to a gay marriage, told me how deeply he had suffered as a child by the raging male hormones other males had directed toward him, taunting and bullying him. And a female friend once told me that as she was giving a male client a massage, he got an erection. He was deeply apologetic and commented that men struggle with testosterone their entire lives.

But what happens to the woman who becomes pregnant when a man just "pops it off" and then takes off? What happens to the fatherless child, to the female child who has been raped by her father or priest, to the innocent child who is kidnapped and sexually trafficked?

All become horribly traumatized. They lose their faith and trust in people. They shrink and contract rather than blossoming and blooming.

Some commit suicide, others take a lifetime to heal. Some never do. A few do overcome their trauma, step into their own spiritual power, and transform their own "experiences" into healing balm to support the struggling survivors of unmastered male testosterone.

# Chapter 5
# Death and Rebirth[32] - Who am I, Separate and Apart from All My Conditioning?

*"But with the familialization of the male, we would see the beginning of the single, great, enduring, and nightmarish task of all subsequent civilization: the taming of testosterone."*

—Ken Wilber

In *Stories Told by The Mother II*, "A Serpent Keeps the Gates of the Treasure," Mirra Alfassa, Sri Aurobindo's female partner and founder of Auroville in Tamil Nadu, India, tells the story of a "tremendous serpent, ten times, fifty times larger than an ordinary one," that "keeps the gates of the treasure."

She said, "Let me pass."

The serpent replied, "I cannot let you pass."

---

[32] Joseph Campbell, in his "Hero's Journey," created the words "Death and Rebirth" as placeholders for the experiential shatteredness of the conditioned self and the birth of the aware authentic self. I have chosen to use Campbell's words "Death and Rebirth" simply for consistency. Others have created different words as placeholders for the same archetypal experience. St. John of the Cross titled his book "Dark Night of the Soul." Related concepts are "positive disintegration" in psychology, "soul loss" or the "descent to the underworld" in Shamanism, "katabasis" in Greek mythology and "nigredo," as Carl Jung symbolically understood it in alchemy. For an excellent discussion of this, see https://medium.com/the-apeiron-blog/the-dark-night-of-the-soul-understanding-amidst-the-absence-of-meaning-3494cb193bc2

The Mother asked, "What must I bring you in order to gain entrance?"

"(If) you could become master of the sex impulse in man, if you succeeded in conquering that in humanity, I could no longer resist."

"That is quite difficult."

In the *Bridges of Madison County*, the character Robert Kincaid states, "The curse of modern times is the preponderance of male hormones in places where they can do long-term damage. Even if we're not talking about wars between nations or assaults on nature, there's still that aggressiveness that keeps us apart from each other and the problems we need to be working on. We have to somehow sublimate those male hormones, or at least get them under control."

## LEGAL MARRIAGE AND COMMITMENT TO THE MAN I MARRIED AND OUR CHILDREN

I did finally fulfill my mother's wishes and married Alexander Stilwell Traub III, on March 22, 1958. Everyone called him Sandy. Stilling my mother's fears that I would become an old maid, we married before I graduated from college. My mother had assured me that if husband and wife each gave 100 percent to the marriage, it would be a wonderful marriage.

On our wedding night, Sandy was intent on having as many orgasms as possible so he could brag to his buddies about how masculine he was. I did not have any.

Having been so thoroughly conditioned by the patriarchal culture into which I had been reared, I blamed myself for my frigidity. I did everything I could to satisfy Sandy's sexual needs. I remained frigid. I kept giving,

giving, and giving, but I remained sexually frigid. What was wrong with me? Was I not beautiful enough?

Years later, in 1975, my mother wrote, "There's no such thing as a frigid wife—just clumsy husbands!" In hindsight, after many years of lived experience, my mother's statement seemed true. Or were the clumsy husbands simply inexperienced and uneducated husbands?

After three years of marriage, our first son was born. Two years later, our second son was born, and finally, two years later, our third son. The children brought me joy. However, it often felt as if I had four sons instead of three sons and a husband.

On weekends, Sandy went off sailing by himself, leaving me to care for home and children. Settling comfortably into the Hestia archetype, I became very good at caring for husband, home, and children. I truly loved my role as wife, mother, and keeper of the hearth, but at times like those, I often felt lonely except for my joy in being a mother. I was also exhausted from the 24-hour-a-day responsibilities. By the time I got to bed, I had little interest in sex.

For the first few years of our marriage, Sandy and I had a functional and often fun marriage, even though it was not sexually intimate. He gifted me with flowers on my birthday. We went sailing together on Penobscot Bay in Maine where his family owned a summer home. We took a trip to Nova Scotia and Prince Edward Island in Canada. We went sailing with our two older sons in the British Virgin Islands, leaving the one-year-old home with a friend. I supported Sandy in finishing college and getting his degree in civil engineering. He always said we had the perfect marriage.

He made me laugh. It was one of the beautiful things about our relationship. I would be serious. He would crack a joke.

We would both laugh, my issue would dissipate, and we would move on together. I still have the birthday and Valentine's cards he gave me and many of our letters to one another.

"'I love the earth with all of myself.'—Kahlil Gibran. Loving you, I love all things."

"For the one I married. Though we've sometimes different points of view—I'm still A-Quiver over you! Happy Valentine's Day, With love."

"Happy Birthday, Keep Smiling. It makes people wonder what we've been up to. Love, Sandy."

## EVOLUTION OF A GROUP MARRIAGE

In 1962, Sandy was offered a job in Vineland, New Jersey. Although we continued to spend time monthly with both sets of parents, we now lived farther away. Getting together with expanded family now required more effort and intentional, focused commitment.

In Vineland, the little, culturally impoverished South Jersey poultry farm town where we had migrated, Sandy and I became good friends with Sandy's boss and his wife. They, too, had three children and what appeared to be a functional marriage. We lived ten minutes apart, had many interesting conversations, and did fun things together. Getting together with them was much easier than getting together with blood relatives who lived two or three hours away. Without even realizing it, we were beginning to form a different kind of family.

The boss, a male, read a book called *The Harrad Experiment*, written by another male, Robert Rimmer. We all read it. It was about group marriage and how, in an intimate relationship with another person, you could discover aspects of yourself that you never knew existed. We were fascinated yet cautious. Among other things, it explored cross-sexual relationships.

Step by step, over a nine-month period, we inched ourselves into what ultimately became a seven-year group marriage. It developed organically. Our interaction became an in-depth education in human dynamics, far more profound than any of us had ever anticipated.

When we first decided to exchange sexual partners, Sandy and the other woman had sex. The other man and I did not. I told the other man I was nonorgasmic. He was caring and compassionate. He did not force himself on me.

When Sandy told me that he and the other woman had had sex, my heart sank. I didn't know why. However, I was so committed to our marriage, family, and children that I brushed the feelings aside. I had made a marital vow to "love, honor, and obey until death do us part" and to dedicate myself to supporting my husband in fulfilling his desires and following whatever path he wanted to pursue.

The next time we were together, the other man and I also had sex. I was nonorgasmic. He was understanding and sympathetic.

The other man commented that Sandy just didn't know what he was doing. I later realized that was true. The other woman later commented that initially, she did not like the way Sandy made love.

The group marriage often felt like an emotional roller coaster with unbelievable emotional highs and gut-wrenching lows. We were co-creating our own little community outside of the cultural norms, with nothing to guide us but our own heads and hearts.

I had never before experienced jealousy. Within the group marriage, I did. It seemed that each of us became jealous in the areas where our own self-esteem and security felt threatened. I felt jealous when I knew that the other man had made love to his own legal wife. She felt jealous over the fluid play, conversation, and co-creativity between him and me.

One evening, a fist fight broke out between Sandy and the other man. I shrank back in horror. The other man later told me it was over me. Really?

My only motivation for becoming sexually involved with the other man was to figure out what was wrong with me sexually, fix it, and bring an "okay" me back into my legal marriage. Was Sandy's unconscious motivation to fit into the cultural, male rhetoric of the time and to feel more "masculine" by adding to the number of women with whom he had sex?

Years later, Sandy commented, "I got married too early. I should have sewn my wild oats first."

Could he not see that he had "sewn his wild oats" with the woman to whom he had made vows; the woman who had welcomed his impregnation because she loved and trusted the man with whom she had exchanged vows; the woman who, through their physical union, had birthed three beautiful sons?

In my sexual relationship with the other man, I *did* discover a highly sensuous, sexy, playful part of myself that I had never before experienced. Our relationship was never just physical. It encompassed mind, body, emotion, and spirit. It was totally co-creative and freeing. For me, there was also an element of surrender, of being overpowered and just letting go. It felt as if we were soul mates.

Suddenly, my self-esteem as a woman soared. Suddenly, I felt sexually okay, even beautiful, and free to play, create, and co-create. I had shifted into the Aphrodite archetype. I was a player in a Kama Sutra sexual relationship. The group marriage solved the precise problem that had motivated me to participate.

With respect to my relationship with Sandy, the result wasn't what I had hoped. My becoming orgasmic with the other man threatened Sandy. It changed our relationship. I had learned that my frigidity was not my fault. Sandy had to start looking at his own role in our sexual relationship if our sexual relationship were to improve. He just wasn't willing or able to do that when he had found another woman ready for sex whenever he wanted it.

I had committed to my legal husband. Together, we had brought three handsome sons into the world. Except for the sexual challenges, we had a beautiful, little, functional, traditional family.

One weekend, the four adults took a weekend trip to Washington, D.C. We left the children with their grandparents. I had promised my parents we would return to pick the children up at 4 p.m. I told Sandy what the arrangements were.

Late Sunday morning, the other man and I were ready to return home. Sandy and the other woman were not. They were still locked together in their motel room.

As the minutes ticked by, my frustration mounted. Being accountable was one of my values. The other man said, "Give them more time."

I was not driving. I had no money of my own. I could do nothing but sit and wait until Sandy and the other woman emerged from their room.

By that time, I knew we would be late. Sandy was driving. The other woman was next to him in the front seat. They were engaged in deep conversation. I was in the back seat sobbing.

Sandy didn't notice. Afterward, he said he thought it was an issue between the other man and me.

In an undated letter, Sandy once wrote, "God dammit – I'm mad - !!!*?—*ZDV!! AAAAARRRGGGGH (watch it). First of all, you wanted to switch last night, not me. I told you that if I had my choice & it was up to me that I'd rather not, but that if everyone else wanted to that I'd go along with it. You are the one that pushed it. You rushed to that phone to call back to & let (the other woman) know that you really wanted to switch because you didn't want to turn (the other man) off. Well, you turned me off!!"

## DEVOLUTION OF THE GROUP MARRIAGE

In 1972, the other man got an exceptional job offer in California—one that he couldn't refuse. He packed up his bags and left with his legal wife and children. He and I were willing to separate, honor our original marital vows, and return to our traditional marriages. Sandy and the other woman were not. Was it because they had not been included in the decision-making process?

Both were determined not to abandon the other. Sandy was not going to abandon the other woman. She was not going to abandon him.

At one point, the other woman told me how confused she had felt, suddenly being deposited in Southern California, having to navigate the high-speed interstate highways and adjust to an entirely new environment and way of life. When she turned to the father of her children for support, he said, "Figure it out."

The next several months were hell. The other woman wrote daily love letters to Sandy, delivered to our Vineland home. I tolerated the influx of letters because I was still dedicated to the group marriage.

However, Sandy was not mentally and emotionally present in his relationship with me. All I was feeling was deep, numbing pain. Why was this happening in a marriage Sandy had always said was "perfect"?

On May 4, 1972, Sandy wrote, "Damn it—I'm mad—or frustrated, or annoyed, or pissed off, or something like that.

I'm not really sure… Why do you have to be continually turned off at something? This time you either don't know why or at what, or you won't say. If this relationship is just continuously bringing upsets and frustrations, is it really worth it? I felt that (the other woman) and I finally made some progress last night toward resolving our relationship only to find that now you and I, whereas I thought our relationship was fine, now apparently have some kind of problem and I don't even know what it is. WHY – WHY – WHY???

"Maybe I am not capable of reacting closely to or emotionally with more than one person at a time. Last night (the other woman) told me of a couple of instances where she wanted and needed my emotional support and I didn't give it—in both cases, I was not aware of her need or, at least, the depth of it, and was also busy working on my relationship with you and the boys those times. Now it appears that maybe while I've been working on my relationship with her that the one with you has suffered. If this is the case, then I don't think I can handle both at once and one of you is always going to be turned off with me."

Did Sandy not realize that, for a relationship like this to work, it had to be carefully structured? Clear structure, intention, and communication were certainly my intentions on that fateful trip to Washington, DC. I had specifically and intentionally told Sandy we had to be home by 4 p.m. to pick our sons up from my parents' home. If there was conflict among needs and intentions, Sandy needed to communicate clearly to all parties involved and choose where he was going to place his own time and focus.

On November 1, 1972, the other woman wrote, "Janet, my love. That sounds like something I should say to (my husband) or Sandy, but it is the way I feel toward you now, ever since our conversation on the phone last night. I understand your feelings about needing to get a job and needing to uninvolve yourself from the group marriage. I've also felt at times it would be easier on all of us if we tried to forget about one another and found other outlets for ourselves instead. I haven't really wanted to do this, however, except as a last resort. I've wanted very much to hold our group marriage together as well as our individual marriages, and everything I've written either to Sandy or to you has been an attempt towards this end… Sometimes I've really been confused and writing to you has helped to straighten me out and clarify my thinking.

"You're right, I did overreact to the subject of divorce & remarriage. I explained to Sandy that probably one of the reasons for my reaction was that I knew nothing about the exchange of letters (between her husband and me) until Sandy told me in Atlanta. It was a total surprise to me that you and (my husband) had discussed it. Anyway, I do understand the reasons behind your discussion now & can accept your thoughts and feelings on the subject as being exploratory and in no way threatening. My 'upset' over it disappeared very shortly after I told you about it.

"I was really sorry to hear that you don't even want to 'switch.' I had no idea you were feeling that badly about our situation. I realize what an emotional state you must have been in, in order to make a decision like that… I know you don't want to see our group marriage dissolve either, but at the same time you also have to make your own life more bearable and satisfying. Janet, my dear wife, please do whatever you must in order to go on living and growing and being. If your job will prevent you from switching, then that's the way it has to be, and I will understand. I still would like to have the opportunity to switch sometime, partly because I am very curious to see how Sandy and I would relate on a husband & wife basis… You must do whatever is best in your situation.

"(My husband) and I didn't get much chance to talk last night, so I don't know how he is feeling… I don't believe he is feeling very good about anything right now.

"I'm really sorry my letters had such a distancing effect on Sandy's relationship with you, but glad that you were able to bring all of this out into the open. I'm glad you told me that these parts of my letters were no help because I want to know what helps and what doesn't.

"In my letter to Sandy of Thursday night I said I felt like the 'other woman' again and did not enjoy that position.

"Your letter today really relieved my worries about you & Sandy. It was good to hear that you were communicating on a rational level, and that Sandy was expressing himself openly to you.

"There's one other thing I wanted to say. In one of your letters to (my husband), which he read out loud to me, you made some comment about 'envying my ability to look up to men, and that this made me very feminine and attractive.' You surely must know, Janet, that you are very attractive to a lot of men. How about Dick, John, and Ben, to name three I can remember. Sandy says a lot of the men at (the party) were obviously attracted to you.

I remember the night we had Ben… over to supper. Ben was drooling over you all night long. It made me slightly jealous because he hardly noticed me at all! I don't need to remind you of Dick, now do I? Sandy says John… is attracted to you. So what is all this business about not being attractive to men? There is a naturalness and spontaneity about you that men find very appealing. I have seen it in you and seen men respond to it. So I know what I am talking about!"

Because of my strong sense of commitment, first to Sandy and our children and second to the group marriage, I continued to tolerate the other woman's daily letters to Sandy. At the same time, I was deeply grieving the lost soul mate relationship I had had with the other man. We were all grieving the loss of something that had become a significant part of our lives.

I still have love letters the other man wrote me. For the first time in my life, I had felt fully alive as a woman, appreciated by a man. Was it also the first time Sandy had felt sexually welcomed and appreciated by another woman?

The other man wrote: "I have thought to myself that perhaps I should not be 'emotional' in writing to you for both our sakes and stick to the factual and other mundane things. But DAMN it, woman, I miss you! and my writing serves as my need to communicate w/you and have a part of you w/me."

We tried to maintain the "group marriage commitment," but it was close to impossible across 3,000 miles. In late December 1972 and January 1973, we engaged in a "wife swap," with me traveling to California for a month and the other woman traveling to South Jersey. All our hearts were aching. It was like putting a Band-Aid on a deep wound.

On January 1, 1973, Sandy wrote: "Hi, Darling, Happy New Year! My God, do I miss you! I didn't think I'd miss you as much as I do, but I sure do. Boy, I wish I could understand my emotions. I was right in my prediction that we'd be opening up a whole new bag of emotions to cope with by going through with this exchange. At least, I was right as far as I'm concerned. "I guess it all boils down to the fact that I'm happiest when both of you are around and when one of you isn't available, then I miss the one who isn't here. The house seems sort of empty without you. It feels as if there is something important missing, and there is!

(Our middle son) "was very quiet for a while this afternoon and it looked like he was in deep thought, but he wouldn't communicate with me. I've been feeling a bit more pressured without you here, I know. I've felt more of the responsibility of the boys on my shoulders. Whenever there's been any friction between them, they always call 'Dad.' It's a big adjustment for all of us.

"(Our oldest son) came home real disgusted yesterday and said that (another neighbor's daughter) wasn't allowed over here for a month because you were away. He said he couldn't understand why not, and neither could her father (a psychologist). (Her brother) was over here this morning. I don't know whether it was with (his mother's) knowledge or not."

When the other man and woman first knew they would be moving to California, I had introduced them to my college roommate and her husband who lived close to their new home. My roommate and her husband were very interested in our group marriage.

In his January 1, 1973, letter to me, Sandy wrote, "(The other woman) has told me some about her intimate relationship with (my roommate's husband). And I guess I was hurt and withdrew from her. I have been going through quite a few emotional reactions since as a result of that, and also as a result of missing you so much. I sure hope they straighten out soon, or I'm afraid I won't be enjoying this month so much. I've been trying to recognize and understand and cope with my emotions.

"Honey, I love you infinitely. Don't tell me that this separation will make me appreciate you more. I already appreciate you and you know it.

"I guess when (the other woman) told me what had been going on with her and (my roommate's husband), I felt very lonely. I felt I'd just lost you and that I was losing her also. Knowing you were out there where he was, and that he would undoubtedly be spending his afternoons visiting you now instead of (the other woman) makes me feel uneasy. It's probably unfair of me, but right now I feel that I dislike (your roommate's husband) very intensely and do not trust him at all.

"I thank you for being you—the you that I love so much."

On January 9, 1973, Sandy wrote: "Your letter that arrived yesterday really meant a lot to me, honey. It was very reassuring to get your support and to know that I wasn't alone in my feelings about the situation between (the other woman) and (my roommate's husband).

"(The other woman) and I have had some long discussions the past two evenings. Just so you know what my present feelings on the situation are, I've told her, as (the other man did) that she is free to do as she pleases. However, I've gone a little further than that and said that if she goes ahead and develops an intimate relationship with (my roommate's husband) that I probably would not want to come to California at any time to visit them. I also said I wouldn't want to have another exchange such as the one we're having now. In other words, it's her choice. She can have an intimate relationship with (my roommate's husband) or she can have one with me, but not both! I know this is a form of controlling her, which I really don't want to do, but at the same time, it's not controlling her because I'm giving her a free choice. I'm not really sure why I feel this way, but emotionally it's just the way things have to be for me now.

"I got no reaction to this other than the fact that she wasn't looking forward to returning to California because then (my roommate's husband) would start pursuing her again. I'm so furious with him right now that if he were to come see us, I'd probably punch him right in the nose. Why can't that bastard leave (the other woman) alone when she tells him to? He just keeps pushing because he knows that if he's persistent enough he'll wear down her defenses. I think at this point the only way for her to discourage him would be to completely break off any communication between the two families, and I don't think she wants to do that.

"Your letter to (the other woman) today made her feel much better, but it sure as hell didn't do any wonders for me.

"Now you're trying to figure out ways for me to accept a relationship between (the other woman) and (my roommate's husband)—well, save your energy, kiddo. If anything, I'm more determined than ever not to even consider accepting such a relationship. They can have it if that's what they want, but count me out.

"Emotions! God damn it! Why does everything have to be so emotional? I told you we were making a mistake switching like this and that we'd open up a whole new bag of emotions to spill over. Mine sure have been spilling over tonight.

"Look how they change, too. In the first paragraph of this letter (written earlier today) I was feeling reassured. Now I feel more threatened than ever. I don't know what the hell to do. I've been cross and angry with the kids. I've deliberately tried to antagonize (the other woman), and now I'm sounding off at you. The one I'm really pissed off at is that gigolo bastard (your roommate's husband). Christ, how many women does he need to have affairs with at one time? He needs a job to keep himself busier, so he won't always be trying to screw other women. At least let him find women I don't know, and he can have all he wants. I only want two, and I don't think that's overly selfish, especially when I'm willing to share them with (the other man). "I have even been toying with the idea of sending (the other woman) home and asking you to come back, but we made an agreement, and it wouldn't be fair for me to ask you to change just because I want to.

"I'm also feeling threatened about you right now, and also community relations have become a bit 'sticky.' (Our oldest son) is continually having to lie to protect us and I don't like putting him in that position.

"The answer to my problem is here—if I can find it.

"I have been trying not to think about anything but my present relationship, here and now, with (the other woman)... "Honey, I miss our relationship and will be glad to re-establish it with you. Right now, I'd like to hold you very close to me and feel the soft warmth of your body. I love you very much...

"(The neighboring wife, a devout Catholic), lets the kids come over here to play, but won't let (the other woman) drive them to school. (The other woman) went over there one day last week to talk to her and got a 'reserved' reception...

"Take care, honey. I miss you and I love you. I'll be sad to see (the other woman) leave, but I'll be glad to welcome you home. Wish I could have you both… "

On January 20, 1973, Sandy wrote, "Your last letter really made me feel good, Honey. Even the part where you said you were risking turning me off didn't turn me off at all. You were completely open and honest about the potential you have for feeling toward (my roommate's husband, middle initial B.) (B for bastard) or toward an awful lot of other males. I can accept that totally and I'm sure the same is true about me and other females. However, as you said, it's the actions that count and I agree wholeheartedly. That's probably what hurt me about (the other woman's) actions, and would do so again in the future if she were to repeat them."

## EXPLOSION OF THE GROUP MARRIAGE AND A TRIPLE DIVORCE

In 1973, the other man received a new job offer back in Southern New Jersey. He was undecided whether to accept.

With my focus on commitment and somehow holding the group marriage together to satisfy Sandy and the other woman, I tried to patch things up by suggesting legal divorces and cross-remarriages while keeping the group marriage intact. That was the tipping point for the other man.

The plan was that he would take the new job and return to Southern New Jersey, I would move in with him, and the other woman would move in with Sandy. The children could choose where they wanted to live weekly.

Each couple would file for a legal, no-fault divorce, a process which, in New Jersey, took eighteen months.

It didn't work.

As soon as I began living with the other man, my once beautiful soul mate became a hell mate. He unilaterally decided he no longer wanted the group marriage, just as he had unilaterally decided to accept the new job offer in California.

He began screaming at me, heaving glasses into the wall, and slamming his fist on the table. He said he wanted to make me angry. My Dr. Jekyll had become a Mr. Hyde. A nurse friend of mine once said she had seen this pattern many times.

There was conflict over the children. Whenever they got into a spat, this "hell mate" would jump into the fray to support his only son, the youngest of all the children, against my sons. He was as abusive toward them as he was toward me.

I later realized how committed both of us were to our sons and families. Did the problems arise because his son and my sons were not *our* sons?

My father told me, "(The other man) is not going to marry you."

I knew I had to get out. But how? I had been out of the job market for 15 years, caring for home and family. I had no independent source of income to continue to care financially for three teenage sons.

The final straw came when the man I once believed was a soul mate began having an affair with another woman.

Our sexual relationship had been powerful, but I had to get out. I did so with precisely the rage that my soul mate, turned hell mate, had tried so hard to instill in me—a fury and passion directed toward freeing myself from his influence.

In the middle of the night, directly behind his new mistress's car, I smashed the beautiful piece of pottery he had so lovingly crafted to symbolize our union.

"Hell hath no fury like a woman scorned."[33] Perhaps that quote should read, "Hell hath no fury like a woman used, abused, and discarded."

Enraged, traumatized, and confused, I spent a few nights in a homeless shelter. Then, still traumatized and confused, but realizing I had the legal right to live in the house titled in Sandy's and my name, I moved back in. The other woman was still there.

While I had the legal right to live there, it no longer felt like my home and our home. It felt as if our once beautiful sanctuary had been desecrated and destroyed by unmastered male testosterone, the other woman's needs and desires, and our patriarchal culture.

Emotionally, I could not stay. I had to get out, somehow, someway. But where could I go?

My parents stepped in and bought a nearby condominium where my sons and I had shelter, beds to sleep in, a kitchen in which I could prepare food, and a small yard for gardening. At least we had an emotionally and physically safe space in which to function, but the road ahead was treacherously hard and steep for all of us.

I sobbed at night for hours. What had happened to Sandy's and my once-functional marriage and beautiful family?

When I tried to remove a few dollars to buy food from what had once been Sandy's and my joint bank account, Sandy had already removed all the money. When I went to what used to be Sandy's and my joint safe deposit box to

---

[33] Congreve, William, *The Mourning Bride*.

remove my personal belongings, he had already cleaned out the contents.

When Sandy and I had a functional, monogamous marriage, he had gifted me with a beautiful refrigerator as a birthday present. Now, he refused to allow me to move it to my parents' condominium where I could continue to use the gift he had given me.

Morally outraged, one day when I knew Sandy was working, I sent movers to the home that had once been ours and had them move a piano that had once belonged to his mother to my condominium. That got Sandy's attention. Ultimately, he got his mother's piano back and I got my refrigerator.

One day, Sandy came to the front door of my condominium, smiling and respectful. Perhaps he was having second thoughts about his adultery and the disruption of our once functional family.

Did he want to renew his marital vows and restore our family? Hoping that this was the case, I invited him in.

Stepping inside, he erupted in violent rage. I had no choice but to call the police. Sandy ran away.

I felt betrayed by three people simultaneously. I divorced three people simultaneously. The pain and betrayal of trust were too great for me to bear.

Sandy later told me that he thought he could have his cake and eat it, too. After all, the mother of his children had always been there to support anything he wanted. Why would she not continue to be that firm foundation from which his life evolved?

The other woman later told me that the father of her children had screamed at her and slammed his fist on the table with her, too. She had never said that during the group marriage when she was still living with him, but within that context, she probably couldn't. As confused and unsupported as she frequently felt, he was still paying the bills and providing food and shelter for her and their children.

Years later, she asked, "Do you remember my asking, 'What if only one of the legal remarriages works?'"

Why, at that time, was she thinking in terms of legal remarriages, rather than the group marriage? Was she, too, desperately trying to get out of an abusive relationship? Was this much of her attraction to Sandy?

The other man once said to me, "I would never have done what you did."

Our sons told me that Sandy and the other woman, once they lived together, constantly nitpicked at one another.

I mailed all the other letters the other woman had sent me back to her. Her words and conduct seemed so totally disparate. I had lost all my trust in my relationship with her. She had subverted and ultimately destroyed the relationship I had with the father of my children and with the beautiful sons we had brought into this world. In my eyes, she *was* the "other woman," the very role she did not want to play.

The other man held his own traumatic history.

As a child, he was the son of a well-to-do Palestinian Arabic Catholic family. During the 1948 Nakba, the family, in fear of being murdered by Jewish Zionists, fled their home in the middle of the night with only the possessions they could pile into their car. Ultimately, they resettled as refugees in Beirut, Lebanon.

"The sins of the parents are visited on the children." The trauma and violence perpetrated by one group of adults on another desecrate everyone involved—particularly the innocent children.

# Chapter 6
# Atonement

*"There is a brokenness*
*out of which comes the unbroken, a shatteredness*
*out of which blooms the unshatterable.*
*There is a sorrow*
*beyond all grief which leads to joy and a fragility*
*out of whose depths emerges strength.[34]"*

—Rashani

## THE RELATIONSHIP BETWEEN "DEATH AND REBIRTH" AND ATONEMENT

The shatteredness and sudden awareness emerging from the "Death and Rebirth" experience gives us no choice but to Surrender into Soul and reconnect with a living, breathing energy that we can only experience and allow to flow through us.[35] When we allow it to flow through us, our thinking and conduct change. We move out of shame, fear, and rage and consciously and intentionally step into our Purpose, Passion, and Power. We become a creator, co-creator, and manifester in each and every moment of pure, present-moment awareness. We shift into Carl Jung's Individuation or Abraham Maslow's Self-Actualization. (See Diagram in Appendix.)

---

[34] https://www.rashani.com/arts/poems/poems-by-rashani.
[35] Humans have created many different placeholder words to point toward an experience that cannot be conceptualized. Some of these placeholder words are: God, Allah, Power greater than myself, Spirit, Awareness, The Eternal Tao.

Atonement requires Commitment—to staying connected and BEING a centered, aware human in each and every present moment of our physical life. It is not easy.

Those still stuck in their own little, culturally conditioned black boxes will not like our spiritual strength and centeredness. They are likely either to attack it or flee from it.

## WEAVING IN AND OUT OF SANDY'S AND MY MARITAL COMMITMENT

In early 1975, Sandy and I were negotiating whether to rebuild our marriage or divorce and move in separate directions. I do not have a copy of the letter I sent to him. I only have a copy of his February 10, 1975, reply.

Sandy asked:

Would you get turned off if I went ocean racing again (i.e., Bermuda Race, etc.)? In order for me to feel totally self-confident with my own abilities to handle boats under adverse conditions (high winds, storms, unexpected occurrences, breakdowns, etc.,) I want to expose myself to these conditions as much as possible. I feel I never stop learning in this area and it's extremely important to me as a person to build this self-confidence. I want to navigate a Bermuda Race someday."

He added, "I know if I really gave you a chance and you were really interested, you'd make a damn good (and naturally efficient) sailor."

I could only remember the time we had sailed around the Island of Tortola in the British Virgin Islands on our little chartered sailboat, with five-year-old and three-year-old sons in tow. The north shore of Tortola is challenging sailing, unprotected from the north seas. Waves were breaking over the bow of our boat as we skimmed along at a 40-degree angle.

Sandy was totally focused on navigating the boat, competent and unafraid. I was hanging on for dear life to the straps of the lifejackets of our two young sons, holding them firmly in the boat to keep them from falling overboard and being washed away by the churning seas.

Neither of us was afraid. We were just doing what needed to be done at that moment, each playing our own role within a functional family setting.

I had often observed that Sandy was most fully engaged in life when he was sailing. I often thought that sailing was his joy and purpose for being. Could he have lived this integrated and purposeful life had he not become an engineer, trading time for money to support his wife and growing family?

Sandy continued,

"Response to what you would want.

Money of your own to make decisions about… I don't particularly like the idea of keeping all the money separate and would prefer it to be ours, instead of yours and mine, but I'd be willing to work that way if you prefer.

Before the group marriage, I had truly felt that Sandy's money and my money was *our* money. I, too, had worked and brought in income before I became pregnant. I had cared for home, husband, and children without any monetary compensation because I was so fully committed to my marital vows and our beautiful family.

Not having money of my own had only become an issue during that disastrous trip to Washington, DC, when I could not fulfill my commitments to my parents and our children because Sandy and (the other woman) were together in their motel room well beyond the time I had told Sandy we would have to leave. I had no money of my own with which to fulfill those other family commitments.

Our money no longer felt like our money. Having no money of my own to fulfill commitments felt like slavery.

Is monetary control sexual control?

Sandy continued: A mutually satisfying sexual relationship – I certainly want that too.

No putdowns in front of friends—'Nuf said. I never meant to hurt you and believe I always said things in a joking manner. I guess I thought it was smart or funny. I apologize for any discomfort I may have caused you and genuinely feel that it was unintentional.

More financial independence. I pretty well covered that in 1. However, I'd be willing to put the Toyota in your name. What, if any, financial obligations would you be willing to bear along with this independence?

Shared responsibilities—I'm willing to help with the "dirty work" much more than before. I know I've changed in this area. I'd like to work as a team as much as possible, particularly if we can establish the same goals. You mentioned not always wanting to be left with taking care of the kids while I went off for a good time. I would hope that more of our "good times" could be together & with the boys. However, we've got to face realities of different interests. I'll never be as interested in gardening…. as you, but I must admit I enjoyed raising vegetables myself last year and know I'll do more in that area. I would be lying if I said I was going to give up sailing. However, I went away much less last year than in the past.

Love and warmth for yourself and the boys—that one's easy!

Things that worry you most—Sexual relationship. That's got to be worked on together. Social Relationships—parties bore you—This one could be a bit sticky at times, but… I don't think it's an insurmountable problem. Some parties bore me too. Some are just a release of tensions—others I find enjoyable. When I think about it, I can recall only 3 of them in the past couple of years where I've really had a "super" time, and 2 of those were with groups of sailors.

Now—What I would want.

I thought this was going to be easy, but now I'm not so sure.

A good, stable, loving relationship with you and the boys. The children mean a great deal to me, and I don't want them to be hurt any more than they already have. I want them to have a normal home life where they don't always have to explain their parents' behavior to their friends.

Stability and less frustration and tension.

No more hashing over of things that happened years ago, or dragging me through the coals of 15 wasted years.

A good working relationship at home between all members of the family.

A good sexual relationship.

Support when I need it.

Not to feel threatened that you become so independent that you may walk out on me anytime you want to.

I very much want to somehow obtain a cruising boat that the five of us could sleep on, cruise on, camp on… probably on Chesapeake Bay…. and make it a family project for having fun on weekends & vacations. I want to do it before the boys grow up & move away. I think it would be a valuable & educational addition to their experiences.

"Things that worry me Same 2 that you listed.

What will our relationship be after the boys are grown up and on their own? Will we enjoy the same things? Will we travel like our parents have?

What if you aren't interested in sailing & can't tolerate my interest?

What if you get bored at a party where I'm having a good time?

What if you want to go to a flower show and I'm not interested, or if I want to go to a boat show and you're not interested?

What if you want to have philosophical discussions and I want to watch a football game?

What about (the other woman and man) & what becomes of our relationship with them?????????????"

Sandy's final question was not *mine* to answer.

My own relationships with the other man and woman were clearly broken and over. I was also done with the group marriage.

Was Sandy willing and able to end his relationship with the other woman and recommit to the woman to whom he had originally made vows eighteen years before, the woman he had impregnated three times, the woman who had birthed their three beautiful sons?

Or did he still want to have his cake and eat it, too? And was the other woman now in a position where she, too, needed financial and emotional support and Sandy was her only support system. Could Sandy now turn his back on her and walk away?

# EVALUATION OF THE GROUP MARRIAGE FROM HINDSIGHT

Robert Rimmer was right about one of the benefits he espoused in favor of the group marriage. In an intimate relationship with another person, you discover aspects of yourself that you never before experienced.

There was such deep love and eye-opening conversation among the four adults and even the six children, as long as we were all fully committed to one another and the group marriage. When only one person put more conventional concerns, such as earning money or having a more prestigious job or returning to a monogamous marriage, ahead of the group marriage, everything began to unravel.

There was clear friction between our group marriage and the conditioned norms of the cultural world around us. Would our deep love for one another have been more stable if it had been culturally accepted by a larger society?

Triangles don't work. You simply don't build a functional relationship with one man and two women or two men and one woman.

We never lived together in a single home. Had this been culturally acceptable, would it have stabilized our relationship?

In a monogamous male/female relationship, you define yourself through your relationships with a single spouse and your children. This type of relationship is much more stable than the emotional fluctuations of a group marriage, where who you are changes depending on the person with whom you are relating. As a result, a group marriage is highly emotional, and who you are constantly shifts.

When different members of the group marriage have conflicting needs or intentions and communication is less than crystal clear, dissonance and trauma occur.

Men marry for sex. Women, particularly after they become pregnant, marry for security.

A good intimate sexual relationship is focused primarily on play and creativity with a playful, creative, and co-creative adult partner.

A monogamous marriage is a commitment focused primarily on co-creating a stable, happy, healthy family, including the welfare of the genetic children born of the physical union of man and woman.

Focus on the welfare of an entire family is very different from focus on a sexual relationship with one other person. You can't do both simultaneously.

If Sandy and I had simply agreed to structure sexual relationship time and family time, would our marriage have become both sexually satisfying and functional for the entire genetic family?

SUBSEQUENT RESEARCH

Years later, I researched polygamy. Even in communities where it was sanctioned, such as the Church of Latter-Day Saints, it appeared that the structure was always a single man with more than one wife, each wife living in her own home with her own children. I did not find any instance where one wife with two husbands was sanctioned and socially acceptable.

I also briefly researched Robert Rimmer, the author of *The Harrad Experiment*. We had had many supportive letter exchanges with him while we were exploring our own group marriage. He was never abusive or critical, rather always encouraging and communicative. I still have those letters.

Had he simply been using us as guinea pigs in his own experiment? Were we all willing pawns on his chessboard? Had that experiment ripped apart two functional marriages and families? Ten years later, it certainly seemed so.

Robert Rimmer died on August 1, 2001, in Quincy, Massachusetts. His obituary appeared in *The New York Times*.

*The Times* stated:

"(The Harrad Experiment) was considered titillating when it was first published, with some heralding it as a ringing manifesto for free love. Sherbourne Press initially printed 10,000 mail-order copies, considering the novel too racy for bookstore distribution. When Bantam issued a paperback edition the next year, it promoted it with sexy billboards and sold 300,000 copies within a month. More than three million were eventually sold. . .

"Mr. Rimmer went on to write more than a dozen more books, almost all on unconventional sexual relationships that he believed would foster fulfillment and freedom...

"His cause was nothing less than revolutionizing the institution of marriage. 'I feel that ultimately, monogamous marriage will not be the only legal, sanctioned form of marriage,' he said in an interview with *Psychology Today* in 1997. 'There will be socially approved group marriages, there will be bigamous marriages, and there will be open-end marriages in which each partner has a relationship outside the marriage.' ...

"In an autobiography appended to a new edition of *The Harrad Experiment*, published by Prometheus Books in 1990, Mr. Rimmer said that as a child, he loved reading fairy tales as well as pouring over *National Geographic* magazines to see photographs of nude women…

"He continued his sexual education with men's magazines and a string of serious romances that he pursued from the age of fifteen. In the fall of 1940, he met his wife, then Erma Richards, a dental technician who cleaned his teeth.

''When she was finished, I asked her point-blank, 'How about a kiss?' he wrote. ''There was no kiss and no date.

"But after his big book, success proved fickle. 'Publishers were convinced I was a leftover hippie,' he wrote. He achieved some fame by writing a guide to pornographic movies with Patrick Riley.

I now understand why the Catholic Church, from the ninth century to the twentieth century, created lists of banned books until, on June 14, 1966, Pope Paul VI formally abolished the practice.

I now understand why "Thou shalt not commit adultery" is one of the Ten Commandments in the Jewish Torah and the Old Testament of the Christian Bible.

## MOVING OUT OF LIMBO, MOVING ON ALONE

Sandy seemed unable to decide whether to recommit to our monogamous marriage and family or whether to continue supporting the other woman. His indecision imprisoned us all in limbo.

I simply could not sit there forever. If Sandy had been willing and able to recommit to our marriage and family, I would likely have eventually moved back to the home we had so beautifully created together. We could have begun doing fun things together with our sons. We could have taken the weekend sailing trips on Chesapeake Bay that Sandy so wanted to take.

Our sons needed stability. The group marriage had created nothing but instability and confusion for all of us. Recommitment to our original marriage and family on new terms based on what we had learned during the group marriage could have provided a stable foundation on which we could have moved forward together. Money, workloads, leisure time, and sexual relationship time could have been easily negotiated.

The longer Sandy sat in limbo, undecided as to how to move forward, the more I simply had to think about my own survival and that of our sons. I had little choice but to go back into the job market to generate a flow of income to buy food, as well as carry the expenses on the condominium my parents had so generously purchased to support their only daughter and her sons.

In rural Vineland, no one cared about my Bachelor of Arts degree from Swarthmore College, one of the best small liberal arts colleges in the United States. I finally found part-time employment where I earned $1.50 an hour. My duties were to file papers, make coffee, and review pension plans drafted by a local male attorney who couldn't write a simple sentence with a subject and predicate. The attorney passed my work on to another attorney who charged his clients $800 for my work.

Our oldest and youngest sons stayed with their father in the home they had always known. Our middle son moved in with me.

I so missed the once functional, caring relationship all of us had had together. I so missed my ability to spend time with and support my oldest and youngest sons as they moved through their teenage years.

Our middle son had been a straight-A student when I chose to move out of the limbo I could no longer endure. I continued to drive him to school every morning, drop him off at the front door, and pick him up at the end of the school day. Little did I know that he was walking in the front door and out the back door.

The school never told me our middle son was cutting classes. Finally, our oldest son told me he was spending his days with a group of other teenage boys who were also cutting classes.

I was outraged that the school had never called and told me. I bitterly complained that I wanted to know if our middle son was cutting classes. The school employees listened politely.

Our middle son continued to cut classes. The school still didn't notify me.

By the end of the year, our middle son had gone from being a straight-A student to a straight-F student and dropped out of school completely. Years later, he told me how confused he had been.

I felt as angry and frustrated as I had at the end of that trip to Washington, D.C. Neither I nor our middle son was getting any emotional support from either his father or the school, and I now had to work during the day for very little money to be able to buy a quart of milk.

At night, deeply grieving, after our middle son was in bed and asleep, I sometimes drove over behind the beautiful little home that had once been his father's and mine. I could hear the man who had once made a commitment to "love, honor, and obey until death do us part," the man who had impregnated me three times, laughing and talking with the other woman in what had once been our family room.

My deep grief transformed into rage and moral outrage. I wanted to murder them both. The only reason I didn't was because I didn't want to spend the rest of my life in jail and didn't want our sons to be orphans.

At age 20, the thought of becoming a lawyer had never entered my mind. At age 40, with all my childhood conditioning smashed by the group marriage, it seemed as if it was the only viable path toward generating enough money to support myself and our sons and bring self-respect and other-respect back into my life.

Other people saw me as courageous. I saw myself as simply fighting for survival, respect, and the people and things I loved.

I was accepted into Rutgers School of Law, Camden, the only school that was close enough for me to commute. I obtained a student loan to pay the tuition for my part-time study.

For the first time in my life, I studied and organized until I had every tiny detail under control. I knew I would have to graduate with very high marks even to be considered for a job in what was then a male-dominated profession. I graduated *cum laude* in 1980 and practiced law in Atlantic City, New Jersey, for twenty-two years.

We were required to do pro bono work as part of our annual licensing requirements. I chose mediation because I was totally incompetent at representing a criminal defendant. I worked in family mediation for years, deepening my understanding of human dynamics.

After twenty-two years, I was burned out. A corrupt city administration had just been elected. My wonderful paralegals transparently told me that by continuing to practice law, I was out of integrity and that they would be able to find other jobs. By that time, I had a financial base from which I could do what I felt driven to do with the rest of my life. I still had questions I had not yet answered.

## NAME CHANGES AND CONDUCT CHANGES

**What's in a Name?**

I had grown up in a generation of women who, when they married, would never have considered *not* taking their husband's surname. At our marriage ceremony, my father "gave me away." Suddenly, I was Janet Traub.

When I filed for a legal divorce from Sandy in my attempt to save the group marriage, I not only went through a horrible financial crisis. I also went through a horrible identity crisis. I was Janet, that "wonderful gift of God," but Janet who?

It seemed clear that the values of the man I had married were not my values. Commitment mattered to me, not only in word but in deed. It seemed that he wasn't even aware of it. Was he still thinking with his penis?

Was he also subconsciously afraid that if I became too independent, I would abandon him? It was a thought that had never occurred to me. The children we had brought into this world tied us together forever.

What were my values and where did they come from? What really mattered?

As I thought more deeply about this, I became aware that, for me personally, integrity, authenticity, transparency, and self-respect were vital. In my relationships with others, clear communication and accountability were vital on my part and on the part of the others with whom I was interacting. I became aware of the strong influence the female goddess psychological archetypes—Artemis, the wild, nature-connected goddess; Hestia, keeper of the hearth; Athena, goddess of wisdom; Demeter, the devoted mother; Persephone, the innocent child, and Hecate, the goddess of the crossroads—had always had on me,[36] each at a different point in my life.

Until the triple divorce, I had always defined myself in relationship to the people in my life. I was my mother and father's daughter. I was my husband's wife. I was my sons' mother. But who was I separate and apart from these human relationships and all my cultural conditioning? What surname was appropriate to symbolize who I was?

My male lawyer told me I had only two choices in the divorce proceeding. I could either retain my husband's surname or retake my father's surname. It felt as if the law created by our patriarchal culture had decided I was either owned by my father or by my husband.

Was the intention behind this patriarchal naming and cultural structure that my father was to be my original protector and the man I married my new protector, expected to step into my father's shoes when he married the woman who would bear his children?

What had happened to all my maternal relatives? What had happened to all my ancestors' maternal surnames? All had been erased by the law and my patriarchal conditioning.

Within the context of my legal choices, I chose to return to my father's surname. At least he had loved me, treated me respectfully, and never betrayed my trust. At the end of the divorce, I again became Janet Smith.

The name Janet Smith, however, symbolized only a small part of who I was. My values came not only from the Smiths. They also came from my maternal ancestors, the

---

[36] https://www.jeanbolen.com/books

Hoffs, Goffs, Perrys, Edwards, and Wilkersons. I was so much more than just Janet Smith.

My mother's maiden name was Warfield. As I ended my legal marriage to the father of my children, I was beginning law school. Warfield seemed like an appropriate name for a new lawyer. I filed the name change application the courts required and became Janet Smith Warfield.

Struggling to survive financially, I desperately needed my tax refund. Do you think the IRS would send it to me? Not until I drove my rickety, old Toyota thirty miles from Vineland to the Cumberland County Social Security Office to change my name on the records of the Social Security Administration.

Men don't have to go through all this aggravation. Why should we women?

I vowed I would never change my name again. I had worked too hard to get it.[37]


## A Woman Practicing Law in a Male Profession

When I first began practicing law, I was hired by one of the largest Atlantic City law firms. In my new job, I phoned a senior male lawyer from another firm about a case where we represented opposing clients. After a short conversation, the other lawyer said, "May I please speak with the lawyer handling this case?"

I let that sentence sink in for ten seconds. Then, I simply said, "I *am* the lawyer handling this case."

His whole attitude changed. Suddenly, I was credible and respectable, simply because I had inserted my credentials into our conversation.

---

[37] There is an after-story here. See The Power of Another Name Change at 140.

Another time, I was representing a client at a municipal council hearing. The municipal officials, all men, were arrogant, overbearing, and pompous. Can you imagine that they were actually demanding that my client camp out in his tenants' yard to make sure they behaved?

I can't say I felt fear before the hearing, but I did feel tension. I was not primarily a litigator and wasn't familiar with the procedures or personalities before I stepped into the municipal hearing room.

I had, however, prepared both law and facts thoroughly. As the hearing progressed, it became clear that the municipal officials were familiar with neither.

I knew the police chief's list of violations was inconsistent with the notices he had sent my client. After he gave his arrogant and condescending opening testimony (which I'm sure was simply a façade for his fear and incompetence), I simply asked him to show me where my client had received notice of the violations. He spent a full two minutes looking through his file. Every eye in the hearing room was on him.

Both my client and I sat respectfully silent while he sorted through his scrambled papers, but we were both chuckling inside. Finally, he had to admit on the record that my client had never received notice. The police chief's arrogance suddenly evaporated.

The code enforcement official, papers in trembling hands, testified that the last time he had viewed my client's property was over four months ago. He nevertheless adamantly testified that the property did not meet the code requirements as of the hearing date. I couldn't believe he had said that.

When I asked him how he could possibly testify that my client's property didn't meet code requirements today when he hadn't viewed it for four months, he backed down, retracted his statement, and suddenly began testifying honestly. Interestingly enough, his hands also stopped shaking.

The complaint was dismissed.

I had been the contract attorney for Atlantic City's in-rem tax sale foreclosures for years. As delinquent properties were foreclosed, resold, and returned to the tax rolls, the city's coffers increased tenfold over what the city paid me. The city could then sell the foreclosed properties to new owners who would renovate them and improve formerly dilapidated neighborhoods.

The new councilman (we'll call him John) strutted around City Hall, ordered the janitor and cleaning lady to work faster, and shouted down anyone who dared to express an opinion different from his own. Rumors circulated that he had beaten his wife so badly that she had been hospitalized.

As obnoxious as John was, I tried to be polite. After all, he was one of the councilmen who would vote on my contract. However, I received neither politeness nor respect in return.

"Why do you care?" he demanded when I suggested a change in the direction of a city street that would have made traffic flow more smoothly. "It's none of your business."

During his campaign, John had asked me to place his campaign sign in the front yard of my home. I politely declined. I was a nonpartisan city contractor. I would not have placed any candidate's sign on my property.

John took my refusal personally. As soon as he was elected, he began attacking both me and my contract. He proclaimed that the city was paying me too much money. John would show the city how to cut their budget.

He pulled my contract off the Council Agenda three times, asserting he needed more information. I had already supplied the information. John refused to return my phone calls. He demanded that I appear before Council to defend myself.

I was terrified. I knew how ugly this man could be and how he hated women. Women attorneys were worse. I felt like an innocent victim being punished for a crime I had not committed.

Would I lose a contract that was a major source of my income? Would I have to let my wonderful paralegals go because I could no longer pay their salaries? Would I lose my own home to foreclosure because I could no longer pay my mortgage?

I still had a son to support and my own bills to pay. Moreover, I was doing an excellent job in an area of law where few attorneys had my expertise.

It was an area of law that John did not understand, nor did he understand the financial ramifications of his actions for the city. However, his ignorance, arrogance, and role authority had become an unpleasant factor in my life.

Sleepless night after sleepless night, I tossed and turned. What would John do and say at the Council meeting? Would I appear incompetent? Would I make a fool of myself?

Would the other Council people agree with John? What defenses could I make? How should I prepare? I trembled as my "what ifs" continued to torment me.

Fortunately, I had participated for several years in Nar Anon, a support group for families and friends of addicts. The more I thought about John, the more I realized his behavior was addictive—bullying, lying, belligerence, anger, manipulation. Nar Anon had taught me I couldn't fix the addict. I could only fix myself.

I needed the help of a "Power Greater than Myself." Nar Anon had taught me to "Let go and let God."

I didn't much like that word "God." It always made me think of an old man with a long white beard, sitting on a thundercloud with a lightning bolt in his hand, waiting to strike me dead if I didn't do some unclear thing he wanted me to do.

I had always considered myself an intellectual agnostic. I liked the words "Power Greater than Myself" better than that word "God."

One morning, still trembling in terror, I sat down on my living room sofa, consciously brought my mind back to the present moment, and repeated over and over, "Let go and let God." Suddenly, my trembling stopped.

Here I was, safe and sound in my own living room. I could manage this present moment. I suddenly knew that I could manage each and every "future present moment," one moment at a time. All I had to do was prepare thoroughly, "let go," and let a "Power Greater than Myself" guide my steps.

On the day of the Council meeting, I sat in the front row with a big, fat file on my lap, glaring at John. Face muscles taut and hands shaking, he refused to look at me. While he made a few half-hearted attempts at blustery remarks, the verbal gusts soon softened as other councilmen and women jumped to my defense. John muttered under his breath, then reluctantly stopped talking altogether.

When the Council finally voted, my contract was unanimously renewed. Even John voted for it.


On September 11, 2001, there was no television or radio in my law office. I was working with my two exceptional paralegals. Our work environment was efficient, harmonious, and productive.

Suddenly, the phone rang. My beautiful staff members became gripped with fear, then terror, as their sons, daughters, sisters, and brothers began transmitting blow-by-blow accounts of the much-too-graphic news broadcasts. The paralysis spread like a plague. What moments before had been a space full of dynamic harmony suddenly became so emotionally dysfunctional that it approached emotional chaos. There was no change in our immediate physical surroundings. There was nothing any of us could do to prevent the World Trade Center from disintegrating into a pile of rubble. Yet, the emotional energy in that office changed in a nanosecond.

What if we had been working in a nineteenth-century office before the advent of telephone, television, and radio? Would the energy in that office environment have been different from our twenty-first-century office with all its modern technologies?

The only difference was the influx of terrifying and gruesome words pouring through microphones into the minds and imaginations of my twenty-first-century employees. The staff in my twenty-first-century office listened to those words and allowed their minds and bodies to absorb that frightful energy. The staff in my imaginary nineteenth-century office would have had no phones through which those gruesome words could pour. There would have been no word plague infecting my nineteenth-century office and no frightful emotional energy with which to deal.

Is it possible that there are some things we don't need to know? Is it possible there are some energies we don't want to invite into our lives? Do you think the 9/11 bombers would have plunged their planes into the World Trade

Center if they hadn't believed they would immediately become media stars?

Why did we all support their dysfunctional behavior by giving it our undivided attention?

The Amish inhabitants of Lancaster County, Pennsylvania, neither believe in nor use modern electronics. Perhaps there is a very spiritual and religious reason for this seemingly strange choice. They simply want to quarantine themselves from the infectious, emotional word energy that plagues our modern world via radio, television, and Internet.

Inhabitants of Glastonbury, UK, also avoid internet and electronics because they disrupt the energetic effects of the amazing and miraculous ley lines beneath that land.

There are many functional ways of dealing with terror energy like that of 9/11. Spiritual masters throughout the ages visualize themselves surrounded by beautiful white shields that insulate them from potentially lethal energies that can paralyze their hearts and minds. They detach from those energies instead of absorbing them. Alternatively, they deflect them back from whence they came, just as the black belt karate masters deflect harmful force back toward its originator.

Perhaps 9/11 was a wake-up call. Perhaps we have spent too many years isolated from our fears. We became complacent, smug, and arrogant. Perhaps the terror plague we experienced on 9/11 awakened us to the need to stop taking things for granted and start appreciating all the things with which we've been blessed. We all need to recognize how very interdependent we are, and how grateful we need to be for every living moment.

**Hard Moral Choices**

My mother spent her last year in a nursing home. I visited when I could. Crippled with arthritis, hard of hearing, mind moving in and out of dementia, one Sunday in a moment of clarity, she blurted out, "I'm just no good to anyone anymore." On Tuesday, the nursing home called. "Your mother aspirated on her food this morning. The doctor has placed an order in her file that she is not to be given food or water by mouth."

My mother had a living will. I was her medical representative. She had written me a letter years before saying she did not want artificial life support. All she wanted was good food, water, and relief from pain.

The enormity of what was happening began sinking in. Had the male doctor imposed a death sentence on my mother? As my mother's personal representative, I had the power to countermand the doctor's order and request a feeding tube.

My mother was 91. Her life had no quality. She knew it had no quality. Yet, she had requested food and water. The doctor had ordered that she not receive it.

The doctor was too busy to speak with me. The compassionate female nurse practitioner spoke with me at length.

My nephew's wife was a nurse. My sister-in-law had worked in hospitals for years. Both had witnessed patients whose families tried to keep them alive, only to have them die excruciatingly painful deaths as pneumonia invaded their lungs. Both said the same thing. "Let it be."

I sat by my mother's bedside and held her hand. She squeezed mine. The following Sunday, she took her last breath.

My mother's body had been in the doctor's hands and mine.

Her soul was in God's.

## A Woman Exploring a Ph.D.

I came into the doctoral dissertation retreat at the beginning of the week with what I thought was great clarity about my dissertation. I was going to have my proposal done by the end of May and spend the rest of the year writing my dissertation. On Monday morning, I volunteered to present first. I had thirty minutes. At the end, the President of the University said that what I had was a perfect D.Min, but certainly nowhere near a perfect Ph.D. He explained the D.Min as the appropriate degree if you wanted to heal people and transform the world.

The Dean of Doctoral Studies later explained that the D.Min was not considered inferior to a Ph.D. The focus was simply different. The Ph.D. was more theoretical or research oriented.

As the presentations continued, I finally understood why it's important to find that "tiny little brick in the great wall of knowledge" if you're going to do a Ph.D. It has nothing to do with scientific, materialistic, objective thinking as I had originally understood. Instead, it's all about setting tight boundaries so you have less to read, less to master, and less to defend.

When I first walked in, the dean of doctoral studies was effusively warm and cordial. I knew somebody had said something to her about my feelings that she was unresponsive to her students' questions.

Good. At least there was an opening for a conversation, although she still didn't seem to have much time.

About halfway through the week, the university president stalked up to me, grabbed me by the arm, and said, "This has to stop. You, the Dean of Students, the Dean of Doctoral Studies, and I are going to meet this evening after the class is over."

I was exhausted. So was the Dean of Students, a good friend.

We nevertheless gathered.

The Dean of Doctoral Studies and I had an opportunity to sit face to face and totally clear the air between us. The University President, on the other hand, became unbelievably verbally abusive toward me, telling me, in effect, that it was time I grew up, looked deep into my own psyche, and stopped talking about the Dean of Doctoral Studies to other students. I was poisoning the well that the staff of the University had so carefully built over the years.

I deliberately and consciously sat there in deep listening mode, looking him right in the eye, even though my whole gut was as tight as a knot. It felt as if he was punching me as hard as he could, over and over again, in my solar plexus.

Every time I refocused the conversation to lack of communication and clarity from University staff about the dissertation procedures, he abruptly cut me off. "This is not about words or communication or the dissertation. **This is about YOUR conduct!**"

After sitting for about twenty minutes on the receiving end of his verbal blasts, he finally ran out of wind and took a breath. I simply looked at him and asked, "Do you have anything else you would like to say?"

"No!" he snorted.

"Well, then we may all just as well go to bed," I responded.

Alone in my own bedroom, I sat with that scene, trying to figure out how a simple request for clarity and consistency about the University's procedures had suddenly become so distorted and transformed, mushrooming into a major vendetta against me.

The relationship between the Dean of Doctoral Studies and I had become clean and clear. The relationship between the University President and me was a nightmare.

All I could figure out was that, as a male, he was afraid of losing control and was also defending and protecting the University that was so near and dear to his heart. It also seemed he was protecting his new Dean of Doctoral Studies.

As far as I was concerned, the conversation between the University President and me was not over, particularly after his brutal comments about my poisoning the University's well and needing to grow up.

The next morning, I stopped him and said, "You and I still need to talk. You set the time."

He said, "Okay."

Two mornings later, when he had still not gotten back to me to set a time to evolve the conversation, I asked, "When are we going to talk?"

"We're not," he snapped, and strode away.

I had deliberately, out of respect for the University President, chosen to keep this conversation private. When he refused to have any additional conversations, the Dean of Students and I continued to talk. She had been as shocked as I over the University President's earlier conduct and was highly concerned about my welfare.

I was consciously and deliberately holding the University President in compassion. There was nothing else I could do.

In the meantime, I was clearly in a holding pattern as far as my dissertation went. Should I try to figure out some way to limit the focus of the Ph.D. or should I reconsider a D.Min?

"Can't" is not a word in my vocabulary. Excellence has always been one of my values. But which path was the path forward?

By Thursday evening, I had a gut feeling that I would never return to the site of the Dissertation Retreat, as beautiful and spectacular as it was. I felt deep grief—the same kind of grief I felt when I divorced Sandy, but also realized that it was far more important to get out into the world with my workshops, keynote speeches, and books than to spend my time putting together either dissertation.

On the final morning of the Retreat, each of us gave a closing statement. I began by stating the clarity I had had at the beginning of the week with respect to my intentions to complete my Ph.D. dissertation. It now seemed clear that neither the Ph.D. nor the D.Min was as important as actually getting out and transferring whatever understanding and wisdom I had acquired to others, and that I saw myself leaving the university completely so that I could put all my time, energy, and resources into other hands-on work, returning primarily to an oral tradition of verbal communication. I already had dozens of credentials. I didn't need another doctorate when I already had one *cum laude*.

I would write books, not as truth, but simply to document as well as I was able, a state of consciousness about which nothing can be accurately stated. I also said that it seemed to me to be neither in the interests of the University nor in my own interests to continue our relationship when I was perceived by the University as poisoning their well.

Poisoning the University's well was not the way I perceived myself. I perceived myself as clarifying and purifying the University's well. It simply made more sense to take whatever understanding I had out to an extensive global community, rather than limit it to the University's little black box.

Before I left, I made a point of seeking the University President out, even though it seemed as if he was still deliberately avoiding me. I asked him if he was up to a hug. He said, "Sure."

It was simply time to move on with much gratitude for what I had received and much sadness for what I would now leave behind.

Years later, I was speaking with a friend who had received her Ph.D. from the predecessor of the same University. When I told her the story of my aborted Ph.D. and mentioned the name of the University President, she commented, "Wasn't he the man who was having an affair with the University Secretary?"

I had no idea. I had never heard that before, but then it was something that no one would have publicly discussed.

I remembered something the Dean of Doctoral Students had once said: "I am quite capable of separating my private life from my public life."

And I recalled noticing how quiet, subdued, and compassionate the beautiful legal wife of the President of the University had been—the mother of the President's two sons.

She was a brilliant woman, daughter of a famous scientist. Her husband had given her a low-level, administrative job within the University.

I later learned that she and the University President were living separately. No one with whom I spoke knew whether they were still legally married or whether they had divorced.

Years later, while spending two weeks in Tamil Nadu, India, exploring spiritual sites, I again had an opportunity to revisit this gut-wrenching, dissertation-ending experience. I wanted the tour facilitator, one of the University Educators, to know the story of my experience with the University President and Dean of Doctoral Studies.

He listened with compassion. "I have seen this very dark side of the University President before. I am so sorry you had to go through that."

Then he added, "Why don't you just be who you are? You are such a role model for the younger women."

A year later, another woman seeking a Ph.D. asked me if I would be her External Advisor. I accepted. How interesting that I was being asked to fill an advisory role for a woman's Ph.D. after being slammed down by a man for trying to write my own.

The woman had paid an exorbitant amount of money to take an enlightenment course from a self-proclaimed male guru. Her experiences had been similar to mine. The man verbally abused her and failed to fulfill the commitments he had made. She, too, had suffered. She, too, had moved on. She, too, wanted to understand her experience and find a way to document it for all the world to see.

# Chapter 7
# Helpers and Mentors

*"To attain Knowledge, add things every day. To attain Wisdom, remove things every day."*

—Lao Tzu

## WHY I SOUGHT OUT HELPERS AND MENTORS

How had I ever fallen into that attempted group marriage and that experience? Clearly, there was knowledge I didn't have, born as I had been into a female body and so beautifully supported and protected by two loving parents and a beautiful, coherent, harmonious family.

I sought out mentors, many of them male, to attain the knowledge, skill, and power I lacked as a female and which the patriarchal culture had refused to allow me to learn. I still felt driven to find answers to my unanswered questions and seek guidance and support for the tasks I felt driven to complete.

I learned something from each mentor: the importance of commitment; how mastermind groups work; how to create a vision board; how to facilitate circles. I broke boards with my hand, ate fire, walked over a bed of hot coals in my bare feet, practiced balancing like a tightrope walker on ropes suspended twenty feet above the ground, was the elder woman in a sweat lodge, participated in an ayahuasca ceremony, and bent a steel rebar with a partner using only our necks. Each exercise centered, strengthened, and empowered me.

## CONNECTING WITH A BEAUTIFUL NEW MALE PARTNER AND HELPER

Shortly after I graduated from law school, I met a wonderful man named Don. We met at a singles group.

Neither of us went to those social gatherings often. We both went that time on the spur of the moment. I later learned that our meeting each other in this strange way was called a synchronicity.

I don't even know why I went. After having been so traumatically betrayed by the two men and other woman in the group marriage, I certainly wasn't eager to get intimately involved with anyone again.

Don tried to start a conversation with me. I was self-protective and standoffish. However, during the circle conversation that followed, he said things that interested me.

Afterward, he asked me to dance. Our dancing was fluid and aware, each of us paying full attention to the other. We were simply enjoying ourselves and the dance we were creating together.

Before we parted, he invited me out for New Years' Eve. I accepted.

There was a part of me that kept saying, "Janet, what are you doing? You don't even know this man!"

Don gave me directions to his home in Avalon, New Jersey. As I was driving down from Atlantic City, the doubts again surfaced. "What are you doing?"

I arrived at a little three-bedroom ranch, right next to the dunes by the Atlantic Ocean. Don had a lovely spread of shrimp and cheeses prepared. I was impressed.

He had made New Year's Eve reservations at a beautiful hotel in Cape May. The evening was spectacular, with an exquisite dinner and marvelous band. Again, we danced fluidly with one another, totally tuned to one another's moods and movements. As we drove back to Avalon after the New Year's Eve celebration, Don invited me to a second home he owned in Avalon. This one was on the bay, overlooking the inland waterway.

That night, we slept together. Many years later, on December 12, 1996, we legally married in Punta Gorda, Florida. We had to wait until Don finalized his legal divorce from the mother of his only son, a woman whom he unexpectedly found in bed one afternoon with another man.

I didn't take Don's surname. It didn't bother him at all.

Except for two temporary breakups, we remained together for twenty-two years—until the day he died. The breakups simply clarified boundaries beyond which neither of us was willing to go. We both knew we were better off together than either of us was alone, just as Sandy, our three sons, and I would have better off together had Sandy been willing and able to relinquish his affair with the other woman and recommit to our marriage.

Don had been estranged from his own son for years. Shocked, pained, and traumatized to suddenly find his wife in bed with another man, he had left wife, home, son, and marriage to understand, heal, recover, and reconnect with his own soul.

He was so very kind to my sons. He treated them with as much fatherly care and concern as if they had been his own. He provided a temporary home for my middle son, confused and traumatized by his parents' physical separation and legal divorce. We took my youngest son on a trip to Cancun, Mexico. We attended and celebrated my oldest son's change-of-command ceremony at Pearl Harbor in Hawaii.

Perhaps it was simply another synchronicity, but I, too, was a piece of the puzzle reuniting Don and his own son a few years before Don died. Don had followed his son's footsteps for years at a distance. He knew his son lived near Huntington Beach, California. I happened to be traveling to an event near Huntington Beach. Don came with me.

It was a wonderful opportunity for Don to reach out to his own long-estranged son. He invited Don Jr. and his wife, Judy, to meet him in the lobby of our hotel. I stayed in our room.

After several minutes, the phone rang. "Don and Judy would like to meet you," Don Sr. said.

I went down to the lobby. We had a wonderful conversation. What a beautiful couple they were! Later, they joined us at my oldest son's change-of-command ceremony at Pearl Harbor.

I had kept my own name. I had been gifted with a wonderful husband and an additional stepson. And I now had my own source of income so that I didn't have to remain subservient to any man, simply to be able physically to survive.

Don and I never merged our money or property. We each retained legal control over our own assets, although whenever it served us both and our aligned interests, we would *use* our assets to support one another.

When I first moved to Atlantic City to practice law, I purchased a three-bedroom duplex. I didn't have the cash to purchase the home outright, so had to finance it. In 1980, mortgage interest rates were 13.5 percent. I had no choice but to accept those rates if I wanted to own instead of rent.

After Don and I had been together for many months in a mutually caring, trusting, and accountable relationship, he offered to refinance my home at 10 percent interest. It benefited both of us. My monthly financial obligation was substantially reduced. He received a steady, reliable stream of passive income to pour back into enhancing our lives together.

In June 2003, Don and I had an opportunity to travel to a weeklong real estate investment retreat in West Bay Beach on Roatan, Honduras. Neither of us had ever been to Roatan.

We both loved to travel. We had both lived in other countries, Don in Haiti and I in Canada and Germany.

We had also both become active real estate investors as each of us desperately struggled to stabilize our lives after our traumatic experiences with adulterous marriages and betrayals of trust. My professional work as an Atlantic City attorney had been focused on real estate. We decided to add a second week to our Roatan trip to explore the island on our own.

West Bay Beach was spectacularly beautiful, with placid, crystal-clear, eighty-degree water for swimming and a magnificent reef not far offshore for snorkeling. We were enthralled with its beauty, but not sure we wanted to buy at the Mayan Princess. We were glad we had decided to stay an extra week.

Don ultimately contracted to buy a lovely little cottage in a community called Sunnyside on the north shore of Roatan. I contracted to buy a spectacular three-acre tract of land on a hillside overlooking the Caribbean, with a beautiful, already-built, Honduran hardwood home and a smaller partially finished two-bedroom bodega and garage. The property was beautifully planted with palms, banana trees, cashew trees, an African tulip tree, a craboo tree, plumeria, birds of paradise, canna, Christmas candles, common peanuts, day lilies, ginger, hibiscus, passion fruit, and wild lime.

It had so clearly been built and planted with deep care and love. The high-integrity seller, as part of our contract, agreed to complete the bodega.

Our intention was to live in the home I had contracted to purchase. Don would rent out his cottage to generate a stream of passive income to sustain our daily expenses and enhance our lives.

I sold everything I owned in Atlantic City. In August 2003, I closed, long distance, on our beautiful new Roatan home.

In September 2003, we returned to Roatan to close on Don's rental property. On September 24th, the day before he was to close, as we were leaving Sunnyside to drive back to our Roatan home, Don suddenly collapsed on the ground.

I ran to get the property manager. A retired nurse living at Sunnyside and a man trained in CPR ran to help.

The property manager called the Roatan emergency medical line. There was no answer.

The nurse and man trained in CPR worked together to resuscitate Don. Someone suddenly remembered a medical center at Anthony's Key Resort.

Together, we managed to lift Don into the back of a pickup truck and drive him to the resort. For thirty minutes, the doctors used every tool at their disposal to bring Don back to life. They shocked his heart. Finally, they announced they could do nothing further. Don's body could not be resuscitated.

The nurse later told me she believed Don had died when his body first hit the ground at Sunnyside. Had he chosen to leave this earth at a place he dearly loved, with people who dearly loved him?

My youngest son and his wife sent me a card with a personal note:

Don was very special to all of us. We cherish the memories we have of him, we do remember him fondly and will make sure the girls know what a special person he was!

Other friends sent a sympathy card with the following personal insert:
Don Bogart was an original,
Words often used to describe an individual
In today's world, but sometimes misused when trying to
Describe the true person. Don Bogart was an original.
I learned so much from him since 1983,
when I first met him.

Don took on any challenge. He stood his ground.
He used his
Very keen common sense in business matters. He was a
Self-made man. He was "Hands-ON" and a Mr. Fix-it.
Don was a collector of "various items." Don was fair and
Thoughtful in his dealings.

I am proud to say that I was a friend of Don Bogart's and
I will continue to tell the stories and remember all that we
Had been through together.

## A WOMAN LIVING ALONE IN CENTRAL AMERICA – CHALLENGES RESURFACING

Again, I walked alone—except for the support of some kind of living, breathing energy in which I had come to believe and learned I could trust.

The sellers of the Sunnyside cottage Don had been about to purchase told me that I could step into Don's shoes and complete the purchase at the original price if I finalized the transaction within two weeks. Roatan prices were skyrocketing as other investors began to discover this beautiful little island. Don had already paid a $24,850 deposit. He would lose his deposit if the transaction were not finalized. If I didn't step into Don's shoes and complete the purchase, the sellers told me they would put the property back on the market at a higher price.

From a financial perspective, I had little choice but to proceed with Don's purchase. I stripped a stock account of my own, which had been providing me $2,000 to $3,000 a month income and stepped into Don's shoes to complete his purchase and save the $24,850 deposit for his estate. The decision limited my own income flow to nothing but $1,100 per month from Social Security.

However, Don's trust had designated me as his lifetime income beneficiary. In addition to receiving annual income, I had the right to request an annual lump sum distribution of 5 percent of the principal of Don's estate. I was only *permitted* to make the lump sum distribution request in December of each year, and was *required* to make it in December if I wanted to receive it.

Desperately needing money to complete the Sunnyside purchase Don had initiated, as well as provide for my own basic living expenses, in October 2003, I spoke with Don's attorney and the trustee his attorney had recommended. My intention was to update them on the Sunnyside situation and inquire when I would begin receiving income distributions from the estate. I knew Don had been receiving regular income from some of the rental properties he had acquired over the years, money that presumably was now flowing into the estate. Why was some of this money not now flowing out to support me as Don had clearly intended?

The trustee could only comment, "You sure put yourself in a lot of doo-doo, didn't you?"

The attorney instructed me the $24,850 deposit Don had paid to purchase Sunnyside was an asset of Don's estate. He asked me to sign a promissory note to the estate in that amount, assuring me that it would be forgiven on December 1, 2003, when I was entitled to make a demand on the principal of the trust. Trusting his verbal assurances, I signed the note.

On December 1, 2003, I requested the lump sum distribution from the trustee. Two months later, I still had not received any money from the trust.

Again, I was beginning to experience the same betrayal of trust and lack of accountability I had previously experienced from the father of my sons and the other man in the group marriage. On the morning of February 2, 2004, as my irritation, frustration, and moral outrage grew, I put on my attorney's hat and wrote a strongly worded, four-page letter to the estate attorney and trustee, hand-delivering the letter that same day.

It got their attention. They agreed to talk with me.

I asked permission to record our conversation. They gave me permission.

I still have that recording. Shortly afterward, I began receiving the money that Don had intended me to receive.


Shortly after Don's death, the local male Honduran authorities began an investigation. They said they suspected foul play.

Did they have nothing better to do with their time? Did they somehow have to find ways to justify their salaries by pointing their fingers "out there"?

A local American-born female real estate agent, who had lived and worked on Roatan for several years befriended me and persuaded the local authorities that there was no foul play. Don had simply died of a heart attack. They left us alone.

In his Last Will and Testament, Don had directed that his body be cremated, and the ashes disposed of at the discretion of his personal representative. I was Don's personal representative. Don had told me in private conversations that he didn't want his ashes buried in some tomb. He wanted them spread on the waters of the places he loved, particularly Avalon, New Jersey, and Manasota Key, Florida.

In Roman Catholic Honduras, cremation was legally forbidden and unavailable. For Don's wishes to be respected, I had to have his body flown back to the States.

More governmental restrictions surfaced. His body could not enter the United States unless it were either cremated or embalmed.

My real estate agent friend helped me fly Don's body for embalmment to Tegucigalpa, the capital of Honduras. My oldest son's wife, through her mother, was able to connect me with a crematory in Florida. I accompanied Don's body from Roatan to Tegucigalpa to Florida, where I relinquished it to the crematory to fulfill Don's wishes.

On May 17, 2004, we held a memorial service at Don's beautiful home on the Bay in Avalon, New Jersey, lovingly surrounded by family and friends. I spread a third of his ashes on the waters there.

Later, alone, I spread a second third of his ashes over the waters off his beautiful Pelican Landing home on Manasota

Key, Florida. I did it surreptitiously, not wanting or needing any male authorities coming in, interfering, and trying to stop me from fulfilling Don's final wishes.

Finally, I carried the remainder of Don's ashes back to Sunnyside on Roatan. The crematory had given me an urn in which to carry these final ashes on the international flight. Again, I was cautious, protective, and secretive. I did not want or need the airport regulators telling me what I could or couldn't do.

When I arrived at Sunnyside, I walked out alone on the dock. Again, I did not want or need obtrusive observers telling me what I could or couldn't do. Gently, I stooped down on the windward side of the dock, said my final farewells to Don, and placed the urn in the water.

I expected it to sink to the bottom. It didn't. My carefully laid plans had again gone awry.

A second time, I stooped down and with urgency, pushed the urn under the dock so it would not be seen by meddling, disruptive intruders. The urn went under the dock, floated up on the other side, and finally stopped in a pile of seaweed.

All I could think was, "Don, you just don't quit, do you?"

Don didn't quit. He was fourteen years older than I. As he aged, doctors had told him he had heart problems. He had begun to lose his balance and fall.

I remember a time when he fell under the orange tree in a home he owned on Manasota Beach Road in Englewood, Florida. I rushed to help. He pushed me away.

He wanted to do it himself. He had done it before. He could do it again. Slowly, with focus, he pulled himself up, scraped and bloodied but able to walk back to the house.

When I look at Don's death from hindsight, I can't help but wonder if the timing and manner were exactly what they needed to be. Have you ever heard of people making agreements before they enter this physical life to relate to one another in a particular way?

I walked out to the end of the Sunnyside dock to watch and wait. As I sat in the shady, covered area, I couldn't help but wonder if Don and I had somehow made that kind of agreement before we entered this physical life. I watched the urn entrapped in the seaweed, hoping it would free itself and drift out to the open seas, as I knew Don would have desired.

I was not dressed to wade into the shallows to free it. I was shortly scheduled to fly out of Roatan. My suitcases were packed, and I was dressed for flying, not wading. I was only able to watch, meditate, and reflect on our time together.

Finally, I had to leave if I was going to catch my plane. Once again, I bid my solemn farewells to my beautiful, supportive partner, walked back to my car, and drove away.

The urn still lay in the seaweed. Was Don unwilling to leave until I left? Was he still with me in spirit, if not in body?

I had done what I could to support Don's last wishes. As I drove away, his soul and final ashes were no longer in my hands. Again, I had no choice but to surrender into my soul.

After Don's death, I holed up in the beautiful home in Roatan I had purchased, and wrote *Shift: Change Your Words, Change Your World*, the book I'd known for thirty-five years I had to write. Would I have had the time and focus to write this book had Don wasted away for years?

I had sold my own properties in the States so I could purchase that spectacularly situated, three-acre property on the north side of Roatan where Don and I had intended to live. Don had placed everything he owned into a revocable trust. The trustee was a financial advisor, recommended by Don's lawyer, who knew nothing about real estate and was intent on selling all of Don's properties and converting the proceeds into stocks and bonds.

Those properties held so many beautiful memories for me. I did not want them sold, but I no longer had any say in what happened to them. I visited each for a final time, removed a few small treasures, and returned to my new home in Roatan. The trustee commented that he would "look the other way."

"Look the other way?" All I was doing was preserving, honoring, protecting, and sanctifying a few small mementoes from my beautiful partner's life. Was the trustee's only interest in selling those beautiful pieces of artwork for money to enrich both the assets of Don's estate and his own pocket?

Is the love of money the root of all evil? Or was it just a game the trustee and I were playing, with the trustee now holding most of the trump cards? Or was it just a dance of self-expression, self-assertion, personal intention, and skill?

In the beautiful little Roatan community in which I now found myself, I soon realized that only about a dozen homeowners lived there full-time. The rest visited for a two-week vacation, renting their properties the rest of the time to generate streams of passive income.

The high-integrity seller of the home in which I now lived had been the original property developer for the entire community. The current property developers had lied, manipulated, stolen from him, and driven him out of his former high-integrity leadership position.

I watched as the current developers unilaterally changed the rules, extracted money from the homeowners to enhance their own pockets and pay for their own projects, failed to follow through on promises made to the community, commingled funds between the homeowners association and their own corporations, and wined and dined the investor homeowners during the two weeks per year they visited.

Is the love of money the root of all evil?

Shortly before an investor was scheduled to arrive, the property manager frantically ran around, attending to tasks that had been neglected for months so that everything would look beautiful before the two-week investors arrived. When they weren't there, he spent much of his time partying and immersed in his sexual relationship with a local Honduran woman.

Is control of the money supply enhancement of power? Is control of the money supply control of the sexual supply?

The full-time homeowners began bonding together as we watched the property manager's incompetence and financial manipulation. We held our own private meetings to brainstorm what we could do to stabilize the community and bring it back into integrity, harmony, and accountability.

Because of my legal training and the fact that I was one of only a few homeowners living in the community full-time, in 2004, I volunteered my services as Secretary of the Homeowners Association (HOA), hoping I could help keep the community fair, functional, legal, and accountable.

The original, high-integrity developer had made it quite clear in the original covenants, conditions, and restrictions that density would never be increased. It was one of the reasons many of us bought where we did.

The property developer wanted to amend the HOA covenants, conditions, and restrictions to double the permitted density so that the Property Manager would have more money to fund his projects.

The resident homeowners drafted a proxy against the density amendment desired by the property developers and sent it out to homeowners whose contact information we had.

The Property Manager danced around the new bookkeeper's questions about HOA deposits and checks. When she asked for financial statements that were being requested by both full-time and absentee homeowners, he kept finding excuses not to provide them. When we asked for homeowner names, email addresses, and telephone numbers, it took eight months before we received them.

There were other tensions between what the group of permanent homeowners wanted and what the property developers wanted. Most of them revolved around money and who was going to pay for the Property Manager's projects.

At a June 2004 HOA board meeting, in my role as Secretary, I offered two proposed agendas, one to be discussed on the record and one to be discussed off the record. The property manager refused to accept either, stating he wanted to make clear that he was running things.

The Property Manager stated that for reasons that had to remain confidential, paving sections of the road could not be done at the present time. I pressed for a time limit on the non-action and questioned what would happen next fall during rainy season if the road issue had not been addressed.

When I asked who was paying for a perimeter survey of the entire property the Property Manager had ordered, he stated, "The HOA." When I questioned the propriety of having the HOA pay for something that pertained to properties other than HOA properties, he withdrew his statement, saying that cost could be discussed and perhaps allocated.

The Property Manager stated that he was considering having the HOA sue the original developer for failure to supply proper electrical service to homeowners. I had seen these kinds of frivolous lawsuits many times before while practicing law.

By using the HOA to initiate the lawsuit, the Property Manager could avoid taking responsibility for his own decisions and actions. If the HOA were to win the case and receive damages or the original developer paid settlement money because he didn't want to waste time and resources going to court, the Property Developers would have more money with which to fund their projects.

The Property Manager stated that he was upset that resident homeowners had mailed proxies to the nonresident homeowners. I responded that if he had provided homeowner contact information to the Secretary of the Board as requested, if Board meetings had been held monthly as required by the Articles of Incorporation, if he had kept HOA members informed about actions he was taking, and if the property developers had stopped trying to increase density, the proxies would never have gone out.

Another topic over which there was substantial controversy was creating a fair system of HOA votes, memberships, and assessments. One homeowner, who owned a home on three lots with 2.7 acres had one membership/vote and was being charged two assessments. Another homeowner, who owned a home on three lots with approximately 2.7 acres had two membership/votes and was being charged three assessments. The membership/votes were established in each owner's individual deed, so changes voted by the HOA would not be controlling, unless agreed to by each property owner.

The Property Manager kept delaying the appointment of a third member of the Design Review Subcommittee until he could find someone who would support his agenda. I pressed for an immediate appointment so that the Design Review Subcommittee could begin its work. The resident homeowners succeeded in having a Colorado architect homeowner appointed.

The Property Manager stated that he would be providing the HOA's new bookkeeper with printouts of the HOA accounts and copies of HOA bank statements by August 13, 2004, so that she could fulfill the HOA bookkeeping responsibilities to which she was appointed at the June homeowners' meeting. She had still not received them by February 23, 2005.

At the September 2004 Board of Directors meeting, we discussed the density issue and what was currently permitted under the covenants. Homeowners who had expressed an opinion did not want either increased density or more duplexes, both of which were also currently prohibited by the covenants.

At the December 2004 meeting, it was agreed that the Property Manager's wife should not be the backup signatory on HOA checks and that the Vice President of the HOA should assume that responsibility.

I and the other homeowner lawyer drafted an alternate proposal for accomplishing the one vote/one assessment structure, to be presented at the April 1st annual meeting for discussion and vote.

By February 2005, I was quite clear that, as beautiful as my Roatan home and property were, I could not continue to thrive in a community run by unaccountable, low-integrity developers who were more interested in using the homeowners to put as much money as possible into their own pockets than they were in developing a beautiful, safe, and sustainable community. By that time, I was already looking at Panama as a better place to live, hoping to find a more coherent, harmonious community there.

By March 2005, the information and money battles between the resident homeowners and development managers escalated. Without the knowledge of HOA board members or board approval, the Property Manager sent out his own agenda for the April 1st homeowners Annual Meeting, including only items the development managers wanted considered. The resident homeowners again sent out a proxy to the nonresident homeowners, including additional items that had been discussed at length at Board meetings, but not included in the Property Manager's agenda. Most important were the increased density and assessment issues.

The Property Managers were not done extracting every possible penny from me to punish me for insisting on transparency, accountability, and integrity. Two days before the Annual Meeting, I received an undated letter from one of the development managers, demanding that I pay three assessments to the HOA for the three lots and one homestead I owned if I wanted to vote at the April 1st Annual Meeting, even though or perhaps because, they knew that a revised version of the Covenants, Conditions, and Restrictions recommending one assessment and one vote per homestead would be submitted for vote by the homeowners at that meeting. I paid the three assessments, two under protest, but I was done with these property managers. It was time to move on.

I listed both Roatan properties for sale. Don's sold first. By that time, I had contracted to buy properties in Panama and needed the money from the Roatan sales to be able to move forward in Panama.

I had the Sunnyside funds wired by the closing realtor to my bank account in the States. The money didn't arrive.

Three days later, it still hadn't arrived. One of the investigative bodies of the United States government had stopped the transfer because they thought I might be laundering drug money.

Give me a break! Do you men have nothing better to do with your time than interfere with and disrupt innocent and transparent private transactions?

When I first moved to Panama in 2006, it was again the stunning beauty of the environment that attracted me as well as the potential for a solid financial investment. I soon discovered Boquete, a little town nestled in the western mountains of Panama where expat Americans migrate. The area is replete with deep river canyons and beautiful waterfalls. Each January, spectacular double rainbows appear.

Temperatures are between 70 and 80 degrees year round. It seemed like the perfect place to build my exquisite dream home where I could invite friends to gather and engage in meaningful, eye-opening conversations.

I contracted to build a beautiful home in what appeared to be a lovely, little, gated community just south of Boquete, The community was surrounded on three sides by a deep canyon. A spectacular waterfall flowed down a gorge on the far side of the canyon. A beautiful clubhouse had already been built.

I found a nearby home to rent and told my landlord (an American) that I needed to stay in his rental property until my own home was built. He agreed. We signed a lease giving him no rights of termination as long as I paid the rent and took care of the property. Under United States law, I could have remained forever.

After two years, my landlord sent me an email saying he had found another tenant who would pay him more money and give him a three-year lease. Could I meet those terms?

The short answer was "No." While I might have paid more money, I couldn't in good faith enter into a three-year lease when I expected to move into my own home within six months.

My landlord gave me notice to leave, commenting he was sure I would understand. Business was business.

Was I livid? Yes. I pursued my Panamanian legal rights in every way possible. I talked with Panamanian friends. I talked with the Corregidor (local district attorney). I talked with my own Panamanian lawyer. They all said the same thing. Under Panamanian law, I had to move out.

"What if I refuse to leave?" I asked.

"You'll get a judgment against you," they replied. Not a good thing for an expat.

I had no legal support and no other worldly options.

However, I had spiritual options.

I left politely and quickly. I wanted my landlord to receive as little additional money from me as possible. I also let everyone in the neighborhood know exactly what he had done. Then I released everything and let the laws of the Universe take over. Hindus and Buddhists would call these "laws of the universe" "karma".

My landlord breached his agreement with me. On the human level, there was nothing fair or reasonable about that. But there *was* a spiritual benefit for me.

I had learned once again that I needed to be more selective in choosing the people to whom I gave my trust and money. This man had helped me step into my own sharpened discernment, assertiveness, and power.

And the spiritual, karmic consequences to him? My landlord's wonderful new tenant breached his agreement with my landlord. The house stood vacant for over a year with no money coming into my landlord's pocket.

I guess business is business. I'm sure he understood.

One of the requirements for building in the community I had chosen for my dream home was that I had to use the builders who owned the land to do the construction. I began running into the same challenges I had experienced with the Roatan property managers: incompetence, lack of transparency, and lack of accountability.

The builders kept the architectural plans off-site. There was little onsite supervision. Workers who had been taxi drivers a few years before were hand-mixing the foundation concrete. When tested by the local university, the strength of the foundation was inadequate to support the building.

I had paid a Panamanian architect to make slight revisions to the plans to accommodate a slightly larger bathtub I wanted to buy and gave the revised plans to the builders. Their workers, nevertheless, began building the home in accordance with the original model plans.

There was a light pole in the middle of the driveway and a wall where the picture window was supposed to be. When the builders tested the water lines, the gauge went down 40 psi in three days.

The builders said the psi drop was due to the temperature and humidity. My American inspector said, "Are you kidding!" The plumber then insisted on pumping soapy water through the water lines to demonstrate that they were not leaking. When my American inspector suggested better ways of testing for leaks, the Panamanian plumber threw his tools across the yard in a fit of rage.

The builders built the septic tank too high so that the capacity was only 20 to 40 percent.

Finally, after twenty-one months of making mistakes and fixing them, they walked off the job in a fit of rage, refusing to finish the house.

Their next ploy was to demand $40,000 if I wanted to finish the house with another builder. Excuse me! Did I hear that right?

Turning to the no-recourse legal system was a waste of time and money. Lawyers are expensive, witnesses can be bribed, judges can be paid off, and getting a decision can take years. The decision is invariably against the non-Panamanian.

Every time I thought about my dream-home-turned-nightmare; I was livid. I had to consider the possibility that I would have to walk away from a $300,000 investment and let it rot. Once again, I had trusted people who didn't deserve my trust.

Yet I couldn't help but notice what my rage was doing to my body. When I focused on the rotting house, I couldn't sleep. My energy was blocked. It felt as if I was banging my head against a stone wall with no solution and no support. I had to let go, not because the builders deserved it, but because I needed to regain and retain my own sanity. I had to find some other way to move forward.

Someone referred me to an auctioneer in Venice, Florida. I agreed to have him proceed with an auction. He, of course, wanted to publicize the auction as widely as possible to attract potential bidders. I was concerned that publicity would only enflame the ire of the builders. It did.

The developers began slandering and defaming both me and the property. They chased away at least three other bidders, sold one of their own homes to one of my interested bidders, and then entered the bidding process themselves to buy my dream home at a ridiculously low price. At the end of the bidding, they were backup bidders to someone who had bid less than half of what I had invested.

While I was horribly disappointed at the amount of the final bid, I had agreed to sell the property to the highest bidders. We finalized the contract.

The developers weren't done. They contacted the high bidders, again defamed me, accused the auctioneer and me of lying and misrepresentation, and persuaded the high bidders that both of us were evil. The high bidders listened to the developers' slander, believed it, and wrote the auctioneer a vicious email repeating the slander, demanding their deposit back, and refusing to complete the purchase. That left the developers in top position at a ridiculously low purchase price. They, of course, were delighted to close that deal.

I wasn't. I told them I wouldn't sell to them.

Their next play was to initiate a foreclosure proceeding in a Panamanian court. I received no notice of the legal action, so didn't even know what they were doing behind my back until I found out by accident. I contacted my wonderful, high-integrity Panamanian attorney who confronted them and stopped the foreclosure.

Finally, another Panamanian couple offered to buy the property at a higher price than the auction offer. We signed a contract, but the developers were still demanding I pay them a ransom before they would settle the lawsuit and agree to the sale. I said no.

I believe the Panamanian buyers finally paid the ransom, but at that point, I didn't care. I had recovered some of my investment, had not succumbed to the developers' bullying, and could move on with my life.

On Christmas night 2009, I was living in a rental home in Jaramillo, reading in bed before I went to sleep. The house was surrounded by a high iron fence along the road and a chain-link fence around the rest of the property. My American landlady lived in the house next door.

Suddenly, I heard a noise outside my window. It sounded as if someone had kicked a pebble. It was enough to attract my attention. I listened for a minute and then, hearing nothing further, went back to my reading.

About two minutes later, I heard a loud pop coming from my landlady's home. Then my cell phone rang.

It was my landlady. "Turn on your lights!" she shouted. "There was a man just peering in my bedroom window. I banged on the window at him, then shot my gun out the back door. He just looked at me and sauntered up toward your home."

I wasn't sure that turning on my lights was a good idea, but I did and stayed away from the windows. Nothing else happened. Finally, both my landlady and I went to bed.

My landlady was afraid to notify the police. Her gun was unlicensed. She was afraid it would be she who would get into trouble with the Panamanian authorities, not the intruders.

Two days later, she finally called the Panamanian police. They barely had gasoline for their cars. They had no forensic tools with which to identify an intruder.

They nevertheless came over, smiled politely, and showed us the hole cut in the chain-link fence at the back of my house. Then, one of them said to my landlady and me, "Let me show you something." He walked up on my back porch and lifted out one of the windows.

That was the final straw. I simply could not live in a place where anyone who wanted to walk into my home anytime he wanted, could do so.

Was there no place where a single woman was safe, where she was not preyed upon by men either sexually or financially?

The next day, I was on a plane back to the States. Within a week, I had found a rental home in Venice, Florida. Within two months, I had packed all my belongings and moved everything I owned back to the States.

## THE POWER OF COMMITMENT

*Until one is committed, there is hesitancy, the chance to draw back, always ineffectiveness. Concerning all acts of initiative (and creation), there is one elementary truth, the ignorance of which kills countless ideas and splendid plans: that the moment one commits oneself, then Providence moves, too. All sorts of things occur to help one that would never, otherwise, have occurred. A whole stream of events issues from the decision, raising in one's favor all manner of unforeseen incidents and meetings and material assistance which no man could have dreamt would have come his way.*

—William Hutchinson Murray[38]

I continued to search for helpers and mentors. I found many, most of them male. All wanted an extraordinary amount of money to teach me what they knew. I paid the

---

[38] https://en.wikipedia.org/wiki/W._H._Murray

money because I still wanted to live and to learn what the patriarchal culture had previously refused to teach me.

Many mentoring activities focused on making a specific commitment before doing some feat you never thought you could do: breaking a board with your hand, eating fire, walking across a bed of hot coals in your bare feet, jumping from a twenty-foot-high telephone pole, or bending a steel rebar with a partner using only your necks. Each time, the commitment was unique because I was at a different time, place, and consciousness state in my life.

Much of what I learned was to watch my own mind, train my own mind, and focus on uncovering and discovering the people and things that would support me as well as protecting myself from the people and things that would not or could not.

Here are some of the practices in which I participated and things I learned.

## Mastermind Groups

I began participating in mastermind groups, where, every two weeks, all mastermind partners exchanged templates. The first section of the template was "My Successes." When I wrote these down, I reminded myself of all the good things in my life, and all of the things I had accomplished. There simply was no room for self-criticism or self-judgment.

Another section of the template focused on "What do I need?" When I asked for help, I almost invariably got that help from my mastermind partners. Someone else would have an idea I hadn't thought of or be able to introduce me to one of their own contacts who might be able to help me.

## Ropes Courses

As I pulled myself up the twenty-foot-high pole, one metal support after another, a part of me was thinking, *Janet, you've got to be crazy! What do you think you are doing, jeopardizing your life climbing this pole and placing your trust in those people down below you don't even know!*

It was precisely the same part of my mind that popped up when I first met Don at that singles group.

Then, I remembered. My intention was to release my pain and anger toward Sandy, who had abandoned both me and our children to spend his life with a woman I once believed was my best friend.

My helmet and harness were securely in place. My belay team held firmly to the ropes that would gently guide me back to earth if I lost my balance and fell. I was determined to do it.

Climbing the pole was manageable until my hand reached the last metal support near the pole's top. Then, somehow, someway, I had to figure out how to get my feet up on top of the pole and stand up straight—without anything to support me but my own courage, physical strength, physical balance, and belay team below.

As I struggled to pull myself upright, I swung sideways off the pole. The ropes, held by my belay team, attached to my harness, stopped what would otherwise have been a disastrous fall.

The experience demonstrated that, once again, I was with people I could trust. Gently, my belay team lowered me down. Now I was more determined than ever to climb to the top of that pole and jump.

Metal support after metal support, I climbed back up to the place where the supports ended. Somehow, I managed to get one foot up on top of the pole, then the other. Slowly, acutely aware of my balance, I stood upright. My belay team cheered loudly. Now I knew I could do it.

For a moment, I stood tall, focused with laser-like intention on what I had come to do: forgive the father of my children for abandoning us. Then, I leaped into space, struck the celebration bell with my hand, and, with the support of my belay team, glided swiftly back to the ground.

I'd done it! Not only had I jumped from the top of a twenty-foot-high pole. I had also surrendered my pain, rage, judgment and blame. The transformation was immense and immediate. In the instant I jumped, I again felt free to move on with the rest of my life.

**Walking Across a Bed of Hot Coals in Bare Feet**

Before I walked across the bed of hot coals, I again committed to forgiving Sandy, my children's father, and the woman I once believed was my best friend for their adultery, which had ripped apart two functional marriages and two beautiful families. For years, I had buried my rage to protect our children during their formative years from being placed in the middle between mother and father.

After I successfully walked across the bed of hot coals without burning my feet, I traveled to Pearl Harbor for my oldest son's change-of-command ceremony. Sandy and the other woman, whom I once believed was my best friend, were there together as legal husband and wife. I asked to speak with each of them—separately—in my own hotel room. I did not want to speak with them as a couple.

In both cases, we had a rational conversation, and I was able to say, "I forgive you." I felt better afterward, not because they deserved it, but because I had followed through on my own commitment. It did not mean I could ever trust either of them again, but it did help release my rage and refocus my energy.

## Breaking a Board with Your Hand

Before you break a board with your hand, you write on the front of the board what you are afraid of or what is holding you back. You write on the back of the board what you will have or be if you break through the blockage.

I still have the board where my fear was losing my sons. If I broke through that fear, I would bring my sons with me to full human potential.

The people who focused on their fears or blockages didn't break the board. The people who focused on what they would have or be if they broke the board slammed right through it.

# THE POWER OF MEDITATION AND WITNESSING YOUR MIND

## Labyrinths[39]

Labyrinths appear throughout history, beginning as early as 2500 BC in Goa, India. Later, they emerged in Greece, Egypt, Italy, France, and Native American cultures.

Labyrinth at Institute of Noetic Sciences
Petaluma, CA

---

[39] As you read through this section, note the analogy to our consciousness diagram and logo—reconnecting with that center point of non-dual consciousness and then manifesting that living, breathing energy with which we have reconnected to the physical world in our own unique, physical form.

The word labyrinth is derived from the Lydian word "labrys," meaning double-edged axe.[40]

The significance of labyrinths differs from culture to culture. Grecian labyrinths were believed to house the minotaur, a mythical creature half man and half bull. Other cultures associated the maze with death and a triumphant return. Today, labyrinths serve as a form of modern pilgrimage for those who can't travel to distant lands. They are walking meditations, allowing each of us to sort out the chaos of everyday life and find that spark of divinity that lies within.

The walk into the labyrinth center provides a beautiful opportunity to meditate on our life purpose. Who are we? Why are we here? What are our unique gifts and talents?

Once we reach the center of the labyrinth and the core of our being, we know who we are, what our unique gifts and talents are, and what we're here to do.

It's not easy. The minotaur, a vicious beast at the labyrinth's center, hides from the world and our own minds. Can we confront and kill that ferocious beast within, meditate on and process the experience, and then move out again to serve rather than slay?

If we succeed, as we wind our way out of the labyrinth, new questions emerge. How can we serve? How can we give back to the world what has been given to us so freely? How can we stay connected with that Living, Breathing Energy at the core of our Being and allow the gifts we are constantly receiving to flow effortlessly through us and back out into the world to enrich and empower all they touch?

---

[40] https://www.merriam-webster.com/dictionary/labrys#:~:text=Definition%20of%20labrys,ancient%20Cretan%20sacred%20double%20ax

The path in and the path out both twist and turn. We think we are reaching the center of the labyrinth and the core of our being, when suddenly, we find ourselves on the outer edge of the circle, far from where we expected to be. We walk next to another spiritual seeker, then suddenly, our paths turn in opposite directions. We separate. As we follow our own path, we repeatedly pass the same people and see the same archetypal patterns from new perspectives.

If you've never walked a labyrinth, try it. I think you'll find it offers new insights into who you are and what your purpose is on this planet.[41]

## THE POWER OF SOUND VIBRATION

### Sanskrit Mantras

Some time ago, a friend sent me an email with a link to a series of Sounds True audios about Sanskrit mantras. Knowing that I was working on another book about word energy, my foreign rights agent had previously mentioned Sanskrit as a language I should explore.

Western language uses symbolism and meaning. Sanskrit uses the pure vibration of sound.

I ordered the audios and began listening. Among other mantras, there was a mantra for bringing abundance into your life.

Phonetically it sounds like "Om shreem kleem Lakshmi ay namaha." It's toned on a single note for the most part with the "ay" one note higher and the "ma" in the namaha one note lower.

---

[41] For more information about labyrinths, see www.labyrinthsociety.org/. To find a labyrinth near you, see www.labyrinthlocator.com/.

The longer mantra is composed of seed mantras. Shreem is the principle of abundance. Kleem is the principle of attraction. Lakshmi is the goddess of abundance, a beautiful woman with abundance flowing from her hands. Namaha means to salute.

According to Sanskrit philosophy, you can attract abundance into your life simply by saying over and over the simple seed mantra "shreem." The longer mantra is supposed to be more powerful. I decided to play with the longer mantra and see what happened.

In 2011, as I drove to Tampa Airport with the intention of flying back to Panama to heal my relationship with the beautiful home I had been unable to complete, I repeated the mantra over and over. Then, I forgot about it.

When I arrived in Panama, there was a penny lying on the ground beneath my feet. Three days later, in Boquete, my travel agent, out of the blue, gave me a free $3 phone card. Then my agent at the bank gave me two free 2011 calendars.

As so often happens in Panama, I fully expected the taxi driver who took me back to Boquete to notice that I was an American and triple his fee. He didn't. It happened a second time.

Greetings, meetings, lunches, and dinners kept flowing in.

The kicker happened shortly before I arrived home. I'd been getting about ten hits a day on my website. Suddenly the hits jumped to over a hundred.

Is there something going on here that I don't understand but that somehow seems to work? Or is it just that, as I focus on abundance, I become more aware of the abundance all around me flowing into my life?

I don't know the answer, but I think I'll continue chanting the mantras.

## THE POWER OF ANOTHER NAME CHANGE

In 2012, I had a numerology study done on the name "Janet Smith Warfield." The results were one of the worst numbers you could possibly imagine. They signified struggle and martyrdom.

I was so tired of struggle and martyrdom. Again, I needed to change my name.

By adding "Dr." at the beginning of my name, which I could legitimately do because of my Juris Doctor *cum laude* degree, the energy of my name changed to magnetizing and attracting.

I liked that energy a lot better. I discovered that by putting the "Dr." at the beginning of my name, people trusted me more.

I somehow had more credibility in their eyes and received more respect.

I like the name Dr. Janet Smith Warfield. I intend to use it for the rest of my life.

## THE POWER OF FOCUSING ON WHAT IS WORKING IN YOUR LIFE

When you're navigating the turbulent emotional waters of a divorce, the death of a best friend, the loss of a job, a forced relocation, or any other major lifetime challenge, how do you stay sane and productive?

The answer sounds simple. Keep your focus on what's working in your life. However, implementing it is not always easy.

In 2009, my book, *Shift: Change Your Words, Change Your World*, had become an Amazon bestseller. It was being translated into Bulgarian, Russian, and Indonesian. It was being distributed in India. The Russian translation alone had sold almost two thousand copies in its first six months.

I was negotiating distributorship agreements with North American and United Kingdom distributors. Radio and television interviews were pouring in. Workshops were bringing participants exciting new insights that suddenly turned their lives around. I simply made a conscious choice to focus on all those good things that were supporting the life path I had been given to follow.

## THE POWER OF STAYING IN INTEGRITY

Between 2013 and 2015, I studied in Chartres, France. I had intended to get my Ph.D., somehow writing a dissertation on the challenge that had been driving my life: How can I use analytical, divisive words to communicate a unifying holistic experience?

We regularly spent time in Chartres Cathedral.

Andrew Harvey, one of our teachers, [42] said, "The cathedral works on you." It certainly worked on me.

The desecration of my marriage to the father of my children had continued to haunt me even more after Don died. Just like being called "queer" by my high school classmate, it felt like an arrow driven deep into my heart.

I could not remove it. More and more, I was seeing marriage and family as a sacred contract where husband and wife held sacred space together so that the children of their union could thrive and flourish.

The issue was not dead. The paternal grandfather of our children had directed Sandy to marry the other woman so

---

[42] https://www.andrewharvey.net/

that everything would look proper to the outside world. I was struggling to survive financially, regain my self-respect, and continuing to support our teenage sons as well as I was able, particularly our middle son, who had been so confused and traumatized over his parents' separation and divorce.

The father of my children was now bringing the other woman into our family gatherings—now as his legal wife. Her energy adulterated the sacredness of our original family.

I sat alone. The wound in my heart split wide open again, my anger again rising. It felt as if they were pouring salt into my still-unhealed wounds.

Sandy and the other woman seemed to be totally oblivious to my pain and their own lack of accountability toward Sandy's and my children, just as they had been on that ride home from Washington, DC. At our family events, all they wanted to do was make small talk as if nothing had happened and everything was fine. I was not interested.

Did they not even care? Did they think their conduct was morally appropriate simply because the paternal grandfather of my children had insisted they legally marry?

Were they burying feelings of guilt they didn't know how to deal with? Were they afraid to face their fear and shame? Were they afraid to face my rage? Was I afraid to bring my rage over the desecration of our once-functional genetic family to the surface for all to see?

I tried to be polite for the sake of our children, but there was unfinished business that needed to surface and be healed. As Thich Nhat Hanh wrote, "... The Buddha never advised us to suppress our anger. He taught us to go back to ourselves and take good care of it."

Being polite wasn't the answer. But what was?

Over and over again, I made a commitment to forgive the father of our children and the other woman. I did it not because I believed they deserved forgiveness, but because I needed to release the terrible burden I was carrying and move on with my own life.

What was I missing? While my intentions were pure, the pain and anger continued to surface. It seemed that something in me was still strongly resisting both forgiveness and walking the spiritual path that seemed to be mine to walk, driving me forward, despite my reluctance and resistance. I simply could not move on with my own life as long as my sons continued to suffer.

Sandy and the other woman continued to attend our family events, hanging all over one another and making small talk. I continued to struggle with my rage and feelings of disrespect.

A few months before I participated in the Chartres Intensive, I found myself waking up in the middle of the night in an intense rage, playing with ways to wake the father of my children and the other woman up and force them to pay attention. The rage was doing nothing for my well-being, but I couldn't let go of principles that mattered so deeply to me: being impeccable with my word, accountability, the sacredness of the marital contract, and holding sacred space in which the children of our union could thrive and flourish.

"The cathedral works on you."

As I sat in the deep stillness, absorbing the energies of the crypt, the Black Madonnas, and the Mary Magdalene window, something shifted.

I didn't need to be a man's wife. That had been my mother's idea.

I had been sexually frigid in my marriage to Sandy. He had often seemed more like a fourth son than a husband. Was my true marriage to God?

Carolyn Myss, one of our Chartres teachers, said, "God, manage me."

Was my natural energy that of the Great Mother, the Divine Feminine? As I sat in the crypt, looking at the serene face of the Black Madonna, my pain began dissipating. Was the energy of the Great Mother, the Divine Feminine, the energy that had been given to me to hold?

## THE POWER OF NONRESISTANCE

A good and spiritual friend of mine once posed the question: "How do you resist insanity?"

Then she answered her own question. "The only way for me, as an individual, to resist is to hold on to who I am amid all of the forces that want to turn me into something else."

At first, I thought: What a great answer! It truly is all about staying centered when external chaos swirls around us. Each of us must stand tall when insanity claws at the core of our being. But then I thought about all the physical forces in my life that have swept me away from what I thought was solid ground into the raging torrent. What was the purpose of those experiences?

Here are some of the things I learned:

I could keep my head above water and swim. When you are struggling to stay alive, you don't feel fear. You're just doing what you need to do to survive. The spiritual benefits were increased self-esteem, courage, and strength.

I began appreciating the chaos of raging waters. They carried me to psychic depths I never would otherwise have experienced. The spiritual benefits were depth of understanding and enhanced clarity.

Raging waters taught me compassion. As I struggled through the physical challenges, I suffered through a soul struggle within myself: anger, fear, frustration, and how to make ethical choices. I could then feel and understand that soul struggle in others. I had walked in their shoes. I understood how traumatic it was to be in that space.

Does one resist insanity or just release it and move on? That has been a regularly recurring theme in my life.

Usually, I'm stubborn. I exhaust every viable avenue for reducing the insanity and retaining the relationship before I'll release it and walk away.

Insanity is the realm of bullies and dictators. Choosing to resist their arrogance, violence, and control issues can have substantial spiritual benefits, both for the individual resisting, for the bullies, and for the world. It levels the playing field and reduces the bullies' dysfunctional power.

However, when one chooses to resist insanity, there are nonfunctional and functional ways of doing it.

**Spotting the Nonfunctional ways**

- Allowing yourself to get sucked into the dictator's insanity.
- Screaming.
- Name-calling.
- Hitting.
- Killing.
- Being nice because you're afraid to set limits and say, "no," and then continuing to feel anger.
- Becoming passive-aggressive.
- Continuing to bang your head against a stone wall that won't budge.

**Functional options**

- Stand firm in your authenticity and spiritual identity. It takes a lot of energy and courage to do this when dysfunctional human beings are battering you. You're just like a lightning rod, standing there all alone, absorbing that dysfunctional energy and grounding it so it doesn't harm you or others.

- You may not have enough energy to do that by yourself.

- If you can trust in and connect with a Power Greater than Yourself, you can access unlimited energy and resources.

- Visualize a shield of white light surrounding you that deflects the negative energy back to the perpetrator.

- Turn the other cheek—sometimes. Turning the other cheek often defuses the negative external energy. Why? Because the dysfunctional person expects you to fight, and you don't. It confuses them. It's like an intervention. The exception is when turning the other cheek is perceived as weakness rather than strength.

- Set boundaries or limits on bad behavior and stick to them. Remove your energy from destructive behavior. Stop enabling it by giving it your attention. If necessary, physically remove the offending person from your environment and let them cope without your support.

- Walk away so you don't continue to feed the insanity with your presence and willingness to listen.

If one does not have enough spiritual centeredness or enough of a support system to resist insanity in functional ways, it may be better to walk away and move on with one's own life. It seems that is often how a spiritual path is intended to go. It shifts you into Abraham Maslow's self-actualization. (See diagram in Appendix.)

## THE POWER OF MAKING THE
## RIGHT CHOICE—FOR YOU

At sunrise, I used to ride my bike along the boardwalk in Atlantic City. When I was riding into the wind, it was slow and challenging, yet I built muscles and stamina. When I was riding with the wind, it was incredibly fast and easy.

Resisting insanity is like riding into the wind. It can be done. Sometimes it needs to be done. It takes a lot of energy, but you become stronger in the process.

Walking away and moving on with your own life is like riding with the wind. It requires no energy at all. You simply trust and allow that "Living, Breathing Energy" to support you easily and swiftly.

Regardless of the decision you make, you will grow spiritually.

## THE POWER OF CHOOSING THE RIGHT WORDS

A visitor to one of my websites, asked, "Is God real?"

What a fascinating question! What does that question mean?

What does the word "God" mean? Are we talking about an old man with a long, white beard sitting on a cloud with a thunderbolt in his hand, waiting to punish sinners? Are we talking about a king seated on a throne? Are we talking about something we've been told is omniscient, omnipotent, and omnipresent, but something that remains a mystery? Are we talking about nature: the chatter of a squirrel, a gorgeous rainbow, a babbling brook, a magnificent sunset? Are we talking about energy, like electricity, which we can't see but somehow know it's there because we can see the results? The lights go on!

Getting clear on what we mean by the word "God" allows each of us to clarify for ourselves our own answer to the question, "Is God real?"

Maybe it's more useful to ask, "In what sense is God real or unreal to me?" You may decide that sunsets and babbling brooks are real, but an old man with a long, white beard sitting on a cloud with a thunderbolt in his hand is not.

A friend of mine who struggled over this question suddenly realized she could believe in God when she substituted the word "good" for the word "God." She somehow knew what good was, even though she didn't know what God was.

What do we mean by the word "real"? Is it what everyone agrees to call real or is it what feels natural and makes sense to each of us?

If you and I are both looking at, smelling, and touching a daffodil, we would probably agree that the daffodil is real. On the other hand, in 1491, most humans agreed that the Earth was flat. Was the Earth really flat just because everybody believed it was?

So, what does it mean to say that something is real? By all means, explore this question, but is the question anything more than simply a way of avoiding surrendering into your own Soul and actually reconnecting with and immersing yourself in the experience or energy of some life force our minds can never conceptualize or understand? When we try to use our minds to understand it, we create a subject/object duality that separates us from the actual *experience* of constantly changing flow.

Sometimes, reconnecting feels like turning a radio dial. At first, there is nothing but static. Then, suddenly, a crystal-clear channel guides our actions easily and effortlessly. Do we know where we're going? No. We simply trust that there is much more to this wonderful life we've been given than any of us can begin to fathom.

## REVISITING ATONEMENT—A LARGER VIEW

On December 24, 2020, I emailed my middle son. He had been so traumatized by the group marriage and his parents' physical separation and legal divorce. I had little doubt that he, too, had experienced his own Death, Abyss, or Dark Night of the Soul. "I want you to join the family gathering tomorrow. You are part of this family, whether you like it or not. Despite your very challenging life, please know that you do matter—to all of us. "I understand how the group marriage ripped what was once a beautiful, functional, and stable family into shreds at a very vulnerable time in your life. I understand your pain, anger, and rage. I understand why you don't want to have anything to do with your parents. Your pain, anger, and rage are justified.

"I, too, have experienced shock, deep trauma, and rage over what happened. It has taken me a lifetime of struggle, hard experience, and thinking about what happened and why to make sense of it all.

"Had I known fifty years ago what I know now, I would never have touched the group marriage. I never expected it to rip two families into shreds. I never intended that. I don't think your father did either.

"If I could undo all the trauma, confusion, and heartbreak we all experienced, I would do it in a minute. I can't. We are where we are.

"If you can find it in your heart to forgive your mother for what she didn't know or understand and help us rebuild what has been lost, please join us."

He texted me back. "Not your fault, Mom. I love you! Have a great rest of your evening!"

My middle son and I stayed in touch. For years, I was his only family contact. I visited him at his home. He visited me at a little cottage I owned about two hours away from his home.

My oldest son's daughter married. She invited Sandy and the other woman to her wedding. She did not invite me or my middle son, nor did she ever thank me for my wedding well wishes.

The wedding was celebrated two hours away from where my middle son lives. Not only was he not invited, but neither his father nor his older brother made any effort to contact him or spend time with him before or after they attended the wedding. He was outraged that neither had cared enough about him and our original family to spend a little time together when they were physically only two hours away.

I felt a twinge of hurt that my oldest granddaughter had treated her paternal grandmother so disrespectfully. However, by that time, I had been so disrespected so many times by so many people that I had learned the art and skill of detachment to protect my own soul and energy field. I simply chose to detach from her dysfunctional conduct toward her own grandmother and her choice to honor the other woman instead.

The same thing happened when my oldest son's son married. The other woman was invited to the ceremony, simply because she was legally married to Sandy. I was intentionally excluded.

In March 2022, my middle son texted me a new phone number. I asked him whether it would be okay to pass it on to his brothers. Still angry with his father and older brother, he instructed me not to give either of them his new number. He told me I could give it to his younger brother, who had not disrespected him. The two brothers have now reconnected.

The sins of the parents are visited on the children.

## ACCEPTING AND STEPPING INTO SPIRITUAL POWER

Several months ago, I woke up in the middle of the night in yet another deep rage. While I'd been angry before over Sandy's abandonment of our children and me; while I'd sat in disbelief over the lying, cheating, stealing, and defamation that had become a way of life for rich, arrogant Panamanians; while I sat stunned when the IRS, without a warrant or probable cause, froze my personal funds and demanded that I prove I was not laundering drug money, the depth of my rage that night was one I had never before experienced.

It felt like a Kali energy, a Samson energy, destroying the temple of the Philistines, a Jesus energy, throwing the money changers out of the temple. My rage wanted to break out and tear down all the arrogant, abusive patriarchal empires that had so wounded me over the years.

My parents were two kind, loving educators. They delighted in exploration, creativity, discovery, and play. As a child, I never knew anger. It was simply not part of my family's world. I know now how blessed I was to have had such wonderful parents.

What to do with my rage? Why had it come into my life yet again? What message was it bringing me?

Was the rage inviting me to step fully into my own ethical, moral, and spiritual power? What did I need to be and do to bring integrity to myself and our planet, to stop the violence, the sex trafficking, the child abuse, to give all children an education, to support female businesses so that women no longer had to sell their bodies for sex to be able to feed and shelter their children?

As I watched in awe, my rage began transforming into gratitude. Thank you, Sandy for abandoning me. Thank you, Panamanian developers for betraying my trust. Thank you, IRS for seizing my money. Without you, I would never have been able to become the strong and powerful spiritual woman I am today.

Each of us has opportunities each and every moment to do just one little thing that makes a huge difference in another person's life. Smile. Hug. Appreciate beauty. Say thank you.

Remember that question that was given to me to answer after that amazing mystical experience I had so many years ago: "How can I use analytic, divisive words to communicate a unifying, holistic experience?"

Suddenly the question changed to "How can I use analytic, divisive words to *facilitate* a unifying, holistic experience?" That was a question I could answer, but it meant stepping into my full personal, moral, ethical, and spiritual power each and every moment. It meant using my words with knife-like precision and great care to serve both myself and the person with whom I was speaking. It meant helping both of us move through our own Death, Abyss, or Dark Night of the Soul, but if, and only if, we were both open to exchanging information and receiving support.

Could I do this? I didn't know. But if I could, I knew I would have to stay aligned with and immersed in that "Living, Breathing Energy" that I could never objectify or conceptualize but had experienced so many times and now fully trusted. I simply had to allow it to flow through me and back out into the world in the form it chose to take in each and every moment, with the intention of supporting myself, those around me, and our planet while, to the best of my ability, doing no harm.

# Chapter 8
# A Gift for a Suffering Humanity

**Using Words Energetically and Alchemically to Facilitate Transformation, Evolution, Creation, Co-Creation, and Manifestation**

*"When soul and purpose come together, when we follow a path with heart, then we are on course."*
—Jean Shinoda Bolen, M.D.

PLAYING THE COSMIC GAME. DANCING THE COSMIC DANCE.

I have always identified most strongly with the archetype of the Goddess Athena. I somehow always seemed to be able to figure out answers to problems, even as a young girl. I loved to play with math and could easily manipulate the theorems and formulas to get the right answers. A fellow junior high school student I once tutored in math said she learned more from me than she learned from our teacher.

Yet, as I have matured and navigated the journey that has been uniquely mine to make, the Goddess Athena has become an even more prominent archetype in my life.

According to Jean Shinoda Bolen, MD, author, psychiatrist, and Jungian analyst, Athena is one of three virgin goddesses along with Artemis and Hestia. Virgin goddesses do not need relationships in order to be actualized. They have minds, hearts, and spirits of their own.

Athena is the goddess of a certain type of wisdom, a strategic kind of wisdom—logically arriving at the best way to do something. She is a warrior, but her armor is rational, intellectual armor. She naturally knows how to make her case well. She combines thinking and feeling and is frequently oriented outward, but her emotions don't control her actions.

She uses her intellectual strength and power diplomatically. She knows how to think things through and negotiate to shape a larger plan.

Even as a child, being alone never bothered me. I was always able to entertain myself, even when Mother sent Jimmy and me to our rooms when we squabbled.

And I always thought strategically, even during some of my most life-threatening experiences, such as two near-death automobile accidents. Although I experienced many strong emotions and was acutely aware of them, those emotions were only messengers demanding that I pay attention to my mind, my focus, and my own action choices. They never took control of my body, even through the turmoil and desecration of the group marriage and the challenge of living in and adjusting to other cultures.

That is the course I have followed as I have navigated the challenges of my own Heroine's Journey and the writing of this book.

Recently, I was driving north from Florida to my youngest granddaughter's high school graduation. I asked my oldest son, who lives in Georgia, whether he and his wife wanted a visit along the way.

He laughed and said, "Well, only if you want to be here with Dad and the other woman."

My quick reply was, "No, I definitely don't want to be there with them. I'll just stay in a motel."

But overnight, while half awake, my brain started thinking differently. What if I accepted my son's invitation?

His father and the other woman could sleep in my grandson's double bed. I could sleep alone in one of the single beds.

The next day, I called my son and told him I was rethinking his offer to visit while his father and the other woman were there. I talked about the archetype of the Goddess Athena, the virgin goddess with whom I so strongly identified, and commented it was the only way I could make sense of the path my life had taken.

He laughed, taken aback. "I was just joking. I don't think *I* could deal with Dad and the other woman sleeping together and you sleeping alone."

That scenario would have fully underscored the infidelity and adultery that had ripped apart two functional marriages. I chose to stay overnight in a motel.

The sins of the fathers are visited on the children.

## OVERCOMING THE CHALLENGE OF WORDS AND WORLDVIEWS

Who Created Words?

We humans created words. Words are a human construct.

Human-created words are not THE WORD or THE TAO or NIRVANA or ETERNITY. The latter are placeholders for an *experience* of an "Energy" or "Beingness" that the mind can neither conceptualize nor understand. As Buddhists would say, those words are fingers pointing at the moon. They are not the immersive *experience* of watching a glorious full moon rise.

## WHY DID HUMANS CREATE WORDS?

To understand. To alleviate pain. To communicate with one another in a new way. To give meaning to our lives. To create, co-create, and manifest.

## WHAT WORDS DO

Words separate, divide, and categorize. High/ low, light/ dark, good/ evil, right/ wrong, black/ white/ oriental/ indigenous, Jew/ Christian/ Hindu/ Islamist/ Taoist. There's an occasional exception, like the word "whoosh," which emulates the sound of rushing water, but for the most part, words separate, divide, and categorize.

Our minds keep separating, dividing, and categorizing our experiences into smaller and smaller parts, creating and co-creating tinier and tinier bricks in the great wall of human-created knowledge.

If understood literally, words separate us from one another. If understood and used consciously, intentionally, energetically, and alchemically, they can focus and refocus our attention, build connections, allow us to communicate, and open our minds to new possibilities. They then transform from placeholders for something "out there" to useful tools for reconnecting us, energizing us, and transforming us into the powerful creators, co-creators, and manifesters of truth, beauty, freedom, and love we were intended to be.

Think of Albert Einstein's formula E=MC2. Words are on the right side of that equation. The words "soul" or "emptiness" or "non-dual consciousness" or "God" or "Allah" or "Jehovah" or "Awareness" or "The Eternal Tao" or "Be here now" or "The Still Point" are fingers pointing toward the left side of that equation. All of us are conditioned into this human-created language.

It's a human-created world of words and concepts drawn from our unique experiences of this "energetic field"— this "First Access"[43] that our neurology has the ability to receive and process.

The word "Mommy" feels very fixed and solid, but it is different from the real, live, warm, loving person who wipes your tears when you cry, hugs you when you're hurting, and tells you that everything is going to be all right.

If somebody asks, "Where is Mommy?" we know exactly what they mean and where Mommy is. We can say Mommy's in the kitchen cooking dinner. We might even say that it's true that Mommy's in the kitchen cooking dinner and everyone around us would agree.

However, the statement that Mommy is in the kitchen cooking dinner is only true right here, right now. Five

---

[43] https://www.businessnlpacademy.co.uk/nlp_what_is_it/

minutes later, Mommy may be in the living room talking to Daddy.

Sometimes, the word "Mommy" does point to the real, warm, loving person who wipes your tears when you are crying. But other times, the word "Mommy" points to the strict disciplinarian who is trying to force you to do something you don't want to do. A word that feels solid and straightforward points to a very complex and continually shifting sensory, emotional, visual, and auditory experience.

Our words are with us every moment of every day. They are part of our lives, whether we are involved in an internal dialog with ourselves, an external conversation with one other person, external brainstorming as part of a team to accomplish a goal, or using words to learn new skills and navigate new life experiences in what we perceive as our outer world.

How many of us pay attention to our words? Do we stop to think about how we allow them to limit us? How we can use them to empower us? How we can use them to create and co-create who we are and the kind of world in which we want to live?

How many of us set a clear and conscious intention about what we want to manifest before deciding what words to speak and what words not to speak, to whom certain words should be spoken and to whom those same words should not be spoken?

We're all conditioned into this human-created world of words and concepts almost from the moment we are born. This is Mommy, that is Daddy, that is the dog, that is the cat.

Those words are simple to understand, and most of us would agree on what each word means.

However, if my mommy is different from your mommy and my daddy is different from your daddy, we now have the same word pointing to a different person. We need to notice that and clarify that. Thus, the creation of pronouns.

Words are useful when both speaker and listener understand the same word as pointing to the same underlying experience. When speaker and listener understand the same word as pointing to different underlying experiences, miscommunication and misunderstanding arise. Words get even trickier and more challenging when we create abstract concepts such as truth, love, joy, hope, good, evil, right, and wrong.

## HOW DO WORDS WORK?

Words, ideas, concepts, and emotions map our experiences. What we perceive and experience depends, among other things, on where we live, our cultural conditioning, education, conscious intentions, unconscious intentions, and expectations. Ultimately, each of us perceives from a unique perspective.

Sometimes, we use different words to structure the same experience. If John and Jane are walking through the same garden, John may be focusing on the paths and trellises. Jane may be focusing on the roses and delphiniums. As a result, the words each of them speaks to describe the same garden walk will be different.

If a listener were to listen to John and Jane talk about the garden, the listener would hear them say very different words. If the listener had never visited the garden, the listener might believe that John and Jane were talking about different gardens.

Sometimes, we use the same words to structure different experiences. If John is standing on the gray sand next to the Atlantic Ocean in Atlantic City, New Jersey, the cold, gray waves will be rolling in as breakers; the beach may be crowded with bathers, bikinis, tan bodies, little children building sandcastles with their fathers; red, yellow, and blue umbrellas; seagulls squawking overhead; black scallop shells; a boardwalk peppered with bikers and joggers; and casinos in the distance. The water is cold, murky, and thick with stirred-up sand. With a land breeze, nasty, biting, black flies appear. John might verbalize this experience as a "day at the beach."

Jane, however, who lives on Roatan, Honduras, might use those same words "day at the beach" to verbalize a very different experience. On Roatan, it is rare to see breakers. The sea is a clear, placid mirror of blues, greens, and turquoises. Seaweed gently washes up on the white sand. Weathered driftwood and palm trees dot the deserted, narrow stretch of sand bordering the sea. An occasional boat accents the skyline.

There are no sun tanners here, for the tropical sun burns tender skin too quickly. Instead of nasty, biting black flies, Jane is tormented by chitres, those dastardly, invisible no-seeums that, with a single bite, can leave a welt the size of a tennis ball. These are very different "beach" experiences, but until John and Jane put the word "beach" in context, they are using the same word, "beach," to describe two very different experiences. Their speech is not as clear as it could be, and their communication becomes as murky as the waters of the Atlantic Ocean.

If John had never experienced the Roatan beach and Jane had never experienced the Atlantic City beach, they might even argue about whether beach sand is gray or white and whether the ocean is gray or blue.

This is how miscommunication and misunderstanding arise.

When we fail to clarify the underlying experience to which the words point, we, just like the words, become separated, divided, and categorized.

Alfred Korzybski wrote, "The map is not the territory."[44]

The words are not the experience. The menu is not the food you eat. Looking at a map of the west coast of Florida is different from driving north on I-75 and breathing in the beautiful bougainvillea, delighting in the swaying palms, or basking in a spectacular sunset.

Once you understand the distinction between the map and the territory and experience the difference between looking at a conceptual map and being in the present-moment experience, you can start dancing with the words, dancing with the maps, and creating and co-creating new maps of the same territory or maybe a similar map of a different territory with a new focus, goal, or intention.

Are we going to continue to dance unconsciously and ignorantly, getting ourselves and others mired in the muck, or are we going to learn to use our words consciously, intentionally, energetically, and impactfully to co-create the kind of world in which we want to live?

When you start dancing with maps, words, and wisdom, it's fun. It's like playing a game.

Sometimes it will feel as if our words and ideas are connecting with and mirroring one another. Other times, it will feel as if they are contradictory and disparate. Can we reconnect the contradictory and disparate words and ideas by telling our own stories, listening attentively and respectfully to the stories of others, and asking clarifying questions?

---

[44] https://en.wikipedia.org/wiki/Map%E2%80%93territory_relation

Think of a moving picture. You are part of that moving picture. It goes where it goes, and you don't really know where it's going. But what our minds do, and what words do is to stop the moving picture at a single frame so that we can chop it up, analyze it, and see how the parts connect. We try to figure out how everything works together and fits together. Our minds create an arbitrary conceptual separation between ourselves and the actual flow of experience. While our minds are doing their mapping, the flow continues on, carrying us with it.

Our creative minds allow us to map our experiences in an infinite number of ways. We can create a road map of Florida, a map of all the waterways, an ecological map, a map from a satellite, or a map of a single house in a single subdivision. My oldest son once told me that our satellites are so powerful that they can read the name of the brand of cigarette that a Russian on a Moscow street is smoking.

The different maps allow us to shift our focus from broad overview to tiny detail in the blink of an eye. We can move in and out at will. The maps change as the focus changes, the experience changes, the conscious or unconscious intentions change, or the needs change. Words and maps temporarily transport us to imaginary and illusory worldviews, but they're fun to play with, can help us meet our needs, and give meaning and purpose to our lives.

Here are some other ways to think about words:

**Grammatica, the First of the Seven Liberal Arts**[45]
Grammatica pertains to the structure of language, its history, and the underlying energy of an idea. Nouns (chair, table, apple, tree) are immobile and passive. Our minds bring

---

[45] https://humanities.byu.edu/the-idea-of-the-european-university-and-the-seven-liberal-arts/

together an experience that we perceive as an object. Then we give it a name. Ordinary consciousness believes the name is the object. Expanded consciousness knows that the name reflects something far more complex.

The name is simply a human-created placeholder for a continually shifting experience. It stops the moving picture at a single frame so we can name it, analyze it, understand it, and feel safe.

Verbs (run, sit, walk, fly) are changeable and active. They can create or transform our perception of time. We ran, run, or will run. Verbs pertain to human will, choice, and action.

Adjectives (beautiful, sad, dysfunctional, harmonic) and adverbs (slowly, quickly, passionately, smoothly) bring emotion into our speech. They add expansion, contraction, and rhythm.

## Dialectica, the Second of the Seven Liberal Arts

Dialectica is an exchange of ideas that persuades us to question words, ideas, concepts, and beliefs we previously believed were true. It requires that we speak clearly and see from many different perspectives. It allows us to move quickly from the depths of hell to the heights of heaven. It enables us to build word bridges between what appear to be opposites.

Like Socrates, it asks questions. Like Zen Buddhist koans, it poses mind-bending puzzles.

## Rhetorica, the Third of the Seven Liberal Arts

Rhetorica evokes emotion. Sometimes, it is beautiful, persuasive speech. Other times, it tells heart-rending stories. Sometimes, it evokes fear or rage. It uses passion and tonality, questions, and pauses. Rhetorica is the intention and power behind our words.

## WHAT WE HUMANS DO WITH WORDS

We have created this immense vocabulary. We use it all the time without thinking about the words that come out of our mouths and how we are going to consciously use those words to communicate, create, co-create, and manifest the kind of world in which we want to live.

How do we use our words? We certainly use our words to try to understand our experiences, pulling ourselves and our minds out of the flow of experience and watching the flow as if it's separate and apart from us. We use words to communicate with one another. We use them to understand our relationships. We use them to distinguish.

Conceptual distinction can be useful, but it can also be harmful. Here is an example of useful distinction.

What if we make a distinction between the concepts of judgment and discernment? This can be very useful if we want to let go of our own self-righteousness and protect ourselves from the self-righteousness of others.

Judgment is about making ourselves or someone else wrong. When we are judging others, we are projecting onto others characteristics within ourselves that we cannot see or may be afraid to face.[46] (See the Johari Window in the Appendix.) When others are judging us, if we allow their judgments to infect our souls or energy fields, we may experience guilt, shame, or feeling not good enough.

---

[46] https://www.psychologytoday.com/us/basics/projection. See, also, The Johari Window in Appendix.

Discernment is about noticing the emotional impact of our own conduct and words, or another's conduct and words, on our own mind, body, spirit, and soul. Once we notice, we can protect that very sacred space from abuse, and support it with kindness and compassion. That requires boundary setting, emotional detachment, and conscious choice of words and actions.

Harmful distinction is very similar to judgment. It is generally unconsciously driven by cultural conditioning and feeling not good enough. If we unconsciously attach emotional content to our words and say, for example, "Black is bad and white is good," we're giving a whole new dimension to our words. While unconsciously, this statement may temporarily make the speaker feel good about himself, it is counterproductive if our conscious intention is to create, co-create, and manifest a peaceful, powerful, prosperous planet.

Sometimes we use words to try to improve our own sense of self-worth. We collect credentials and accomplishments and celebrate the goals we've attained. These credentials may support our own self-esteem, but if we flaunt them, they may cause others who do not hold them to feel inferior and resentful.

We are right and good. The other is wrong and evil. Unconsciously, we play worldly power games—power over, power under, and power against—because we feel less than and not good enough. We want to feel loved. We want others to like us and admire us. We want to control others who are doing things that irritate us.

"Billy, if you don't pick up your toys right now, I'm going to spank you."

"If you want to eat and have a bed to sleep in and a roof over your head, you will do whatever I tell you to do."

This is something I call power over. It subjugates one person to the control of another.

Sometimes, the person who is on the underside, who is in a power under position in this power-over/power-under dynamic, rebels and becomes full of rage. They are going to fight back. They use their words in a fight against others. "You idiot! How can you possibly say that?" I call this power against.

The territory or experience is what it is, but we tend to fight with one another over our maps. This shifts us into a power-against dynamic.

When used unconsciously, power over, power under, and power against games can have deadly consequences. If we want to survive as a species, each and every one of us must learn the wisdom tools and practices to consciously shift into a Power With dynamic.

When our minds and emotions start sucking us down into some rabbit hole that drains the life out of our souls, we can consciously choose to surrender, allowing soul and spirit to work through us, turn things around, and reconnect mind, body, and emotions with those beautiful, peaceful, powerful, and prosperous unique human beings we naturally are.

When our minds try to analyze an experience rather than just allowing ourselves to be in the experience, our minds separate us from the experience. We perceive ourselves as being here, looking at some object over there rather than just experiencing the flow.

However, we can learn to use our words to create, co-create, and manifest wisdom practices that support us in reconnecting with our souls, functioning from our souls, and manifesting out into the world as a peaceful, powerful, prosperous person with true empowerment within, respect and compassion for others, and respect for the planet and cosmos that support our lives.

How can we use the analytic, divisive words we humans have created to guide us in returning to that very comfortable flow of Beingness? It's not easy.

Words and maps, including mine, are not Truth. They are only reflections that support us as we walk along our unique life path, striving to answer the question "Who am I, " evolving and growing our unique meaning, purpose, and gifts we have been given to offer back in service to the world and to one another.

## POWER OVER AND POWER UNDER

The Atlantic City councilman, who physically abused his wife to the point where she had to be hospitalized, is an excellent example of unconscious, uncontrolled eruption of power over.

Because of his own deep feelings of inadequacy and inferiority, which he had never had the courage or ability to examine and transform, the councilman violently beat his wife so he could feel important and in control. He could have killed her.

Conscious use of power over looks very different from unconscious, uncontrolled eruption of unexamined power over. The clear intention of conscious use of power over is to enhance and preserve life.

When I was three years old, my mother and I were walking along Roosevelt Boulevard in northeast Philadelphia, hand in hand. Suddenly, I jerked my hand out of hers and started to run across the multi-lane, highly trafficked highway.

My mother used power over to grab me, yank me back to safety, and spank me. I was clearly in a power under position. She knew much more than I about the lethal impact of cars on humans. She had no intention of allowing the only child she would ever have to ignorantly kill herself. She may have saved my life.

If I am on a plane that is having engine trouble, I willingly put myself into a power under position and listen to the instructions of a pilot with forty years of piloting experience. I do what I am told because I want to live. I know the pilot has many years of training and experience that I do not have.

If, on the other hand, the plane is, for reasons unknown, being piloted by a five-year-old, that may be precisely why it is having engine trouble. Who in the world gave that child permission to play the role of pilot? A child's ignorance and inexperience will get us all killed if that child is given role power that the child has not lived long enough to experience, understand, and master.

Are these examples of Sigmund Freud's Eros and Thanatos?[47]

------

[47] https://www.verywellmind.com/life-and-death-instincts-2795847

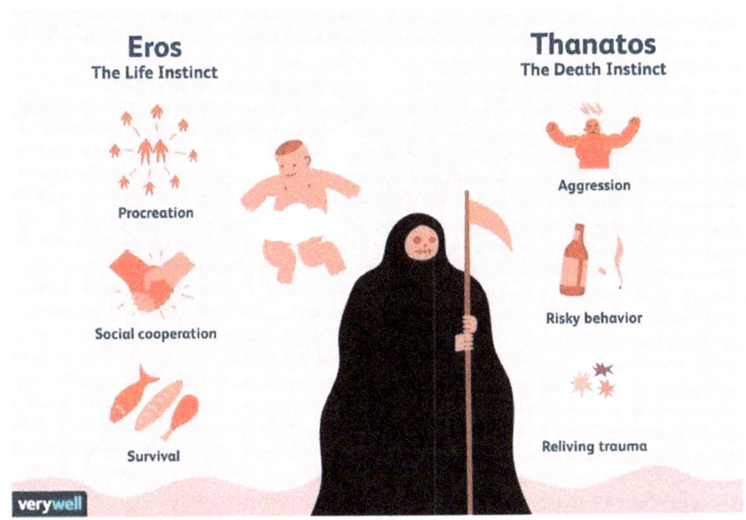


Is this Life Instinct what the Buddhist Eightfold Noble Path[48] directs us all to practice?

## POWER AGAINST

When used unconsciously, power against can have deadly consequences. It begins with ignorant, unconscious power over. World War II is a perfect example.

When the Japanese bombed Pearl Harbor on December 7, 1941, the worldly, patriarchal intention may have been to rule the world. Ultimately, however, the effect was very different.

On August 6, 1945, Hiroshima, Japan, was devastated by the first atomic bomb. Three days later, on August 9, 1945, Nagasaki was devastated by a second atomic bomb. Over

---

[48] https://www.britannica.com/topic/Indian-philosophy/Early-Buddhist-developments#ref314587: (1) right view, (2) right intention, (3) right speech, (4) right action, (5) right livelihood, (6) right effort, (7) right mindfulness, and (8) right concentration.

100,000 Japanese died. Six days later, the Japanese surrendered.[49]

The Nazis, who came to power in Germany in January 1933, believed that Germans were racially superior. Their worldly, patriarchal intention was to create a racially pure state through world domination, and physically kill those they considered inferior—Jews, gypsies, homosexuals, Germans with disabilities, and some of the Slavic peoples (especially Poles and Russians). Other groups were persecuted on political, ideological, and behavioral grounds, among them Communists, Socialists, and Jehovah's Witnesses.[50]

On September 1, 1939, inflamed by the rhetoric of Adolf Hitler, Nazi armies invaded Poland.

On April 30, 1945, after annihilating defeat, Hitler took his own life in his bunker underneath the Reich chancellery. Two days later, on May 2, 1945, Berlin surrendered to the Allies. Five days later, on May 7, 1945, German army commanders surrendered all forces to the Allies.

Between 1939 and 1945, an estimated six million Jewish men, women, and children were murdered by the Nazi regime as well as millions of other Nazi-designated inferior people. During the entire Second World War, an estimated total of 70-85 million people perished, about 3 percent of the world population in 1940.

When used consciously and intentionally for life-enhancing and life-empowering purposes, power against can

---

[49]

https://en.wikipedia.org/wiki/Atomic_bombings_of_Hiroshima_and_N agasaki

[50] https://encyclopedia.ushmm.org/content/en/article/documenting-numbers-of-victims-of-the-holocaust-and-nazi-persecution

become a vehicle for both self-improvement and other-improvement.

When two football teams compete against each other, if the competition is done with the intention of improving each team's own skills and performance, they play with an attitude of good sportsmanship. At the end of the game, they congratulate a winning opponent who has challenged them to improve their own skill and self-mastery.

That was the way we children played softball in the summers with my father on the street in front of our Glenside home. We were playing to be the best we could be. When someone hit a home run, everyone cheered.

This is the way we played board games with my birth family in the evenings or Red Rover or I See Something Red outside in the summers. Even though there might be a game winner or loser, it was only a game. Everyone who played was there only to enhance her own ability. Everyone was part of an interactive team where everyone won because each player gave her all, increased her skill and experience, and learned and grew.

WORDS ABOUT WORDS FROM SEMANTICISTS

## Alfred Korzybski[51]

Alfred Korzybski was an acclaimed Polish American scholar who developed a field called general semantics. This field discusses how human knowledge is limited due to the development of different languages. Korzybski hypothesized that different languages prevented a person from knowing absolute reality.

---

[51] https://quotes.thefamouspeople.com/alfred-korzybski-3568.php

Korzybski studied engineering. He served in the Second Russian Army during the First World War. Later, he served in the French-Polish Army.

These war experiences drove him to question the purpose and value of this savage human destruction and desecration. He began studying the difference between human and animal behavior. Friends encouraged him to publish his studies.

He did so in his first book, *Manhood of Humanity: The Science and Art of Human Engineering*. The book's success motivated Korzybski to research psychology.

His second book was called *Time-Binding: The General Theory*. He soon became a prominent figure in the field of psychology and traveled widely to present his theoretical lectures.

**Alfred Korzybski's words:**

- The map is not the territory.
- The only usefulness of a map depends on similarity of structure between the empirical world and the map...
- Whatever you say it is, it isn't.
- The objective level is not words and cannot be reached by words alone. We must point our finger and be silent, or we will never reach this level.
- Thus, we see that one of the obvious origins of human disagreement lies in the use of noises for words.
- We see what we see because we miss all the finer details.
- I want to make clear only that words are not the things spoken about, and that there is no such thing as an object in absolute isolation.
- If we gamble on verbal structures that have no observable empirical structures, such gambling can never give us any structural information about the world.

Therefore, such verbal structures are structurally obsolete, and if we believe in them, they induce delusions or other semantic disturbances.
- Man's achievements rest upon the use of symbols… we must consider ourselves as a symbolic, semantic class of life, and those who rule the symbols, rule us.
- There are two ways to slide easily through life: to believe everything or to doubt everything; both ways save us from thinking.
- If a psychiatric and scientific inquiry were to be made upon our rulers, mankind would be appalled at the disclosures.

## John Grinder[52]

John Grinder is the co-creator of Neurolinguistic Programming (NLP) and co-creator of New Code NLP. His ability to model and code the performance of geniuses was a fundamental influence in the development of Classic Code NLP.

His academic prowess underpins the core coding of NLP models that emerged in the 1970s. His desire to continually develop the field, combined with his inherent innovation, stimulated the emergence of New Code NLP as a natural extension to Classic NLP. New Code NLP refined many of the original NLP models and brought to the field exciting new processes for change.

John Grinder's words:

---

[52] https://www.johngrinder.com/

- Wisdom comes from experience, but experience is not enough. Experience anticipated and experience revisited is the true source of wisdom.[53]
- Creative geniuses are:
    1. Comfortable with uncertainty
    2. Able to hold seeming opposites or paradoxes
    3. Persistent[54]
- One of the strategies that they taught us was how to generate an even greater amount of learning and choice from every experience or life situation. We were instructed to review the events of the day and identify the significant choice points. We were to reflect on the choices we had made at those points and whether they were successful or unsuccessful in reaching our desired outcome.
- The only justification for the application of NLP patterns is the creation of choice and precisely in the context in which choice presently does not exist.
- Remember: the journey is the destination.
- The greeting of risk, the willingness to discover through (certain classes of non-lethal) trial and error, the subordination of success to exploration and discovery, and the insistence of finding the edge of patterns; where they fail, all of these seem to contain echoes of field work in Special Forces and related intelligence organizations, the passion for languages, the recognition that much of what passes for effective communication can be

---

[53] https://www.azquotes.com/author/28040-John_Grinder#:~:text=John%20Grinder%20Quotes&text=Wisdom%20comes%20from%20experience%2C%20
[54] https://www.goodreads.com/work/quotes/24026280?error_code=100&error_message=picture+should+represent+a+valid+URL#_=_

achieved with very little actual understanding, the primacy of nonverbal communication in influencing face-to-face communications, a tolerance for ambiguity and vagueness, and a fascination with the unknown.

- So, what every parent would want their college kids to know: Look for patterns, they are always there. Challenge all my assumptions. Change can be good. Use all my senses, even the ones I am not aware of. Understand the world from another's perspective, not mine. Listen more, talk less; if I do talk, ask questions.

- Everyone is doing the best job they can, given the limitations of their beliefs. My job is to get people to use the best of themselves to get better, to improve. Everyone has a chance; if something didn't work, it's because of my limitations, not the other person's. I am ultimately accountable for and own the outcomes of my choices. All of them.

- The problem is NOT the problem. The problem is the state that the client goes into as s/he approaches the context where s/he thinks the problem is.

## Carmen Bostic St. Clair[55]

Carmen Bostic St. Clair is the co-creator of New Code NLP and principal designer of many of the New Code processes. Her innate creativity is emphasized in the dominant philosophy of New Code NLP of streamlined NLP processes to create maximum choices in an individual's life.

Carmen's steadfast business background brings a grounded approach, and her work is highly results orientated. Carmen's ingenuity in course design brought a different style of NLP Training to the field, a style which is

---

[55] Ibid.

now a key feature in Classic Code and New Code NLP Training.

Carmen Bostic St. Clair's words:

- Study the patterns. Know the content. Know what's going on behind.[56]
- Come and experience it. You'll find that your experience will lead you to states of high performance and focus that you have not yet achieved before.[57]

## Whispering in the Wind[58]

"Whispering in the Wind" is a rich, entertaining, and precise presentation of a number of topics and issues that define the enterprise called Neuro-Linguistic Programming (NLP… a scientifically based endeavor with its precise focus on one of the extremes of human behavior: excellence and the high performers who actually do it.[59]

## Whispering in the Wind's words

- First Access (FA). First Access is defined as the first point where we gain access to the information about the world . . . and which most people call reality or the territory… This is equivalent to what we understand Freud to be referring to as primary experience. These are linguistically unmediated mental maps.[60]
- … it is literally impossible for an NLP practitioner to function as a congruent agent of change unless he or she has cultivated an ongoing positive relationship with his

---

[56] https://www.youtube.com/watch?v=CsVvk10Nu50
[57] Ibid.
[58] Bostic St. Clair, C., and Grinder, J. – Whispering in the Wind, J & C Enterprises, Scotts Valley, California (2001).
[59] Ibid. Back cover.
[60] Ibid. p 57.

or her own unconscious—the source of so many insights in the field of NLP.

- . . . it is clear how the translation of an artistic expression from the form of a primary experience to a secondary representation (language) fundamentally changes the meaning.

## Richard Bandler[61]

Richard Wayne Bandler is an American author and trainer in the field of self-help. He is best known as the co-creator of Neuro-linguistic programming, a methodology to understand and change human behavior-patterns. He also developed other systems named Design Human Engineering and Neuro Hypnotic Re-patterning.

## Richard Bandler's words:[62]

- The greatest personal limitation is to be found not in the things you want to do and can't, but in the things you've never considered doing.
- If you can't enjoy what you have, you can't enjoy more of it.
- Why be your real self when you can be something really worthwhile?


[61] https://en.wikipedia.org/wiki/Richard_Bandler
[62] https://www.goodreads.com/author/quotes/34924.Richard_Bandler

**The Tao Te Ching**

The Tao Te Ching, as rendered in English by Dr. Wayne W. Dyer:[63]


Verse 1


The Tao that can be spoken
is not the eternal Tao
The name that can be named
is not the eternal name.


The Tao is both named and nameless.
As nameless it is the origin of all things;
As named it is the Mother of 10,000 things.


Ever desireless, one can see the mystery;
Ever desiring, one sees only the manifestation.
And the mystery itself is the doorway
To all understanding.


**Hinduism**

Hinduism speaks of "piercing the veil of illusion."[64] The word the Hindus use to refer to what they call the illusion of duality is "maya."

The word "maya" is derived from Sanskrit roots. "Ma" means "not" and "ya" means "that." In short, when the

---

[63] Dyer, Dr. Wayne W., (2009). *Change Your Thoughts, Change Your Life.* Hay House USA
[64] https://psychology.wikia.org/wiki/Maya_(illusion)

student asks whether something is True, the teacher will reply "Maya," not that.

Why does the teacher always say "Maya," no matter what words the student has spoken? Because words—all words—are illusions!

The goal of enlightenment is to understand this illusion—or more precisely, to experience or pierce it. Maya is something to be seen through, like an epiphany or aha experience. When we have this aha experience, we have the power to end our suffering.

When we eliminate the static of human words and tune the dials of our minds into an energy that lies beyond words, everything flows effortlessly and spontaneously through us. We are transformed.

Words are illusions, dancing at a masked ball. Look, not at the words, but at the underlying energy and meaning—for you. Then explore what underlying energy and meaning those same words have for others. Just ask.

If you would like to delve deeper into an experience of piercing the veil of illusion, jump to page 201. Or play with us here: https://www.youtube.com/watch?v=XVCg4ahjwes

## Sri Ramana Maharshi

Sri Ramana Maharshi[65] lived his entire life around Arunachala in Tamil Nadu, India. After what many of us would think of as a tortuous life—being pelted with stones by urchins, living in an underground vault never penetrated by sunlight, being bitten by ants and vermin, he taught only through presence and silence.

Once a devotee asked him to at least write on paper what he had to say. Maharshi wrote:

---

[65] https://www.sriramanamaharshi.org/ramana-maharshi/at-arunachala/

The Ordainer controls the fate of souls in accordance with their past deeds. Whatever is destined not to happen will not happen, try how hard you may. Whatever is destined to happen will happen, do what you may to stop it. This is certain. The best course, therefore, is to remain silent.

**The Old Testament**

The Book of Genesis in the Christian and Judaic Old Testament[66] tells the story of Adam and Eve disobeying God's orders and eating of the Tree of Knowledge. Suddenly, they created words and began using words. Suddenly, they became aware of their shame and were expelled from the Garden of Eden, that pure flow of constantly changing experience.

The Old Testament also tells the story of the Tower of Babel.[67] According to Genesis, the Babylonians wanted to make a name for themselves by building a mighty tower with its top in the heavens. God disrupted their work by so confusing the language of the workers that they could no longer understand one another. The people were dispersed over the face of the Earth.

**Buddhism**

Buddhists are reported to have said, "Words are fingers pointing at the moon. They are not the moon."[68]

Words cannot give you the moon. That is something you must discover for yourself, through your own unique efforts and your own unique spiritual path. What words can offer,

---

[66] Gen. 2:17 – 3:24.
[67] Gen. 11:1-9.
[68] https://www.goodreads.com/quotes/843488-bhikkhus-the-teaching-is-merely-a-vehicle-to-describe-the

however, are guidelines. They may point in directions you may want to explore.

One of the paths in the Buddhist Noble Eightfold Path is Right Speech.[69]

What is right speech? Does right speech emerge from present moment awareness of the contexts and content of a physical, worldly dynamic?

If the conscious intention of the speaker is to manifest a dynamic harmony, right speech flows effortlessly from both passion and compassion for both self and others. It will be different in each and every context, which is one of the things that makes it so challenging, so hard to talk about, and so fascinating.

Each and every context is unique. It must be free, but it must also be very conscious and intentional.


**The Quran**

The Quran describes itself as a book of guidance for mankind ( 2:185).[70]

It sometimes offers detailed accounts of specific historical events, and it often emphasizes the moral significance of an event over its narrative sequence.

Supplementing the Quran with explanations for some cryptic Quranic narratives, and rulings that also provide the basis for Islamic law in most denominations of Islam, are hadiths—oral and written traditions believed to describe words and actions of Muhammad.

A verse is sometimes recited with a special kind of elocution. In order to extrapolate the meaning of a particular

---

[69] https://www.britannica.com/topic/Eightfold-Path
[70] https://en.wikipedia.org/wiki/Quran

Quranic verse, Muslims rely on exegesis or commentary rather than a direct translation of the text.

The Quran states, "Evil words are for evil men, and evil men are subjected to evil words. Good words are for good men, and good men are an object of good words. Those good people are declared innocent of what the slanderers say, for them is forgiveness and noble provision."[71]

HELPFUL FORMS OF LANGUAGE

**How can we use words to know ourselves?**

We can't say there are right or wrong words, but there are words that are useful or helpful or words that will suddenly give us a new idea or a new perspective that fits in with, and helps solve, something we are struggling with.

If we want to choose to use words to facilitate knowing ourselves and partnering with others in co-creating a peaceful, powerful, prosperous planet, what personal word wisdom practices might work best? Here's my experience:

### *First-Person-Singular Language*

Why? It focuses our mind on the way we perceive the world (or want to perceive the world), not on what our minds and emotions project outward. It keeps us out of generalizations. (There are always exceptions to every generalization.) It supports us in owning our own experiences and the words we have chosen with which to manifest them. It keeps us out of self-righteousness. It connects us with our own spiritual power—our own soul.

---

[71] https://corpus.quran.com/translation.jsp?chapter=24&verse=26

183

"I think this. I feel this." We could add "in this moment" because what we think and feel may change as we have new experiences or receive new information.

"I think, I feel, I need," (if we have needs). Then we can ask questions such as, "What do I need to know? Where can I find the answers I need? Whom can I trust?"

A final question might be, "What are my choices in this situation?" That shifts our focus to decision-making and action. Using first-person singular language empowers us to know ourselves. Then, through freedom and choice, first person singular language empowers us to be the very best people we can be. We shift into Abraham Maslow's self-actualization[72] or Carl Jung's individuation.

### *Stories*

Why? Because each of us owns his or her own experiences and the words we have chosen with which to share them. Stories keep us out of self-righteousness. They are a wonderful way to communicate a deeper meaning without sounding authoritarian. Through story—particularly stories with a real twist at the end that opens the mind—the reader is invariably drawn into an archetypal pattern that humans have experienced throughout history. The story may culminate in comedy or tragedy, but in either case, it contains a deep life lesson. The reader comes to identify with one role or another and frequently discovers new ways to solve old problems.

Stories empower us to manifest our own unique perspective and soul. Jesus taught using stories or parables.

---

[72] See Diagram in the Appendix.

Why? They open our minds and the minds of others. They offer us a deeper understanding of another person and more clarity around the dynamic going on between us or among us. They put us in deep listening mode and the Buddhist "beginner's mind," a mind of inquiry. They keep us out of self-righteousness. Socrates used questions.

However, questions alone are not enough. We need to ask the right questions to get the answers we need.

To ask the right questions, we first need to answer the question: What do I need? No one can answer that question but you.

If you ask, "Why doesn't he pick up his clothes?," you may never get an answer. You'll only create frustration. If you ask, "What can I do about the clothes on the floor?" you've got lots of answers.

When you are focused on what another person is doing wrong, you are going to be asking yourself questions like, "Why does he not put his tools away when he's finished with them? Why can't he cut the grass when it needs to be cut?" Those are disempowering questions.

If you shift those questions to "What do I need?" or "What would I like to see happen?" the answers become, "I would like to see the grass cut." "How can I get the grass cut?" There are lots of answers to that question.

I can go out and cut it myself. I can ask my husband to cut it. I can ask my kids to cut it. I can hire somebody to come in and do it for me. By changing disempowering questions to empowering questions, answers emerge.

If you start complaining to your husband about the fact that he's not cutting the grass, you will probably just create greater separation between you and your husband. You might get the grass cut, but what do you want your relationship with your husband to be?

### *Koans*

A koan is a paradox to be meditated upon that is used to train Zen Buddhist monks to abandon ultimate dependence on reason and flip them into gaining sudden intuitive enlightenment.[73]

Examples of koans:[74]
If you practice sitting as Buddha, you must kill Buddha.
What do you call the world?
What is this?
Out of nowhere, the mind comes forth.
Wash your bowls.

### *Metaphor*

A metaphor [75] is poetically saying something is something else.

All the world's a stage, And all the men and women merely players.[76]

These are wonderful, artistic, creative linguistic tools that help clarify what we mean.

There is a beautiful parable, allegedly told by the Buddha, about a man who arrived at a vast expanse of water. The land where he was standing felt dangerous. The land on

---

[73] https://www.merriam-webster.com/dictionary/koan
[74] https://www.huffpost.com/entry/zen-buddhism-koan_n_563251dce4b0631799 115f3c
[75] https://www.masterclass.com/articles/metaphor-similie-and-analogy-differences-and-similarities#whats-the-difference-between-metaphor-simile-and- analogy
[76] https://literarydevices.net/all-the-worlds-a-stage/

the other side appeared safe. However, there was no bridge or boat he could use to cross the water.

The man collected twigs and grass and leaves and branches, bound them together, and by paddling with his hands and feet, reached the other side.

The Buddha then compared the raft to the dharma or teachings. The raft was useful for reaching the other side of the water. The teachings are useful for attaining enlightenment. However, the raft is to be let go of once the man reaches the safety of the opposite shore. The teachings are to be let go of after enlightenment is attained.

### *Analogy*

An analogy[77] is saying something is like something else to make an explanatory point. An analogy is more complex than a metaphor.

What you're doing is as useful as rearranging deck chairs on the Titanic.

## HELPFUL WORD WISDOM PRACTICES

Be aware that a conscious conversation with self is very different from a conscious conversation with one other person. Both are different from conscious conversations within a larger group.

Conscious conversations with self can and should be totally uncensored.

Conscious conversations with one other person vary, depending on who that other person is and the resources you

---

[77] https://www.masterclass.com/articles/metaphor-similie-and-analogy-differences-and-similarities#whats-the-difference-between-metaphor-simile-and- analogy

personally have available when the conversation takes place. Conscious conversations within a larger group are most effective when evolving within a consciously created structure with the intention of facilitating clear speaking, deep listening, equal time for each participant, mutual compassion, and mutual respect.

## Individual Word Wisdom Practices
### *Affirmations*
Affirmations are a valuable practice whenever you're feeling not good enough, stupid, or something's gone wrong in your life. It's a way of shifting you back into that positive energy of feeling centered and part of the creative and co-creative flow.

Rather than talk about affirmations, which creates a separation between me, you, and the affirmations, we[78] would rather offer you an experience of what affirmations can do for you if you start using them in your life, as needed, as a wisdom practice.

Begin by giving yourself permission. Note! I am not saying, "Do this," I am saying, "Begin by giving yourself permission," if you are willing and able to do so. If not, now is not the right time for you to be saying affirmations. Put the book down and do whatever is more pressing in your life.

If you are willing and able to give yourself permission, please get comfortable in your chair. You can place both feet on the floor if you'd like, so that you feel more grounded and more connected with the earth. You can rest your arms on your lap, palms up, which allows you to receive energy from the Cosmos or universe. Relax and give yourself permission

---

[78] Co-created with my friend Donna O'Toole.

to breathe easily. Just absorb these words and know that this is who you are.

Notice: I am using first-person-singular in these affirmations, not because I am making statements about myself, but because I want you to feel the truth of these statements within yourself.

*For those reconnecting with their soul by releasing what no longer serves them.*[79]

My life is purposeful and meaningful.

My health is excellent because I take good care of my body, mind, and spirit.

I listen.

I ask questions. I observe.

I change the things I can.

I surrender the things I cannot change.

I have the wisdom to let go of what I cannot change and the courage to change the things I can.

I am grateful.

I am aware.

I am respectful, both toward myself and others.

I am compassionate, both toward myself and others. I trust my Soul completely.

### *For those reimmersed in their soul*[80]

I AM listening to my soul. I AM peaceful.

I AM living with clear eyes and an open heart.

I AM loving life.

I AM connected with all that is.

---

[79] On the consciousness diagram, these are the little black dots of culturally- conditioned worldviews.

[80] On the consciousness diagram, this is that center point, which Buddhists call "awareness," T.S. Eliot calls "the still point," Ram Dass refers to as "Be here now," and I call "Non-Dual Consciousness.

*__For those called to create, co-create, and manifest from their soul__*[81]

I experience my soul as purposeful and meaningful.

I experience my soul as intelligent.

I experience my soul as confident, relaxed, and poised.

I experience my soul as positive, enthusiastic, and infectious.

I experience my soul empowered to serve humbly.

I experience my soul resolving all challenges and doing whatever it has been given to do with ease and grace.

I experience my soul attracting abundance into my life.

I experience my soul attracting rich rewards.

I experience my soul opening to all who want to join in this adventure.

I experience my soul interacting with all people and drawing out the best in them.

My soul supports and teaches those who want to grow with me, and learns from those who know things I do not.

I experience others responding to my soul in positive ways. I experience my soul empowering all with whom I have contact to be all that they can be.

I experience my soul fulfilling its destiny in each and every moment and being provided with everything it needs to do so.

Together, our souls co-create marvelous new worlds of beauty, love, truth, and freedom.

Together, our souls are a living, breathing universe, fulfilling universal principles of love, respect, creativity and justice.

---

[81] On the consciousness diagram, these are the rays manifesting outward from that center point of non-dual consciousness. Each ray is unique. In Buddhism, these would be called "Bodhisattvas."

Together, our souls are catalysts for creating, co-creating, and manifesting planetary peace, power and prosperity, forever and ever.

We are all part of the universal creative flow.

### *Journaling*

Journaling is a wonderful word practice for permitting and documenting a conscious conversation with self. It is vital that it be done without censorship.

No one else ever has to read what you write unless you choose to share your words. You can stop anytime it gets too frightening. You can burn your writing when you are done if you so desire.

However, I would strongly suggest that you save your journaling if you have a safe place to keep it. Years later, you may find it interesting and helpful to go back to that original consciousness time, place, and space, and look at it from your new perspective of enhanced expanded consciousness. That is precisely what I did when I saved all those writings from that group marriage of so many years ago.

Journaling is a practice within Ken Wilber's upper left quadrant.[82] It is very personal, individual, and subjective. It helps answer the question, "Who am I?" If you journal without censorship, I guarantee you will end up with deeper understanding and greater clarity.

### *How do you journal?*

You start by writing down a challenge you are facing. Then allow your mind to go where it will, and document your thoughts, one after another as they fly through your mind. It is a conversation with self—a very private

---

[82] See diagram in the Appendix.

conversation. These are your words to you going through the paper. Whatever comes into your mind goes down on the paper.

The process is somewhat analogous to the "Witness" in Buddhist thought: "Big Mind" is watching "little mind."

It is not straight-line thinking. It is tapping into your subconscious.

You may be surprised at what emerges. You'll start seeing connections between experiences and thoughts, thoughts and thoughts, and experiences and experiences.

You may not want to look at some of those thoughts. That's perfectly normal. Just notice your resistance, note it, and continue to allow the thoughts to flow through without censorship. Continue to write them down.

You will likely come out in a totally different place from where you started with many new ways to move forward.


### *Poetry*

Writing poetry shifts you away from the literal meanings of words. It allows you to touch, even if for only a moment, a deeper connection with the mystery of life.

Once you experience something deeply, the words somehow pour out of your mind and onto the page to reflect that very deep experience in ways that your literal, analytic mind could never realize. Then, you simply play with form, alliteration, and simile, until something emerges that symbolically reflects or mirrors that very deep experience.

A form of Japanese poetry I like is called "haiku." Haiku is fun to write and fairly simple. Five syllables in the first line. Seven syllables in the second line. Five syllables in the third line, with a twist of meaning at the end.

MIND

Terror and trembling
body's rebellion against
mind rigid commands.

Mind, logical tool
analyzes, deduces
from faith in premise.

### Sanskrit Mantras

For my own experience with Sanskrit mantras, see my story on page 138.

From a more conceptual perspective, according to Thomas Ashley-Farrand, Sanskrit mantras are sacred words of power.[83] According to others, they are energy-based sounds embodying the highest spiritual state. Yet others refer to them as sound mysteries that change consciousness.

### Meditation[84] – Listening Deeply. Listen to the Silence. Listen to the Soul. Be Here Now.

Meditation is another practice that changes a person's state of consciousness so that they shift into calm, relaxation, clarity, concentration, and an expanded state of spiritual awareness, mental well-being, complete freedom, and self-realization. On the consciousness diagram, it is that center point of non-dual consciousness, beyond any attachment or aversion.

---

[83] https://www.amazon.com/Mantra-Sacred-Words-Thomas-Ashley-Farrand/ dp/1591791472
[84] https://en.wikipedia.org/wiki/Meditation

A practitioner can focus intensively on a single object or on anything that enters the field of awareness. The intention is simply to just be a knower-seer.

One of my own deep meditation experiences occurred in Chinchero, Peru, when we were ushered into the Womb of Pachamama and directed to listen to the silence. I became so very aware of a tiny little plant struggling to survive in the crevice of a rock and the deep beauty and peace of the natural environment.

Does anything more really need to be said here, other than perhaps to point to some famous words written by others:

From T.S. Eliot
At the still point of the turning world. Neither flesh nor fleshless;
Neither from nor towards; at the still point, there the dance is,
But neither arrest nor movement. And do not call it fixity,
Where past and future are gathered. Neither movement from nor towards,
Neither ascent nor decline. Except for the point, the still point,
There would be no dance, and there is only the dance.[85]

---

[85] The Four Quartets, Burnt Norton.
https://www.brainpickings.org/2015/11/18/t- s-eliot-reads-burnt-norton/

From Ram Dass

Remember. Be Here Now. Now Here Be.[86]

From Thich Nhat Hanh

We have to continue to learn. We have to be open. And we have to be ready to release our knowledge in order to come to a higher understanding of reality.[87]

### *Vision Boards*

Vision boards have intentions very similar to affirmations. One of the intentions is to help you feel good about who you are and support you in creating what matters most in your personal life—your personal purpose. A second intention is to help you get clear on what your own intentions are. This correlates with one of the guidelines in the

--------

[86] https://www.amazon.com/Remember-now-here/dp/B000728SR8/ref=pd_lpo_14_ img_0/144-7117407-0057817?_encoding=UTF8&pd_rd_i=B000728SR8&pd_rd_r=08576471-fe0a-445d-8016-bd3ffa4f03dd&pd_rd_w=Ca0i3&pd_rd_wg=p6beB&pf_rd_p=16b28406-aa34-451d-8a2e-b3930ada000c&pf_rd_r=0PMBZ1Y1JZT4TR8G2S3J&psc=1&refRID=0PMBZ1Y1JZT4TR8G2S3J

[87] https://www.goodreads.com/quotes/843508-we-have-to-continue-to-learn-we- have-to-be.

Buddhist Eightfold Path—right intention or right resolve. A third intention is connecting all of our unique intentions to help all of us co-create the kind of world in which we would like to live.

### What is a vision board?

A vision board is your own unique collage at a particular moment in your life. You create it from words and pictures that bring you joy, purpose, and meaning. It is your vision of what your life would be like if it were exactly the way you wanted it to be.

### Why create a vision board?

It refocuses your attention and intention on all the good things you want to bring into your life. Your right attention and intention help manifest those good things.

A fascinating energetic shift happens as you focus on the good things in your life and set clear intentions about where you want your life to go. Somehow, your life goes in that direction. I don't know why it works that way, but I know that it does.

### How do you make a vision board?

Allow yourself a couple of hours. Get yourself a big piece of poster board, a pile of old magazines[88], a pair of scissors, and some glue. Look through the magazines and cut out anything that attracts you, whether it's pictures of nature, words, beautiful homes, scenery, exotic places. You can add photos of beautiful and supportive family members if you would like. When your pile of cut outs and photos is large

---

[88] Check your local library. Many libraries give away old copies of magazines at no charge.

enough, arrange them in any way you desire on the poster board. It's your collage, your poster board, your vision board, so you can design it any way you want.

When you have a design you like, paste the words and pictures down. If you want, you can have your vision board laminated for more durability.

You can even host a vision board party and let each participant do his or her own vision board. Since you're all in the same space, you can easily look at one another's vision boards, talk about them, and share ideas about them.

***What to do with your vision board once you have completed it.***

Hang it on a wall where you will see it every day. Hanging your vision board on a wall is a maintenance practice. It's a constant reminder of what really matters to you, what you want to bring into your life, and how you want to live your life.

You can make new vision boards as more information comes into your life. As your focus and life purpose change, your vision boards change. As you mature, receive more understanding, more education, and have new experiences, new visions will open up for you.

Don't expect a single vision board to last for your entire life.

Look for new patterns and insights. Invite your friends to look at your vision board and tell you what they see.

Once you get your vision boards up on your walls, you can sit back and be amazed as the words and pictures on your vision boards start manifesting in your life.

I began creating vision boards twenty years ago. I've done seven to date and have manifested every single item on every single vision board I have ever created. I don't know why, but somehow, whatever I have envisioned on my vision boards shows up in my physical life.

How does it happen? I haven't the foggiest idea, but I know that it does.

## Group Wisdom Linguistic Practices
### Circle Work

> I live my life in widening circles
> that reach out across the world.
> I may not complete this last one
> but I give myself to it.
> I circle around God, around the primordial tower.
> I've been circling for thousands of years
> and I still don't know: am I a falcon,
> a storm, or a great song?
> — R.M. Rilke, *Book of Hours*

### *Intentions behind circle work*

To bring disparate worldviews and perspectives into alignment through a safe structure, a focused topic, and transparent, conscious, respectful sharing of stories, thoughts, and experiences.

### *What does a circle look like?*

As the name suggests, those participating in circle work sit either on the ground or in individual chairs in a circle. Sometimes, there is an altar in the center where each participant can offer a personal gift.

Sometimes there is simply a talking stick, picked up and held by whomever is speaking. Only the person holding the talking stick speaks. Everyone else listens.

Participants are dressed in clothes in which they feel comfortable. A circle always has a clear structure, although each structure is different, depending on the circle facilitator.

### *How does a circle work?*

The structure with which I am most familiar is the Vistar Method of metaphysical circles, [89] created by Ron and Victoria Friedman. In this structure, there are three roles: facilitator, support person, and participant. There are four guidelines: raise your hand if you want to contribute, limit your contribution to two minutes, no questions, and no cross talk. There are three sections to the circle structure: enunciation, development, and recapitulation.

When done well, the experience is a coming together in resonance at an almost metaphysical level. The effect is intimacy and harmony. No one wants to break the bond and leave when the circle is formally over.

---

[89] http://www.vistarfoundation.org/

***Other recommended Circle Groups***
*The Millionth Circle*[90]
*Widening Circles, A Memoir*[91]
Gather the Women[92]


***Mastermind groups***

One plus one doesn't equal two. One plus One equals Eleven. I first heard that statement over twenty years ago from Mark Victor Hansen.

Mastermind groups are a collaborative vehicle for moving individual projects forward with clarity and speed. Each member may have a unique focus or purpose. Other members provide positive support, new perspectives, and helpful connections.

Recommended size - three to eight people

Recommended frequency of meetings - two times a month for 60 to 90 minutes, as determined by the group

Location of meetings - determined by group members. Can be in person or via video conferencing.

Recommended structure – One-page templates are exchanged by email 24 to 48 hours before each meeting. Templates include:

- My successes over the past two weeks
- My intentions or goals
- Where I need help from the group
- What I have to offer to the group (skills, education, training, connections, support)

---

[90] https://millionthcircle.org/
[91] https://www.amazon.com/Widening-Circles-Memoir-Joanna-Macy/dp/1897408013
[92] https://www.gatherthewomen.org/

At each meeting, one person volunteers as a facilitator and one as a timekeeper. The allotted time is divided among members present. Each participant may use his or her time as s/he pleases. However, usually, the most beneficial focus is a focus on the third item—where I need help from the group.

### *Why this Structure Works*

Templates are primarily for the benefit of the writer. Listing successes helps each member appreciate what s/he has accomplished over the previous two weeks, increasing self-confidence and a sense of forward momentum. Listing goals and intentions helps him or her get clear on next steps. Asking for help unblocks frustration and opens doors for new ways of moving forward.

Limiting the time each member has to receive feedback from others encourages focus and priority setting. It also prevents any one member from monopolizing group time.

## TRANSFORMING OURSELVES

### *Transforming Ourselves – Answering the Question "Who am I?"*
An Exercise in Piercing the Veil of Illusion[93]

---

[93] For another thread and more context about Piercing the Veil of Illusion, see page 179.

Created by Punya Mishra

Good | Evil ambigram design by Punya Mishra

www.punyamishra.com

Used by permission

## WHAT DO OUR MINDS DO WITH WHAT WE EXPERIENCE?

What do you see?

If you see the word good, how do you feel? If you see the word evil, how do you feel?

What happens when one of us sees only good and another sees only evil? Will we fight over who is right and who is wrong?

If so, why do we do this? Is it because we have confused the map with the territory?

Is what we see a projected reflection of how our minds are shaping our world?

Experience is what it is. When we enjoy or at least accept what is, we experience unity. We are in the flow. If we don't like what is, our words and choice of focus have the power to change what we experience.

To better understand the map is not the territory, here's a game to play in a very safe space to explore how our words and perceptions affect our emotions, actions, and well-being, as well as the emotions, actions, and well-being of those around us. You can then take whatever you learn here and play with it in your own very safe space, in your very own time, and at your very own pace.

"LOVE" by John Langdon,
1999 (used by permission)

What do you see?

If you see the word "hate" what do you feel? If you see the word "love" what do you feel?

Note how nothing in the image changes. All that changes is what your mind does with what it perceives to be there.

Once you can see both "love" and "hate," you can choose the word on which you prefer to focus.

Which focus makes you feel better? Is it your focus on love or hate? Which do you choose to focus on and why?

203

Can you simultaneously hate injustice and love justice? Which focus gets better results, and why?

"All Is Vanity," by Charles Allan Gilbert, 1902

(Ecclesiastes 1:2)

What do you see?

If you see the beautiful woman sitting in front of her mirror, what do you feel?

What other thoughts or images come to mind?

If you see a skull, what do you feel? What other thoughts or images come to mind?

As you engage more fully with the picture and see both images clearly, please notice that nothing in the image changes; all that changes is your focus and what your mind does with what is there.

You can choose what you focus on. Which makes you feel better? To focus on the beautiful woman or to focus on the skull? Which do you choose to focus on and why? Does it depend on your intentions? Your needs of the moment?

In the previous optical illusions, I asked you to look at an image, notice what you saw, what words you used to describe what you saw, and any emotions the words or images generated. I intended to strengthen your awareness of all the different words and emotions that can emerge from a single, fixed image or experience.

My intention with the next image is different. In the following image, I will use words to give you an instruction. Your challenge is to correctly understand the meaning of the words in the instruction.

"The Hidden Tiger" by R. Rusty Russ
(Used by permission)

Find the hidden tiger. What do the words "Find the hidden tiger" mean? What are you being directed to look for? A hidden shape? A shadow?

Eyes peering from the underbrush?

When you see the hidden tiger, you will absolutely know you have found it. You may even chuckle at yourself for not having seen it sooner. Once you find the hidden tiger, you will always be able to see the hidden tiger.

Suppose I were to tell you that you are not being directed to look for a hidden shape, a shadow, or eyes peering from the underbrush. What if I were to tell you to look for words?

As before, nothing in the image changes. Nothing in the instruction changes. The only thing that changes is the amount of information you have received and what your mind does with that information.

***Transforming Ourselves – Answering the Question "Whom do I choose to be, right here, right now?"***

The world is full of choices, illusions, and perceptions. How many can you see? On which do you choose to focus, right here, right now? Which supports your soul? Which drains it? Which desecrates it?

What are you going to do with your one open mind, right here, right now?

What are you going to do with the power of your words, right here, right now?

What are you going to do with your one precious life, right here, right now?

The present is your point of personal power. It is the only moment you can choose and act.

***Transforming Our Planet—Shifting power over, power under, and power against to Power With through Conscious Conversation***

If each and every one of us were to bring peace, power, and prosperity into our own life, right here, right now, peace, power, and prosperity would instantaneously become planetary.

The question then becomes, "How do we maintain planetary peace, power, and prosperity forever and ever?

Here's how.

Each of us, in each and every moment, lives and models personal peace, personal (em)power(ment) and personal prosperity (abundance). When interacting with others, we exchange thoughts, ideas, and personal stories, through conscious, creative, co-creative, mutually respectful, and deeply compassionate conversations.

How do we use our minds and words to bring these qualities into our own lives and the lives of all around us?
1. We listen deeply.
    i.   Within and without.
2. We speak clearly.
    i.   We ask questions.
    ii.  We ask the right questions to get the answers we need.
    iii. We clarify our referents, the territory toward which our words and conceptual maps are pointing, so that we don't misunderstand one another, start arguing with one another about whose words are right and whose words are wrong, and start feeling unheard, misunderstood, and not good enough.
    iv. We tell our own stories from our own perspectives.
    v. We own our own words and the impact they have on ourselves, others, and the planet that sustains us.

3. We keep learning, growing, creating, co-creating, and manifesting while doing no harm.

That is what wisdom practices are about. Regardless of the form, the intention is always the same: to shift a dysfunctional power over, power under, or power against dynamic into a functional Power With dynamic that serves life.

We can, of course, choose to use our words to try to change someone or something "out there," whether it be people or environments or systems or human-created physical structures. Sometimes that's useful and sometimes it works. But we can also use words to change and master ourselves, which is much more effective, although not necessarily easy. It's a way of shifting us into a "power with" energy consciousness—a Beingness. This is an internal power within oneself—being comfortable in one's own body, in one's own skin, in one's own mind, in one's own emotions.

There are some human dynamics and contexts in which power over, power under, and power against are aligned with and integrated with Power With. This happens when all are serving life. (See page 157, et seq.)

However, what do we do about worldly, bully/coward, ugly, abusive relationships that serve only death and separation from soul for all participants? We are all absolutely entitled to healthy relationships, both within ourselves and with others, so how do we get them?

We simply choose the relationships that support us and walk away from those that do not. We don't need to justify our actions. We don't need to explain unless we want to. All we need do is walk away.

Nobody deserves abuse. Nobody. But as long as we stick around, we are enabling the abuse and it is likely to continue. If we simply walk away, there is no one left to abuse. Our power lies in changing ourselves.

I first learned about the power of walking away from a very dear friend of mine, The Honorable Anthony Gibson, an Atlantic County chancery court judge, who had offered me a job when I first graduated from law school. I should have taken Judge Gibson's offer. Instead, I chose to work for a large, prestigious, Atlantic City law firm.

The partner for whom I worked had me working eighty hours a week. He would send me off on a research project only to change his mind and send me off on another. He never seemed to be able to decide what he wanted. He never seemed satisfied. Even worse, he always seemed frustrated, angry, and irritable.

One evening at a bar dinner, I was chatting with Judge Gibson and began complaining about this abusive partner who was totally exhausting me. After about a minute, the judge simply excused himself and walked away.

My tirade stopped immediately. I had lost my audience and rightly so. I was wasting both my time and the judge's time with ineffective complaining to someone who could do nothing to change the dysfunctional dynamic between me and the law firm partner.

What I should have done was quit the law firm job. I did that six months later, willingly taking a pay cut to gain the advantage of better working hours and more respectful treatment.

Walking away is not easy. After all, we're strong, right? And smart, right? And committed, right? And we can handle anything, right? And if we walk away, outsiders may perceive us as weak cowards, afraid to fight back against bullies. If we don't master the dysfunctional dynamic and don't choose to see ourselves as standing for peace, like conscientious objectors, rather than running away in fear, we only add shame, rather than courage to our Beingness.

Perhaps the shadow we don't want to look at is our own vulnerability, pain, and feeling not good enough. When we notice these and don't want them anymore, it's quite easy to change them.

The power lies fully within each of us. While we can never change another person directly, if we change ourselves, the dynamics of the relationship change. Sometimes, the other person changes indirectly as a result of our own direct change.

# Chapter 9
# Creating, Co-creating, and Manifesting Planetary Peace, Power, and Prosperity – Together and Forever

Being a Bridge between the World of Matter and the World of Energy, Spirit, and Soul.

*"We have the beginning of a new age. The earth gets a new skin. Better still, it finds its soul."*

—Teilhard de Chardin

## OUR PRESENT STATE

Patriarchal systems are breaking down. Top-down communism no longer works. Top-down democracy, bought by top-down corporations, no longer works. Monarchies and dictatorships are being challenged and overthrown.

Women are waking up and starting to think for themselves. They are no longer willing to accept the roles into which men have placed them: sex object, subservient wife, mother, cook, housekeeper, babysitter. Women are no longer willing to sit idly by and watch their husbands and sons be slaughtered by other women's husbands and sons.

As women take back their power, men are waking up, too. They are beginning to respect the formidable female collaborative and cooperative power that can lead our entire planet away from war and violence and into global peace, power, and prosperity.

Throughout the world, men and women are aligning to bring about reform. Occupy Wall Street has spread across the globe as the 99 percent challenge the 1 percent whose decisions have led us to the brink of destruction.

Together, we have allowed the major news media to shape our minds, thoughts, and emotions. People are tired of a steady stream of violence, verbal abuse, and news about what's wrong with the world.

Good news media are springing up everywhere to replace the naysayers and spread the good news about what is working. People everywhere seek a return to sanity, both in their personal worlds and their collective worlds. They are starting to think for themselves, to release their fear and depression, and take positive action to recreate themselves and our world.

## CONCEPTS – HOLONS AND NOOSPHERES

Here are two concepts that can help us understand what's happening so that together, we can consciously co-create a world that works for all of us. One is holons. The other is Teilhard de Chardin's Noosphere.[94]

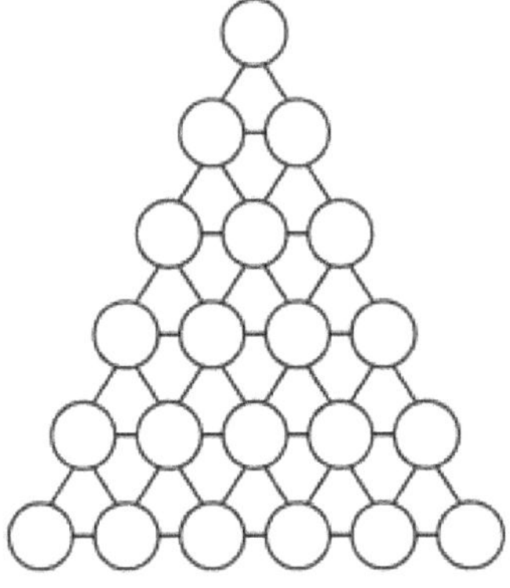

---

[94] P Teilhard de Chardin, (1959), *The Phenomenon of Man*, Collins, St James Palace, London.

The first concept, a holon, can be represented by the image on the previous page. If energy is inherent within each circle, and each circle is its own complete system (whether an atom, a cell, a heart, a human being, a planet, etc.), we have a holarchy, or pure democracy, or pure communism. Another way of thinking of this is that we have undivided wholeness, with power and creativity flowing in all directions, top-down, bottom-up, and all around. Each circle/system (e.g., each human being) connects to and is part of other more encompassing circles/systems (families, communities, nations, our planet, our galaxy, our universe). All participate in an energetic exchange that affects every part. The challenge is to align them and bring them into harmony and balance.

For the past two thousand years, this has been accomplished through patriarchy. It is interesting that this image can also be viewed as a hierarchy when the underlying energy is flowing only from the top down.

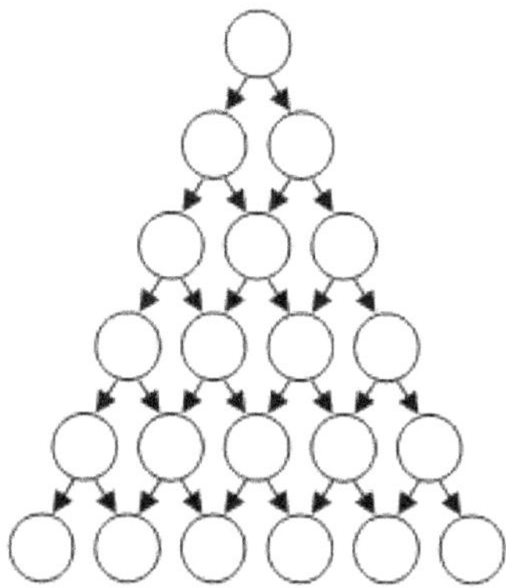

A functional hierarchy emerges when the person at the top is the most experienced and the wisest, a steward of the energetic flow, a facilitator, a shepherd of the entire flock of less experienced people, a servant leader. A dysfunctional hierarchy emerges when a person with little experience or wisdom manipulates his way to the top through lying, stealing, bullying, and sucking the energy from those below him solely to enhance his perception of his worldly power.

The first map above is the Noosphere or Teilhard de Chardin's thinking layer of earth. If each minuscule part of a holon is complete in itself, and yet connected to all other holons, then each is connected to every other holon at a thinking level beyond itself. The Noosphere might also be referred to as the Akashic Records or the Field or Indra's Web.

If we use our words not to judge and condemn, but simply to share information, there are no right or wrong words. There are only creative perspectives.

Some perspectives work better than others for particular purposes. Some perspectives are more encompassing and inclusive than others. No perspective is any more encompassing and inclusive than the perspective that everything is perspective.

The perspective that everything is perspective is freeing. The way we see the world is okay.

It is also terrifying and humbling. The way others see the world is also okay. If we believe that everything is perspective, we have to listen to and respect ourselves and others. We also need to be very aware, conscious, and accountable for all of our own actions.

There's a fine line between chaos and heaven on earth. That line is non-violence and awareness. It's a choice - for each and every one of us.

## TAKING ALIGNED ACTION AS A TEAM TOWARD A COMMON GOAL OR INTENTION

There are so many examples of what this might look like: The Los Angeles Dodgers; the Philadelphia Symphony Orchestra; the Russian Ballet.

On the surface, these look very different from one another, yet the underlying pattern is the same: setting a goal or intention and working in harmony with aligned team players to manifest that goal or intention.

With the Dodgers, the goal was winning the 2020 World Series. With the Philadelphia Orchestra under its mid-1950s Conductor Eugene Ormandy, when the Swarthmore, Bryn Mawr, and Haverford College choruses sang with the orchestra, the intention was to co-create an exquisite, immersive, and mesmerizing musical experience.

With the Russian Ballet[95], the original intention was to separate ballet from opera to allow more focus on movement. After the Russian Revolution, the arts were temporarily restricted into a power under position, as the new, judgmental, bullying role authorities required ballet to reflect socialism if ballet were to survive.

Companies like the Bolshoi Ballet created the ballet "Ivan the Terrible" to pacify the bullies playing power-over roles, although this did not prevent dancers from continuing to focus primarily on movement. In the 1960s, as many dancers from the Bolshoi became more aware of the power over limitations into which top-down socialism had imprisoned them, they defected to the West with the intention of expanding their artistic freedom.

---

[95] https://www.lansingstatejournal.com/story/sponsor-story/wharton-center/2016/06/09/why-russia-epicenter-ballet/85493900/

Notice how the goal or intention shifted, depending on how prominent the bullies/cowards were within the cultural structure of the time. Despite this, the commune of conscious creators, co-creators, and manifesters continued to survive and thrive. The connected team of unique individuals always remained intact.

## THE MORAL IMPERATIVE—A SIMPLE RULE FOR LIVING

The moral imperative is not about creating a system of ethics to be imposed on everyone from above. It is an internal, soul directive to each and every unique human being on this planet to know oneself, keep learning and growing, and live life full out without harming oneself, others, or the planet that sustains all of our lives.

The Moral Imperative—A Simple Rule for Living is simply to do whatever you want as long as you do no harm.

Yet even those words are generalizations—only fingers pointing at the moon. They are not the moon.

Every time we eat a meal, we kill another life. Is this the origin of the Christian ritual of grace before eating a meal? "Thank you for the life that has given its life so that I may live."

And even when we try to live according to that simple rule—do whatever you want as long as you do no harm—we often don't know when we are doing harm. We are so conditioned into our own worldviews that we always believe we are doing the right thing. Yet, a pure belief and intention may not have a positive effect on another person functioning from a different worldview.

I remember a time when I was participating in a retreat for friends and families of addicts. Recovering addicts were participating in their own retreat in an adjacent building. Toward the end of the retreat, the two groups came together.

I had recently learned the left-side-to-left-side hug, where, if you allow yourself to relax, give, and receive, you can feel the energetic exchange of that heart-to-heart connection. I wanted to offer what to me was a gift to everyone I met.

I approached one of the addicts in the room, opened my arms wide, and began hugging her. She recoiled and pushed me away. I was stunned!

My best guess is that she had lived such a challenging life that she didn't trust anyone. Why would she want to hug a stranger she didn't even know and trust?

I had a similar experience with one of my daughters-in-law. To me, it often felt as if her hugs were nothing but formalities—quick pecks on the right cheek.

One day, I said, "Let me show you something." I showed her the heart-to-heart hug.

For years afterward, she wouldn't hug me at all. What had I done wrong?

It was awkward. When I left their home, I would always give my son a beautiful, warm heart-to-heart hug. My daughter-in-law would stand on the opposite side of the room, her arms crossed, just watching.

Finally, one time when I left, as always, my son and I exchanged warm heart-to-heart hugs. Then, I looked across the room at my daughter-in-law, standing perfectly still, and just said, "And you don't like to hug, do you?"

"Oh, I hug, but I just don't like to be told how to do it."

Oh, so that was it. She had thought I was telling her how to hug, rather than offering her an opportunity to explore something new that for me had been a beautiful gift.

I stood motionless. The ball was in her court. She thought for a moment, then quickly came over and gave me a quick peck on the right check.

My son later told me that his wife likes herself the way she is.

She sees no reason to change.

I can certainly respect that. I, too, like myself the way I am. But we are different women, with different relationships to the man (my son, her husband,) who is so important to both of us in vastly different ways.

When situations like this happen, how do you move beyond the dissonances? Here are some understandings that have helped me:

1. I am not going to change anybody but myself.
2. We are both doing the best we know how, based on the information we have, the experiences we have had, our cultural conditioning, and the resources we have available.
3. My worldview is different from another's worldview. My needs are different from another's needs.
4. Our energies and paths are not always fully aligned.
5. I can serve both of us best by surrendering to the other person's needs of the moment, as long as those needs don't throw me out of integrity with who I am and desecrate my own soul. If the other person's needs throw me out of integrity with who I am and desecrate my own soul, I need to say no and set boundaries that do not infringe on my own integrity.

Here are some questions that have helped me:

1. What is this relationship teaching me?

2. What is this relationship giving me?
3. What values are essential to my own sense of integrity?
4. Am I living these values every moment of every day to the best of my ability? If not, why not?
5. What do I require in a healthy relationship?
6. What is my purpose on this planet and how can I fulfill it?

Here are some action steps that have helped me:

1. Make a decision to forgive. (This does not mean you condone what the other person has done. It does not necessarily mean that you go back into the relationship. It simply means that you are ready to release the past, mentally and emotionally, so you can fulfill your own purpose on this planet in each and every present moment.)
2. Think about why you are on this planet. (What is your purpose? What are your skills? What gives you joy?)
3. Create a vision board.
4. Write out affirmations and put them where you can read them every day.
5. Notice your thoughts. (If they are negative and critical, consciously choose to reword them.)
6. Notice the connection between your thoughts and emotions. When your thoughts are negative, how do you feel? If you want to feel joy, what changes can you make to your thoughts and focus?
7. Choose to stop focusing on what s/he did and start focusing on what you can do, right here, right now.
8. Ask yourself what you are willing to die for. Whatever you are willing to die for is what you must live for. Life is not a dress rehearsal.

9.  Your uniqueness is the gift you have to offer the world. Don't allow another human to strangle it.

10. Always stay in integrity with yourself. Personal integrity is the most valuable asset you own.

11. Be a spiritual warrior. Be aware that there are energies that will support your creative spirit and energies that will drain it. Surround yourself with supportive energies.

12. When you find yourself in the midst of destructive energies, protect yourself. Remove yourself from those people and that environment. Being a spiritual warrior is little more than staying centered on your own creative path.

13. Envision yourself surrounded by a beautiful field of white light that shields you. Notice how calm you feel.

14. Make a conscious effort to detach emotionally from cutting, sarcastic remarks. Don't use sarcasm on others.

15. Don't be afraid to say no when you are asked to take inappropriate action. If you don't say no, you may be asking for a painful universal lesson.

16. Know that the only person you need to work on is yourself.

17. Understand that sometimes less is more.

An understanding of what we do with our words can open up portals to personal, community, and global transformation:

- Releasing fear and anxiety.
- Mastering anger and rage.
- Letting go of shame.

Shift into and live from that creative and co-creative, present-moment state of consciousness that Buddhists call "emptiness" and Ken Wilber calls Non-Dual Consciousness.

Transformation (also labeled salvation, piercing the veil, transcendence, awareness, samadhi, consciousness shift, being in the present moment) happens when we reconnect *experientially* with Non-Dual Consciousness. It is a sudden consciousness shift from conditioned dual consciousness to Non-Dual Consciousness.

Suddenly, in the context of a particular experience, we see the world through new eyes. We hear through new ears.

There is no linear way of shifting from conditioned dual consciousness to Non-Dual Consciousness. It's simply a jump, a leap of faith, a letting go of old beliefs, and moving back into the flow of experience out of which new

worldviews emerge. It's like staying focused on the "Light of God" and Dove of Peace in St. Peter's Basilica in the Vatican.

Only then can we tune into a pure channel of unlimited energy that supports and flows through us - allowing new words and thoughts to emerge, take form, and transform like a kaleidoscope of beautiful colors. Finally, together we co-create a dynamic dance of consciousness and a peaceful, powerful, prosperous, abundant, and sustainable planet.

At first, the Abyss or Dark Night of the Soul is a terrifying place to be. We don't want to give up our limiting beliefs and slide into what feels like a void. There *is* a light at the end of the tunnel, a light called "Faith." We believe,

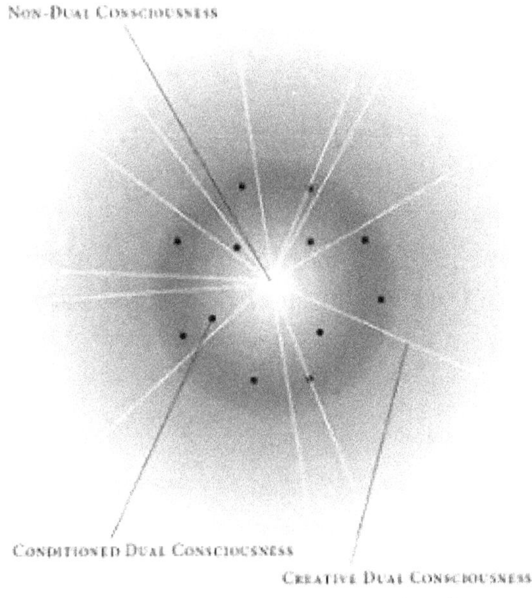


not because we know our belief is true, but because it's too terrifying not to believe that there has to be some "Higher Intelligence" running this show.

Once reconnected with Non-Dual Consciousness, we can use our analytical abilities to move in any direction from the center, playing, creating, co-creating, and manifesting anywhere we please, with whatever tools and resources we have available at any particular time, in any particular location. What a listener can hear depends on what they've been taught, what they believe, and the emotional content with which they infuse particular words based on their own experiences. In short, the effect can be different from the intent when the two are not fully aligned.

Telling another person how to live their life or what they should do simply doesn't work. We *do* need to listen to and respect one another's freedom of choice. However, it is equally important that each of us protect our own souls from abusive and violent attacks by those still stuck in a single worldview.

## PLANETARY PEACE, POWER, AND PROSPERITY LEGACY FOUNDATION, INC.

On April 17, 2020, we filed articles of incorporation in the State of Florida for a new educational foundation, Planetary Peace, Power, and Prosperity Legacy Foundation, Inc.

**Our Vision**
To consciously and intentionally use our co-creative power to develop ideas, present solutions, and promote action for the greater good of humanity and the planet.

**Our Mission**
To attract each human consciousness, through deep listening, clear speaking, and conscious conversation:

| Away From | Toward |
| --- | --- |
| Feeling not good enough | Stepping fully into our own, unique personal power, while not harming others or the planet that sustains us. |
| Abusing others or allowing ourselves to be abused | Self-compassion and other compassion |
| Fear and terror | Inner strength and courage |
| Rage | Standing firmly in right action |
| Shame or guilt | Making amends by changing conduct |
| A transactional economy of lack | An abundance economy of giving and receiving |
| Planetary war and desecration | Deep inner, community, and planetary peace |

To fully use each of our unique gifts, skills, talents, and passions to connect, shift, transform, evolve, expand, manifest, and maintain, creatively and co-creatively, a peaceful, powerful, prosperous planet—together and forever.

This is the logo we created together. It reflects the final phase of our consciousness diagram, the manifestation outward of our unique gifts and talents after we have reconnected with Non-Dual Consciousness and our core being.

This is our website, https://planetarypeacepowerand prosperity.org/, where you can find a wealth of information, free videos, and a carousel of our current partners, each offering their own skill or service.

If you would like to create your own legacy by helping us manifest sanctuaries and educational centers all over the planet and are able to share a voluntary skill or service, please contact us here:

https://planetarypeacepowerandprosperity.org/contact/

If you would like to partner with us and amplify the good work we are all doing on this planet, please fill out the same contact form and let us know. Partnership is simply an exchange of logos, website URLs, and a short phrase (five words or less) describing the service you offer. To see how it works, please look at the current carousel of partners on our website.

# Appendix of Useful Maps

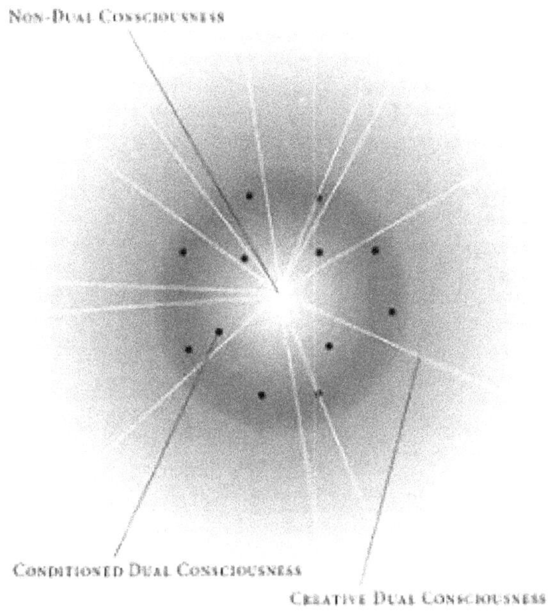

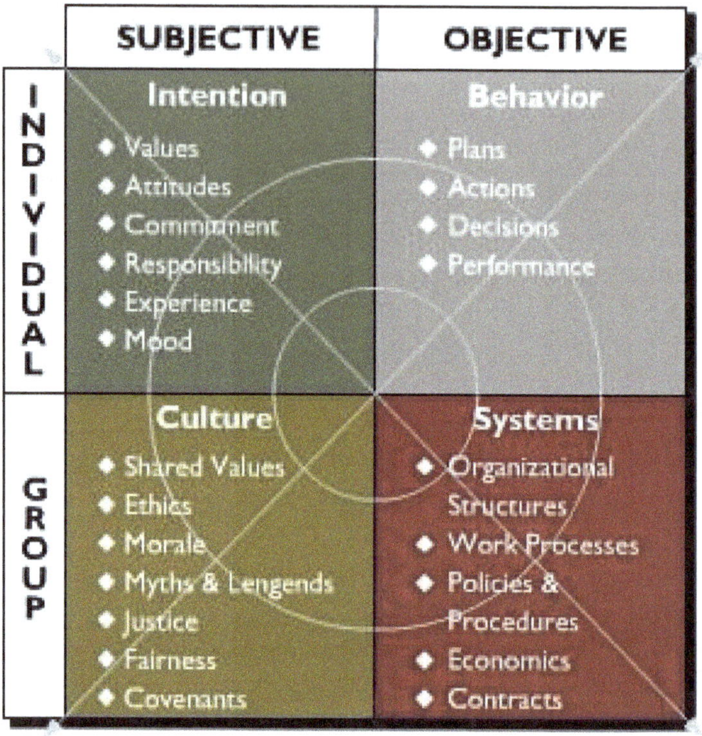

**Ken Wilber's AQAL Diagram**

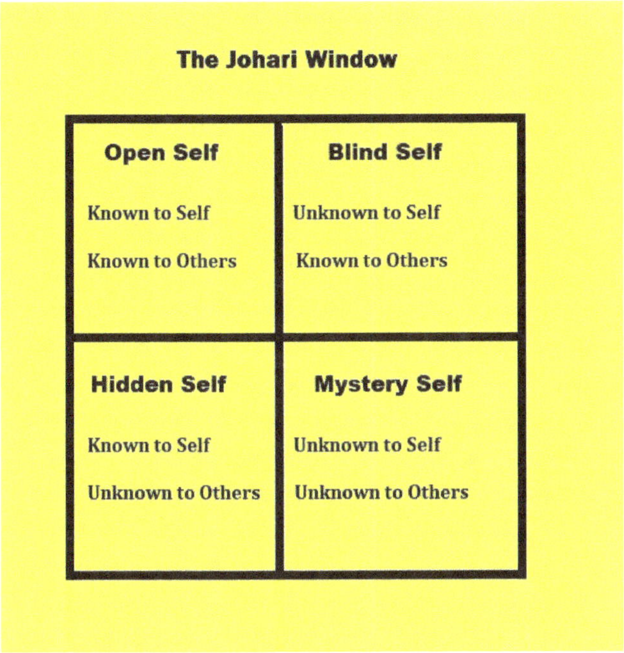

The Johari Window

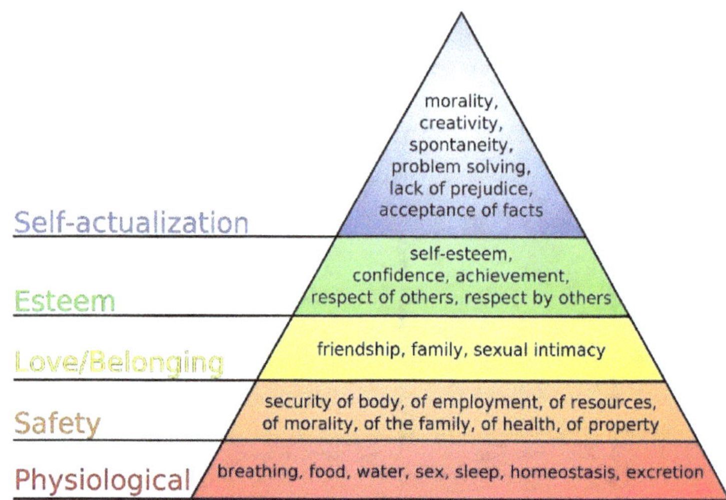



**Maslow's Hierarchy of Needs**

**Human Personality Types**

# Reconnection, Integration, and Expansion

Back on page 100, I shared my story, *A Woman Exploring a Ph.D.* Based on my recollection, photos, and notes, this event occurred in May 2016, at a PhD Dissertation Retreat held in a spectacular private home overlooking Monterey Bay in Scotts Valley, California.

I came into the Retreat with great clarity about completing my PhD dissertation. I left the Retreat with all my plans shattered and my PhD Dissertation Proposal never completed and submitted.

On October 9, 2024, Hurricane Milton made landfall on Siesta Key, Florida, ten minutes from where I was hunkered down. My new publisher and I were in the process of brainstorming this Second Edition. Knowing that my electrical power would likely go down any moment and with no guarantees that I would physically survive Milton's fury, I quickly searched a file folder on my computer entitled Sacred Journeys, pulled the two longest writings, and emailed them out to my new publisher. Two minutes later, our power disappeared. The outage lasted for almost 48 hours.

I didn't know what I had sent my new publisher. I didn't have time to read it before Milton struck. I just knew I had to get it into their hands.

I survived Milton and the tornado swirling overhead only a mile away. Finally, our power returned.

After surveying the external devastation Milton had strewn, I finally had time to read what I had sent my new publisher. It was my never-completed PhD dissertation proposal.

It was the perfect way to end this Second Edition. What an amazing synchronicity!

# Abandoned Dissertation Proposal Resurfaced

## DICHOTOMY AND INTEGRATION

Draft Proposal for a Thesis in the Fields of Mysticism, Language and Non-Dual Consciousness

Dr. Janet Smith Warfield

7339 Royal Birkdale Drive

Sarasota, FL 34238

USA

"Submitted in partial fulfillment of the requirements for the 'DEGREE OF DOCTOR OF PHILOSOPHY IN WISDOM STUDIES' at Wisdom University."

Course title:

Doctoral Writing and Research Methods

Instructors:

Mark B. Ryan, Ph.D.
Carolyn Atkinson, Ph.D.
Ginger Clarkson

Dates:

August 10-15, 2014
Post-paper

# Proposed Title

The Dichotomy between Dualistic Words and an Integrated State of Non-Dual Consciousness

# Abstract

This dissertation emanates from several personal, consciousness-shifting experiences, thinking about those experiences, trying to understand those experiences, trying to conceptualize those experiences, trying to communicate those experiences, reading about similar experiences, noticing the ways others have conceptualized those experiences, and attempting to put together the pieces of the word puzzle we humans have created into an integral, theoretical whole where every conceptual piece fits. For the pieces to fit, we must give each piece its proper experiential, contextual meaning.

It is the position of this dissertation that:
1.  Words structure experience.
2.  The manner in which each person structures experience is determined by genes, childhood conditioning, education, culture, personal experience, and personal mental processing of experience.
3.  There is no right or wrong way to use words to structure experience. There are, however, more or less effective ways to use words to structure experience to manifest particular intentions.

4. What our neurology can access is limited.

5. The terms "objectivity," "truth," and "knowledge" can be given meaning only as tentative agreement among all "subjects" or persons, based upon information currently available.

6. What has been termed "Truth," and "Knowledge" (with a capital 'T' and 'K') refers to a Non-Dual State of Consciousness that transcends words and concepts.

7. We live in a holographic universe where each of us is a mirror, both of one another and the whole.

8. What has been termed a "spiritual path" is a series of consciousness-shifting experiences that open up new and more expansive ways of thinking, being, and doing. We become aware. We know that in each and every moment, we have a choice as to how to act. Rather than re-acting based on fear, anger, past conditioning, and lack of education, we take responsibility in the present moment for our choices of action. We step into our personal power. When fully developed, that personal power is always "power with," not "power over."

9. Each of us must think for ourselves in whatever way makes sense to us. If we want to think for ourselves, we must also allow others to think for themselves. If we are willing to stay open and listen to one another's thoughts without judgment and stop fighting over whose words are right and whose words are wrong, we can continue to expand our own consciousness and that of others through respectful dialogue.

# Introduction

**Statement of Purpose**

This dissertation has several inter-related purposes:

1. To elucidate mystical experiences by using the lens of my own mystical experiences as focal points for discussion.
2. To elucidate what we humans do with words.
3. To develop a theory about language and its relationship to experience.
4. To shift our focus from a search for conceptual truth to the experiential, contextual *meanings* of the words we use.
5. To develop tools for clearer communication.
6. To facilitate the co-creation of a peaceful, powerful, prosperous planet.

Ever since I had a mystical experience many years ago, I have been trying to find ways to communicate that experience to others. I have included a detailed description of that experience, "How It All Began," and several other personal, transformational experiences in Appendix A.

The experience was spontaneous, happened in an instant, and offered immediate clarity and understanding of words I had been taught as a child many years earlier in Unitarian Sunday School: "But I say unto you, that ye resist not evil; but whosoever shall smite thee on thy right cheek, turn to him the other also." Matthew 5:39.

Nothing outside me changed. What changed was the way I understood those words. My consciousness had suddenly shifted, just as consciousness suddenly shifts when one sees a new image in an optical illusion.

LOVE
acrylic and enamel on canvas
John Langdon, 1999
used by permission

When I tried to conceptualize the mystical experience, I found myself faced with paradoxical questions I couldn't answer. Did I know or did I know nothing? Was my life the same or was it different?

I somehow "knew" in the sense that suddenly everything was clear, connected, and integrated. For the first time, I saw every detail of every moment with beauty and wonder. For the first time, I felt both ecstatic with understanding and entirely peaceful.

However, as soon as I tried to conceptualize the experience, there were no "right" words. There were many different words that expressed different aspects of the experience. There were words that pointed toward the experience. None of the words could fully capture it. As the 21st verse of the Tao states:

The Tao is elusive and intangible.
Although formless and intangible,
it gives rise to form.
Although vague and elusive,
it gives rise to shapes.
 Although dark and obscure,
it is the spirit, the essence,
the life breath of all things.

(Dyer, W., 2007). In short, you cannot capture it conceptually, but you can experience it and express it artistically.

My life was the same in the sense that I still washed clothes and cooked meals. However, the focus, appreciation, and attitude with which I performed those activities had totally changed. I was fully present in performing those activities. I was no longer doing them by rote while thinking about what clothes I needed to buy for my children the following day.

Emotionally, I felt ecstatic, passionate, and somehow driven to pass the clarity and understanding emanating from that experience on to others. As I began talking about the experience, I quickly realized that no one understood a word I was saying. That caused me to pull back and look at the words I was using, their contextual meanings, and ask, over and over again, why I was having this communication problem.

Mystical experiences are traditionally described as ineffable (James, 1902; Underhill, 2005). I was embarking on mission impossible. No matter what words I chose through which to express my experience, they were limited and partial.

I am still embarking on mission impossible, but I haven't stopped trying. If every person on this planet were to have a similar unifying, holistic experience, we would all be living together in peace, power, prosperity, understanding, compassion, and mutual support.

After noticing that my words were not communicating, a question arose—one with which I sat for many years: "How does one use analytical, divisive words to communicate a unifying, holistic experience?" The experience itself had a noetic quality or essence, yet as soon as I tried to conceptualize and verbalize it, that noetic quality disappeared.

As I delved into religious, spiritual, and philosophic literature in my search to discover how others had conceptualized similar experiences, I understood the contextual meanings of most of the different words I read, but each set of words was focusing on a different aspect of the experience or conceptualizing it differently. There was a sense in which the concepts were fingers pointing at the moon. There was another sense, when the concepts became solidified into doctrinal truths worshiped by believers, that they were nothing but illusions and false idols. When that happened, the words became more important than the experiential meanings and functional, ethical conduct toward which they pointed.

It was as if we were all part of a moving picture, when suddenly someone detached himself from the flow, stopped the flow at a single frame, became a subject looking at an object, and mentally separated the parts of the "object" so he could understand and analyze it. He may have mentally understood that single frame in great depth, but while he was focusing on that single frame, he was missing all the rest of the movie that continued to flow by, carrying him with it.

Perhaps all words are illusions, mine included. This does not mean they are not *useful*— for understanding our lives, giving meaning to our lives, and communicating with one another.

However, words are only useful if our intention is to use their power to understand ourselves and one another, to deepen the meanings of our lives, and to communicate more clearly. If our intention is to use words to shame, judge, or manipulate one another, we only create tension, suffering, and dysfunction.

As I read Zen Buddhist literature, I realized that the Zen Buddhists were often using analytic, divisive words, not to *talk about* the unifying, holistic experience, but to *facilitate* it in others. This was an entirely different use of language requiring different words and methodologies. I then toyed with a new question: "How does one use analytical, divisive words, not to *communicate* a unifying holistic experience, but to *facilitate* a unifying, holistic experience?" At that point, I was equating the word "communicate" with the words "talk about" and making a distinction between using words to talk about the experience and using words to help make it happen.

I have now returned to the original question that was given to me to answer: How does one use analytic, divisive words, to *communicate* a unifying holistic experience. The reasons for this return are threefold:

1. There seems to be no good reason to change the original form of the words. It focuses on the way we *use* words, the *intention* with which we apply them, and the dichotomy between dualistic words and a unifying holistic experience.

2. One of my advisers thinks that academics, my audience for this dissertation, may react adversely to the word "facilitate." It is not my intention to ruffle feathers. It is only my intention to open minds.

3. Clear communication *is* facilitation. It makes a concept easier to understand and apply.

Through my study of religious, spiritual, and philosophical texts, I became acutely aware of how masters of religion, spirituality, philosophy, and language used their words to engage their audiences and initiate them onto a path of personal discovery and self-mastery. Engaging a listener was the first step toward clearer communication. As Underhill (2005) states, "His audience must be bewitched as well as addressed, caught up to something of his state, before they can be made to understand." Is this not the use of *Rhetorica*, as illustrated in Plato's *Phaedrus*? (2012).

Each unique master engaged his listener in a unique way. Socrates used questions and dialogue. Moses used the Ten Commandments. Jesus used parables. Hindu masters used mantras. Christians used rituals. Rumi and Kahlil Gibran used poetry, imagery and metaphor. Hermann Hesse used novels. Zen Buddhists used paradox. Friedrich Nietzsche used thesis and antithesis to point toward a synthesis that transcends words and concepts.

Each method was context and culture specific. All were carefully crafted to shift the listener into a more open-minded, self-respectful, and other-respectful state of consciousness.

Through my study and practice of law, I became aware of the different levels of depth through which a topic can be conceptualized. Legal texts frequently have several tables of contents, each with a different degree of detail. For example, the summary table of contents might include the topic Constitutional Law. A more detailed table of contents under Constitutional Law might include the First Amendment, the Second Amendment, the Third Amendment, etc. An even more detailed table of contents under each Amendment might include the texts of specific cases discussing each amendment as applied to a particular factual situation.

Any conceptualization can be developed at any level of detail. The level of detail I offer in this dissertation will vary, depending on my own interest in the topic. It may or may not meet the reader's desire for more detailed development of a particular topic. I see no way around this dissonance in communication other than to note the dissonance and open it up as a focus for future research and dialogue.

## Why This Would be an Original and Substantive Contribution

If I focus on my own life experiences, the fact that I have personally experienced many consciousness-shifting experiences and spent years thinking and reading about these experiences and the words used to articulate them automatically makes this an original contribution. No one else on this planet has my genes, my rearing, my education, and my life experiences and perspectives. How many people on this planet are a mystic, a divorcee, a widow, a mother, a grandmother, a poet, an author, and a retired attorney? How many people on this planet have broken boards with their hand, eaten fire, walked on hot coals with their bare feet, and, with a partner, bent a steel rebar using only their necks?

This does not mean that my contributions are better than others. It simply means they are original and unique.

If I focus instead on the words written by Carol Roberts (2010) in *the Dissertation Journey* where she describes a doctoral dissertation as "an original contribution to theory or practice," and her further clarification of the meaning of the term "original," as implying "some novel twist, fresh perspective, new hypothesis, or innovative method that makes the dissertation project a distinctive contribution," (12%), I believe what I write here will be an original contribution in a different way. While I don't offer a new hypothesis about language, I do offer a new twist to an old

243

hypothesis (that words structure experience) by connecting mystical experiences, language, and non-dual consciousness. I have created several diagrams to illustrate my theories about consciousness, which I have discussed in the section entitled Conceptual or Theoretical Framework. To my knowledge, these diagrams are also original. I also offer a fresh perspective on the writings of Friedrich Wilhelm Nietzsche, that, to my knowledge, no one has ever offered before. And finally, I have recreated some 2,000-year-old archetypal stories of human dynamics within the cultural context of the 20th and 21st centuries.

It might be useful here to comment briefly on the concept of adding my brick to the great wall of knowledge. I have heard this repeated many times over the past several months by advisers telling me to limit my focus to a narrow topic.

When I research "brick in the great wall of knowledge" on the Internet, it appears to apply primarily to scientific research. In that kind of "objective" research context, the metaphor may make sense. If I have to apply it to the subjective, qualitative kind of research I have done and continue to do, the only way I can think of my brick in the great wall of knowledge is as follows.

There are seven billion people on this planet. If, as this dissertation posits, each one of those seven billion people is unique, with different genes, cultural conditioning, rearing, education, opportunities, and lifetime experiences, and if, as this dissertation also posits, each sees the world from a slightly different perspective, then each of those seven billion people has a unique brick to contribute to the great wall of knowledge. I am only one of those seven billion people. Yet, my unique perspective is the brick I can contribute.

This will be a substantive contribution if, and only if, as a species, we mutually decide to set an intention to co-create a peaceful, powerful, prosperous planet. If our conscious or unconscious individual and collective intentions are to use power over rather than power with, to treat one another as objects, to control one another, to wage war against one another, to exacerbate climate change, and to decimate ourselves and our planet, this dissertation is useless.

If our mutual intention is to co-create a peaceful, powerful, prosperous planet, this dissertation can offer major clarifications and understandings about how we use words and concepts and how we can use them more effectively to co-create a more sustainable and harmonious world that has the potential to nurture every living being, both individually and collectively. It can also offer major clarifications of the experiential meanings of words used by spiritual masters and philosophers throughout history. This dissertation would then make a substantive contribution to the *meanings* of words and concepts, the *meanings* of our lives, clear communication, aligned intention, co-creative dialogue, and dynamic co-creative interaction to manifest almost anything we desire. It would strongly support freedom of speech and thought as well as freedom of action as long as the action was non-violent. It would also open up unlimited opportunities for creative research, both quantitatively and qualitatively, to further enhance our individual and collective wellbeing.

# Research Question/Thesis

## Research Question

How does one use analytic, divisive words to communicate a unifying, holistic experience?

## Thesis

Words and concepts structure experience. Each of us uses words differently, even when our words structure the same experience.

## The Social Problems

Misunderstanding, hurt feelings, suffering, unclear and inadequate communication, fighting over right and wrong words, using words to intimidate, manipulate, and control, physical violence, using power over rather than power with.

## Author's Philosophical Worldviews

In *Research Design* (Creswell, J., 2014), John Creswell suggests that individuals preparing a research proposal make explicit the larger philosophical ideas they espouse. He recommends:

- The philosophical worldview proposed in the study
- A definition of basic ideas of that worldview
- How the worldview shaped their approach to research

I prefer to present these in a different order, beginning with how my life experiences shaped my worldviews, intertwined with how those worldviews shaped my approach to research, followed by the four philosophical worldviews proposed by Creswell, and finally, within the context of

Creswell's conceptual structure, a focus on those worldviews with which I most agree. To give more focus to my own worldview, I will also briefly discuss the three questions that Kate Turabian states dissertations try to answer and offer my own answers.

My worldview can be viewed as my bias. From a legal perspective, it can be viewed as my position.

There have been three major patterns in my life: (1) a love of exploration, learning, and problem-solving, (2) a low level of tolerance for dysfunctional authority, and (3) a love of words and their ability to help me process, reframe, and clarify my experiences and give meaning to my life.

**Love of Exploration, Learning, and Problem-Solving**

I was always an excellent student, even though I never tried. I just played and explored.

My parents, while holding the official titles of fourth grade teacher and high school music teacher, were far more than teachers. They were educators. They knew how to draw out the best in the daughter they had birthed. They held her safely within a stable, functional, and creative family environment. It is what I term a "power with" environment.

In Unitarian Sunday School, we read stories from the Bible. We were invited to think about how miracles might be explained in ways other than by supernatural intervention.

In high school, I loved geometry because it was visual and integrative. I could see how the theorems and corollaries all fit together. I tutored another student for a semester. She said she learned more from me than from our teacher.

Like Ken Wilber (2000), my own particular theoretical orientation has developed primarily from my own experiences, thinking about those experiences, reading the words of others who appear to have had similar experiences, and dialoging with others who have brought their own original ideas in for cross-fertilization.

While I could position the content of this dissertation within the non-dual level of consciousness in Wilber's upper left quadrant in his Theory of Everything (Wilber, 2000), I prefer to think of it as an independent and frequently parallel process that has evolved my own thinking to similar conclusions. When positioned as a parallel process, it is simply a different experiential path to the same end result. Thought of this way, it is simply a triangulation that supports many of Wilber's conclusions and perhaps offers a further synthesis of Wilber's concepts through a focus on words and what we do with them.

A *conceptual* understanding of what we do with words can synthesize all concepts from all cultures and all time periods. An *experiential* understanding of what we do with words transcends words and concepts. We then function from a State of Being that I term Non-Dual Consciousness. (For diagrams and a more detailed discussion of Non-Dual Consciousness, see Conceptual and Theoretical Framework below.) Non-Dual Consciousness can *use* dualistic words and concepts creatively and effectively to manifest peace, power, and prosperity on this planet.

According to Wilber (2000, 46-47), ". . . males tend to make judgments using ranking or hierarchical thinking, whereas women tend to make judgments using linking or relational thinking." As I woman, I agree that my own thought processes are inherently relational rather than hierarchical. However, I have also been exposed to the *use* of hierarchical thinking during my 22 years of law practice and can use it when necessary and appropriate.

## Low Level of Tolerance for Dysfunctional Authority

This has been, and continues to be, a major pattern in my life. Perhaps it is because, as a woman, my thought processes are innately relational rather than hierarchical. Perhaps it is because I was fortunate enough to be reared in a family that modeled functional authority. Perhaps it is because my Unitarian upbringing encouraged skepticism of anything that didn't make sense. Perhaps it is because my undergraduate liberal arts college, Swarthmore, introduced me to the functional, contemplative, and informative meditative silence and emergent speech of a Quaker Meeting.

Whatever the factors that contributed to my low level of tolerance for dysfunctional authority, it is clearly part of who I am. It has led me along a very challenging life path.

My educator parents used authority in functional ways—ways that benefited everyone. They used "power with." As I began interacting with people outside my family, I learned that not everyone uses authority in functional ways. All too many try to use "power over" to mask their subconscious fears and insecurities.

When I was three years old, the little girl next door tried to bully me. I can remember physically grappling with her on the floor of our garage. My parents wanted me to learn to fight my own battles and successfully defend myself. Instead of interfering, they stood on the sidelines and cheered. I punched and kicked so hard that the neighbor's child fled in tears. I knew I was being supported as I defended myself against the abusive attack of another three-year-old. "Power over" was all that she understood. "Power over" was what her own parents had taught her.

In ninth grade, I was editor of the junior high school newspaper. I wrote an editorial about freedom of speech. The teacher in charge of the newspaper rewrote what I'd written, explaining why what I'd written was "wrong." She stated that she would be publishing the "corrected" version, but would be kind enough to publish it under my name.

For the first time in my life, I experienced Kali rage—totally out of character with my family experience and the model student I believed myself to be. Fury contorted my face. Tears flooded my eyes. My voice exploded, "You wrote it. You put *your* name on it." Then I stormed out of the room, slammed the door, retreated to the girls' bathroom, locked myself in a stall, and sobbed.

During my years of law practice, my low level of tolerance for dysfunctional authority was tested many times as I dealt with local New Jersey politicians and unaccountable clients. See Appendix A for narratives of two of those experiences, one with an Atlantic City Councilman and one with an Avalon Police Officer and Code Enforcement Official.

**Love of Words and Their Ability to Help Me Process, Reframe, and Clarify My Experiences**

In junior high school, I was newspaper editor. In senior high school, I was yearbook co-editor. My writing always flowed creatively from my own perceptions and experiences. I learned how to play with words, embellishing them with my imagination. What a joyful dance with words!

It was only many years later, after I had my first sudden, unexpected mystical experience, that my attention turned to the words themselves, their many different contextual meanings, and the many different creative ways I could use them to structure and communicate my perceptions, emotions, and experiences in order to shift and expand both my own consciousness and that of others. My own consciousness had shifted to a subject/object duality. Before, I had simply played, allowing the words to flow through me. Now I stepped back into a Witness role and began analyzing the words and their effects. Now, I was playing with a very serious focus and intention—personal growth for both myself and those with whom I came in contact.

My 22 years of law practice further deepened my understanding of how words could be used creatively to make a point and win an argument. Asking the right question was vital to getting the answer one needed. Knowing where to focus and how to structure an argument were also essential. The law practice taught me many word skills, as well as deepening my understanding of archetypal human dynamics.

**Philosophical Worldviews Proposed In This Study**

In *Research Design* (Creswell, J., 2014), John Creswell distinguishes four worldviews or sets of beliefs that determine a research approach:

1. Postpositivist
2. Constructivist
3. Transformative
4. Pragmatist

From my perspective, these are not necessarily clear cut, separate categories. However, if I must choose a primary worldview, I would choose Pragmatism, with Constructivism a close second. Some of Creswell's definitions for Postpositivism and Transformativism also apply to my worldview.

According to Creswell (2014), pragmatic researchers are concerned with application—what works and solutions to problems. Instead of focusing on methods, researchers emphasize research problems and use all approaches available to understand the problem. Pragmatism "arises out of actions, situations, and consequences rather than antecedent conditions." (10). It focuses "attention on the research problem in social science research and then (uses) pluralistic approaches to derive knowledge about the problem." (11).

In this dissertation, I am clearly focused on two related research problems: how does one use analytic, divisive words to communicate a unifying, holistic experience, and how does one use analytic, divisive words to create a peaceful, powerful, prosperous planet? One focus is on the individual. The other is on the collective. I am equally focused on solutions to these interrelated problems. What words work? I have used many experiential and conceptual approaches to understand these problems.

According to Creswell (2014), pragmatism is not committed to any one system of philosophy and reality. Individual researchers have freedom of choice as to methods, techniques, and procedures of research that best meet their needs and purposes. Truth is what works at the time. Pragmatist researchers look at an intended consequence—where they want to go. They look at the social, historical, political, and other contexts. They believe they need to stop asking questions about reality and the laws of nature. Pragmatism opens the door to multiple methods, different worldviews, and different assumptions, as well as different forms of data collection and analysis (10-11).

My pluralistic approach to research fits quite comfortably within the category of pragmatism. I am also quite clear about where I want to go. I want to be part of the co-creation of a peaceful, powerful, prosperous, sustainable planet. I also understand from my years of practicing law, as well as my years of exploring my own consciousness, how important it is to ask the right questions to get the answers you need. Asking the wrong questions simply sends the mind spinning around in endless circles of non-productivity. Two of the most productive questions any of us can ask are: (1) What is my intention, right here, right now? (2) How am I going to manifest it in a non-violent way?

According to Creswell (2014), constructivists believe that individuals seek understanding of the world in which they live and work. Individuals develop subjective meanings of their experiences. These meanings are varied, multiple, and complex rather than narrow and categorized. Meaning matters and frequently emerges out of discussions or interactions with other persons. Studies take place within historical and cultural settings. Researchers recognize that their own backgrounds shape their interpretation. They position themselves in the research to acknowledge how their interpretation flows from their personal, cultural, and historical experiences. The research process is conducted inductively. Theories or patterns of meaning emerge as the research progresses.

Creswell's descriptions of constructivism clearly describe my own theoretical and practical positioning. I have used an inductive process to understand my consciousness-shifting experiences. Theories and patterns of meaning around words and concepts have emerged. The meanings have been subjective, varied, multiple, and complex. Many meanings have emerged out of discussions or reading the writings of others. Historical and cultural settings are always part of the relevant experiential context.

Creswell's statements about Postpositivism that reflect my own worldviews are that knowledge is conjectural. Absolute Truth can never be found—at least not conceptually. (I would, however, posit that what has been termed "Absolute Truth"—something I would term Non-Dual Consciousness—can be experienced and spoken from.) Evidence established in research is always imperfect and fallible. (This dissertation is imperfect, fallible, and incomplete.) Researchers do not prove a hypothesis. Rather they indicate a failure to reject the hypothesis. Research is the process of making claims and then refining or abandoning some of them for other claims more strongly warranted.

The aspect of Postpositivism that most strongly supports this dissertation is that I know I cannot prove my hypothesis. I can marshal evidence to support it, just as a lawyer gathers evidence with which to support her case, but I cannot prove it. The verdict is up to the jury of world citizens who will have to decide for themselves whether or not the hypothesis and its corollaries make sense and whether or not they want to use the suggested practical applications to co-create a peaceful, powerful, prosperous planet.

While I cannot prove my hypothesis, at the same time, I cannot disprove it. I welcome the input of anyone who believes they can.

Creswell's statements about Transformativism that reflect my own worldviews are that the inquirer is concerned about issues of power and social justice, discrimination, and oppression; researchers are critical theorists and participatory action researchers; and the research contains an action agenda for reform. This is not very different from the Pragmatist's worldview that truth is whatever works.

I am very concerned about issues of power and social justice, discrimination, and oppression. In my particular case, the focus has been primarily on discrimination against and oppression of females, because I have personally experienced so much of it. I see it as emanating from the almost uncontrollable male, biological sexual drive and perceived need to ensure that a sexual supply is always available. To ensure a constant sexual supply, men have, for centuries, disempowered women by paying them less or no money for their labor, refusing to allow them to own land, and refusing to educate them. Women have enabled this dysfunction by accepting and submitting to it.

However, that narrow focus is not the subject of this dissertation. The broader focus is whether, both individually and as a species, we intend to use power over or power with. Power with includes refusing to enable power over. It means knowing how to set boundaries and limits on what we will and will not do. In short, it means living a life of integrity. The path is not easy.

**Questions that Researchers Ask and My Answers**

According to Kate L. Turabian (2013) in *A Manual for Writers of Research Papers, Theses, and Dissertations*, there are three kinds of questions that researchers ask:

1. Conceptual questions: what should we think? (The answers to those questions don't tell us how to change the world, but they do help us understand it better.)

2. Practical questions: what should we do? (Practical questions are most common outside the academic world, especially in business.)

3. Applied research questions: what must we understand before we know what to do? (This raises the question whose answer is not the solution to a practical problem but only a step toward it.)

My answer to question one is simple. We should think whatever we want. Thinking is creative and constantly changes.[96]

My answer to question two is almost as simple. We should do whatever we want, as long as we do not hurt either ourselves or others.[97]

---

[96] A more focused form of this question would be: What should we think about (focus of interest) if our intention is . . . An example would be: what should we think about war if our intention is to create peace. The more focused question may well have a specific answer based on the structure of the question and the empirical data and research. At least, there could be an answer in the sense that the perceptions of all researchers agree.

[97] I am indebted to A.S. Neill's *Summerhill* (1960) for this idea. I am well aware that the words are simply a general guideline. They are only fingers pointing at the moon, but fingers that have been immensely helpful to me. However, in a particular circumstance, what is hurtful and what is helpful may not be easy to discern. Choosing a course of

My simple answer to the third question is that we must understand why and how we use words before we know what to do. Unpacking the *meaning* of that answer is fraught with paradox, because I have to *use* words to discuss the dichotomy between words and experience. If I can adequately articulate a theory of why and how we use words and concepts, that understanding would open up limitless opportunities for additional creative research and application within a societal context of non-violence, creative dialogue, and free exchange of information.

Clearly, I have no intention of undertaking all the creative research that could be undertaken once we understand what we do with words and the dichotomy between concepts and experience. I don't have enough physical years left in my life. I don't have the skills or education in many fields of endeavor, such as health, biology, physics, or chemistry. I leave that creative research to the passionate minds and hearts of others more highly trained than I in specific fields of inquiry.

---

action that benefits all is ideal, but not always possible without pain to some.

## Conceptual or Theoretical Framework

My personal experiences, the conceptual framework, the literature review, and the research methods have all evolved together. In short, I have moved back and forth among these focuses in very practical ways. Each focus has informed the others.

It has been very much like putting together the pieces of a jigsaw puzzle, grouping similar patterns together and figuring out how they all fit. They *do* fit, although not necessarily in ways that are emotionally comfortable.

It is the position of this dissertation that the noticing we call "consciousness" underlies all concepts, including mine. If consciousness is, in fact, the noticing from which all concepts arise, it cannot be defined. To define means to limit. Consciousness has no limits.

It *can*, however, be experienced, spoken from, and expanded. It can also give our lives meaning. Sudden shifts in consciousness can give our lives transformational meaning. What we term "consciousness" can be conceptualized in many different ways, depending on the intention of the speaker or writer.

This noticing or awareness that psychologists and philosophers call "consciousness" (De Quincey, C., 2011, 13%) has been conceptualized throughout religious and spiritual history using many different terms. Jews call it YHWH, Christians call it God, Muslims call it Allah, Buddhists call it Awareness, Taoists call it the Tao. Hindus seem to be more focused on the many aspects through which "consciousness" manifests: a variety of religious beliefs, rituals, Gods, Goddesses, and festivals. Aristotle's editor called it "metaphysics."

One of the intentions of this dissertation is to synthesize theories or concepts into a unified whole where each fits and has meaning. To do this, we need to understand these concepts or theories in their proper experiential context and clarify the author's intention. The position of this dissertation is that the general, psychological intention of any particular author is will to power or will to life.

Will to power can be exercised either "over others" or "with others." Saints and mystics, who have struggled along the path to Non-Dual Consciousness, have exercised it "with others." They have been through enough Dark Nights of the Soul to understand that if, as a species, we are going to survive, there is no other choice.

Both "consciousness" and the words that attempt to conceptualize it cut across all disciplines. Obviously, a single dissertation cannot analyze in depth the experiential context, author intentions, and linguistic choices of every single theory or concept that has ever been developed. It is not the intention of this dissertation to do so. It *is* the intention of this dissertation to offer an integral theory and simple practices within which concepts can be developed and research performed, while simultaneously honoring ourselves and others through dialogue, collaboration, non-violence, and "power with."

In the Literature Review, I have selectively chosen to review, with one exception, only those seminal writings which have given me great clarity in understanding my own transformational experiences. The exception is Evelyn Underhill's *Mysticism* (2005). I include that book because it is a recent treatment of mysticism that many consider a classic. It is my intention both to applaud the well-written parts and to question the parts that appear to me to be less than fully understood.

The fact that I do not review every book written on the topics that interest me does not mean that other books are less important. I may never have read some very significant writings. I do not know Hebrew, Aramaic, or Sanskrit. However, the fact that I have not read every book ever written about language, mysticism, or non-dual consciousness does not, in my view, negate the conclusions I reach. As Wilber (2000) notes when discussing his Maps of the Kosmos, ". . . the basic *capacity* for integral, second-tier thinking does not demand that you master all these different maps. You do not have to memorize the various levels, or know all of the civilization blocks we will discuss . . ." (109).

Underhill (2005) states: "The true mystic—the person with a genius for God—hardly needs a map himself. He steers a compass course across the 'vast and stormy sea of the divine.'" (75).

Similarly, it is my position that I don't need to read every book that has ever been written on every subject I discuss. Intimately knowing the territory frequently makes maps unnecessary and irrelevant, particularly when the maps have been developed, not from the territory itself but from other people's maps. The books and practices that have added depth to my understanding of the territory and helped me navigate it better are included in my Literature Review.

As I've moved along what I call my "spiritual path," I have intuitively used a qualitative research approach. There are many methods within that approach, and I have used most of them depending on my intention, focus, and resources of the moment. I have occasionally used logic. I have used induction and deduction. I have not used quantitative research methods, because I have no training or experience in those methods. That does not mean they could not be used by others who do have that training and experience. (For example, interesting quantitative studies might measure the changes in brain waves, blood pressure, or pulse before and after a person performs the practices of Ho'oponopono, meditation, or prayer.) The multi-method approach I have used has allowed me to triangulate processes and conclusions to support their validity and credibility.

As previously stated, I can position this dissertation conceptually within Ken Wilber's non-dual, transpersonal or spiritual wave in his Upper Left Quadrant (Personal, Subjective, Intentional, first person singular language). I will discuss Wilber's Four Quadrant Theory or Theory of Everything in the Literature Review below. That positioning may be appropriate conceptually. If, however, as this dissertation posits, the *experience* of non-dual consciousness is the ground from which all concepts arise, then perhaps Wilber's Four Quadrant Theory should be positioned within experiential non-dual consciousness, as should the concepts presented in this dissertation. Both can then be thought of as Creative Dual Consciousness emanating from a State of Non-Dual Consciousness. See diagrams and discussion below.

If we use Wilber's Four Quadrant Theory as our conceptual map; if I position this dissertation within Wilber's non-dual wave of the Upper Left Quadrant; if we then zoom into that non-dual wave of the Upper Left

Quadrant, Figure 1 below is a single, pictorial representation of a more focused Conceptual or Theoretical Framework for this dissertation.

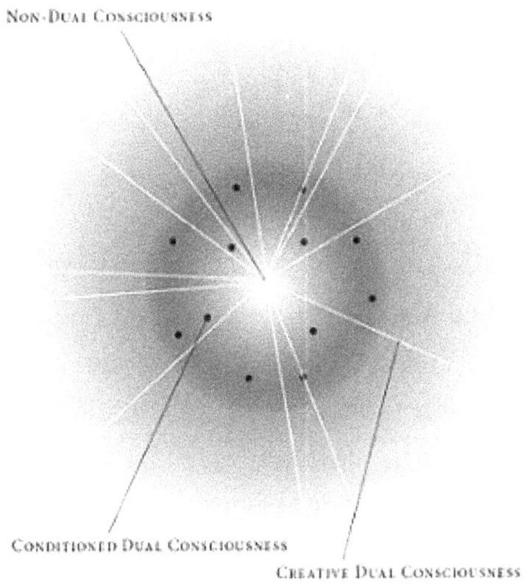



*Figure 1*. Consciousness diagram. This figure illustrates the relationships among Non-Dual Consciousness, Conditioned Dual Consciousness, and Creative Dual Consciousness.

A newborn baby begins physical life in Non-Dual Consciousness. In the child's first year, Mommy and Daddy eagerly teach the child words: Mommy, Daddy, ball, milk, toy. These words are useful for purposes of transmitting learned meaning and enhancing communication. However, they are still human concepts created by human minds. This is where Conditioned Dual Consciousness begins.

Words divide. They focus the child's mind on a single aspect of the whole and distinguish that aspect from other aspects. Beyond that, the child is taught that the words stand for something "out there" that is real. That certainly appears to be true.

That is not to say that this kind of distinguishing is not useful for particular purposes. It clearly is. We just need to be aware of what we're doing.

"Stop!" may prevent a child from running out into the street in front of an oncoming car. "Please get dressed now," ensures that the child is ready when the school bus arrives.

However, as the child matures, he notices that many different words and concepts are abstract and unclear. Some appear to be opposites: right and wrong, good and bad, knowledge and ignorance. Perhaps the child is spanked if he doesn't do the "right" thing—if he dares to defy Mommy and Daddy. This may initiate emotions of fear and anger. Perhaps the child is praised when he picks up his clothes and puts them in the laundry basket. This may initiate emotions of pride and self-righteousness. The child's parents, aunts, uncles, grandparents, teachers, and friends are constantly conditioning his conduct and concepts. The concepts he ought to believe are separated from the concepts he is not allowed to believe. He gets stuck in one of the little black dots of Conditioned Dual Consciousness in the above diagram. Of course, the parents and teachers who taught him are also stuck in one of those little black dots of Conditioned Dual Consciousness.

As the child begins school and moves out into the larger community, he notices that other children don't believe what his family taught him to believe. His Catholic friends have been taught one set of concepts, his Buddhist friends another, and his Jewish friends a third. Which concepts are right? Which concepts are wrong? He has lost his connection with Non-Dual Consciousness, as have his friends, and finds himself in painful and conflicted situations. Emotionally, he has shifted into a situation where everyone is fighting over whose concepts are right and whose concepts are wrong. Figure 2, below, depicts what has happened.

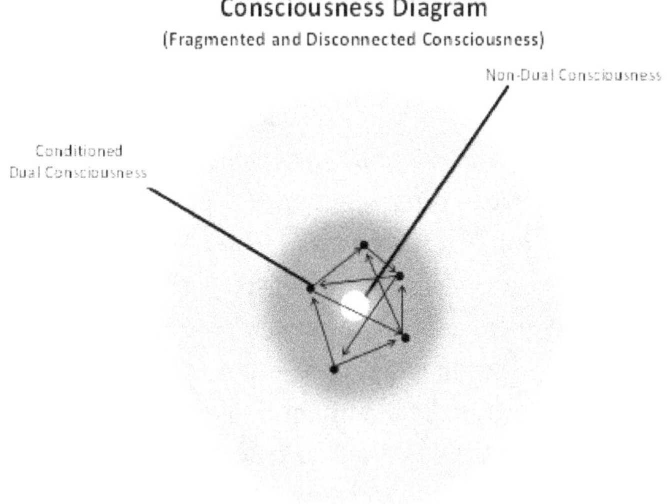


*Figure 2*. Consciousness diagram (fragmented and disconnected consciousness). This figure illustrates what happens when humans become separated from Non-Dual Consciousness by "Eating of the Tree of Knowledge" and creating dualistic language.

Everyone is stuck in Conditioned Dual Consciousness. People are calling one another names, hitting one another, and killing one another as they fight over whose words are right, whose words are wrong, who knows, who is ignorant, who is good, who is evil, and who has the "right" conception of "Reality." People are fighting wars against terror, wars against cancer, and wars against poverty. No one is living in peace, health, and abundance. No one is connected with Non-Dual Consciousness.

Throughout history, an occasional person has experienced an unexpected consciousness shift. He suddenly sees life from new perspectives, perhaps from somebody else's black dot of Conditioned Dual Consciousness. Perhaps he tries something new and different and it works. He moves from one black dot in the diagram to another, looking at "what is" from different perspectives. The meanings of words shift as he understands those meanings from new perspectives and within new experiential contexts. Relationships shift. The meaning of life shifts.

No one knows where these consciousness shifts come from or why they happen. They are mental events, not physical events, yet they happen within the context of our everyday physical lives. William James (1994), in *The Varieties of Religious Experience*, states that the experience is passive. Christians conceptualize it as the Grace of God. The Buddha, after years of searching, simply said, "I am aware." Is the fact that these events are mental events rather than physical events the underpinning of the philosophical school of Idealism?

The person who experiences such a consciousness shift feels driven to communicate it, but there are no right words. There are only creative words.

Attempts to conceptualize the experience are nevertheless made. Because the words are creative, they are all different. To someone stuck in Conditioned Dual Consciousness there is a great temptation to turn the words of someone speaking creatively from Non-Dual

Consciousness into "right words" as well as rules and doctrines that must be obeyed at any cost. The words then become yet another dysfunctional use of "power over."

To the extent that any of the major world religions or spiritual traditions understands that its words are creative but not right, the Consciousness Diagram looks like Figure 3.

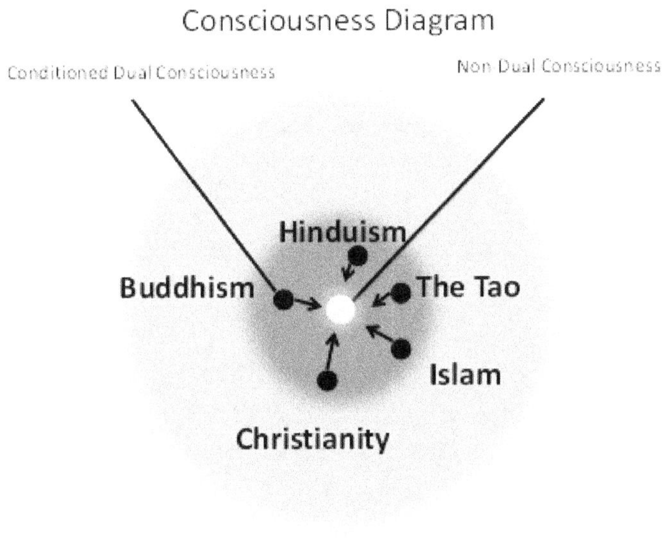

*Figure 3.* Consciousness diagram of functional religion. Functional religion recognizes that its words are guides for reconnecting with Non-Dual Consciousness. They are not Truth.

To the extent that any of the major world religions or spiritual traditions does not understand that their doctrines are creative but rather pontificates that they are somehow the only true and right words using "power over" to enforce their beliefs, the Consciousness Diagram reverts to Figure 2.

Every person who has released Conditioned Dual Consciousness and returned to alignment with Non-Dual Consciousness can speak or write *using* Dual Consciousness words in new and creative ways to shift the consciousness of those still stuck in Conditioned Dual Consciousness and help them realign with Non-Dual Consciousness. He always uses "power with." The Consciousness Diagram then looks like Figure 4.

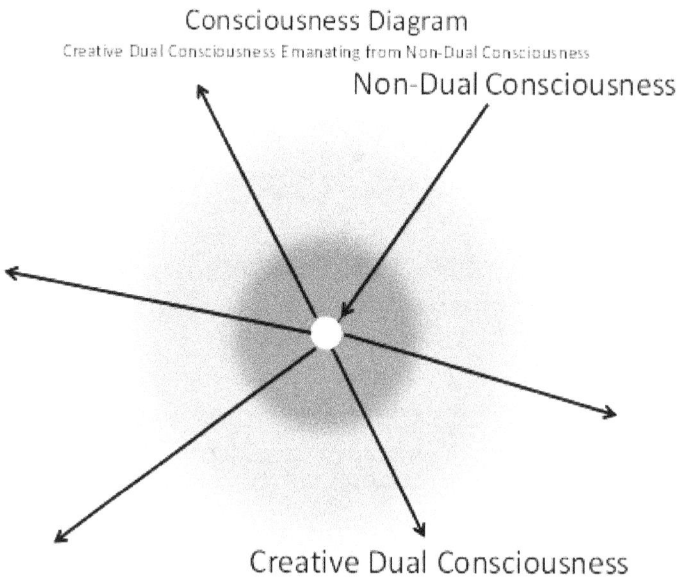

*Figure 4.* Consciousness diagram (creative dual consciousness emanating from non-dual consciousness). This diagram illustrates what happens when a human reconnects with Non-Dual Consciousness. She can then *use* dualistic words in many different ways to create in the physical world. The intention is always to shift people stuck in conditioned dual consciousness into a reconnection

with Non-Dual Consciousness so that they, too, can become co-creators in functional ways.

If each and every person were to live in Creative Dual Consciousness aligned with Non-Dual Consciousness, we would shift, as a global community, into Co-Creative Dual Consciousness. Each person would be thinking for herself. Each person would be respectfully sharing creative thoughts with others. The Consciousness Diagram would then look like Figure 5.



*Figure 5*. Consciousness diagram. (Co-creative dual consciousness emanating from non-dual consciousness). This figure illustrates what our world would be like if everyone on the planet were reconnected with Non-Dual Consciousness. We would no longer be fighting over whose words were right and whose words were wrong. We would simply be exchanging information and perspectives to solve problems and benefit all to the greatest extent possible.

How interesting that this diagram looks something like Internet images of the Vedic/Hindu/Buddhist Cosmology of Indra's web.

Retrieved from http://webofliz.files.wordpress.com

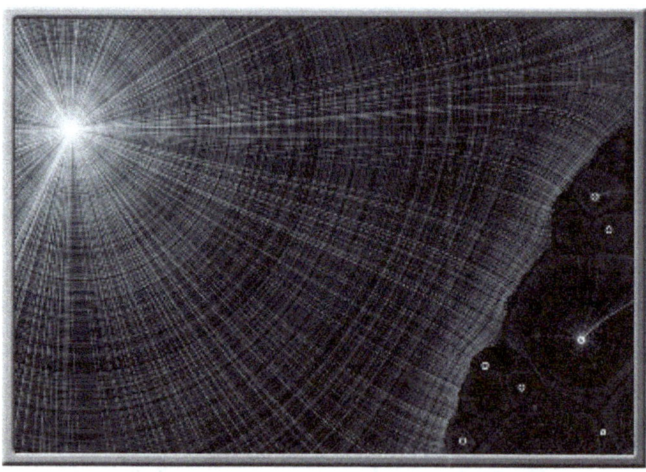

Retrieved from http://shop.toporek.com

This may also be thought of as Teihard de Chardin's Noosphere where information and creative thoughts are freely exchanged and shared in an atmosphere of clear speaking, deep listening, and mutual respect.

**Ethical Considerations**

Within the context of this dissertation, I am not planning to do any case studies involving other people. My case study has been and is my own life and spiritual path. This does not mean that case studies could not be done to support or discredit the thinking in this dissertation. They certainly could and probably should be done by social scientists far more skilled than I in designing and performing case studies. However, because I am not personally planning to develop my dissertation through case studies, I do not need to be concerned with the usual ethical concerns surrounding use of other people in my study.

What I *do* need to be concerned about is the other people who played active roles in my narratives. Since my intention in telling these narratives is to elucidate meaningful, archetypal human interactions and dynamics and the consequences of particular human action choices, it is not at all necessary to use real names that might identify the people who actually participated in these dynamics. It is not my intention to embarrass anyone. I will therefore be using pseudonyms or generic names.

**Research Process**

My research process began approximately 45 years ago when I had my first consciousness-shifting experience. See

Appendix A, "How It All Began." I couldn't stop thinking about what had happened and trying to understand it.

I can think of my research process as pure inductive thinking. I experienced something I didn't understand, wanted to understand, and couldn't stop thinking about. I read every relevant text I could get my hands on, started looking for patterns in my experience and the experiences of others, played with different ways of conceptualizing the experience, played with theories, tested the theories, revised the theories, and retested the theories. The process was and is open-ended, rife with possibilities for creative thinking. However, there is also a sense in which there was and is a conclusion. There is ultimately a "knowing" that we know nothing. We are simply creators—of words, of concepts, of human dynamics.

"Knowing this" confers a very special kind of knowledge. If I "know" I know nothing, I know that you also know nothing. Our words can then be used to exchange thoughts and understand one another's perspectives or alternatively, to engage in word skill games with life and death consequences for the thriving or extinction of our species on this planet. *Cf.* Hesse, H. *The Glass Bead Game.*

**Research Method or Approach**

One of the macro focuses of this dissertation is how we use words, the contextual meanings of our words, and our ability to communicate with one another using words. I distinguish this focus from one that purports to offer conceptual, objective truth. Clearly, this puts me in the camp of those questioning the absolute validity of reductionistic, logical, objective, cause-and-effect-oriented, deterministic

methods of research for all purposes. (See Atkinson, 2014).
I am *not* saying these methods and concepts are not *useful*
for *particular* purposes. Clearly, they are. However, it is the
position of this dissertation that they are not useful when
dealing with topics like mysticism, non-dual consciousness,
power relationships, or the meanings of words in
experiential context.

I would like to distinguish between the methodology I
used to reach my conclusions and the methodologies I have
been and will be using to communicate those conclusions to
others.

As stated in the previous section on research process, in
my attempts to understand my mystical experiences, I used
induction—what would be understood as a normal scientific
method. I had experienced a mental phenomenon—a
consciousness-shifting experience—that I could neither
understand nor conceptualize. I wanted to understand it and
conceptualize it, and I used every possible way I could think
of to do that. I thought about it. I tried repeating my own
personal conduct in new situations to see if the same thing
would happen. I read literature about similar experiences
others had had. I tried to talk about it with others. After much
trial and error, I understood a great deal about the
experience, about the human consciousness that tries to
conceptualize it, about human communication, and about
human power dynamics. I came to understand the dichotomy
between the experience—in fact, any experience—and the
words we use to conceptualize it. Ultimately, I was able to
formulate a hypothesis about what we humans do with words
and develop corollaries to that hypothesis. To the extent the
hypothesis and corollaries make sense to others, we can

collaborate to develop practices, applications, and structures that support both ourselves and one another in a living, breathing, dynamic community of unique human beings on a living, breathing, dynamic planet.

Communicating my conclusions requires the understanding of and the ability to use many different methodologies. Using Ken Wilber's Four Quadrant Theory as a conceptual framework (see more detailed discussion below in the Literature Review), what others will hear and understand will depend on the perspective and conditioning from which they are hearing my words. The optimal method of communication is one-on-one in the context of a particular situation, where I can choose to speak the worldview language and methodology of the other participant. However, within the context of a dissertation, I cannot use that optimal method of communication. I have to choose from a number of standardized, categorized, qualitative or quantitative research methods, as if there were only one form from which to speak. There is not. I view each of these methods simply as a conceptual lens through which we shape our experiences, give meaning to our lives, and communicate with one another.

I could use any of the *traditional*, qualitative research methods: narrative research, phenomenology, grounded theory, ethnography, case study, historical, reflexivity, philosophical, hermeneutic (Atkinson, 2014) (WU Dissertation Manual), given the fact that I am able to view the world through many lenses. I could also use any of the *emerging* qualitative research methods: arts-based research, organic inquiry, indigenous research, or integral methodological pluralism. (Atkinson, 2014).

If I shift my focus away from how best to communicate with an unknown readership and toward the most honest and high integrity form of writing I can use without knowing the level of consciousness of my readers or the extent to which my words and concepts will be heard, I have to use narrative autoethnography as a primary method. By doing so, I transparently own my own lenses and biases. This does not mean I will not use other methods as appropriate to particular discussions.

Narrative autoethnography would eliminate the subject/object duality I find so unconsciously conditioned into the traditional dissertation process and would allow me to write from a unified, integrated, state of non-dual consciousness. It would acknowledge up front my *use* of creative dual consciousness throughout this dissertation. That means I would not claim my words were true. They are simply word art. I *do* claim they have meaning and significance, in the same way that Hermann Hesse's *Siddhartha*, Kahlil Gibran's *The Prophet*, or Shakespeare's *Hamlet* have meaning and significance.

Ken Wilber says in part 8 of his video dialogue with Brother Wayne Teasdale about The Mystic Heart (downloaded from https://www.integrallife.com/future-christianity/mystic-heart), "The part of the public relations dilemma of coming up with integral spirituality, a spirituality that deals with these deeper, higher dimensions, is to find ways to present those to the world at large in a way that diffuses their very legitimate concern that this is some other form of ethnocentric, oppressive mythology and dogma." My concern in writing this dissertation is similar. I want to use words in a way that honors and includes all perspectives, both scientific and religious. It seems to me that viewing what I write as word art, not truth, is the optimal way to do this. It is not perfect.

In the same video, Stewart Davis, whom Ken Wilber describes as a brilliant singer/songwriter and integral, trans-rational musician, adds, "I do think that art is uniquely equipped to facilitate what you just described. . . . . I think there is a new kind of artistic technology that is being developed. . . . all human beings accessing and unfolding this artistic dimension of themselves to make this happen."

I will have to write extremely transparently and vulnerably to achieve any degree of credibility and validity. Any credibility I might achieve would come, not from the words themselves, but from whatever depth of meaning they might evoke for the reader. Can I find a way to communicate, in Martin Buber's words, from "I to Thou." (Buber, M., 1923).

To the extent I succeed, I will have communicated my mystical experience to others, not simply at a conceptual level, but at a deeper cellular, experiential level, where it ultimately can make a real ethical and moral difference, both individually and culturally. I may also include dialogue to broaden the autobiographical material out into a social and cultural context. It is the position of this dissertation that we are mirrors of one another. There are others who will be able to see through the same perceptual and conceptual lenses through which I see. Perhaps some of my lenses will offer them new ways of thinking and being. Whether or not others use these lenses is not in my hands.

As previously stated, when I look at my impactful religious, spiritual, and philosophical texts (my "Literature

Review"), there are certain forms of speaking and writing that are most often used by the greatest spiritual and philosophical masters: stories or parables (Jesus), questions and dialectic (Socrates), poetry (Hafiz, Kahlil Gibran, Rumi), novels (Hermann Hesse), thesis, antithesis, and synthesis (Hegel, Nietzsche). All are word art, not scientific, "objective," "conceptually true" analysis or theory.

In *Method Meets Art: Arts-Based Research Practice*, Leavy (2008) states that the artistic turn to narrative in the social sciences can be viewed as the evolution of more conventional research practices. If this is so, then autoethnographical writing may be on the cutting edge of the evolutionary research front.

Referencing Pinnegar and Danes (2007), Leavy notes four broad themes that pertain to the expansion of the qualitative paradigm: (1) the relationship of the researched to the researcher, (2) the move from numbers to words as data, (3) a shift from the general to the particular, and (4) the emergence of new epistemologies. (Leavy, P., 2009). If, as is the position of this dissertation, we live in a holographic universe, a focus on the details of any particular will be mirrored both in other particulars and in the whole. A focus on the details of any particular can bring clarity, not only to that particular, but also to other particulars and to the whole.

The relationship of the researched to the researcher is relevant to my concerns about the subject/object duality conditioned into traditional research processes. The use of words as data is equally relevant, since it is the position of this dissertation that all words are data, and the meanings of words shift depending on experiential context. This dissertation also suggests a new epistemology. After navigating years of challenging spiritual seas, we "know" we know nothing. We are only co-creators. Brought to our knees intellectually, we unshackle our power to co-create.

Autoethnographic methodology clearly focuses on the particular, at least as a starting point. That does not mean it cannot expand outward and embrace the general. To the extent that patterns in the particular are mirrored in other particulars, general cultural, archetypal, and anthropological patterns emerge.

It is also the position of this dissertation that "objective knowledge," per se, is an illusion, and the only *meaning* that can be given to the words "objective knowledge" is a tentative concept with which all agree that enhances understanding and enables us to function more effectively, both individually and in community.

Leavy (2009) describes autoethnographic narrative as follows:

Autoethnography is a method of self-study in which the researcher is viewed as a viable data source. Autoethnographic writing is distinct. Ellis (2004) notes, "*Autoethnography* refers to writing about the personal and its relationship to culture. It is an autobiographical genre of writing and research that displays multiple layers of consciousness" (p. 37, quoting Dumont, 1978, original emphasis). Pelias (2004) suggests the purpose of autoethnographic writing is *resonance* (p. 11). As with all arts-based research, this kind of writing creates "me too" moments for readers (Pelias, 2004). Moreover, this method accesses the "nexus of self and culture" using the "self as a springboard, as a witness" (p. 11).

Leavy (2009) adds:

As researchers working from critical perspectives such as feminism have challenged the subject-object, rational-emotional, and concrete-abstract dualisms that have historically guided social scientific inquiry, the space has opened for researchers to create methods and methodologies that not only account for a researcher's subjectivity but also refashion the researcher as the primary subject of investigation (or one of several overlapping sources of data).

While I consider myself and my mystical and transformational experiences as the primary subject of my investigation, I am not the only source of data, nor is autoethnography the only methodology I use. Numerous mystics have written about their experiences. Their words are also sources of data. I suspect that many philosophers and scientists were or are closet mystics. Their words, too, are sources of data.

Autoethnography allows me to use first person singular language. First person singular language is the language that Ken Wilber identifies with the Upper Left Quadrant of his Four Quadrant Theory, the individual, subjective quadrant of mysticism and Non-Dual Consciousness. (See a more detailed discussion in the Literature Review below.) It is also the only language I have discovered that I can use and still stay in integrity. (See a more detailed discussion in the Literature Review below under Al-Anon's Twelve Steps & Twelve Traditions.)

Referring to Jones (2006), Leavy notes that the surge in narrative inquiry is linked to increased awareness of the role social science has in maintaining or resisting current relations of power. Another layered macro theme of this dissertation is relations of power and the importance of maintaining collaborative relations of power rather than win/lose relations of power—what I term "power with" rather than "power over." Narrative inquiry rejects the "codified language" starkly used in academia and gives multi-layered meanings to words within experiential context.

The sharing of narratives in daily life occurs when a person wants to tell others "about something" and that something is "an event — something that happened" (Labov, 2006, p. 38). Clandinin and Connelly (1989) suggest that the term narrative inquiry "names a fundamental structuring and quality of experience, both personal and social." Narrative can be viewed as a frame through which people make sense of their lives.

The events I speak of are not physical events. They are mental events. The language we humans have developed to describe physical events is inadequate to describe mental events. We can do a translation of sorts by resorting to storytelling, poetry, symbolism, and metaphor with the intention of conveying meaning.

The narrative method is a collaborative method of telling stories, reflecting on stories, and (re)writing stories. Participants are simultaneously telling and retelling the stories as they are living them. They re-story or re-plot these stories through their own reflective process over the passage of time. What results is multidimensional meanings and authentic and compelling rendering of data. It relies on small sample studies with rich results. I have used this methodology extensively in my Appendices.

**Literature Review**

In *The Dissertation Journey* (Roberts, C., 2010), Carol Roberts suggests that the purpose of the literature review is to find out what is already known and what is unknown. (13%). Besides the fact that this stated purpose makes questionable epistemological assumptions, it has not been the intention with which I have conducted a literature review. I have conducted a literature review to understand my personal transformational experiences and find ways of conceptualizing them.

Focused on this intention, the literature review has become a major portion of my research. As Leavy (2009) suggests, both my own words and the words of authors discussed in the Literature Review become data to be explored. The data offer thick descriptions of human experiences with multiple layers of meaning. My focus is not on the truth or falsehood of what has been written. Rather, my focus is on the experiential context from which it was written and the possible experiential meanings of the written words that also give form and meaning to my own transformational experiences.

There are a few pieces of seminal literature that have given me great clarity as I have moved through my transformational experiences and the process of making sense of them. While I have read many more books than those presented in this Literature Review, it is my intention here to focus only on those that have offered me sudden and exceptional clarity or confirmation. As previously stated, the single exception to this focus of limiting my literature review to seminal literature that has given me great clarity and understanding is a book by Evelyn Underhill (2005),

*Mysticism: A Study in Nature and Development of Spiritual Consciousness*. While parts of this book capture well the ecstasy of the mystical experience, I question whether Underhill fully understands some of the more esoteric concepts that point toward the experience of non-dual consciousness.

I will be presenting this Literature Review, not in alphabetical order, not in the chronological or historical order in which the books were written, but in the chronological order in which I read them, beginning with the first book that substantially impacted my understanding. I continue to read, only to find additional confirmation and creative expression in many new books and articles. It is a never-ending process. I have not discovered anything that disproves the ultimate conclusions I reach.

Figure 6 below is a tentative Literature Review Map of those writings or practices that have been seminal in helping me understand and give meaning to my many transformational experiences.

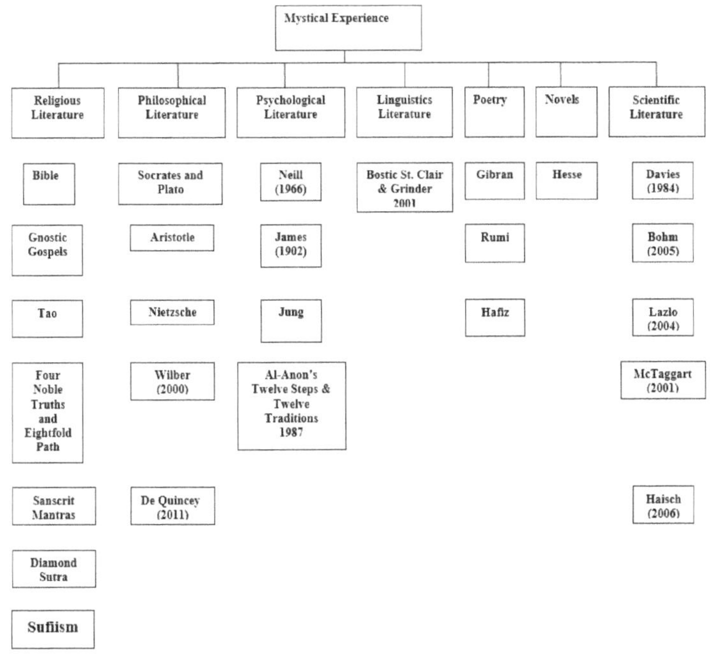



*Fig. 6 Literature review map* (subject to change). This map categorizes and lists books and practices that have been seminal in helping me understand and give conceptual form to my transformational experiences.

## Neill, A.S. (1964). *Summerhill, a Radical Approach to Child Rearing*
________ (1966). *Freedom, Not License*

Neill's classic alternative-education book *Summerhill* fell into my hands at a time when I was struggling with my five-year-old son Bill's bed-wetting. (See Appendix I, "How it All Began.")

By narrating story after story, Neill demonstrated how he had shifted his students' behavior from reactivity and classroom disruption to cooperation and a renewed interest in learning simply by giving each misbehaving child a penny. This radically different way of dealing with dysfunctional behavior gave me a new option to try with my son.

Changing my *own* conduct brought me my first consciousness-shifting experience and started me on the path I continue to walk today.

One of the aspects of *Summerhill* that attracted my attention was the way Neill used language. He taught by telling stories. Instead of telling his readers what they should or shouldn't do in rearing their children, he just told stories about what the problems were, what he did, and what the results were. He left the reader free to follow his example—or not.

## James, W. (1994). *The Varieties of Religious Experience, a Study in Human Nature*

After that first consciousness-shifting experience, I was conceptually confused. It was not a physical event. It was a mental event. My Unitarian rearing hadn't given me any vocabulary with which to understand and conceptualize my experience. I couldn't even give it a name.

I later understood that this lack of a built-in vocabulary was both a disadvantage and an advantage. Had I been reared in a religion that offered a ready-made vocabulary, I might simply have adopted that vocabulary to conceptualize the experience. The fact that I didn't have a ready-made vocabulary forced me to look for one. What I found was not one but many.

When I read James' description of mysticism and the four marks of mystic states, I finally had a name for my experience—a mystical experience. My experience included all four of James' marks of mystic states:

1. Ineffability (incapable of description)
2. Noetic quality (a profound sense of knowing)
3. Transiency
4. Passivity

I couldn't describe or communicate the deeper meaning of the experience.

I somehow just knew that I knew.

The experience happened and passed.

It was not an experience and consciousness shift I chose, although I did choose the actions that preceded it.

Adopting the term "mysticism" gave me a focus for further conceptual exploration.

**Holy Bible, The, containing the Old and New Testaments, Authorized King James Version. (Undated)**

The Unitarian Church I attended as a child was more theistic than most. Attending Sunday School had already familiarized me with most of the Biblical stories.

As a child, many of those stories did not make sense. My parents and Sunday School teachers had always encouraged me to think beyond the literal words and try to figure out how the stories *could* make sense in our materialistic, objective world.

After that first transformational experience, which I now felt comfortable calling a mystical experience, words that had not made sense to me as a child suddenly did. In addition to the words that popped into my head when I had that experience, "But I say unto you, that ye resist not evil; but whosoever shall smite thee on thy right cheek, turn to him the other also," (Matt 5:39), another set of Biblical words suddenly made sense: "The Kingdom of Heaven is within you" (Luke 17:21). "Of course!" I thought. "Heaven is not some physical place we go after our bodies die. Heaven is a state of consciousness, right here, right now." The contextual meaning of the words had changed.

According to Gen. 1:1, "God created the heaven and the earth."

According to Gen. 1:27, "God created man in his own image, in the image of God created he him."

God was the Creator, but so was man. Man was a microcosm of the macrocosm, a holon in a holographic universe, a reflection of God.

As I struggled unsuccessfully to try to communicate my experience to others, other Biblical words caught my attention.

"They have ears, but they hear not:" (Ps(s) 115:6; Ps(s) 135:17).

"Yea, thou heardest not; yea, thou knewest not;" (Is. 48:8).

"Having eyes, see ye not? And having ears, hear ye not? And do ye not remember?" Mark (8:18).

"He that hath ears to hear, let him hear." (Matt. 11:15. Mark 4:9).

"He that hath an ear, let him hear what the Spirit saith unto the churches." (Rev. 2:7).

The authors of several of the Biblical texts also were not heard. I was not alone in my inability to communicate my consciousness-shifting experience.

Related to the experience of not being heard and understood was the Biblical admonition "Give not that which is holy unto the dogs, neither cast ye your pearls before swine, lest they trample them under their feet, and turn again and rend you." (Matt. 7:6). Words spoken from Non-Dual Consciousness or wholeness will not be heard or understood by people still stuck in conditioned dual consciousness. Instead, they will misinterpret the meanings of those words, feel threatened, and will likely react with condemnation, judgment, and perhaps even murder.

Jesus was crucified by men stuck in conditioned dual consciousness. Socrates was commanded to drink hemlock. Gandhi and Dr. Martin Luther King were assassinated.

Speaking from a State of Non-Dual Consciousness is not easy. History has shown us how often those who spoke from a State of Non-Dual Consciousness were killed by those who did not understand.

On many occasions, I have had to choose between caving in to dysfunctional authority or standing in integrity and saying, "No, I will not do that." As a woman culturally conditioned to support men, yet faced with the hierarchical and autocratic thinking of many dysfunctional men, standing in integrity has not been easy. I have frequently experienced fear of not being sexy enough, being ostracized, ridiculed, shamed, screamed at, physically attacked, even assassinated for thinking differently. When I lived in Panama and was saying "no" to the extortion demands of Panamanian developers and defending myself against their attempts to steal my money and my dreams, the thought that I might end up at the bottom of Panama Bay with my hands tied behind my back and a concrete block around my neck was frequently in my awareness. (Some of these stories are included in Appendix A.) I have only been able to stand in integrity by choosing to believe that there is some kind of God, Higher Power, or Universal Energy supporting me, just as my parents supported me as a child in my struggle with my three-year-old next-door neighbor. As a result of these challenging experiences, the words of Psalm 23:4 have become very meaningful to me: "Yea, though I walk through the valley of the shadow of death, I will fear no evil, for thou art with me."

As I struggled to find ways to integrate what appeared to be opposite words and concepts, words from the Book of Revelation kept coming to mind: "I am Alpha and Omega, the beginning and the end, the first and the last." (Rev. 22:13).

And as I braced myself against the frustration and anger directed toward me for not conforming to how other people thought I should think and act, I could only note the warning in Luke 6:41 against self-righteousness: "And why beholdest thou the mote that is in thy brother's eye, but perceivest not the beam that is in thy own eye?" It was so much easier for others to blame and judge me than to work on themselves. It's simply not that easy. Who is up to the challenge of looking hard at his own thoughts, emotions, and actions? Who is willing to explore the emotional depths of her own terror, so that she can move through that hell to the psychological heaven on the other side? "Narrow is the way, which leadeth unto life, and few there be that find it." (Matt. 7:14).

Delving deep into one's own consciousness is a terrifying and humbling experience. How many of us are willing to undertake the journey? "It is easier for a camel to go through the eye of a needle than for a rich man to enter into the kingdom of God." (Matt. 20:24). By rich man, I mean someone surrounded by physical comfort. What possible motivation would someone surrounded by physical comfort have to look at his own consciousness? Perhaps this was why many churches recommended a life of poverty. The purpose was not to be poor. The purpose was to position spiritual sojourners so that they would have to look at their own consciousness from a challenging physical position.

There are, nevertheless, many humans throughout history, who have taken the plunge deep into the depths of their own personal hells and emerged experiencing this constant awareness of the influx of sensory data and their own mind's creative structuring of that data. Many have labeled their resurrection from dualistic words "salvation" or "piercing the veil of illusion" or "transformation," and their human, non-dual consciousness "heaven" or "nirvana." All felt somehow connected to an Energy far greater than their own, an Energy many have called "God."

Many of those same humans, when looking back on their previous lack of awareness and imprisonment behind the rigid bars of conditioned dual consciousness, language, and fear, have labeled their previous mental and emotional state "hell." Words like "heaven" and "hell" have experiential meanings, right here, right now.

The myths of the expulsion of Adam and Eve from the Garden of Eden (Gen. 1:3) and the attempts of the Babylonians to build a tower to reach heaven (Gen. 11:1-9) also suddenly made sense.

God told Adam and Eve they could eat anything in the garden, except the fruit of the Tree of Knowledge. When Adam and Eve disobeyed God, they suddenly realized they were naked and suddenly became ashamed. Absolutely nothing changed about Adam and Eve except the way they perceived themselves and their environment. They had lost their connection with Non-Dual Consciousness and shifted into Dual Consciousness.

Before, they had been one with God. Now they were separate and apart from God. If they hadn't eaten of the Tree of Knowledge, the concepts naked and ashamed would have meant nothing. Because they ate of the Tree of Knowledge, those concepts suddenly became divisive and derogatory.

Language separates and divides. Can the concept naked have any meaning except in relation to the concept clothed? Can the concept ashamed have any meaning except in relation to the concept unashamed? If it weren't for language, wouldn't we simply be experiencing sensations and feelings? Before Adam and Eve ate of the fruit of the Tree of Knowledge, weren't they simply experiencing sensations and feelings?

Eating of the fruit of the Tree of Knowledge—creating opposite words from the whole cloth of experience—caused man's exile from the symbolic Garden of Eden. Can words be used as catalysts for a return to that Garden of Eden, a return to reunification with that Non-Dual Consciousness that some have called God?

In the Tower of Babel story, the Babylonians decided to build a tower to reach God. When God learned about it, he confounded the language of all the earth and scattered the people abroad. Perhaps the Tower of Babel should have been called the Tower of Babble.

Our language is still confounded. We believe a single word has a single meaning. We believe that different words have different meanings. We believe that every word stands for some object "out there."

In the Biblical Book of Revelation, it is Babylon, symbolic of our confused speech that is ultimately judged and burned with fire. (Rev. 18:2, *et seq.*).

If we understand words within their experiential contexts and listen for the underlying meanings, linguistic confusion disappears, and we are once again able to communicate with one another, support one another, and live in harmony.

I continued returning to the Bible, over and over, as my understanding deepened and I continued to be faced with challenging human experiences. I was particularly fascinated as I began reading the work of Wilhelm Friedrich Nietzsche (see below) and could see how he had used Biblical words and phrases symbolically to integrate and point toward a synthesis of what appear to be opposite concepts such as Christ and Antichrist. I was beginning to understand that the synthesis I was trying to verbalize transcended words and concepts. It could be experienced but not conceptualized. It could be spoken from, but not about. Yet, there *was* an experiential synthesis. It is what I have chosen to call "Non-Dual Consciousness." (See Conceptual or Theoretical Framework.)

Another Book in the Bible that fascinated me was The Book of Revelation. While I didn't understand all of it, there were many references to overcoming. My own mystical path had been rife with overcomings: the adultery of the father of my children, a divorce after 21 years of marriage, becoming a lawyer when few women were practicing attorneys, the drug addiction of one of my sons, saying 'no' to dysfunctional political authority, many betrayals of trust, two daughters-in-law who barely tolerated me, one who banned me from "her" home for over two years and refused to let me see "her children" because I was "dangerous." On many occasions, I struggled with fear, even terror, and had to learn how to understand and release those emotions. I also struggled with rage and had to learn how to transform it into constructive action. See Appendix A for some of these stories.

**Nietzsche, W. (1954).** *The Philosophy of Nietzsche.* **"Thus Spake Zarathustra," translated by Thomas Common. "Beyond Good and Evil," translated by Helen Zimmern. "The Geneology of Morals," translated by Horace B. Samuel, M.A. "Ecce Homo," translated by Clifton P. Fadiman.**

**———— (1954).** *The Portable Nietzsche.* **"Twilight of the Idols," "The Antichrist," "Thus Spoke Zarathustra," translated and edited by Walter Kaufmann.**

I can't begin to tell you how excited I was when I began reading the works of Friedrich Wilhelm Nietzsche. I recognized a fellow mystic, striving somehow, someway, to synthesize what appear to be opposite concepts and point to the experience and essence of Non-Dual Consciousness—a consciousness that transcends words and concepts.

To my knowledge, Nietzsche never openly identified himself as a mystic. However, the term may not have been available to him. Nietzsche had a mental collapse in 1889 and died in 1900. It was not until two years later, in 1902, that James focused a spotlight on mysticism by lecturing on it in *The Varieties of Religious Experience*.

In trying to figure out how to use analytic, divisive words to communicate a unifying, holistic experience, I had become so frustrated with the inadequacies of language that I began drawing pictures.

Here is one:

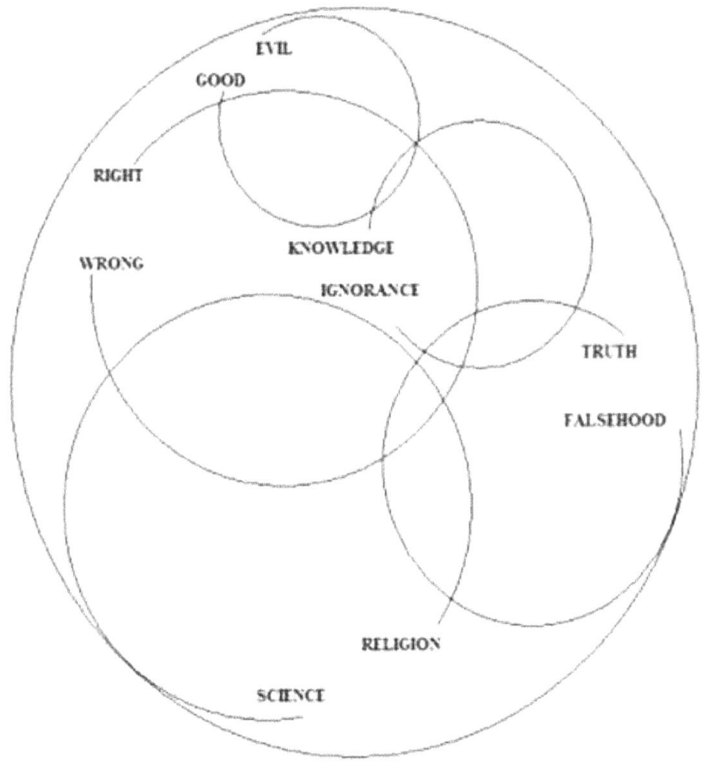

Here is another:

GOOD
GOD

ANARCHIST
CHRIST

FAITH
TRUTH
GOD

LOVE
HATE

COLD
PEACE

SKEPTICISM
FAITH

BEGINNING
ENDING

As I read Nietzsche, he seemed to be struggling with these same linguistic paradoxes.

In *Ecce Homo*, Nietzsche wrote:

I know my destiny. Someday my name will be bound up with the recollection of something terrific—of a crisis quite unprecedented, of the most profound clash of consciences. (923).

. . . it seems to me indispensable to declare here who and what I am. As a matter of fact, this should be pretty well known already, for *I have not allowed myself to be "without witness."* (Emphasis supplied.) But the disparity between the greatness of my task and the smallness of my contemporaries is made plain by the fact *that people have neither heard me nor seen me.* (811). (Emphasis supplied.)

I am the Antichrist. (858).

It is likely that Nietzsche was familiar with the work of Georg Wilhelm Friedrich Hegel. Hegel, like Nietzsche, lived in Germany. Hegel was born in 1770 and died in 1831. Nietzsche was born in 1844 and died in 1900.

Hegel developed a method of thought called the dialectical method, which posited that progress occurs through the conflict of opposites. First, there is an idea, called the thesis. Because the thesis is always incomplete, it draws forth an opposite idea, called the antithesis. Thesis and antithesis then become reconciled through a third, more encompassing idea, called synthesis. The trouble with the synthesis that both Nietzsche and I were struggling with was that it transcended words and concepts. There were no words or ideas that were adequate to describe it. The synthesis was not an idea. It was not a concept. It was a unifying, holistic moment in time that shifted a person into a non-dual state of consciousness.

Was Nietzsche using Hegel's dialectical method when he wrote that he was the Antichrist? Was he presenting himself conceptually as antithesis so that a synthesis that transcends words and concepts could emerge?

In *Beyond Good and Evil* (1954), a title that also implies a synthesis beyond words and concepts, Nietzsche wrote:

Everything that is profound loves the mask.... Should not the contrary only be the right disguise for the shame of a God to go about in? . . . Every profound spirit needs a mask; nay, more, around every profound spirit there continually grows a mask, owing to the constantly false, that is to say superficial interpretation of every word he utters, every step he takes, every sign of life he manifests. (425-26).

In *Ecce Homo* (1954), Nietzsche wrote, "I know both sides, for I am both sides." (817).

Nietzsche termed himself the "Antichrist." The term sounds like the antithesis of the term "Christ." Few have understood Nietzsche. Jesus Christ, linguistic thesis. Nietzsche Antichrist, linguistic antithesis. Are these "opposite concepts" simply two aspects of the same, non-dual spiritual consciousness?

Nietzsche's words, "I am the Antichrist" come from his essay *Ecce Homo*. "Ecce homo" were Pontius Pilate's words as he handed Jesus over to be crucified. (John 19:5). These Latin words mean "Here is the man."

In *Beyond Good and Evil*, Nietzsche wrote:

How could anything originate out of its opposite? ... This mode of reasoning discloses the typical prejudice by which metaphysicians of all times can be recognized.... The fundamental belief of metaphysicians is the belief in antitheses of values. It never occurred even to the wariest of them to doubt here on the very threshold (where doubt, however, was most necessary) ... For it may be doubted, firstly, whether antitheses exist at all; and secondly, whether the popular valuations and antitheses of value upon which metaphysicians have set their seal, are not perhaps merely superficial estimates, merely provisional perspectives... It might even be possible that what constitutes the value of those good and respected things, consists precisely in their being insidiously related, knotted, and crocheted to these evil and apparently opposed things—perhaps even in being essentially identical with them.

Was knowledge crocheted to ignorance, truth to falsehood, Christ to Antichrist?

How does one separate these insidiously knotted concepts? No matter what conceptual form one chooses with which to express non-dual spiritual consciousness, the form is only a single creative conceptualization of the whole, a single linguistic and symbolic expression of that which contains the possibility of an infinite number of linguistic and symbolic expressions.

Did Nietzsche put on the outer garments and trappings of the Antichrist to symbolize the conceptual and linguistic divisiveness of the human experience? It was surely a disguise that no one who thought divisively could penetrate. It was a disguise that only individuals who had experienced the unity and non-dual consciousness underlying linguistic form could access.

While Nietzsche's words took the form of antithesis, they were sprinkled with clues pointing to the identical and creative nature of truth and falsehood, knowledge and ignorance, Christ and Antichrist.

One of Nietzsche's themes was "the overman." "Behold, I teach you the overman. The overman is the meaning of the earth. Let your will say: the overman shall be the meaning of the earth."

The German word Nietzsche used was "Übermensch." Thomas Common translated the word "Übermensch" as Superman. Walter Kaufmann translated it as "Overman." Common totally missed the Biblical symbolism. Kaufmann's translation is clearly correct.

How strikingly the word "Overman" parallels the words in the Christian Bible's Book of Revelation.

"To him that overcometh will I give to eat of the tree of life." (Rev. 2:7). "He that overcometh shall not be hurt of the second death." (Rev. 2:11). "To him that overcometh will I give to eat of the hidden manna, and will give him a white stone, and in the stone a new name written, which no man knoweth saving he that receiveth it." (Rev. 2:17). "And he that overcometh and keepeth my works unto the end, to him will I give power over the nations." (Rev. 2:26). "He that overcometh, the same shall be clothed in white raiment." (Rev. 3:5). "Him that overcometh will I make a pillar in the temple of my God, and he shall go no more out: and I will write upon him the name of my God, and the name of the city of my God, which is new Jerusalem, which cometh down out of heaven from my God: and I will write upon him my new name." (Rev. 3:12). "To him that overcometh will I grant to sit with me in my throne, even as I also overcame and am set down with my Father in his throne." (Rev. 3:21).

Did Nietzsche have Christ consciousness? Buddhist awareness? Was he writing from that creative state of Being that I have termed Non-Dual Consciousness? Was antithesis the only way he could humanly express the conceptual paradoxes emanating from our human consciousness? Has he been unheard, misunderstood, and unrecognized, because the words with which he expressed himself were so unlike the forms that believers expected?

Do we all have this same potential for Christ consciousness, for Non-Dual Consciousness? Can we all overcome our conditioned thinking, shift into Non-Dual Consciousness and start using dualistic words creatively, rather than authoritatively?

Is it possible that the second coming in the Bible's Book of Revelation, the overcoming, has always been possible throughout that continuum we call time? Is the second coming and return to the Garden of Eden an individual human consciousness shift? Does it symbolize the ability of each of us to remove our blinders and attune ourselves to that creative energy or power that directs our lives harmoniously if we allow it to do so?

Friedrich Nietzsche termed himself the Antichrist. He peppered his writings with Biblical references and clues symbolizing his Christ identity. Do his writings evidence the blinders our reductive, dualistic thinking straps onto our creative consciousness?

Do we see, but not see, hear, but not hear? Do we expect events to take a different form? Do we expect external things to change, rather than the consciousness within each one of us? Do we expect trumpets and brilliant lights and angels? Are we all wearing blinders and missing what is there for all to see? Is everything written in the Bible and other religious and philosophical writings simply artistic and symbolic expression of this expanded creative state of consciousness, this Non-Dual Consciousness, a consciousness available to every person on this planet?

Is it possible that, when perceived through this expanded, creative, non-dual state of consciousness, that the events in the Book of Revelation occur, not 2,000 years after the physical birth and death of Jesus, but in eternity, where eternity symbolizes a Non-Dual State of Consciousness, possible for every human at every moment in what scientific thinking perceives as time?

Has this overcoming always been possible? If so, it requires the participation of every human on this planet.

**Hesse, H. (1981). *Demian*. Translated by Michael Roloff and Michael Lebeck.**

**——— (1969). *Magister Ludi*. Translated by Richard and Clara Winston.**

**——— (1951). *Siddhartha*.**

*Siddartha* is a novel about a man's search for answers to life's largest questions. *Magister Ludi*, also known as *The Glass Bead Game*, is about the conflict between and the need to synthesize thought and action, intellect and flesh.

Hesse was as profound a thinker as Nietzsche, yet used a different form of writing, the novel, to question conditioned values and challenge conditioned systems.

It was a few sentences in *Demian* that caught my attention.

. . . on my table lay a few volumes of Nietzsche. I lived with him, sensed the loneliness of his soul, perceived the fate that had propelled him on inexorably; I suffered with him, and rejoiced that there had been one man who had followed his destiny so relentlessly. . . . (W)hat nature wants of man stands indelibly written in the individual, in you, in me. It stood written in Jesus, it stood written in Nietzsche.

Had Hesse, too, seen the symbolism in Nietzsche's writings? Had he seen Non-Dual Consciousness in the personas of both Jesus and Nietzsche? Was Hesse himself writing from a state of Non-Dual Consciousness, using his novels as artistic art forms?

**Al-Anon Family Group (1987).** *Al-Anon's Twelve Steps & Twelve Traditions.*

As I continued to struggle with how to use analytic, divisive words to communicate a unifying, holistic experience, I also struggled with the drug addiction of one of my sons. The struggle with the drug addiction forced me to look at my own co-dependency and threw me into Nar-Anon, a support group for families and friends of addicts. We used the same literature that members of Al-Anon use.

I had never much liked the term "God." It had always reminded me of an old man with a long white beard sitting on a cloud with a thunderbolt in his hand waiting to strike me dead if I didn't do some unclear thing he wanted me to do. While the twelve-step programs used the term "God" in steps three, six, and eleven, they also used the term "Power greater than ourselves" in step two and often used the term "Higher Power" during group discussions. I liked the latter terms better.

Until I joined Nar-Anon, I had been trying to use second and third person language to communicate my mystical experience. They just didn't work. I couldn't stay in integrity while using either one.

Second person language sounded judgmental. "You ought to pick up your clothes." "Why *are* you doing that?" "You shouldn't do that." The last thing a mystical experience was about was judgment. If anything, it was about releasing judgment and self-righteousness.

Third person language didn't work either. While it might be effective for scientific measurement—"His blood pressure is 120 over 80"— it didn't work when one was trying to communicate a mystical experience. The mystical experience was an internal, subjective experience, a consciousness shift, a mental event, where nothing in the external world changed and everything in the internal world changed. Perception radically shifted.

It was in Nar-Anon that I learned the value of using first person singular language when talking about these kinds of internal, subjective experiences. We were required to use first person singular when we shared in the group. We were not there to fix our addicts or the world. We were there to heal ourselves. To do so, we needed to be aware of our own thoughts, emotions, and conduct, and how each of us, individually, needed to change.

If I used first person singular, I could speak about my own thoughts, feelings, needs, and choices without sounding either authoritarian or judgmental. I could also listen to other people's first person singular language about their thoughts, feelings, needs, and choices, hearing those words simply as information about the other person that gave me a better understanding of them. I didn't have to agree or disagree. The words were pure information. I was beginning to learn to communicate honestly and transparently from my own heart and soul as I listened to others communicating honestly and transparently from their own hearts and souls. We were developing I—Thou relationships.

**Great Dialogues of Plato: Complete Texts of THE REPUBLIC, APOLOGY, CRITO, PHAEDO, ION, MENO, SYMPOSIUM, a Modern Translation by W.H.D Rouse (1956). New York: The New American Library.**

When I read the allegory of the cave in *The Republic*, I could only think that Socrates had beautifully captured the mystical experience.

Before that experience, I had seen the world in the same way the prisoners in Socrates' cave saw the world. I saw nothing but shadows. The shadows were the conflicting concepts of conditioned dual consciousness into which I had so unknowingly been conditioned and indoctrinated. However, because I was experiencing nothing but shadows, I believed the shadows were real.

After the experience, I saw the world entirely differently. It was as if I suddenly saw it for the first time. I can remember watching rain drops fall into a puddle of water— really watching. Poetic words suddenly popped into my mind. Everything was alive and vibrant. Everything suddenly made sense and fit together.

The only difference between what Socrates described and what I had experienced was that at least in that first experience, I didn't feel dragged into it. It felt more like an unexpected gift that had been laid at my feet. Christians would have used the term "Amazing Grace."

In later experiences, I did feel dragged and pushed up the slope. Why me? I did not want to go there. It was too bright. I did not want this job. It was too difficult. Yet something seemed to be pushing me along a path I had never planned to take. Did I have the skill to do this? Did I have the stamina? Did I have the integrity? I did not know. I still do not know.

It is interesting to note the form of Socrates' language in this dialogue. Much of it consists of questions. In addition, he frequently uses first person singular language. For example:

"I will try to explain," said I, "what I, at least, believe. Whatever points I distinguish in my own mind as leading in favour of or against what we are speaking of, pray look at them with me and agree or disagree; then we shall see more clearly if this study is what I divine it to be." (320).

**The Four Noble Truths and the Noble Eightfold Path of Buddhism**

Here is a highly simplified summary of The Four Noble Truths and the Noble Eightfold Path of Buddhism. The Four Nobel Truths are:

1. The nature of perceived and experienced existence is suffering.
2. The cause of suffering is:
    a. Greed and desire.
    b. Ignorance or delusion.
    c. Hatred and destructive urges.
3. It is possible to liberate oneself from suffering by extinguishing attachment to desire, ignorance, delusion, and hatred. This liberation is manifested as the signless.
4. There are means by which suffering is recognized and realized, the cause of suffering is known and understood, and the disappearance of suffering and realization of freedom and peace are attained. These

practices are called the Noble Eightfold Path. They
are:

    a.   Right view or understanding.
    a.   Right aspiration, aim, intention, or thought.
    b.   Right speech.
    c.   Right action or doing.
    d.   Right living or livelihood.
    e.   Right effort.
    f.   Right mindfulness.
    g.   Right concentration or focus.

This Noble Eightfold Path leads to vision, calm, enlightenment and "Nirvana." It entails just observing the nature of things without becoming entangled in views and theories. Conceptual dualities cease to hold any reality.

From my perspective, Buddhism is one of the simplest and most transparent practices for shifting into Non-Dual Consciousness because of its simple focus on non-violence—in thought, word, and deed. In addition, it notes that once one functions from a state of Nirvana or Non-Dual Consciousness, one no longer needs the concepts of the Four Noble Truths or the Eightfold Path. One is simply living them and being them.

**The Diamond Sutra: The Perfection of Wisdom, Text and Commentaries translated from Sanscrit and Chinese by Red Pine (2001). New York: Counterpoint.**

(To be developed.)

**Dyer, W. (2007).** *Change Your Thoughts—Change Your Life: Living the Wisdom of the Tao.* **New York: Hay House, Inc.**

I chose this version of the Tao for three reasons. First, I have met Dr. Wayne W. Dyer personally and highly respect his integrity. Second, I respect the care with which he poured through the historical records of the Tao and ten of its translations to piece together the 81 passages in his book. Third, I respect the transparency with which he owns his own role in piecing together the 81 passages, based on how they resonated with him. I am far more interested in the actual verses from the Tao as pieced together by Dr. Dyer than I am in Dr. Dyer's interpretations of those verses. Many of those verses beautifully express my own experiences and understandings.

The Tao that can be told
is not the eternal Tao.
The name that can be named
is not the eternal name. (1st Verse.)

What the Chinese call the Tao is what I call Non-Dual Consciousness. It cannot be conceptualized because it is a unified, holistic experience or state of being that transcends words.

So the sage lives openly with apparent duality
and paradoxical unity. (2nd Verse.)

Words and concepts, by their nature, are dualistic. Apparent duality happens only when our minds chop experience up into words and concepts. Anyone who speaks from a state of Non-Dual Consciousness, will, by necessity, use paradoxical language.

The Tao is empty
but inexhaustible,
bottomless,
the ancestor of it all. (4th Verse.)

The Tao is void of "true" words and concepts, yet inexhaustible in meaning and potential creativity.

Thirty spokes converge upon a single hub;

it is on the hole in the center that the use of the cart hinges.

. . . .

The usefulness of what is

depends on what is not. (11<sup>th</sup> Verse.)

The first two lines of this verse appear to offer a very good verbal description of my non-dual consciousness diagrams. It is on the hole in the center, Non-Dual Consciousness, that the *usefulness* of everything else depends. To be effective, we must be aligned with and speaking from Non-Dual Consciousness.

The master observes the world

but trusts his inner vision.

He allows things to come and go.

He prefers what is within to what is without. (12<sup>th</sup> Verse.)

This is an excellent description of Ken Wilber's upper left quadrant (subjective, personal), within which Non-Dual Consciousness arises. See discussion below.

Approach it and there is no beginning;

follow it and there is no end.

You cannot know it, but you can be it,

at ease in your own life. (14<sup>th</sup> Verse.)

The first two lines of this verse seem to mirror the Riddle I created about beginning and end. See Appendix C.

The last two lines express the experience I had when I tried to conceptualize my consciousness-shifting experiences. I couldn't do it. The noetic essence I experienced faded as soon as I tried to express it in words. I found myself mired in conceptual paradoxes. I could *be* it, I could *speak from* it, but I could not speak *about* it because the experience transcended human-created concepts.

(To be further developed.)

**Davies, P. (1984).** *God and the new physics.* **New York: Simon & Schuster, Inc.**

(To be developed.)

**Gibran, Kahlil (1986).** *A tear and a smile.* **Translated from the Arabic by H.M. Nahmad. New York: Alfred A. Knopf.**

———— **(1973).** *Jesus, the son of man, His words and his deeds as told and recorded by those who knew him.* **New York: Alfred A. Knopf.**

———— **(1986).** *The prophet.* **New York: Alfred A. Knopf.**

———— **(1966).** *The wanderer, his parables and sayings.* **New York: Alfred A. Knopf.**

(To be developed.)

**Wilber, K. (2000).** *A Theory of Everything. An Integral Vision for Business, Politics, Science, and Spirituality*

Wilber uses a four quadrant conceptual model to present an integral vision. The two quadrants on the left are subjective perspectives. The two quadrants on the right are objective perspectives. The two upper quadrants are individual perspectives. The two lower quadrants are collective perspectives. Subjective perspectives use "I" and "We" language. Objective perspectives use "It" language. A highly simplified perspective looks like Figure 7 below.

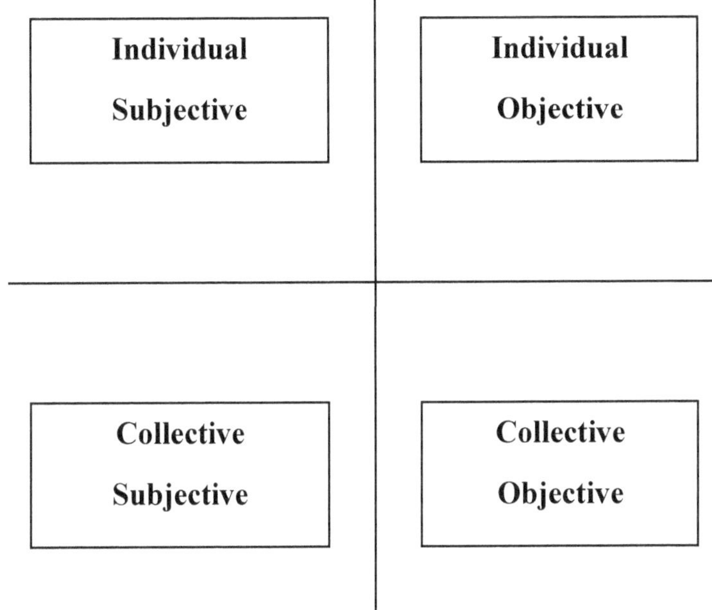

*Figure 7*. Simplified rendering of Ken Wilber's Four Quadrant Theory. This figure illustrates the four quadrants through which Wilber distinguishes subjective from objective and individual from collective.

Wilber terms the upper left quadrant self, consciousness (43), intentional (102); the lower left, culture and worldview (43); the upper right, brain and organism (43); and the lower right, social system and environment (43).

I clearly function by choice from the two subjective perspectives for the reasons stated above about my experiences in Nar-Anon. I function within the upper left quadrant when I am thinking about personal experiences and my conceptualizations of them. I function within the lower left quadrant when I am in dialog or thinking about what someone else has written. I have no problem taking the position that all we *mean* by the term "objectivity" is that to which all "subjects" agree, when everyone is looking at the same information from the same perspective using the same rules of interpretation. What we consider "objective" at one time and place changes as new information or new ways of putting together old information enter our awareness.

That does not mean I cannot function from an "objective" perspective. For example, in writing this dissertation, I have to distinguish myself, as author of these words, from useful conceptual categorizations that I use, such as "words", "concepts", "mystical experiences", and "Non-Dual Consciousness." As I have previously stated, I consider the words in this dissertation creative, dual-consciousness art forms. I know only too well the danger of proclaiming them as "objective truths." They are not "objective truths." I hope rather that they may be meaningful and useful in offering new ways of thinking about how we use words and concepts.

Most of the time, I function from the upper left quadrant of Wilber's Four Quadrant Theory, the quadrant that, according to Wilber, contains the eight levels of development identified by Clare Graves and further refined by Don Beck and Christopher Cowan in their Spiral Dynamics Theory, plus four "higher, transpersonal, or spiritual waves (psychic, subtle, causal, and nondual)." (43-44).

Wilber (2000, 64) writes: "The uppermost realm is the nondual ground of all the other realms so that ultimate spirit suffers no final dualisms."

Because this nondual ground suffers no dualisms, it cannot be spoken *about*. It is simply a State of Being that transcends words and concepts. When spoken *from*, the dualistic words *used* are art forms. Wilber (2000) writes, "Art refers to the aesthetic/expressive realm, the subjective realm described in first-person or 'I' language." (70). That is clearly the realm within which I am most comfortable. As Al-Anon suggests, "You are free to take what is useful for your own life and leave the rest."

**Bostic St. Clair, C. & Grinder, J. (2001). *Whispering in the Wind*. Scotts Valley, CA: J&C Enterprises.**

I came across this book recently, in 2014, after another Wisdom University doctoral student recommended it. I had, long ago, as the result of all my transformational experiences, come to the conclusion that words and concepts simply structured experience and that we all did it differently. The only meanings that could be given to the words "knowledge" and "truth" were whatever concepts everyone agreed to call knowledge and truth.

Bostic St. Clair and Grinder took my own thinking to much greater depths in their chapter on the epistemology underlying Neuro-Linguistic Programming (NLP). NLP was co-created by Grinder and Richard Bandler in the mid-70's in California and was offered as a technology for modeling what they refer to as excellence in human behavior.

In their epistemology, Bostic St. Clair and Grinder argue for "a sharp distinction between the set of neurological transforms that process the incoming data stream from the world up to the point where we as humans first gain access to it (primary experience) and the set of transforms subsequent to that point, focusing on the linguistic mapping and their effects (secondary experience)." (ix). It was clear that my own focus had been only on the second set of transforms—the linguistic mapping of what Bostic St. Clair and Grinder term First Access (FA).

Bostic St. Clair and Grinder argue, first of all, that there are limitations to the data streaming into First Access.

. . . the vast majority of the events occurring around us in the gale of electromagnetic movement as possible sources of experience are simply NEVER detected by us as they fall outside the narrow bands of access that we call our sensory channels. (15) . . . . (Our) eyes are capable of detecting wavelengths between 400 nanometers and 700 nanometers. (Our) ears register . . . sound waves generated between 20 cycles per second and 20,000 cycles per second. (Our) tactile sensitivity . . . responds to differences in position, temperature, and moisture . . . within extremely limited ranges. The rest of what is happening – indeed, the vast majority of those events that occur in the electromagnetic spectrum that defines the actual world – occur without any awareness . . . (17).

What we as individuals consider the world to be is a set of complex, dynamic relationships between what is actually out there (unknown) and our sensory and neurological processing abilities as we sense a small and selective portion of those events that are occurring. (22). The conclusion is clear enough – that FA is already a set of transformed representations: products of transforms defined over the incoming data stream. (23).

Not only is the linguistic map not the territory. The territory is not the territory because of the neurological limitations our neurology imposes on what we can experience.

This was simply further confirmation of the conclusions I had already reached—that we humans can know nothing about any kind of Reality or "objective world" out there. All we can "know" or experience or perceive is what Bostic St. Clair and Grinder term "First Access"—what our neurology can take in.

Bostic St. Clair and Grinder then move on to a discussion of the linguistic transforms that our minds impose on the neurological transforms already limited through First Access. This is the area of focus to which all my transformational experiences had taken me. I can only agree with Bostic St. Clair and Grinder's conclusion: ". . . language is an additional layer of distortion in perception. It is another source of illusion – an apparently uniquely human transform layered on top of the neurological transforms. . . " (27).

On top of our neurological limitations then, all we are doing conceptually is playing with words and exercising our will to power and will to life.

This is not to say that we cannot give experiential meaning to concepts. Clearly we can. Perhaps that is simply another exercise of will to power or intention to create.

Bostic St. Clair and Grinder include two fascinating quotations from two top scientists, Albert Einstein and Niels Bohr to support their argument, as well as a quotation from a major writer, philosopher, and intellectual, Aldous Huxley.

I see on the one side the totality of sense-experiences, and on the other, the totality of the concepts and propositions. The relations between the concepts and propositions among themselves and each other are of a logical nature, the business of logical thinking is strictly limited to the achievement of the connections between concepts and propositions among each other according to firmly laid down rules, which are the concern of logic. The concepts and propositions get "meaning" viz., "content" only through their connection with sense-experiences. The connection of the latter with the former is purely intuitive, not itself of a logical nature. The degree of certainty which this connection, viz., intuitive combination, can be undertaken and nothing else, differentiates empty fantasy from scientific "truth". The system of concepts is a creation of man together with the rules of syntax, which constitute the structure of the conceptual system. (28).

**Albert Einstein, Autobiographical Notes, p. 13**

It is wrong to think that the task of physics is to find out how nature is. Physics concerns what we can say about Nature.

**Niels Bohr, quoted in The Ascent of Science, Brian Silver, page 36.**

To make biological survival possible, Mind at Large has to be funneled through the reducing valve of the brain and nervous system. What comes out the other end is a measly trickle of the kind of consciousness which will help us to stay alive on the surface of this particular planet. To formulate and express the contents of this reduced awareness, man has invented and endlessly elaborated his symbol-systems and implicit philosophies that we call languages. Every individual is at once the beneficiary and the victim of the linguistic traditions into which he has been born – the beneficiary inasmuch as language gives access to the accumulated record of other people's experience, the victim in so far as it confirms him in the belief that reduced awareness is the only awareness and as it bedevils his sense of reality, so that he is all too apt to take his concepts for data, his words for actual things.

**Aldous Huxley, *The Doors of Perception*, New York, Harper and Row, 1954, pages 22-23**

**Underhill, E. (2005). *Mysticism; A Study in Nature and Development of Spiritual Consciousness*. Stilwell, KS: Digireads.com Publishing.**

I had a difficult time getting into this book because of the form of some of the sentences. Statements such as ". . . no responsible student now identifies the mystic and the ecstatic; or looks upon visionary and other "extraordinary phenomena" as either guaranteeing or discrediting the witness of the mystical saints" sounded dictatorial, authoritarian, and dysfunctional. Unlike other texts I had read, those words did nothing to support and clarify my own understanding of my own mystical experience. Rather, they obfuscated it.

The words were clearly not written from a state of Non-Dual Consciousness. Rather, they seemed to be written from a state of conditioned dual state consciousness of which the author may perhaps not even be aware. I found no acknowledgment of this limited state of consciousness from which some of Underhill's words appeared to have been written. In short, the perspective appeared not to have been made transparent.

I noticed the same limitation in the chapter on Mysticism and Magic, which separated and derogated Magic, as well as the exaltation of Christian Mysticism and the denigration of pantheism in the Chapter on Mysticism and Theology. Underhill appears not to fully understand the vehicles of magic and pantheism. I see her view, not as wrong, but simply as limited and not fully understood and clarified.

That having been said, Underhill exquisitely captures the mystical experience when she shifts her linguistic form from judgment to description. Her chapter on the Characteristics of Mysticism is brilliant.

For example, she writes:

Try how he will, his stammering and awestruck reports can hardly be understood but by those who are already in the way. But the artist cannot act thus. On him has been laid the duty of expressing something of that which he perceives . . . . By means of veils and symbols he must interpret his free vision, his glimpse of the burning bush, to other men. He is the mediator between his brethren and the divine, for art is the link between appearance and reality.

And:

The earthly artist, because perception brings with it the imperative longing for expression, tries to give us in colour, sound or words a hint of his ecstasy, his glimpse of truth. Only those who have tried, know how small a fraction of his vision he can, under the most favorable circumstance, contrive to represent. The mystic, too, tries very hard to tell an unwilling world his secret. But in his case, difficulties are enormously increased. First, there is the huge disparity between his unspeakable experience and the language which will most nearly suggest it. Next, there is the great gulf fixed between his mind and the mind of the world. His audience must be bewitched as well as addressed, caught up to something of his state, before they can be made to understand.

And:

The true mystic claims no promises and makes no demands. He goes because he must, as Galahad went towards the Grail: knowing that for those who can live it, this alone is life.

**Conclusions**
**Hypothesis**
Words structure experience.

**Observations**
***What we do with words and the results***

- Sometimes, we structure experience the same way, using the same words. We seem to experience aligned group perceptions. When we do, we experience harmony and clear communication. The creative patterns we perceive and artfully communicate give meaning and purpose to our lives and focus to our destinies. Often, we are tempted to term or word-label these aligned group perceptions "Truth," because we all seem to agree.

- Other times, we structure experience differently, depending on our perceptions, the culture in which we were reared, our conditioning, and our conscious and unconscious needs. When we do this, we often fight over whose words are right and whose words are wrong rather than focusing on communicating, cooperating, and working together to solve problems and meet needs.

### *Why we have created words and concepts*

- To communicate with one another.
- To understand our physical world.
- To meet our individual and societal needs.
- To give meaning to our lives.

### Primary Corollary

There are no right or wrong words. There are only more or less effective words for particular purposes or intentions.

### Other Corollaries

- Words and concepts emerge from individual need, intention, and/or purpose. Most of these needs, intentions, and purposes are unconscious.
- Words are creative art, not Truth. This includes the words of religions and the words of scientists. They are conceptual maps that help us organize and understand our experiences.
- Words have meaning only within the context of particular experiences.
- Two people who experience the same phenomena at the same time in the same place may conceptualize the phenomena differently depending on how they perceive the phenomena and their differing needs and intentions at that moment. Example: two people looking at the same optical illusion may see different images. One person sees an old hag. Another sees a

young woman. The perceptions are different, the words are different, the emotions are different, and the actions are different. Example: two people at a crime scene will conceptualize the experience differently. The thief may be desperately trying to feed his hungry children. The victim feels violated without her consent.

- Words can be used to point to what I have termed "Non-Dual Consciousness," which can never be accurately captured or labeled or limited using words. Even the term "Non-Dual Consciousness" is nothing but a placeholder for something much more complex. (See Clark, A., 2000 for a discussion of words as placeholders.) Words by their nature divide (high/low, right/wrong, knowledge/ignorance). The State of "Non-Dual Consciousness" unifies. Using analytic, divisive words to try to describe Non-Dual Consciousness is like using a screwdriver to hammer a nail.

- Another way of thinking about this State of "Non-Dual Consciousness" is that it transcends words and concepts. It can be experienced, spoken from, and pointed to, but never fully conceptualized or spoken about.

- The words of every religion that has ever been created are art forms and tools pointing to this State of "Non-Dual Consciousness." Other word-labels for what I have termed "Non-Dual Consciousness" are "God," "Brahma," "Allah," "NoThing," "The Tao," "Essence," "Higher Power," "Universal Intelligence," "Universal Energy," Power Greater than Ourselves."

- Quantum physics is also pointing toward this underlying "Energetic Field", which appears to emerge differently depending on the intentions of the person perceiving and the way an experiment is structured. See the wave/particle debate in quantum physics.
- According to Dr. Will Taegel in private correspondence, "indigenous wisdom and science see words as actual living beings that pass through us and collaborate with us as they pass through."
- Perhaps conceptual dualities only integrate experientially at a point of individual creative choice and action.

**Theoretical Implications**

Words are creative vehicles to manifest particular intentions. They can take us to the depths of hell or the heights of heaven. We can use them to destroy the human race or we can use them to cooperate, collaborate, and co-create a dynamic, peaceful, powerful, prosperous planet. The choice lies within each and every one of us.

**Practical Implications**

If, and only if, our intention is to co-create a dynamic, peaceful, powerful, prosperous planet, we need to learn to:

- Speak with as much specificity and clarity as possible.
- Listen deeply to one another
- Clarify the meanings of our words by putting them into experiential context.
- Get clear on our personal needs and intentions and

ask for what we need.

- View words not as truth, but as creative art forms and personal self-expression.
- Satisfy our own needs and the needs of others to the best of our ability.
- Co-create a dynamic, all-inclusive, non-violent society of unique human beings.

# Works Referenced

Al-Anon Family Group. (1987). *One day at a time.* New York: Al-Anon Family Group Headquarters.

__________________. (1987). *Al-anon's twelve steps & twelve traditions.* New York: Al-Anon Family Group Headquarters, Inc.

Atkinson, C., (2014). "Ways of Knowing," "Research Methods, 2014," "The Literature Review," "Ethics APA Resources." PowerPoint presentations. Private correspondence.

Bostic-St.Claire, C. and Grinder, J. (2000). *Whispering in the wind.* Scotts Valley, California: J&C Enterprises.

Buber, M. (1970). *I and thou,* translated by Walter Kaufmann. New York: Charles Scribner's Sons.

Clark, A., (2000). *Mindware: An introduction to the philosophy of cognitive science.* USA: Oxford University Press.

Creswell, J.W. (2014). *Research design: Qualitative, quantitative, and mixed methods approaches.* Los Angeles: Sage Publications, Inc., 6-11.

Davies, P. (1984). *God and the new physics.* New York: Simon & Schuster, Inc.

De Quincey, C. (2011). *Radical knowing: Understanding consciousness through relationship.* (Kindle version). Retrieved from Amazon.com, 13%.

Dyer, W. (2007). *Change your thoughts—change your life: Living the wisdom of the Tao.* New York: Hay House, Inc., 234.

Hesse, H. (1981). *Demian.* Translated by Michael Roloff and Michael Lebeck. Toronto: Bantam Books, 112, 116.

———— (1951). *Siddhartha*. New York: New Directions Publishing Corporation.

Holy Bible, The, containing the Old and New Testaments, Authorized King James Version. (Undated). Cleveland and New York: The World Publishing Company.

James, W. (1994). *The varieties of religious experience, A study in human nature*. Modern Library Edition. New York: Random House, Inc., 414.

Leavy, P. (2009). *Method meets art: Arts-based research practice*. New York: The Guilford Press (Kindle version). Retrieved from Amazon.com, 11%.

Neill, A.S. (1966). *Freedom, not license*. New York City: Hart Publishing Company.

———— (1964). *Summerhill, a radical approach to child rearing*. New York City: Hart Publishing Company.

Nietzsche, Friedrich Wilhelm (1954). *The philosophy of Nietzsche*. "Thus Spake Zarathustra," translated by Thomas Common, "Beyond Good and Evil," translated by Helen Zimmern, 382-83,425-26. "The Geneology of Morals," translated by Horace B. Samuel, M.A. "Ecce Homo," translated by Clifton P. Fadiman, 811, 817, 858, 923. "The Birth of Tragedy from the Spirit of Music," translated by Clifton P. Fadiman. New York: The Modern Library.

———— (1954). *The portable Nietzsche*. "Twilight of the Idols," "The Antichrist," "Nietzsche contra Wagner," "Thus Spoke Zarathustra," 125, translated and edited by Walter Kaufmann. New York: The Viking Press, Inc.

Plato (1956). *Great dialogs of Plato*. "The Republic," "Apology," "Crito," "Phaedo," "Ion," "Meno," "Symposium," translated by W.H.D. Rouse, edited by Eric

H. Warmington and Philip G. Rouse. New York and Toronto: The New American Library.

______(2012). *Phaedrus*, translated by Jowett, B. Kindle version). Retrieved from Amazon.com.

Roberts, C. (2010). *The dissertation journey: A practical and comprehensive guide to planning, writing and defending your dissertation, second edition.* Thousand Oaks, CA: Corwin.

Turabian, K. (2013). *A manual for writers of research papers, theses, and dissertations, eighth edition: Chicago style for students and researchers (chicago guides to writing, editing, and publishing).* Chicago: University of Chicago Press. (Kindle version). Retrieved from Amazon.com, 4%.

Underhill, E. (2005). *Mysticism: A study in nature and development of spiritual consciousness.* Stilwell, Kansas: Digireads.com Publishing, 55-56, 75.

Wilber, K. (2000). *A theory of everything. An integral vision for business, politics, science, and spirituality.* Boston: Shambhala Publications, Inc., 43-44, 46-47, 64, 70, 84, 102, 109.

# Works Consulted

Apatow, R. (2012). *The spiritual art of dialogue: Mastering communication for personal growth, relationships, and the workplace* (Kindle version). Retrieved from Amazon.com.

Abram, D. (1996). *The spell of the sensuous.* New York: Vintage Books

Allen, J. (1942). *As a man thinketh.* New York. Grosset & Dunlap.

Armentrout, D. (1996). *Canvas in the mirror.* Boise, Idaho: The Creative Lure.

Baring, A. (2013). *A dream of the cosmos: A quest for the soul.* Dorset, England: Archive Publishing.

Bartholomew (1987). *From the heart of a gentle brother.* Channeled by Mary-Margaret Moore. Taos, New Mexico: High Mesa Press.

BBC (2009). "The Four Noble Truths." Retrieved from http://www.bbc.co.uk/religion/religions/buddhism/beliefs/fournobletruths_1.shtml

Beattie, M. (1987). *Codependent no more.* New York: Harper/Hazelden.

Bennett, H. (2007). *The lens of perception.* Berkeley, California: Ten Speed Press.

Bernardi, T. (2011). *Dialogues: The courage and wisdom to ask and hear.* Bethesda, Maryland: HAP21.

Bhaktivedanta Swami Prabhupāda, A.C. (1986). *Bhagavad-Gita as it is.* Australia: The Bhaktivedanta Book Trust.

Bohm, D. (2005). *Wholeness and the implicate order.* London and New York: Routledge.

Bucko, A. & Fox, M. (2013). *Occupy spirituality: A radical vision for a new generation.* Berkeley, California. North Atlantic Books.

Buddhism (1961). Edited by Richard A. Gard. New York: George Braziller.

Butterworth, E. (1989). *Discover the power within you: A guide to the unexplored depths within.* New York: Harper & Row, Publishers, Inc.

Cameron, J. ( 2002). *The artist's way.* New York: Jeremy P. Tarcher, Inc.

Campbell, J. (2003). *The hero's journey.* Novato, California: New World Library.

Camus, A. (1963). *Notebooks: 1935 – 1942.* New York: Alfred A. Knopf.

Chodron, P. (1997). *When things fall apart: Heart advice for difficult times.* Boston: Shambhala Publications, Inc.

Curry, D. & Wells, S. (2006). *An organic inquiry primer for the novice researcher: A sacred approach to disciplined knowing.* Kirkland, WA: Liminal Realities

De Quincey, C. (2011). *Consciousness from zombies to angels: the shadow and the light of knowing who you are.* (Kindle version). Retrieved from Amazon.com.

Eliot, T.S. (1964). *T.S. Eliot selected poems.* New York: Harcourt, Brace & World, Inc.

Emerson, R.W. (no date). *Essays.* New York: Merrill and Baker.

Fox, M. (2002). *Creativity: Where the divine and the human meet.* New York. Jeremy P. Tarcher/Putnam.

——— (2012). *Hildegard of Bingen: A saint for our times.* Vancouver, Canada. Namaste Publishing.

———— (1983). *Meditations with Meister Eckhart.* Rochester, Vermont. Bear & Company.

———— (1980). *Passion for creation: The earth-honoring spirituality of Meister Eckhart.* Rochester, Vermont. Inner Traditions.

Gibran, Kahlil (1986). *A tear and a smile.* Translated from the Arabic by H.M. Nahmad. New York: Alfred A. Knopf.

———— (1973). *Jesus, the son of man, His words and his deeds as told and recorded by those who knew him.* New York: Alfred A. Knopf.

———— (1986). *The prophet.* New York: Alfred A. Knopf.

———— (1966). *The wanderer, his parables and sayings.* New York: Alfred A. Knopf.

Glass-Coffin, B. & Miro-Quesada, O. (2013). *Lessons in courage: Peruvian shamanic wisdom for everyday life.* Faber, Virginia. Rainbow Ridge Books, LLC.

Gnostic Gospels, The (2006). Translated by Alan Jacobs. London: Duncan Baird Publishers.

Gutiérrez, C. (2008). *Wisdom in action.* United States of America. Xlibris.

Haisch, B. (2006). *The God theory: Universes, zero-point fields, and what's behind it all.* San Francisco, California: Weiser Books.

Hanh, T. N. (1993). The fourth precept: Deep listening and loving speech. Reproduced from *For a future to be possible: Commentaries on the five wonderful precepts.* Reprinted with permission of Parallax Press, PO Box 7355, Berkeley, CA 94707.

Hawkins, D. (2012). *Power vs force: The hidden determinants of human behavior*. West Sedona, Arizona: Veritas.

Hesse, H. (1969). *Magister Ludi*. Translated by Richard and Clara Winston. Toronto, New York, London: Bantam Books.

Hicks, E. & J. (2009). *The vortex: Where the law of attraction assembles all cooperative relationships*. United States of America: Hay House, Inc.

Hollowell, B. (2011). *The quantum gateway: The Intersection of Science and Religion*. Lakeland, Florida: New Leaf Press.

Holmes, E. (2010). *The science of mind: The complete edition.* (Reprint edition.) New York: Jeremy P. Tarcher, Inc.

Jung, C.J. (1971). *The portable Jung*. Edited and with an Introduction by Joseph Campbell. Translated by R.F.C. Hull. New York: Viking Penguin Inc.

Langley, N. (1967). *Edgar Cayce on reincarnation*. New York: Warner Books, Inc.

Laszlo, E. (2004). *Science and the akashic field, an integral theory of everything*. Rochester, Vermont: Inner Traditions.

Leonard, G. and Murphy, M. (1995). *The life we are given: a long term program for realizing the potential of body, mind, heart and soul*. New York: G.P. Putnam's Sons.

Lerner, R. (1985). *Daily affirmations*. Pompano Beach, Florida: Health Communications, Inc.

Macy, J. & Brown, M. (1998). *Coming back to life: Practices to reconnect our lives, our world*. British Columbia, Canada: New Society Publishers.

McTaggart, L. (2001). *The field: The quest for the secret force of the universe.* Great Britain: HarperCollins Publishers.

Medhurst, C. S. (1972). *The Tao-The-King: Sayings of Lao Tzu.* The United States of America: The Theosophical Publishing House.

Myss, C. (2009). *Defy gravity: Healing beyond the bounds of reason.* United States of America: Hay House, Inc.

Perricone, J. (2005). *Zen and the art of public school teaching.* Baltimore: PublishAmerica, LLLP.

Prather, H. (1970). *Notes to myself.* Moab, Utah: Real People Press.

———— (1980). *There is a place where you are not alone.* New York: Doubleday.

Qur'an, The (2001). Translated by Abdullah Yusuf Ali. Elmhurst, New York: Tahrike Tarsile Qur'an, Inc.

Red Pine (2001). *The diamond sutra,* text and commentaries translated from Sanscrit and Chinese. New York: Counterpoint.

Redfield, J. (1993). *The celestine prophecy.* Hoover, AL: Satori Publishing.

Rico, G. (1983). *Writing the natural way.* Los Angeles: J.P. Tarcher, Inc.

Roberts, J. (1978). *The nature of personal reality.* New York: Bantam Books.

Ruiz, D.M. (1997). *The four agreements.* San Rafael, California: Amber-Allen Publishing, Inc.

Ruiz, D.M. and Mills, J. (2001). *Prayers: A communion with our creator.* San Rafael, California: Amber-Allen Publishing, Inc.

Schaef, A. (1986). *Co-dependence, misunderstood—mistreated*. San Francisco: Harper & Row.

————— (1985). *Women's reality, an emerging female system in a white male society*. San Francisco: Harper & Row.

Shakespeare, W. (1928). *The complete works of shakespeare*, edited with a Glossary by W.J. Craig, M.A., London: Oxford University Press.

Shibayama, Z. (2000). *The gateless barrier: zen comments on the mumonkan*. Boston: Shambhala Publications, Inc.

Suzuki, D. (1956). *Zen Buddhism: Selected writings of D.T. Suzuki*, edited by William Barrett. Garden City, New York: Doubleday & Company, Inc.

Svoboda, R. E. (2002). Speaking truth: The art of sacred speech. Retrieved from http://www.drsvoboda.com/sacredspeech.htm

Tan, P. (2003). *Learning and being: thoughts on overcoming problems and living.* Roselle Park, New Jersey: Bright Light Publishing.

Tolle, E. (2006). *A new earth: Awakening to your life's purpose*. London: Penguin Books, Ltd.

————— (1999). *The power of now: A guide to spiritual enlightenment*. Novato, California: New World Library.

Warfield, J. (2007). *Shift: Change your words, change your world*. Las Vegas: Word Sculptures Publishing, L.P.

Williamson, M. (1997). *Illuminated prayers*. New York: Simon & Schuster.

Zukav, G. (2010). *Spiritual partnership: The journey to authentic power*. New York: HarperCollins Publishers.

———— (1989). *The seat of the soul*. New York: Simon & Schuster.

Works to Be Consulted

De Quincey, C. (2010). *Radical nature: The soul of matter*. (Kindle version). Retrieved from Amazon.com.

Gangadean, A. (2008). *Meditations of global first philosophy: Quest for the missing grammar of logos*. (Kindle version). Retrieved from Amazon.com.

Wilber, K. (2011). *A brief history of everything: Revised edition*. (Kindle version). Retrieved from Amazon.com.

————(2011). *Sex, ecology, spirituality: The spirit of evolution (second edition, revised)*. Boston: Shambhala Publications, Inc.

# List of Figures

# Appendix A

**Transformational Stories from My Spiritual Path**

**How It All Began**

I don't remember who came to my door. I don't remember what he said. I do remember he was angry, arrogant, and rude.

I had just finished reading a book called *Summerhill* by an English schoolmaster, A.S. Neill. Its theme was "freedom, not license." Each student in Neill's school was free to do whatever he wanted as long as he didn't hurt anyone else. The community Neill had created was a free, creative, loving, respectful, responsible interaction of unique human beings.

The behavior of the man at the door was obnoxious, but he wasn't hurting me. I decided to allow him to vent his anger. I didn't do it because it was something I ought to do. I did it because I chose to do it. I experienced acceptance of the anger and no desire to retaliate. Suddenly, the anger stopped.

Nothing changed. My house, the door, the living room, and the man, were all still there, just as they had been five minutes before.

Yet everything changed. Suddenly, I understood the meaning of words I'd been taught as a child: "But I say unto you, that ye resist not evil; but whosoever shall smite thee on thy right cheek, turn to him the other also." (Matt. 5:39).

My five-year-old son Bill began wetting the bed after his youngest brother was born. This new, irritating behavior made hours of extra work for me at a time when I was already exhausted caring for three preschoolers.

At first, I ignored the bedwetting. Perhaps it would stop on its own. When it didn't, I explained to Bill why he was too big a boy to wet the bed. The wetting continued. I reasoned with him, threatened him, shouted at him, and spanked him. The wetting continued. I felt angry and frustrated.

Neill frequently dealt with problem behavior by rewarding his students. Rewards for bad behavior didn't make sense, but nothing else had worked and I was desperate. Neill's ideas had worked with the man at the door. I decided to try them with the bedwetting problem.

The next time Bill wet the bed, I gave him a penny. He stared at me in confusion. This was not normal mother behavior. The following morning, his bed was dry. He never wet the bed again. My anger and frustration disappeared.

Wow! What a powerful tool! I began using Neill's ideas with neighboring children.

One day, two of Bill's friends were calling each other names in the backyard and threatening to fight. Instead of trying to stop them, I took each aside and asked him if he wanted to fight.

Each said the same thing. "I don't want to fight, but he's making me do it. He's calling me bad names."

"Do you want to fight?" I repeated. "If you do, go ahead and do it."

The boys mumbled to themselves and looked at the ground. Two minutes later, they were happily playing together.

What I was doing contradicted everything society had taught me, but it brought the peace and harmony I desired. Society had taught me to punish people for "bad behavior," but I wasn't punishing them. Society had taught me to resist "evil," but I was no longer resisting. Society had taught me to fight for peace, but I wasn't fighting.

Instead, I was simply detaching from the anger and turmoil around me and allowing it to happen without responding to it. The anger and turmoil disappeared, and my life and relationships worked. By allowing myself to remain peaceful and harmonious, everything around me became peaceful and harmonious.

As a child, I had understood Matthew 5:39 as a puzzling and unattainable moral commandment, requiring subservience of my own needs to the needs of others. Suddenly, in a personal experiential context, those same words took on an entirely new meaning. They didn't require subservience of my own needs to the needs of others. Rather, they suggested extremely effective action I could take all by myself, that benefited both me and others. There was no self-denial in my actions. There was nothing but self-affirmation and life affirmation. I had never before felt so free, so strong, so powerful, so integrated, so fully in control.

Nothing outside me changed. All that changed were my perceptions, thoughts, actions, and emotions.

What I experienced has been called a "mystical experience." It contained all four of the characteristics William James described in his book *The Varieties of Religious Experience*. Those characteristics were:
1.  Ineffability (incapable of description)
2.  Noetic quality (a profound sense of knowing)

3. Transiency

4. Passivity

My experience was certainly ineffable. Nothing outside me had changed, so I couldn't talk about objective, external changes. There were none. To try to describe the inner changes in my psyche, the perspective from which I now understood, and the deeper transformational meanings I now had was close to impossible with the dualistic, subject/object language we humans had created. There was no subject/object duality to conceptualize. There was only a unified sense of being.

I somehow just knew that I knew. The religious, spiritual, and ethical concepts I had been taught as a child that had made no sense at age six now made sense at age 30. All were conceptual tools that pointed toward ways of overcoming our limited understandings of life, expanding our perspectives, and living together in harmonious community.

The experience was transient. It happened and passed. I continued to do the objective, physical activities I had previously done. I washed dishes, baked bread, tended the family garden, cleaned house, went shopping, and cared for our children. Yet the experience had left an indelible mark on my psyche—one that I would never lose. I now washed dishes, baked bread, tended the family garden, cleaned house, went shopping, and cared for our children with a far greater sense of presence. My life suddenly had a deeper meaning and purpose. It was vital to bring this presence, meaning and purpose to others.

The experience was passive in the sense that it was not an experience and consciousness shift I chose. It simply happened. It was like an unexpected gift. I had, however, chosen the actions that preceded it. The actions I had chosen were different from the actions into which society had conditioned me.

As a child, I had been taught to doubt, question, and trust my own judgment. My rearing didn't include education about mystical experiences, but I knew that many religions contained words describing similar experiences. As I read texts from Christianity, Buddhism, Zen Buddhism, Confucianism, Taoism, Islam, Hinduism, Plato, and existentialist philosophers, I could recognize my own experience in all the different words.

It was as if different people were describing the same beautiful flower garden. Some talked about roses, some spoke of delphiniums, some noticed the color patterns, and some focused on the trellises and paths. If I hadn't seen the flower garden and were just listening to the words, I would have thought the people were talking about different gardens. Having seen the flower garden, I knew they were all giving verbal structure and form to the same underlying experience, just as our minds give form and meaning to the fixed lines of optical illusions or ink blots.

I couldn't stop playing with these ideas. Was my life the same or was it different? Externally, not a thing had changed. Internally, my life was totally transformed. My perceptions, emotions, and actions had suddenly shifted. Words and their experiential meanings had changed. Suddenly, I was looking at and understanding the externals from a sparkling new perspective.

Did I know or did I know nothing? I wasn't sure. There was a sense in which I absolutely "knew," because I could relate my own experience to other people's words about similar experiences. There was another sense in which I "knew" I knew nothing. There were no correct words with which to communicate what I had experienced.

Religious words are gorgeous art, reflecting this universal underlying transformational experience. Offered as guides, they serve humanity well. Presented as Truth, they become false idols that separate and divide.

The meaning of words depends on the human consciousness that hears and understands them. Words have meaning only in the context of particular experiences and mindsets.

**Overcoming Fear**

As a child, I attended Sunday school at the Unitarian Church of Germantown in Philadelphia, Pennsylvania. My parents had migrated to Unitarianism from Presbyterianism and Methodism. Both had rebelled against being forced to accept obtuse religious doctrines as a prerequisite to belonging to a spiritual community.

Unitarianism is freethinking and intellectual. It encourages questioning, skepticism, and a search for deeper and more comprehensive answers. That training has been a valuable part of my education. However, there are aspects of Unitarianism that have failed to support my spiritual development.

Unitarianism is skeptical of everything. For example, no one in Sunday school ever talked about mystical experiences. When I had a mystical experience, I had no frame of reference within which to think about it. When I experienced fear, even terror, there was no one to talk with, because emotions were just not discussed. There is a very different energy in a Unitarian Church from the spiritual energy I have experienced, for example, in Unity and Science of Mind congregations. I like to refer to the Unitarian energy as intellectual energy and the Unity and Science of Mind energy as heart energy.

The purpose of this background is simply to provide a reference point for where I was coming from, mentally and emotionally, when I participated in the following two weekends of personal growth workshops.

Before the first workshop, the facilitator asked us to make several commitments—to ourselves and to the other participants: don't chew gum; don't interrupt; be on time; do whatever we were told.

I didn't object to not chewing gum. I rarely chewed it anyway. I didn't mind not interrupting. I wanted to be on time, because accountability was already one of my values.

However, I absolutely refused to commit to doing whatever I was told without clarification.

"From whom are we to take our direction?" I asked.

"From any of the facilitators in the room," the lead facilitator responded.

Immediately, my Unitarian skepticism kicked in. It wasn't an answer I could accept. I'd had bad experiences following the direction and advice of other human beings. Moreover, history taught me that humans had directed other humans to murder, commit suicide, and lay waste to valuable human resources.

The facilitator refused to continue unless I agreed. I finally backed down and agreed simply so that the workshop could continue.

My decision nagged me the entire week before the second workshop. I had been out of integrity during the first workshop by going along with a request I believed was wrong. I knew the facilitators would make the same demands before the second workshop. I knew that if I refused to do what the facilitators demanded, I would incur the wrath of the other participants. I was terrified.

The entire week before the second workshop, I felt trapped between two impossible and painful choices. Was I going to give in to my fear of human wrath and capitulate to the demands of the facilitators or stand alone and refuse to submit?

If I chose to stand alone, I knew I couldn't do it by myself.

Faith is not knowledge. Faith is a choice.

If I were going to overcome fear, I needed help. I didn't trust other people. I'd been betrayed too often. To whom or what could I turn?

Sitting alone in my living room the week before the second workshop, I agonized over what seemed like an impossible choice. Tears were streaming down my cheeks. I didn't want to ask for help. I didn't want to believe in something I couldn't understand and couldn't see. I didn't want to humble myself, but I knew I couldn't stand alone against the wrath of the other participants without support. At the same time, I had to say no to the demands of the facilitators in order to stay in integrity with myself.

In desperation, sinking to my knees, I cried out: to something, somewhere, somehow; to something I couldn't see; to something I couldn't hear; to something I couldn't understand, "God help me."

Suddenly, I was calm and centered. My fear was gone.

When I returned to the second workshop, the facilitators made the same demands. We were to commit to not chewing gum, not interrupting, being on time, and doing whatever we were told. Calmly, without fear, I refused to agree to do whatever the facilitators told me to do.

The room immediately turned surly.

Sue had paid a babysitter to watch her four year old while she attended the workshop. My refusal to commit was wasting her time and squandering her money.

Sam had taken time off from work to attend. I was wasting his time and money by refusing to commit to doing whatever I was told.

Sue screamed that I was a jerk who was making her lose money. Sam began shouting and pounding his fist on the table.

The facilitators walked out, leaving me alone with the other furious participants. I was doing exactly what I was being told—but not by the facilitators and not by the other participants.

I had gone to the workshop because I wanted to overcome fear. I was afraid of criticism, afraid of anger, afraid of what other people would think.

I was skeptical of the concept of God. I couldn't believe in an old man with a long beard, sitting on a cloud with a thunderbolt in his hand, waiting to strike me dead if I didn't do some vague, unclear thing he wanted me to do.

As the other workshop participants screamed and shouted at me, I felt no anger, no hurt, no fear. I felt only centeredness and compassion.

The facilitators returned. They asked me to leave the workshop. It didn't matter. I had received what I came to receive—release from my fear.

A friend later told me that the other participants spent the rest of the weekend looking at their own rage and violent conduct toward me.

What is this thing called faith? Isn't everything faith? Whether faith in other humans, faith in God, or faith in self, it's just a choice, isn't it?

**Standing in Integrity, Courage and Strength**
**The Atlantic City Councilman**

When I opened my law practice, one of my first clients was the City of Atlantic City. One of the City Councilmen (we'll call him John), arrogantly strutted around City Hall, ordered the janitor and cleaning lady to work faster, and shouted down anyone who dared to express an opinion different from his own. Rumors circulated that he physically abused his wife. People said she had been hospitalized.

During his political campaign, John had asked me to place his campaign sign in the front yard of my home. I politely declined. I was a non-partisan City contractor. I would not have placed *any* candidate's sign on my property.

John took my "no" personally. As soon as he was elected, he began attacking both me and my contract. He proclaimed that the City was paying me too much money. He pulled my contract off the Council Agenda, asserting he needed more information—information I had already supplied. He refused to return my phone calls. He demanded that I appear before Council to defend myself and my contract.

I knew how ugly this man could be and how he hated women. Would I lose a contract that was a major source of my income? Would I have to let my wonderful paralegals go because I could no longer pay their salaries? Would I lose my home to foreclosure because I could no longer pay my mortgage?

I was doing an excellent job in an area of law where few attorneys had my expertise. It was an area of law that John did not understand. He also did not understand the ramifications of his conduct. His hubris had, however, become a hugely disruptive factor in my life.

After struggling with my own fear and rage and examining my own conduct for things I could have done better, I simply stepped into my own power and integrity. The man was an incompetent bully, misusing the power the citizens had entrusted to him.

On the day of the Council meeting, I sat in the front row with a fat file on my lap glaring at John. He refused to look at me. His face muscles tightened. His hands shook. While he made half-hearted attempts at blustery remarks, the verbal gusts soon dissipated as other councilmen jumped to my defense. John muttered under his breath, then reluctantly stopped talking. When the vote was taken, my contract was renewed—unanimously. Even John voted in favor of the renewal.

## The Borough of Avalon Code Enforcement Officer

While I was a practicing lawyer, I was representing a client at a municipal council hearing. The municipal officials were arrogant, overbearing, pompous, and making ridiculous demands. Can you imagine they were actually suggesting that my client camp out in his tenants' yard to make sure they behaved?

I can't say I felt fear before the hearing, but I did feel tension. I was not primarily a litigator, and I wasn't familiar with the municipal procedures or personalities before I stepped into the hearing room.

I had, however, prepared both law and facts thoroughly. As the hearing progressed, it became obvious that the municipal officials were familiar with neither.

I knew the police chief's list of violations was inconsistent with the notices he had sent my client. After he gave his arrogant and condescending opening testimony (a façade for his fear), I simply asked him to show me where my client had received notice of the violations. He spent a full two minutes looking through his file. Every eye in the hearing room was on him.

Both my client and I sat respectfully silent while he looked, but we were both chuckling inside. Finally, he had to admit on the record that my client had never received notice. The police chief's arrogance suddenly vanished.

The Code Enforcement Official, papers shaking in his trembling hands, testified that the last time he had viewed my client's property was over four months ago. He nevertheless adamantly stated that the property did not meet the Code requirements as of the hearing date. I couldn't believe he had said that.

When I asked him how he could possibly testify that my client's property didn't meet Code requirements today when he hadn't viewed it for four months, he backed down, retracted his statement, and suddenly started testifying honestly. Interestingly enough, his hands stopped shaking.

**The Power of Intention.**

A few years ago, I made a wish list of things I wanted. One was a beautiful home overlooking the ocean, surrounded by tropical plants, fruit, beautiful flowers, and birds. I visualized Hawaii, couldn't imagine how I could ever afford it, put the list aside, and forgot about it.

Three years later, my husband and I visited Roatan, Honduras. We both fell in love with the island. He bought a condominium, and I bought a home on a three-acre parcel of land, overlooking the Caribbean, beautifully landscaped with tropical trees and flowers.

A few weeks later, in the middle of the night, I suddenly awoke with goose pimples all over my body. My Roatan home was the manifestation of my visualization, but it cost only one-tenth of what it would have cost in Hawaii. My wish had come true.

# Healing

The peak of Volcan Baru, western Panama's dormant volcano, loomed majestically out of the clouds in the early dawn as I pulled a card from my friend Donna's bowl of affirmations. It said, "Allow yourself to grieve."

I got it. I was certainly here to grieve. Despite all my efforts to complete a beautiful home midst mountains, waterfalls, and rainbows, the house sat unfinished and rotting. I had suffered verbal abuse, defamation, evictions, robberies, and floods. The final straw had been robbers in the back yard of my rental home on Christmas night 2009.

Shelley Darling, www.goldenlightdowsing.com, had dowsed a plan of the property before I left the States for Panama. She immediately noted that the plan was missing its relationship corner. "Have you been having challenges

with relationships recently?" she asked. I certainly had –
over and over and over.

Through dowsing, Shelley had discovered two negative
vortexes (one minor, one major) and five geopathic stress
lines. She plotted these carefully on the property plan and
sent me off with nine copper rods to place in the ground to
redirect the negative energies. "Make sure you don't pack
them in your carry-on luggage," she cautioned. "TSA will
confiscate them."

Before I left, as Shelley and I visualized, some
interesting symbols appeared. Simultaneously, Shelley and I
saw an American Indian chief with a full headdress of
feathers. This made no sense in the context of Panama.
Shelley explained that he was "White Eagle", a spirit guide
who would support us through challenges.

One of the visualization exercises we did was intended
to open a portal so that trapped negative energies could
ascend to their proper places in the Universe. I saw a figure
in a fetal position. I couldn't tell whether it was male, female,
adult, or child, but the curled-up position was unmistakable.
Why did this fetus suddenly show up in my mind? None of
this was fitting together or making sense.

Later, Shelley emailed me that she had intuited there was
a female spirit on the property – a woman who had
transitioned – who did not want to leave. This didn't make
sense either. The only woman I could think of who didn't
want to leave was the female owner of the corrupt and
incompetent construction company.

Steven Northcraft, another friend and healer, had told me
to buy four pink quartz crystals and sage. The pink quartz

crystals symbolized love. The sage would be used for purification.

Donna loaned me her own dowsing rods to help me check the positioning of the copper rods Shelley had given me. I had never used dowsing rods before and needed to practice.

On the morning I left to do the healing work, Donna, a Usui Reiki Master and a Karuna Reiki Master, used a pendulum to clear spirit entities, lesser demons, giant demons, shape-shifting giant demons, fallen angels, and dark ETs from me, the property, my corporation, the developers, the builders, and anyone connected in any way with the property. I have no idea what this meant, but I was more than willing to receive any help that was freely offered. John, my young American friend, was there to help bury rods and hold the space for healing.

I spent the first day working on the minor negative vortex. Beginning with the visualization exercise Shelley had taught me, I visualized white, blue, rose, and purple lights supporting both me and the property, and finally a golden dome covering everything. I soon discovered I needed clarification as to how to place the copper rods I had brought with me. I was still learning how to use Donna's dowsing rods, but I developed a tentative placement.

The next day, I pulled the "Moving Forward" affirmation card. It certainly didn't feel as if we were moving forward. I had been blocked over and over in my attempts to build this home, having made the mistake of trusting Panamanian builders who mixed foundation concrete by hand, didn't have my architectural plans on site, paid no attention to the plans, had inadequate onsite supervision, used workers who five years before had been farmhands and taxi drivers, built the septic tank so high that only 1/3 of it was usable, and totally ignored the terms of the contract they had signed.

I had forgotten to bring Shelley's compass with me. As a result, I could only estimate the placement of the rods in the minor negative vortex. John was there to hammer a 10" deep hole in each corner of the property in which, once we had completed the dowsing, we would place the rose quartz crystals Steven had told me to buy. We positioned the hole in the missing relationship corner outside the property line to heal the missing relationship piece.

The third day, I pulled the "Push for Change" card from Donna's bowl. This made no sense either until one of the development security guards swaggered onto the rear of my property where John was loudly hammering trenches in which to place the copper rods. Accusingly, the guard demanded in rapid Spanish, "What do you think you are you doing?" (Note: this was on property I owned on which he was trespassing.) In Spanish, with gentleness and firmness, I explained that we needed silence and respect for the property.

At first, he didn't know what to do with my response. Then he tried the same conduct again, repeating his conditioned belligerence of asking demanding and intimidating questions. I looked him directly in the eye and repeated that we were requesting his silence and respect for the property, a sacred space and sanctuary. After several moments of indecision, he spun abruptly on his heel and marched off. Shelley had told me that once the healing began, negative energies would leave the property.

Finally, we had completed all the dowsing except for the major negative vortex. Shelley had said this was in an enclosed storage area under the stairwell and directed me to visualize the dowsing ascension ring and portal in the middle of that space.

The energies in the storage area were intense. The dowsing rods were flying chaotically around. As John hammered the concrete, there was a deep ringing sound that seemed to extend to the bowels of the earth.

As I invited the trapped entities to ascend through the portal, I suddenly made the connection between the figure in the fetal position and the woman who did not want to leave. That woman had lost her child on the property and would not leave without her baby. Tears streaming down my face, I invited the woman to cradle her dead child in her arms, ascend through the portal, and release both of them to their rightful place in the Universe.

Then suddenly, I was that woman. The figures in the fetal positions were my own sons, wounded through their parents' divorce and struggling through the dynamics of their own marriages. Gently, I cradled each one in my arms, carried him through the portal, and released him to his proper place in the Universe. My tears would not stop flowing as my own intense pain began to dissolve.

Simultaneously, I was releasing myself from my attachment to a dream that would never be, despite my pure intentions and dedicated effort. It was time to move on. Was I also the figure in the fetal position, waiting to be born to my purpose on this planet?

The only thing left to do was to place the rose quartz crystals in the holes John had dug the day before, cover them with dirt, and sage the perimeter of the property. Then, we prayed for rain – to cleanse everything and to obliterate the traces of our work.

As the raindrops fell, a beautiful rainbow appeared over the healed relationship corner. A white falcon sat at the top of the tree. As we drove away, I knew I would never return.

The next day, I pulled my final card from Donna's bowl: "Completion." I knew my work was done.

### Transforming Rage into Right Action

I have always had to go deeply into my own rage in order to bring it into the light to heal. If I don't allow myself to *feel* the rage, I cannot heal either myself or others. Not allowing myself to feel it is like clamping a lid on a boiling pot of water. Eventually, it boils over in uncontrolled torrents.

Feeling the rage does *not* mean acting it out against others. But what then do we do with this powerful emotion?

When my husband refused to leave his mistress for the sake of our marriage and family, at first I felt shock, disbelief, and deep numbing pain. I sobbed at night for hours. I had given my whole heart and soul to this marriage and family, only to watch it being trashed by my husband's adultery—conduct I had no power to change.

Suddenly my pain transformed to rage. I felt disrespected and betrayed, not only by the man I had married and trusted, but also by the woman I had once believed was my best friend. I deserved so much better, as did our children. Together, my husband and his mistress had relegated me to nothing more than a convenient maid, cook and babysitter. I felt used without my consent so that they could go off and play.

I felt like buying a gun and killing them both, but didn't want to spend the rest of my life in jail; nor did I want to leave my children orphans. What was I to do with this boiling rage which had suddenly appeared in my life? I had hard moral decisions to make.

Rage serves valuable spiritual purposes.

One, for me, was the release of self-righteousness. I knew from personal experience how it felt to want to murder. If I were capable of murder, how could I ever judge another person who was going through a similar traumatic inner struggle?

A second was the realization that rage was a messenger. It was telling me I needed to grow and change. But how?

Change does not mean getting rid of rage. Change means transforming rage into constructive, passionate, nonviolent action that supports values of fairness, safety, justice, mutual respect, and courage.

The children and I had needed my husband's financial and emotional support and protection while the children were growing up. He had abandoned us all mentally and emotionally. I had no choice but to learn how to protect myself and our children as well as I could.

I divorced my husband, dropped his surname, went back into the job market, fought for half of our assets in court, took care of our children as well as I could, applied to law school, graduated cum laude, and was offered a position as an associate attorney with a large Atlantic City law firm. Later, I opened my own law practice.

People to whom I've told this story often comment about how courageous I was. I wasn't courageous. I was livid with rage and fighting for my survival and that of my children.

Ultimately, my rage transformed into a deeper understanding of what the Buddhist Eightfold Path calls "right action." There is conduct that supports human cooperation, respect, love, justice, harmony, abundance, and peace and conduct that destroys these values. "Right action" supports the values we all cherish when everybody wins. It is the arena of morals, ethics, and the Ten Commandments. Adultery destroys marriages and families.

Going through this experience was not a path I desired. It seemed to have chosen me, and yes, it has been challenging and a constant overcoming.

I have had to learn to stop enabling injustice without myself being unjust, stop enabling disrespect without being disrespectful, stop enabling abuse, control, and manipulation without myself becoming abusive, controlling, and manipulative. I have had to learn to be very transparent in expressing my needs, listening to the needs of others, and offering support where I can.

I have also had to learn to be just, respectful, loving, forgiving, and grateful toward myself so that I know how to be just, respectful, loving, forgiving, and grateful toward others. I have had to walk out of many unjust, disrespectful, and abusive relationships to protect my own soul and sanity. Only then have I been able to re-engage these same people from a more expanded, deeper, and transformed consciousness.

Under no circumstances do I believe others are evil. Their intentions, in ignorance and lack of awareness, are simply directed toward goals that serve only themselves at the expense of others. They have their own spiritual lessons to learn and their own karma to live, but mess with my family and I become part of your karma.

Has my path been the path of the spiritual warrior? It certainly feels that way. Are we all spiritual warriors grappling with the rage within so that we can transform it into passionate purpose?

**Abundance**

According to Thomas Ashley-Ferrand, mantras are sacred words of power. According to others, they are energy based sounds, embodying the highest spiritual state. Yet others refer to them as sound mysteries that change consciousness.

Some time ago, a friend sent me an email with a link to a series of SoundsTrue audios about Sanskrit mantras:

http://www.soundstrue.com/shop/STSearch.do?searchTerm=Thomas+ashley+farrand&searchDomain=author&selectedType=All+Products&searchPage=0&selectedComponentGroup=All&selectedItem=bestsellers

Knowing that I was working on another book about word energy, my foreign rights agent had previously mentioned Sanskrit as a language I should explore. Western language uses symbolism and meaning. Sanskrit uses the pure vibration of sound.

I ordered the audios and began listening. There was a mantra for bringing abundance into your life. Phonetically, it sounded like "Om schreem kleem Lakshmi ay Namaha." Most of it was toned on a single note, with the "ay" one note higher and the "ma" in Namaha one note lower.

This longer mantra was composed of seed mantras. "Schreem" is the principle of abundance. "Kleem" is the principle of attraction. "Lakshmi" (pronounced "lockschmee") is the Goddess of abundance, a beautiful woman with abundance flowing from her hands. "Namaha" means to salute.

According to Sanskrit philosophy, you can attract abundance into your life simply by saying, over and over, the simple seed mantra "schreem." The longer mantra is supposed to be more powerful. I decided to play with the longer mantra and see what happened.

As I was driving to the Tampa airport to fly to Panama, I repeated the mantra over and over. Then I forgot about it.

When I arrived in Panama, there was a penny lying on the ground beneath my feet. I picked it up. Three days later, in Boquete, my travel agent, out of the blue, gave me a free $3 phone card. Then, my agent at the bank gave me two free 2011 calendars.

As so often happens in Panama, I fully expected the taxi driver who took me back to Boquete to notice that I was an American and triple his fee. He didn't. It happened a second time.

Greetings, meetings, lunches, and dinners kept flowing in.

I had wanted to facilitate healing workshops and had always wanted to go on a cruise. Suddenly, I was offered opportunities by PacificOrient Caribbean Cruises out of Australia and WhaleWatchingPanama around Coiba and Contadora Islands off the southern coast of Panama.

The kicker happened shortly before I arrived home. I'd been getting about ten hits a day on my website. Suddenly, the hits jumped to over 100.

Was there something going on here that I didn't understand but that somehow seemed to work? Or was it just that as I focused on abundance, I became more aware of the abundance all around me flowing into my life? I don't know the answer, but I think I'll continue chanting the mantra.

**The Universe as a Living, Breathing Organism**

Before the Shamanic ceremony, we had been asked to refrain from pork, red meat, spicy foods, spicy peppers, citrus, nectarines, caffeine, dairy, prescription medications (particularly MAIO anti-depressant drugs) and sex for several days. The day of the ceremony, I consumed only a small glass of juice and some water.

As I approached the reception area, the first thing I noticed was the kindness in the faces of the assistants. They gently looked me in the eye. Some of them gave me a hug.

I was the only person in the room permitted to sit in a folding chair. I had received reluctant but compassionate permission to honor my arthritic knees that would no longer easily bend.

When the Shaman entered the room, he gave a short introduction. The ceremony was about finding the larger self in each one of us. There was a reason we were there. Each person's experience would be unique and exactly what each of us needed.

As the ceremony began, I simply observed as those sitting to my right in circle, one at a time, approached the Shaman to receive their little shot glass of medicina. Some prostrated themselves before him before accepting the drink. Then, one at a time, they returned to their back rests on the floor and sat quietly, some with eyes closed, waiting for the medicina to purge their impurities and open their souls and spirits.

Then it was my turn. I looked the Shaman in the eyes and told him it was my first time. He nodded with a kind smile. The thick, brown medicina did not taste good. I did not want to drain the glass.

We sat quietly in circle as those to my left received their medicina. Nothing seemed to be happening.

Then, the Shaman began chanting. The chants were repetitive, mesmerizing. It was as if he were teasing us, inviting us to purge whatever was blocking us and discover our full presence and power. Chants were followed by silence, then a teasing flute, then rattles, then more chanting.

My attention was drawn to the flickering sunlight on the floor. The colors seemed more intense than before and there were more moving patterns. It seemed as if the floor were mirroring the dance of the leaves in the trees outside. Veils of shadow and light seemed to open and close, beckoning me to explore deeper depths of myself.

As I closed my eyes, it was as if I were enveloped in huge red DNA strands, constantly moving around me like a kaleidoscope.

Suddenly, I became aware of my hands. It was as if I were seeing these hands for the first time. I was mesmerized as I watched the fingers stretch, retract, wiggle. My hands were alive.

People were beginning to purge into the buckets that had been provided. There was no odor. I, too, was beginning to feel nauseous. At first I resisted the feeling, then wanted to get the medicina out of my body. I vomited gently four times, continued with a couple of dry heaves, still had a bad taste in my mouth, spit a couple of times, and then knew I was done. I was.

My body was suddenly very alive. I wanted to move every muscle. I rotated my head and shoulders, stretched my legs, rotated my ankles, shifted my torso.

I again became aware of my hands. As I stretched my arms and fingers out before me, they suddenly began to tingle. It was as if electric current were shooting out from my fingertips into the room. My hands had the power to heal and I had never before been aware of that power, nor had I ever used it.

I began to feel a sense of presence and power within me, a feeling that I AM. There was nothing I needed to do and yet everything was magnificent. The room was alive with light and brilliance. It was as if pinpoints of light were dancing with one another, all part of a living, breathing universe, and I was part of the dance.

I looked around the room. Some people were sitting quietly. Others were violently vomiting. A young man to my left was convulsed with vomiting, bent over in agony. The Shaman stood over him, spoke with him, shook rattles over him, compassionately and firmly supported him as he purged the poison from his soul. Gradually, gradually, the vomiting subsided and the man sat peacefully, quietly.

I began using my hands to send power and compassion into the room. I was helping to hold the sacred space as others purged their poisons. One of the guides to my left was also using her hands to hold the sacred space.

My friend Johanna was sitting next to me. She had not vomited. She was simply sitting stoically.

About half way through the ceremony, the Shaman asked if anyone would like more medicina. About a dozen people stepped forward, one after another. Johanna was among them. I was clear that I did not want any more.

After about ten minutes, Johanna suddenly arose and stalked out of the room. It was clearly not a bathroom break. Something major was happening.

I turned my palms upward and spread my fingers out toward the center of the room holding Johanna in my thoughts and prayers. Then I waited.

It felt as if twenty minutes or more had passed. Johanna had not returned to the room. Suddenly, the Shaman bolted from the room. We sat in silence and waited.

A few moments later, Johanna returned, followed by the Shaman. The chanting, flute, and rattles resumed. Johanna sat with her head in her hands. I knew she was processing something major. Then, she began purging.

"Medicina, medicina," The Shaman was chanting. Most participants were sitting quietly now, simply processing what was happening.

The song turned to "te amor." I knew enough Spanish to know that it was a dedication of self to the Divine. We sat in deep, profound silence.

We had started the ceremony at 3 p.m. It was now dusk. The only illumination in the room came from a large candle in the center of the circle. I marveled at the Shaman's dedication and perseverance. He had been constantly serving us for more than five hours—chanting, playing the flute, shaking rattles, attending those who were having an intense experience, allowing us to absorb the profound silence.

As I relaxed my eyes to drink in the profundity of the moment, it seemed as if light was streaming down from the heavens into the center of the candle, then flowing out into my heart. I welcomed that light. I knew my heart needed healing. It had been so deeply wounded. The light felt like my personal connection with the Divine.

Then, the candle began to undulate, moving up and down and in gentle circles. It was as if the candle itself was a huge, dynamic, living, breathing heart. The universe around me was alive with beauty and I was part of that beauty. I was part of the living dance.

The Shaman formally closed the Ceremony at 9 p.m. I sat for a few more moments in silence. Many devotees were flocking to the Shaman's feet. A few minutes later, I left.

As I was packing my belongings and walking toward the stairs, I realized that I had not been to the bathroom once during the seven hours of ceremony, nor had I had any need to sip water or apply salve to my lips. As I began walking down the steps, I was walking straight down rather than in my usual crab descent, one step at a time. My legs felt alive and flexible again.

I thought I would sleep well. I was wrong. I lay in bed, my mind processing the experience of the past several hours.

They had told us they would waken us at 4:15 a.m. for a Puja—a fire ceremony. We were required to shower before participating. I was disgusted that I couldn't sleep. It must already be 3 a.m. I turned on the light and looked at my watch. It was only 12:30.

I decided to take my shower then. Finally, I slept.

During the Puja, we were required to walk outside in our bare feet. The ground was rocky and hurt my feet. Everyone was chanting a chant I did not know and could not understand. The Shaman now appeared as his alter ego, a Hindu Avatar. We were required to prostrate ourselves as we received grains of rice in our right hand to offer into the flames. My feet hurt, my knees hurt, and my body was unstable. A young woman assistant noticed my struggles and came over to guide and support me. She was so kind and compassionate that my eyes filled with tears. As I stared at the fire, it suddenly fanned out into a huge guiding flame.

We returned to the place of ceremony for some ParaShakTea made of raspberries, raspberry leaves, and rose petals, and a delicious vegetarian breakfast. It was then that Johanna told me her story.

Her mother had lost four babies before Johanna was born. It was the custom at that time to hold a mother's legs closed until the doctor arrived. Johanna was trapped in her mother's birth canal, struggling to be born, for twenty minutes. She could still feel the rage of being trapped in that birth canal.

After her second helping of the medicina, she had experienced the same rage. She had desperately needed to get out into nature, a place that had always healed her. She had walked downstairs and out the door, only to be met by one of the Shaman's assistants, insisting that she remain inside.

"What is this?" she demanded. "A Catholic girls' school?"

The assistant was about to restrain Johanna physically when Johanna warned, "Do not touch me. I need to go outside." She realized she was not being very nice and was creating a scene. She didn't care.

Then the Shaman appeared. He didn't touch her. He simply looked at her with love and compassion. She repeated, "I need to go outside."

The Shaman responded, "Well, you can certainly do that if you want, but then you will miss the most healing part of the ceremony."

Johanna stopped short, turned around, and followed him back into the room. She told me later that it wasn't what he said. It was the way he had looked at her. "He is a true Avatar," she said. "I would follow him anywhere and learn what he has to teach me. I definitely want to do the ceremony again."

After breakfast, we again sat in circle to share our experiences of the day before. The Shaman was no longer present. One of his assistants facilitated. We were each limited to two minutes.

Everyone except one woman had had a life-altering experience. All were different. The woman stated she had had a horrible experience, couldn't wait for it to be over, would never do it again, and just wanted to go home.

On the long drive home, I did not listen to one tape nor turn on the radio. I was still processing. I expect to continue the processing for months into the future.

Will I ever do it again? I don't know. I feel no need to repeat the experience right now, but if I shift into a space where I feel confused and need to be reminded of the power that is available to each and every one of us, I would have no hesitation repeating the ceremony.

# Appendix B

## Transformational Poetry from My Spiritual Path

### Babylon

First came the experience
Then came the word.
The word conveyed the experience
Or did it?
Perhaps, it only pointed.

First came experiences
then came words,
The words divided and distorted.
We listened to the words, and
we, too, became divided and distorted.

Good fought with evil,
knowledge with ignorance,
truth with falsehood,
science with religion.
Each man chose word weapons,
hurling his words against others
dividing,
distorting.

The words fought and contradicted
and we fought and contradicted.
Each word wanted to reign supreme, and
each man wanted to reign supreme.

**Mind**

Monsters created
by machinations of mind
self-destruct. Let go.

Mind forms false idols,
creating separation.
Analysis splits.

**Words**

Words reflect

unique time
place
experience
perspective

Words jangle

unique time
place
experience
perspective of another
and create fear.

Words mirror

unique time
place
experience
perspective of another
and soothe.

Words clarify

unique time
place
experience
perspective of another
and transform.

**The Fall**

In the beginning
the earth was without form and void, and
darkness was upon the face of the deep.

Then man's senses experienced
dividing light from dark
and man's mind created words
"light" and "darkness"
and man moralized
that light was good and
darkness was evil.

Man saw the brilliant scarlet of the poppies
and created red.
He felt the warmth of the sun
and created security and comfort.
He experienced the anguish of death
and created grief.
He experienced pain and created the Devil.
He experienced serenity
and created God.

Then man became enamored of his creations
exalting them into moral doctrines.
Pain was bad and serenity was good.
The Devil was bad and God was good.
Man posed as God
proclaiming his word creations right
and other word creations wrong.

Each man created his own tree of knowledge
of good and evil
and each man believed that
his tree of knowledge was
The Tree of Knowledge
applicable to all.

An occasional man extracted himself
from the human creations and word idols
into which he was born
and returned to the experience
from which they evolved.

Freeing himself from the word shackles
binding humanity
he returned to the experience
from which all arose.

Free to experience the beauty of the poppies.
Free to experience the warmth of the sun.
Free to experience the pain and joy of human existence.
Free to use mind to create
in the image of his Maker.

Experiencing
through cleansed eyes
he created fresh word forms
radiating with honesty

Human words.
Individualized words.
Unique words.
Pure words.

Men who still worshipped false idols
parroted the pure words
desecrating them into false idols.

From the mouths of idolators
the pure words became profanity.


From the mouths of idolators,
the pure words became instruments of control.


From the mouths of idolators,
the pure words became the opposite
of what saviors and saints intended.


From the mouths of idolators,
the pure words became shackles to bind mankind
rather than tools to free him.


Author's note: If language is an instrument of mind, how does one use divisional language to synthesize? How does one become whole through separation?

**Metamorphosis**

Strangled, suffocated,
by words, thoughts, teachings,


my mind lets go, and


I, cradled in now,
absorb the sunset's soothing pinks and reds
each moment unrepeated

breathing again

a tiny speck of eternity

## Awakening

Today, I listen,
hear it for the first time—

a cardinal greeting the sun.

And then, as I release all thoughts
of yesterday, tomorrow,
spring suddenly surrounds me

and I am.

## Scylla and Charybdis

Enmeshed in the web of imperfection,
silence denies my purpose;
speaking distorts.

Absurd and foolish is my speech,
yet speak I must.

Answers have I not,
but only an awareness.

**Haiku**

Spikes we call knowledge
ruthlessly crucify our
creativity

**Questions**

"There are no wrong questions," he said
with certainty in his voice.
"There are only wrong answers."

Perhaps

But

If I ask a meaningless question,
can I expect a meaningful answer?

If I ask an ambiguous question,
can I expect a clear answer?

For are not question and answer
corollaries of a single idea?

and does not the right answer
lie in the right question?

**Rules**

Man's rules of right and wrong
Brew bitter fights in

court
battlefield
street
home

consuming

court
battlefield
street
home

with

tension
fear
anger
frustration

God has no rules of right and wrong

God only releases

       tension
          fear
             anger
                frustration

to free
      love
         acceptance
            respect
              creativity

## Haiku

Words twist and distort
the perfect imperfection.
Wholeness divided.

# Master Sculptor

We

blessed with
mind, choice, language

struggle

to shape
eternity
to our wills.

Against it,

we hurl
our finite selves
straining.

To no avail.

The Sculptor,
silent,
watches

as we chip away our impurities
against the immovable void

until perfected
we acquiesce

in defeat
in mastery
in harmony

## Limitation

When man defines God
god is no longer God

## Freedom

Why do we dream of becoming free when
we have always been free.

We worship words and thoughts,
our own creations,
tricking us into thinking
we are not free.

How will we use our freedom?

# PERSPECTIVE

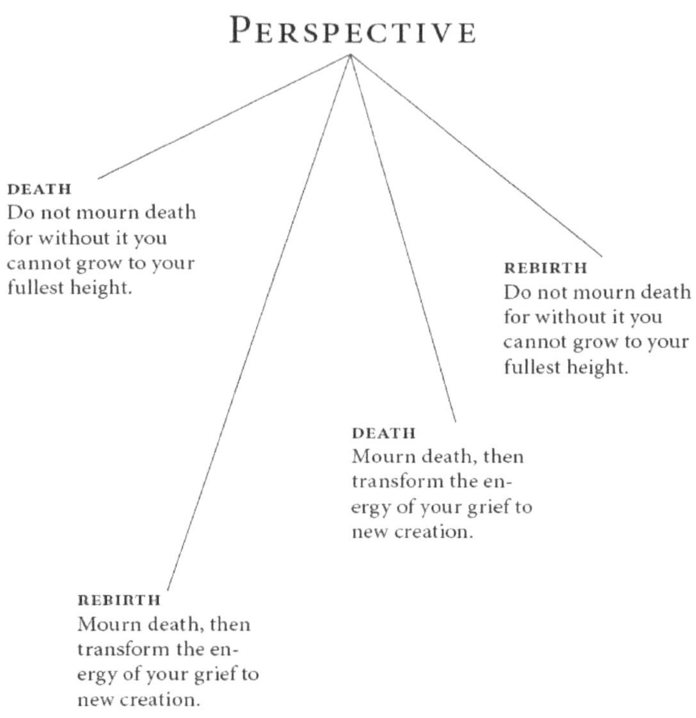



## Co-Creation

When I know myself,
I know others.

When I know my fears,
I understand the fears of others.

When I notice my masks,
I can penetrate the masks of others.

When I forgive myself,
I can forgive others.

The only power I have
Is the power to change myself,

But when I work on what I can
I co-create with my Maker.

**Haiku Couplets (If)**

Thought starts with premise
How can man then think thought is
universal truth?

Thought starts with premise
is not thought naught but Godlike
creativity?

**Free Will and Predestination**

Fumbling,
stumbling
past beckoning doors,
we haltingly wonder

which one to open,
which, disregard?

Silently, destiny, unknown, awaits, and
manifests only when all doors are chosen.

## Paths

A principled man
followed the straight, narrow path of discipline.

A free-thinking man
followed the winding path of exploration.

The principled man
stumbled across a roadblock called I can no longer do
it.

The free-thinking man
discovered a better way.

And together, they joined hands,
setting forth on the path where discipline and freedom
merge.

## Haiku

Cat, tensing, twitching,
focused on innocent prey
soon to awaken.

## Reflections

Reflections of reality
twisted and skewed by motion
mirror faithfully
only when motion ceases.

## Global Harmony

Life is a sphere
with each of us
somewhere
in the mass of that sphere
striving to reach the center.

We can watch each other
touch each other
love each other
learn from each other

but when we uncenter and
lose our direction
we get in our way
and the way of others.

The path you must follow
is different from
the path I must follow.
Only the center
can give us direction.

## Haiku

Teacher and student,
both teaching, learning, thriving—
catalytic growth.

**In His Image**
**(Bridges)**

The left brain plods along
with its rigidly accurate logic
except for its premise
that always begins with "if."

The right brain will,
perhaps must,
make that leap of faith
from which it absorbs the courage to risk

absurdity,

creativity.

**A Single Tear**

A single tear flowing
cleanses
releases
merges with other tears
streaming in sorrow
rushes in rivers
sweeping impurities
out to the calm
of the infinite sea.

**Rain**

Tears dampen my cheek
washing the pain from my soul—
Refreshing shower!

**The Other Side**

Digging deep
in the depths of my psyche
aghast

my terror entombs

when suddenly
exploding into brilliant light and play
astounded

my terror chuckles

**Moment of Truth**

Insane with rage,
Betrayed by two trusted friends,
My fantasy grabbed a pistol and shot them dead,
Trashing them from my life and this earth.

Reason returned.

Was it I feeling this anger?
Was it I wanting to murder?

Never again can I judge a murderer!
Never again can I condemn in others
The fury I felt that passionate moment
When I lost my sanity
And found my truth!

**Doormat**

Today

I noticed
my anger and pain
directed outward,
blaming.

Again

I'd laid myself down
like a doormat,

walked on,
trampled,
scuffed.

I didn't deserve that treatment.

But who put me there?

**Prayer**

May mind become conscious.

Mind creates its own emotion and conduct,
constructive or unconstructive.

May mind become conscious.
May it choose its creation.

**Reconciliation**

Fog
silently
jolts my senses
demanding reconciliation
of surrealistic scenes.

The ocean is gone,
erased by a single stroke of fog.
Sand alone
stretches to gray horizon
where once waves played.

Where is the ocean?

A silhouette of man and dog appear
where sand meets sky,
and suddenly I know
the ocean is still there,
beyond the horizon of my senses,
reconciled.

**Monastery of the Soul**

alone
in silence
we think unlimited thoughts
breathe unlimited possibilities
commune with self.

together
with others
we share limited thoughts
limited possibilities
codifying the fluidity we call self
into words
rules
form
anything solid to cling to

graven images
we idolize

feeling fear
afraid to face our fear
in ignorance
not knowing our ignorance
forgetting creation
from which all springs

## Blessings

Silver rain strings
its tiny pearl droplets
glimmering beads
upon shimmering wire

Magnificent artistry
offered to all
but nurturing only
seekers who notice.

## Renewal

Soft Avalon bay mud
oozes through toes
soothes anxieties
as a crab scuttles away
seeking safety in the same muck
from which I seek release

Clams sucking the silt
pop clean in hands
dirty fingernails happy

as the cool tide swirls inward
over toes
rooted
homed

## Keys

It was easy with knowledge
to use words carelessly.

To change "I was naked" to
"You sinned."
To change "I share responsibility" to
"You're guilty."

It is still easy without Knowledge
to use words carelessly.

To change "I'm afraid" to
"Stop that!"
To change "I'm angry" to
"Shame on you!"
To change "I believe" to
"You're wrong."
To change "I'm frustrated" to
"Damn you!"

It is still so easy
to use words carelessly

and lock oneself out
of the Garden of Eden.


**Abundance**

Drop
                by
                        drop
                                by
                                        drop
the
        dew
                drips
                        onto
                                alabaster
                                        lily
                                                petal

Drop
        by
                drop
                        by
                                drop
the
        flower
                fills           flow
                to over          i
                                        n
                                                g
releasing
            to
                the
                        universe
                                what
                                    it
                                        cannot
                                                h
                                                    o
                                                        l
                                                            d

**Facets**

Within my being I hold the

terror of the coward
violence of the criminal
obsession of the addict, the

gentleness of the parent
devotion of the spouse
spontaneity of the child

I embrace the
ecstasy of the lover
neediness of the thief
ruthlessness of the dictator

treachery of Judas
intellect of Socrates
compassion of Christ
To which facets of self
do I choose to give form?

**Today**

To d a y

I noticed myself
worrying
about future catastrophes

Missing

the brilliant sun
shining on azure bays

Now

## It Is All Very Simple

Each of us has only one soul to fix . . .
Each of us has only one heart to heal . . .
Each of us has only one head to clear . . .

our own

But we need all of us

Without one, there is disorder . . .
Without one, there is imperfection . . .
Without one, there is a hole in harmony . . .
no whole.

It is all very simple.
We all matter.

## Dawn

A cardinal trills
its welcoming reveille
through stillness of mind.

# Cities

<blockquote>

**Therefore is the name of it called Babel;**
**because the Lord did there confound the language of all the**
**earth.**
**—Genesis 11:9**

**Thus, with violence shall that great city Babylon be thrown**
**down,**
**and shall be found no more at all.**
**—Revelation 18:21**

**And he carried me away in the spirit to a great and high**
**mountain,**
**and shewed me that great city, the Holy Jerusalem,**
**descending out of heaven from God....**
**—Revelation 21:10**

</blockquote>

Words
bricks of the Tower of Babel
glued together by human mortar
struggle toward Heaven like Sisyphus
only to tumble divided to the depths of Hell

We have a City to build

We search for bricks
but find only bricks of Babylon
the polarized language of humankind

Our City is complex, holistic
a gestalt of inexpressible relationships

How does one describe the color blue
or the smell of lilacs?
How does one share the warmth of a hug
or the pain of prejudice?

As we ponder the impossible in silence,
the City of Jerusalem descends,
each life a precious gem of shifting facets
kaleidoscoping through moments in time,
bound to each and one another
by the mortar of eternity.

We have a City to build.

# Appendix C

## Transformational Images from My Spiritual Path

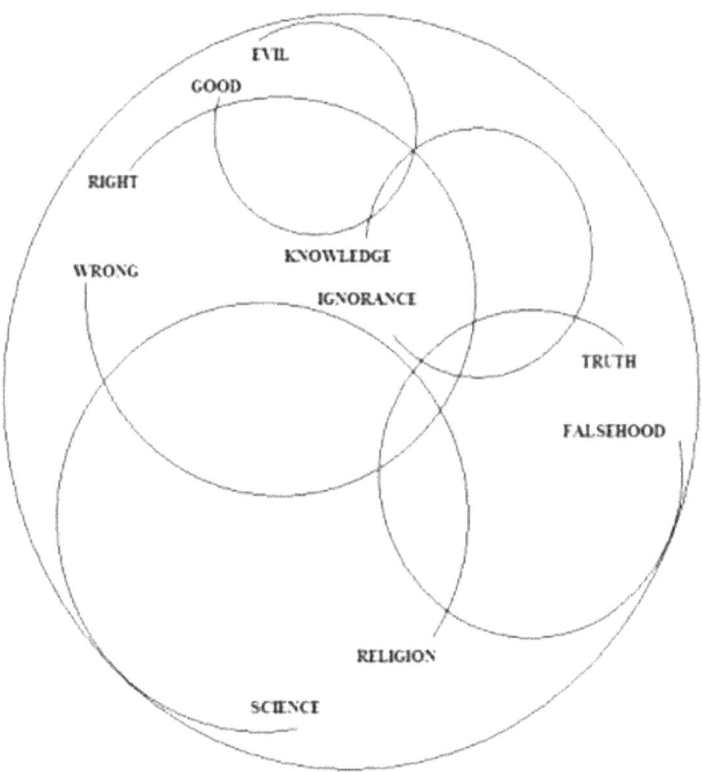


392

GOOD
ANTICHRIST
FALSEHOOD
LOVE
PEACE
SKEPTICISM
BEGINNING

# RIDDLE

If beginning and end are points on a circle and where does beginning begin and end end?

# Appendix D

**The Transformational Power of Fear**

**Things I Have Feared**

- What other people may think
- What other people may do
- Trusting other people
- Trusting a power greater than myself
- Conflict
- What might happen in the future
- Not being perfect (inadequacy)
- Losing relationships
- Losing money
- Losing possessions
- Being different
- Being alone
- Being overly dependent on others
- The void (losing all familiar bearings)
- The unknown (what we don't understand)
- Bullies
- Making a fool of myself
- Spending my last days in a nursing home
- Heights
- Physical death
- Living fully
- Taking risks
- Non-action (sitting still and doing nothing)
- Success (fully using my unique skills and powers)
- Fear

## Fear of Criticism – A Single Condemnatory, Crippling Word

When I am afraid of criticism, who is the critic: the person out there or the person in here?

When I was fifteen, I overheard a classmate call me "queer." The word then didn't have the same meaning it has now. It simply meant strange or peculiar. Nevertheless, that word of condemnation felt like a knife through my heart. I so wanted to belong.

I could only think that there must be something dreadfully wrong with me. I *was* different. Boys rarely asked me out. I wasn't part of the clique. I liked school and wanted to learn. I got good grades. My parents adored me and my teachers praised me as one of their better students.

Many of my classmates had abusive parents, hated school, hated homework, cracked jokes, gossiped, clowned, dated, and got drunk. Yes, maybe I *was* queer.

Unconsciously, I absorbed that "queer" label with all its pain and negative connotations. For years, the belief crippled me. My hands shook. I had knots in my stomach. I hid my talents and abilities for fear of offending others. I was afraid to reach out and build friendships. I thought of committing suicide.

I had allowed one foolish little word, spoken by another without thought or conscious intention, to destroy my spirit. I was terrified to be who I was because others might not like me.

## Releasing Fear by Refocusing—Breaking the Board

I wanted to please others, but I soon noticed that not all people were pleased by the same things. I had a small group of friends who loved to learn. We were the minority, both envied and despised by our classmates. Who was I supposed to please: My friends? Other students? My parents? My teachers? Who was right? Who was wrong? I lived in a hell of confusion, chaos and conflicting doctrines.

Many years later, I began focusing on my own personal growth and what I wanted to do with my life. I attended a workshop where one of the exercises was breaking a board with my hand. The purpose was *not* an idle exercise in physical strength. The purpose was to overcome fear.

On the near side of the board, we wrote what we were afraid of. On the far side of the board, we wrote what we would have or be if we overcame our fear. On the near side I wrote, "Fear of losing my relationship with my sons if I pursue my vision and purpose." On the far side, I wrote, "I am going to pursue my vision and purpose and I'm bringing my sons with me into full human potential."

As I took my stance to break the board, the instructors told us to focus on the far side of the board: what we would have or be if we overcame our fear. My long years of listening to my teachers stood me in good stead. I focused on pursuing my vision and purpose and bringing my sons with me into full human potential. The board snapped. Students who focused on their fears didn't break the board.

I have been criticized and verbally abused many times. I know now that critical, verbally abusive, judgmental, angry words say nothing about me. They say volumes about the speaker. His energy is blocked. She is powerless and ineffective. How can I feel anything but compassion and forgiveness? That does not mean I must remain in this destructive energy.

I still have moments of fear and contraction when I hear someone's angry, judgmental words. Now, however, I know how to release the fear so I can function again. All it takes is a simple shift in focus from an outside authority to my own inner authority. For me, that inner authority must be aligned with a Higher Power I have chosen to believe in. My mind can neither understand nor explain it. My experience, however, tells me the belief makes a difference in what I can accomplish.

Is it selfish, arrogant, narcissistic, insane to trust my own inner authority? There go those critical words again, spinning around in my brain.

No! I choose to believe that relying on that inner authority is as sane as any of us is ever going to get. I intend to keep breaking the board of my self-imposed limitations and focusing on the vision beyond.

Now when I notice an energetic shift in my body into fear and contraction, I simply detach from the speaker's words, whether that speaker is me or someone else. Then I notice where my mind is. (This is sometimes called the Witness.) I can promise you my mind is either in the future or on what someone else may think, say or do. When I notice where my mind is, I can make a conscious choice to bring it back to the present moment. Perhaps I'm in my own living room, my office, or my car. I'm safe there. It's only my mind that is off on sabbatical, terrorizing me with its fantasies of future catastrophes.

Once I consciously bring my mind back to the present moment, I simply ask, "What, Janet, is your next step? What can you do right here, right now, to move your vision forward?" Then I do it.

### Fear as a Catalyst for Transformation

On September 11, 2001, there was no television or radio in my law office. I was working with two exceptional paralegals. Our work environment was efficient, harmonious, and productive. Then the phone rang. My beautiful staff members became gripped with fear, then terror, as their sons, daughters, sisters, and brothers began transmitting blow by blow accounts of the much-too-graphic news broadcasts. The paralysis spread like a plague. What moments before had been a space replete with dynamic harmony suddenly became so emotionally dysfunctional that it approached emotional chaos.

There was no change in our immediate physical surroundings. There was nothing any of us could do to prevent planes from crashing into the World Trade Center. Yet the emotional energy in that office changed in a nanosecond. Why?

What if we had been working in an office before the invention of telephone, television, and radio? Wouldn't that office environment have been different from our $21^{st}$ century office with all its modern technologies?

The only difference between the two environments was the minds and imaginations of the two staffs and the words or lack of words pouring into those minds and imaginations. The staff in my $21^{st}$ century office heard emotionally-charged words pouring through microphones, believed those words, and absorbed that frightful energy into their bodies. The staff in my imaginary $18^{th}$ century office had no phones through which those gruesome words could pour. There was no word plague to infect the office and no frightful energy to absorb.

The Mennonites or Amish neither believe in nor use our modern gadgets. Perhaps there is a very spiritual/religious and practical reason for this seemingly strange choice. They simply want to protect themselves and their communities from the infectious, emotional word energy that plagues our modern world. The Catholic Church likely censors books for the same reason.

I'm not advocating burning phones and TV's. I'm not even advocating censorship. I *am* advocating awareness of the potential for words to contaminate the flow of positive emotional energy into our lives. This positive emotional energy is our birthright. We can choose to foster it or destroy it.

There are many functional ways of dealing with terrorizing words and frightening emotional energies like those of 9/11. Spiritual masters throughout the ages visualize themselves surrounded by beautiful white shields that insulate them from potentially lethal energies that can paralyze hearts and minds. They detach from those energies, instead of absorbing them. Alternatively, they deflect them back from whence they came, just as the black belt karate master deflects the harmful force directed toward him back to its originator.

Perhaps 9/11 was a wakeup call for complacent, smug, arrogant Americans who never before had any reason to begin walking a spiritual path. Being immersed in the 9/11 terror plague made many of them suddenly aware of the loss of all those beautiful things they had previously taken for granted: trust, safety, accountability, even life itself. Perhaps for the first time, they began to recognize how very interdependent we all are, how very important it is to nurture that interdependence, and how grateful we need to be for every living moment.

**Benefits of Releasing Fear**
- Freedom to live from one's own inner voice.
- Passion for using one's uniqueness to make a difference
- Living full out
- Ability to bring about win/win solutions
- Power to help others by helping oneself
- Integrity—The courage to speak and live one's truth
- Creativity
- Inner peace in the midst of external turmoil
- Awareness and creative problem-solving
- Mastermind ability
- Synchronicities. The support of the entire universe. It is there to help one if one allows it to help.